BONDS THAT BIND
CAN EITHER
BEND OR BREAK

BREAKAWAY

STOLEN AWAY SERIES

BOOK TWO

WILLOW PRESCOTT

Copyright

Breakaway Copyright © 2024 Willow Prescott

All rights reserved.

Any unauthorized reprint or use of this content is prohibited. No part of this book may be reproduced or transmitted in any form or by any means, electronic or mechanical, including photocopying and recording, or by any information storage and retrieval system without the express written permission of the author except for the use of brief quotations in a book review. This book is protected by international copyright laws.

This is a work of fiction. Names, characters, businesses, events, and incidents bearing any resemblance to actual persons living or dead or actual events are purely coincidental.

Cover design and formatting by Books and Moods.

To my favorite professor, CHM. Thank you for sharing your infectious love of dead English poets. And I apologize profusely for the following literary sacrilege.

Note from Author

Dear Reader,

This is the second book in the Stolen Away Series. If you haven't read the first book, please turn back now and give Hideaway a read for the sake of your sanity. Breakaway cannot be read as a standalone unless you're fond of extensive confusion with a healthy dose of really good smut.

This is a dark romance that contains themes and situations that may not be suited to some readers. The story focuses heavily on the physical and emotional aspects of BDSM. Please don't expect perfection from these characters—because they're flawed as hell—but I assure you they are trying their best. The bounds of safe, sane, and consensual won't always be adhered to, and if that's something that makes you uncomfortable, I would ask that you reconsider your decision to dive into the deep end. Because this is the dark side of kink. This story contains violence, power play, dubcon, forced proximity, emotional trauma, mention of suicide and murder, and a shopping list of BDSM including: pain play, bondage, knife play, degradation, impact play, and edging. A full disclosure of trigger warnings can be found on my website. For the sake of your own mental health, please read them before turning this page. For those of you who like your MMCs to be morally grey bastards, your fictional relationships to be tortured, and you like a little bit of pain, let's dance together in the dark.

Happy reading, my loves.

Yours always,

Willow

Love will not be constrain'd by mastery;
When mastery 'comes, the god of love anon
Beats his fair wings, and farewell! He is gone!
Love is a thing as any spirit free;
Women by nature love their liberty

-Geoffrey Chaucer, The Canterbury Tales

Chapter 1

KARA

Never ask a woman if she's ready yet. If you have to ask, there's a good chance she's not and an even greater chance she'll spend the next few hours plotting your murder. Tread carefully with stupid questions.

"Are you ready, yet?" Cade asks from behind me as he bends down to kiss my shoulder, the warmth of his breath against my exposed skin causing shivers to dance along my spine. Even after six months, the bastard still inexplicably wreaks havoc on my nervous system. The softest words, the smallest touches, the slightest commands still set the blood in my veins aflame. I am an unwilling captive to his needs and desires in more ways than one. And I still fucking hate it.

Mostly.

I glare up at his too attractive reflection in the mirror, the size difference between us almost laughable as he and his six feet of British deliciousness towers over me while I sit on my plush stool in front of the vanity. "It's still not perfect," I reply with a small huff of annoyance as I survey my own reflection in the mirror for perhaps the hundredth time tonight. I reach for the brush, viciously raking it through my pale, blonde hair until it hangs in glossy waves down my shoulders. I've let it grow out over the months I've been with Cade, the long tresses a testament to the surprising endurance of our relationship.

I scrunch up my nose in irritation as I critically judge every facet of my appearance from my dark brown eyes that stand out even more with the smoky, charcoal shadow to the blood-tinged hue of my lipstick. Something still isn't quite right.

"I beg to differ," Cade says with a soft laugh as he bends to place another kiss on the sensitive curve of my neck, the slight stubble of his cheek tickling me until I struggle beneath him. "You are always perfect, no matter how much unnecessary time you spend putting on makeup and doing your hair and whatever the hell else you conjure up in here."

Cade's mouth slides down to my shoulder, his lips hot and distracting as he kisses and nips his way along my skin. I can't help the moan that escapes as his teeth graze my collarbone and bite down. "Cade," I breathe, the chastisement sounding more like a beg for more. And it is a plea he is more than happy to satisfy. He trails soft, languid kisses down the exposed length of my back before his fingers deftly reach for the zipper that lies slightly above the curve of my ass.

"Cade!" I squeal, this time a little more frantic. As enticing as that sort of diversion sounds at the moment, there is no way I could escape a proper fucking with my makeup still intact. "Stop," I demand, a note of sternness in my voice. My protests soon turn to giggles as Cade's fingers find the sensitive spots on my hips, and he proceeds to torture me until I conceded to his demands.

"What was that, love? I couldn't quite hear you," Cade taunts. He pulls me against his chest and continues to incite unbecoming squeals and screeches with his damned fingers in my sides. Trapping my flailing arms against my back, Cade once again reaches for the zipper on my dress.

"Caden Ashford, if you get me naked again, we are not leaving this manor tonight," I admonish, my chest heaving from the painful exertion of forced fits of giggles.

"That sounds almost like a command, Miss Caine," Cade chides, his tone sharpening. "Only one person gives the commands in this house, and it certainly isn't you." I feel a quick sting of teeth against my neck. It is the subtlest of warnings that such behavior will not be tolerated where we are going.

Well, he can shove the warning up his ass because we won't be going anywhere if he keeps trying to slip his cock inside me. "Someone needs to stop thinking with their dick if we are ever going to make it to Pandemonium."

Pandemonium is the kink club owned by Cade's friend, Finnian Holt, the gorgeous bastard who saw me half naked and on my knees while I served the two of them for the night. It was, without a doubt, the most awkward experience of my life and the most sadistically creative punishment Cade has ever contrived. Yet.

I've seen Finn quite a few times since that night—fully clothed, thankfully—and I'll admit he's beginning to grow on me. When we're together, the three of us get into a fair amount of mischief. And as Cade's closest friend, he and I have formed a tenuous friendship of our own. One that will undoubtedly be tested when I experience Cade and Finnian in their element for the first time tonight.

It was my idea to go to Pandemonium. I have been begging Cade to take me for months, and, after much pleading and a fair amount of cock sucking sorcery, he finally caved.

"You sound quite eager to be paraded around a filthy sex club, tonight." Cade's smile is teasing, but I know he's proud of me for being willing to step out of my comfort zone. "I fear I've thoroughly corrupted you."

"Don't give yourself so much credit, Lord Ashford," I snark, swatting away his lingering hands from my hips. "I'm merely interested in scoping out your competition. Think there are any available Doms who are a little less endowed in the assholery department?"

"If there are, I'll make sure they're *unavailable* by any means necessary before the night is over," Cade threatens with a surge of venom in his voice. His fingers twist in my hair and jerk my head to the side, forcing me to look into his melded green and gold eyes. The sparks of fury in his molten gaze twist and warm my insides in unusual ways. "And you had better watch that mouth before it earns you a punishment that you definitely won't consider worth the amusement of provoking me."

"Yes, *sir*," I respond, my eyes still sparkling with machinations in spite of Cade's threats. He gives one last, firm tug against my tender scalp before releasing me, his beautiful features contorting with discontent. There is nothing I enjoy as much as getting under his thick skin. And I will enjoy it even more when he leaves his marks on *my* skin later as payback.

I frown when I look at my reflection in the mirror once more. The damned man mussed up my hair. Rolling my eyes, I reach for the brush again.

"Kara, if you touch that fucking brush *one* more time, I will put you over my knee and use it to redden your arse."

I blanch, my hands quickly falling to my lap for fear that he might mistake any movement as an invitation to make good on his threat. "You're a bastard," I retort with a pout.

"And you're gorgeous," Cade responds in a serious tone as he captures my chin in his grasp. "You could show up tonight in a bloody burlap sack, and you would still outshine every single person in the room. In fact, I haven't quite decided if I'll allow everyone to leave with their eyes intact after being allowed to look at you the entire evening."

"That's a little dramatic," I answer with a nervous laugh. I'm terrible at accepting compliments as it is, so I have an even more difficult time finding an appropriate response to the *you're so beautiful I could kill anyone who looks at you* sort of compliments Cade likes to regularly throw at me.

"I never claimed to be anything but," Cade says with a smirk, tracing a single finger along my bare throat. "I think something is missing," he comments with a cryptic insinuation.

Those few words incite panic, morphing the butterflies in my stomach into carnivorous creatures with pointed teeth and claws aimed to draw blood from my insides. "I knew it," I agree in distress. "Is the makeup too much? Should I put my hair up? Maybe wear the red dress instead of the black?"

"Your dress is lovely," Cade answers with a smirk as he reaches into his coat to pull out a large, black velvet, square box. "Though I would like to see you in red." He hands me the unexpectedly heavy box, his features marked by an indiscernible mixture of emotions.

With trembling fingers, I open the top, gasping when I discover what lies within. It's a necklace fit for gracing the neck of a queen—a choker composed entirely of large, oval rubies, the deep red stones haloed with diamonds that glimmer strikingly in the light. It's without a doubt the prettiest piece of jewelry I've ever seen. And I'm terrified to even touch it.

"Cade—I can't wear this," I respond as anxiety creeps up my throat at the thought of holding something so precious and valuable. Something that doesn't belong anywhere near the neck of a simple librarian. "It's too much." I try to hand the box back to him.

Ignoring my protests, Cade snatches the outrageously expensive necklace from the box and drapes it across my neck. "You *will* wear it because it pleases me beyond words to see you claimed as mine." Cade's fingers expertly fasten the clasp at my nape, leaving me with an almost uncomfortable weight against my throat.

"What exactly is that supposed to mean?" I ask in confusion. The choker is tight, loose enough for me to breathe, but constricting enough for me to be reminded of its presence with every intake of breath.

"This is more than just a pretty piece of jewelry, love. This is your collar," Cade says, slipping a single finger beneath the choker and tugging me toward him. The pressure of the jewels against my throat is tighter now, and I struggle to breathe steadily. "It serves as my mark of ownership, and you will wear it anytime we go to Pandemonium. The other submissives and slaves will be wearing collars as well. It is a sort of code to establish who is taken and who is free game."

I gape at Cade, waiting for the punchline of his ridiculous joke. As usual, there isn't one. I'm left rolling my eyes as he stands there expectantly as though he didn't just normalize his Dom shit for the sake of seeing me squirm beneath the literal weight of the submission he demands. Because why give a girl a necklace and call it a necklace when you could call it a fucking *collar of ownership*?

Damn kinky bastard.

Cade uses his hold on the choker, or *collar*, to pull me to my feet. Catching me by surprise, he steals the last of my breath with his mouth, his warm tongue coaxing my surrender in a way only he can as he kisses me into light-headed bliss. He pulls harder, the pressure of the necklace against my throat causing my vision to tinge with darkness, and I moan into his mouth, more desperate for the taste of him than actual air in my lungs. Just as I start to sway in his arms, Cade releases his hold, his lips unlatching from mine as I gasp for oxygen, my blood singing with an indescribable high from having its life-source momentarily deprived. Cade runs his thumb over my now swollen bottom lip, seeming to enjoy smearing my red lipstick against my skin. "There," he says in a soft rumble, his voice filled with warmth mingled with a strange sort of awe. "Perfect."

Chapter 2

CADEN

The drive to Pandemonium is about thirty minutes from Ashford Manor along dark country roads lit only by the faintest hint of moonlight. We are so far outside the city that you can see the stars glimmer against the blackness of the night sky on a clear night, and tonight the summer air is dry and warm.

I look over at the beautiful girl that I get to call mine, her small hand intertwined with my own. Kidnapping an archivist from a library and holding her prisoner in my home was hardly the makings of a match made in heaven, but fate decided to have a little irony. Now, my little librarian lets me take her to the hideaway beneath my library and fuck the propriety out of her in deliciously filthy ways. Turns out, my good girl has quite a taste for being a bad girl.

Unfortunately, she's expected a few changes out of me as well. Namely—no more stealing. I'm not going to lie, it hurt to retire from black market acquisitions. Not because of the money; God knows I inherited more than enough wealth from my grandfather along with the title of Lord. But robbing museums and private collections of their treasures gave me a challenge—something to do with my time. Now, I'm left with nothing to do other than Kara. So if her delightful cunt ever gets tired of being stuffed with my cum, the blame is entirely hers.

The mouth-watering thought of her bare pussy has me staring down at the slit in Kara's black dress. I move our joined hands up her thigh, forcing her to spread the inky silk of her dress until both of her full, creamy thighs are showing. I stroke my thumb over her skin, watching as goose flesh erupts under my touch. She shivers, biting down on her perfect red lip as she looks over at me. Her dark eyes are wide and pleading.

"Are you nervous?" I ask, continuing to caress her while her legs jostle against the leather seat.

Kara stills, her knees no longer bouncing up and down. "Yes," she answers, her voice soft and hesitant.

"Why are you nervous, love?"

"I don't want to do it wrong." The words tumble rapidly out of her mouth, like she's been holding them in the whole night.

I give her a knowing smile. How very typical that her anxiety is about wanting to be perfect. "There's no wrong way to do kink, Kara. As long as it's safe and consensual, anything goes. You know that."

"I know." She bites down on her lip, and I'm worried she might break the skin.

"Hey," I chide, using my thumb to tug her bottom lip from the prison of her teeth. "The only person who's allowed to make this pretty skin bleed is me. Understood?"

She nods. "Yes, sir."

"You're perfect," I remind her, chucking her under the chin. "When have you ever been anything less, Dr. Caine?"

That gets a begrudging smile to tug at her lips. I never call her by her formal title. In spite of her having earned more than one Doctorate of Philosophy, I tend to demote her just for the sake of annoyance. Few things get under my little librarian's skin more than calling her Miss Caine when she wants to be taken seriously. And it's one of my many joys in life to get under her skin as well as inside her.

"Are we doing away with the usual power play for the evening, Lord Ashford?" Kara asks with an arched brow and a cheeky little smirk on her face.

"Not at all," I retort, pinching her cheek until she winces and the smugness on her face wavers just a bit. "It was simply a reminder that just because you're submissive doesn't mean you're any less powerful."

Kara's expression softens, and I can read the tension leaving her body, like darkness being excised from the soul. My girl is stronger than anyone; she merely needs to be reminded of it every once in a while.

"Thank you, sir," she replies after a moment of reflection. Her brown eyes are warm with adoration as she gazes up at me. She's no longer nervous. She's willing to trust me with her limits and trust herself with her endurance. The peace of her submission radiates off her body with an effervescent glow, enrobing her like the mantle of a goddess.

And she is my fucking goddess.

"You're most welcome, love." My eyes turn to the bright blaze of torches writhing in the distant darkness. "We're here."

Pandemonium. Milton's name for the capital city of Hell in Paradise Lost. A land of perpetual flames and darkness. It's an oxymoron, of course, but Finn tried his best to make the city of hellish revelry a reality.

A palace of darkness sits on top of a hill. The shadowed mansion is an imposing structure composed of black stones, four rounded turrets, pointed spires, and not a single window. And while the outer facade is a beautiful nightmare, the inside is a deviant's dream paradise. Once we pass through the black, iron gates literally inscribed with the word *Hell*, flaming torches light the way on either side of the winding drive leading to the sprawling estate. There are no signs or directions to find your way in the near darkness. After all, Hell has no need of a roadmap. Those who belong merely have a way of finding it.

This version of Hell comes with a chauffeur, so I toss the Aston Martin's keys to the attendant wearing a black demon mask and help Kara from the car. She stands stunned in front of the enormous brass doors ornately detailing the fall of Satan and the angels into the fiery lake on one side and the serpent's seduction of Eve on the other.

"It's beautiful," she says in awe.

"It is," I agree. Apart from Ashford Manor, Pandemonium is the only place where I'm truly allowed to embrace my whole self. It's very freeing, and

I hope Kara grows the same fondness for Finn's little slice of Hell.

Kara runs her fingers over the carved metal reverently, not even bothering to use the large, serpent's head knockers.

"You're not the only one who prides themselves on their excessive literary knowledge," I whisper against her ear, pressing my body against her back. "Though Finn keeps his strictly to the theological variety. Did I tell you he meant to join the priesthood at one point? This was sort of his middle finger to God for making him choose between his faith and his cock."

Kara nods her head in feigned interest, still enraptured with interpreting the artistic narrative. My hands slide down her hips; I'm teeming with excitement to give her a tour of my private room and do ungodly things to her. I bury my lips in the crook of her neck, running my tongue over her skin and lapping up the taste of salt and sweetness. The scent of violets and berries floods my senses, and I want to drown myself in the intoxicating essence of her.

"Want to see the inside, love?" I ask, biting down on her pulse point and feeling it throb against my tongue.

"Yes, please," Kara answers, her voice raw and needy as she grinds her arse against me.

"Then let's go to Hell."

The doors are opened by another attendant in a black demon mask, this one unmistakably feminine. Black is Finn's dress code for every Pandemonium employee, as is the mask. It's as much to preserve the identities of the workers as it is to allow them to blend seamlessly into the background. Finn wants the experience to feel as real as possible. What can I say, theatrics are one of his kinks.

The inside of Pandemonium is nothing like its dark, foreboding exterior. It is lavish, decadent, a tainted mirror of heaven. The room is a quatrefoil—rounded on all four sides. Three of the spheres contain a different collection of equipment or implements for various kink play. The fourth sphere is the club bar. Like many establishments that mix alcohol and sex, there's a two drink limit.

The floors and the arched ceiling are gold, the finish so gleaming that they reflect off each other. There are four golden, carved pillars forming a circle in the middle of the seemingly endless room, each depicting a scene from Milton's epic. Each pillar has a suspension ring at the top for the addition of ropes, cuffs, or chains.

And at the center of the circle is Satan's golden throne—intricate metal work composed of twisted serpents.

The most striking detail of the entire club is the element of hellfire. Every wall is encased in flames. Massive, floor to ceiling fireplaces shielded in glass run along the whole length of the room. Thanks to the reflective surfaces of the floor and ceiling, the entire room appears to be consumed by fire. The flames are the only source of light in the dim room, and the effect is positively hellish.

Beneath the large public playroom fondly referred to as "Hell," there's a sensory deprivation sauna. It's pitch black and kept scorching hot—Finn's interpretation of Milton's hell being a furnace of flames that emit no light. Perfect for all the deviants who like to pretend they're writhing in hell as they fuck. It's Finn's favorite part of Pandemonium, but I don't like to play on the lower level. After all, what's the point of fucking Kara if I can't see her?

"Where does that lead?" Kara asks as we make our way through the throng of people in various states of undress. She's looking curiously at the staircase beside the bar. It's the first time she's spoken. And since she hasn't screamed in terror yet, I'll take that as a good sign.

"Those are the private rooms," I answer, wrapping an arm around her waist and drawing her close. "There are six in total. It's a sort of hierarchy within Pandemonium. The highest level members are given extra privileges, one of which being a private space outfitted with everything needed to indulge in their specific tastes. One for Satan, obviously reserved for Finn. One for Eve, our esteemed Dominatrix. And four for the higher demons of Hell."

"So Beelzebub, Belial, Mammon, and Maloch, I'm assuming?" Kara asks, her face adorably scrunched with the concentration of skimming through the texts in her head and plucking the aforementioned characters found in *Paradise Lost* from her memory.

"Have I ever told you how sexy you are when you slip into student mode?" I answer, laughing at her almost competitive need to be well-versed on every subject of literature.

"Yes, I believe we've delved into your sexual fascination with *schoolgirls* quite thoroughly," Kara retorts with a grimace of annoyance.

I smile at the memory of Kara splayed over my desk with her bare arse peeking out of her short little schoolgirl skirt. "If you ever want me to teach you a lesson again, just say the word, Miss Caine," I breathe against her ear. Kara shivers beneath me, but she makes no move to touch me. She's still too uncomfortable to perform under the intrigued gaze of strangers, but she'll get over it soon. I'll make sure of it.

"So are you one?" she asks, jolting me from pleasurable fantasies involving her on her knees, begging for my cock in front of the entire club.

"Am I what?" I've no fucking idea of what our conversation was about before the word schoolgirl was thrown into the mix.

"Are you a *demon* level Dom? Is one of those private rooms yours?" she clarifies, giving meaning to the current furrow of her brow and the observable hesitance in her expression.

I pause, now understanding her wariness. She's probably thinking of all the subs that might have come before her and all the debasing things I might have done to them if one of those rooms happens to be mine. Which it is. And there were countless others before her, although no number of them combined could ever measure up to the feelings I have for her.

"Yes," I respond in answer to both her questions. "Can you guess which moniker our gracious dark lord bestowed upon me?"

Kara appraises me with studious concentration—a perpetual academic positively salivating at the thought of a potential homework assignment. "Mammon," she answers after a long pause, seeming quite certain of her assessment.

I scoff at the inferred insult. "Mammon? Is that what you think of me? I hardly think greed is my primary motivator."

"Says the man who literally kidnapped me for the sake of monetary gain," she retorts with a smug smile.

"Maybe I kidnapped you because I thought you'd look good in my bed," I reply, lowering my head until my lips hover directly above hers. Taunting her with the possibility of a kiss.

"Well, I can't argue with you there," she quips in a cheeky tone. "I am an exquisite bed accessory." Taking the bait, she meshes her lips with mine. She tastes heady and sweet, like a full bodied wine with subtle notes of berries and chocolate.

"That you are, love," I agree with her, moving from her lips and placing a doting kiss directly on the tip of her nose. Kidnapping her has been the best questionable decision I've made in my entire goddamn life.

"So who *did* Finnian pick for you?" she asks, still stuck on literary metaphors while I'm fully erect and consumed with fantasies of fucking her into oblivion.

"Beelzebub, obviously. And you'll get into quite a heap of trouble if he hears you calling him by his first name here. In his sanctum, all underlings address him as *my lord*. Many Doms here refer to him as Satan. They like playing into the whole theme; honestly, I think Finn gets off on the theatrics of it too."

"Please tell me you're not serious," Kara responds, a slight flush of embarrassment tinging her cheeks. I knew she would be *thrilled* about that part. Kara's stout sense of pride doesn't take well to the submissive aspect of our relationship when it is outside the confines of the bedroom. Kara Caine bows to no man. And that is what makes breaking her so much more delectable.

"I am more than serious, but please feel free to test me on it and see what happens. We haven't had a public whipping in quite some time, and I'm sure everyone would appreciate the show."

Kara blanches, her pale skin turning an even lighter shade as the blood drains from her face in horror. And she should be frightened. I've seen what happens when Finn feels he's been disrespected in his dominion, and it's not pretty. Although, I suppose that would depend upon your definition of pretty. Finn's skill with a single tail can be quite lovely.

"Don't worry," I soothe, stroking my knuckles along the edge of her jaw. "If in doubt, just keep silent." The glare she shoots me can only be described as of the murderous variety.

"Ashford!" a familiar voice calls from behind me. I turn to find Finn striding toward us, his flavor of the month—a curvaceous, red-headed beauty—crawling as fast as she can on hands and knees to keep up with him.

Finn is one of the few people in the room taller than me, and his commanding presence immediately captivates anyone in his vicinity. He is fair and blonde with pale blue eyes the color of icy waters and sometimes just as cold. He looks the very epitome of an angel before the fall, and he has his father's Danish genes to thank.

"Satan," I greet, my tone full of patronizing derision. He knows I hate the fucking nicknames.

"I haven't seen you for a month, and you're already being a cunt," Finn retorts with a good humored laugh. "And I see you've finally brought the little librarian with you." His eyes rove over Kara's exposed skin with an appreciative interest, and I can't resist wrapping my hand around her throat just above her new collar. My touch is gentle, for the moment anyway.

"Say hello, Kara," I command in a soft tone, my lips brushing against the silkiness of her hair.

"Hello," she answers with a quiver of nerves.

I squeeze my fingers a bit tighter around her neck as a reminder of our recent conversation regarding how to address Finn. I'm torn between wanting her to comply and being interested in how he will react if she doesn't. I feel her swallow hard against the pressure of my thumb digging into her windpipe.

"Hello, my lord," she rectifies, her body warming with humiliation. And I bet if I trailed my hand from her throat down to her cunt, she'd drench my fingers with her arousal.

"Good girl," I whisper so only she can hear, not missing her slight moan in response. I happen to know exactly what those two little words do to her, and if she wasn't craving my cock before, she sure as hell is now.

"Well, someone is on their best behavior," Finn says with a doting smile and a pinch to Kara's flushed cheek. They've seen each other many times since Kara's punishment dinner, and they always seem to engage in good-natured bickering. Kara is probably tortured with the effort to remain submissive and polite when her usual retort to Finn's riling is to tell him to *fuck off*.

"Thinking of poisoning me the next time I'm at the manor for dinner?" he asks her, reading the vengeful intent in her gaze.

"Perhaps, my lord," she answers with the sweetest of smiles. Like a fucking angel with the heart of a demon and the tongue of a serpent.

"Nonsense," I interject, feeling a little jealous that she would share her threats of death with anyone other than me. "If she was going to poison anyone, I would have been dead six months ago. Isn't that right, love?" I ask, wrapping both of my arms around her and pulling her close enough that her familiar scent intoxicates my senses.

"Yes, sir," she answers, twisting in my arms to look up at me. "Although, how do you know I haven't been doing it slowly?"

Finn bellows with laughter, and I smirk too because, honestly, neither of us would put it past her. "I think someone is begging for a spanking," I threaten, reaching down and squeezing the perfect plumpness of her arse. "Want me to put you over my knee right now, cheeky girl? Let everyone here see your arse turn a pretty shade of pink?"

"No, sir," she answers in an instant, her eyes quickly lowering to the floor in submission. Or *feigned* submission.

"Pink?" Finn scoffs. "The Ashford I know likes his girls red at the very least. Is the little librarian turning you soft?"

I scowl at him, hating that he brought up my past submissives in front of Kara. And because he's probably right. Not wanting to discuss my personal weaknesses in front of present company—or fucking anyone—I search for a diversion.

"Well, the *Satan* I know wouldn't let his lowly slave look at other Doms as though she deserves to suck their cocks," I retort with a pointed glance at the girl on her knees shamelessly eye-fucking me in front of her own master and my submissive. The redhead and Kara both jolt violently as though met with the lash of a whip. In Red's case, she'll likely know the feeling pretty soon.

Finn looks down at his slave in disapproval, looping a single finger through the large metal ring on the front of her collar and jerking the girl up until she is nearly dangling in the air with her knees just barely brushing the floors. I feel Kara stiffen in front of me, probably worried that Finn will hurt the girl. Which he probably will, and the redhead girl will enjoy every minute of it judging from the excited gleam in her eyes.

"Did you look at Beelzebub?" Finn seethes with a jerk of the leather collar around her neck. He likes to enforce high protocol among his slaves while at the club, so a slave looking another Dom in the eye is a cardinal sin in his book.

"Yes, my lord," the girl admits with a sheepish grin, having the good sense to look a bit frightened.

"I thought I taught you better than that, slave," Finn reprimands with a tsk.

"Yes, my lord," she answers, her eyes obediently trained on the floor. "Please give me the punishment I deserve."

"I did have more enjoyable plans for you this evening, slave, but I suppose they will have to wait. Come." Finn drags the girl by her collar as though it were a leash. "I'm sorry to abandon you to this bastard for the night, Kara darling, but this naughty little kitty needs a whipping," he says, pulling the girl in the direction of his private room. "I'll find you later, Ashford," Finn calls before disappearing down the hall with the girl crawling behind him.

"Well that was entertaining." I turn Kara around to face me and lift her chin so that her eyes meet mine. "How are you feeling?" I ask her gently. I'm aware that this sort of scene can be overwhelming when you're inexperienced.

Her eyes flit around the room, taking everything in. I know what she sees. Carnality. Nudity. Raw sexuality. Inhibition. Vulgarity. Passion. A collage of so many pure, unfiltered emotions and interactions that compose the natural state of humanity. When I look around the room, I see freedom. I see a community of people brave enough to reveal their truest selves. It's a beautiful thing, and I hope she is able to embrace that beauty alongside me.

"It's mesmerizing," she says in awe, her warm brown eyes wide with wonder. "They're so open and comfortable with their bodies and each other. It makes me wonder why anyone could think sex is meant to be had in the dark. It belongs in the light where every aspect of such intimacy can be seen and celebrated."

"That's very progressive of you, Dr. Caine," I reply, teasing her to mask the overwhelming pride I feel at her ability to accept all of the sexual deviance happening around us without judgment.

"So, what do you want to do?" Kara asks, looking up at me with large doe eyes that appear a great deal more innocent than they should. I want to wipe every fleck of innocence from those eyes and fill them with tears as she gags on the cock straining against my pants.

"You," I answer, my voice dark and savage with need.

"And how would you like to do me, Lord Ashford?" she questions in a sultry tone that has me licking my lips for a taste of her sinful mouth. "Would you like me on my back, my legs spread wide so you can take me and fuck me hard and deep?" Her fingers trail along the roughness of my jaw, outlining the sharp edges. "Or maybe you'd like to take me to your private room, tie me up, and fuck me against the wall while I'm helpless and at your mercy."

Her fingers slip down my neck to my tie, wrapping it around her hand and pulling me against her. "Or maybe," she tempts, her low voice like a siren's call as she drags her teeth over her full bottom lip. "Maybe you would like me on my knees." She drops to her fucking knees in front of me and anyone else in the club who wants to watch. "So you can grab my hair and fuck my face like I'm your good little slut." She reaches for the buckle of my belt, and I haven't the fortitude or the inclination to stop her.

"Jesus fucking Christ, Kara," I growl, running my fingers through my hair as I look down at her, and it's taking all of my self control not to come on the spot when I feel her hands brush teasingly against my cock. "Take it out," I command in a sharp tone, my fingers slipping into her hair and twisting the strands at the roots.

She obeys without hesitation, nimble hands loosening my belt, unfastening my pants, and allowing my aching cock to spring free. She rubs her thumb over the tip, smearing the first drops of pre-cum in a circular motion and setting every nerve in my body ablaze. I shiver at the sensitive touch before shaking myself out of the haze of arousal. She shouldn't be able to control my body so easily. She's meant to be serving me, not dragging me around like a drooling dog begging for a fucking pet.

Turning fierce, I fist my fingers in her hair and pull hard. "Now choke on it like a good little slut," I order, thrusting my hips and forcing her head down, groaning when the tip of my cock hits the back of her throat and she swallows me down. She doesn't fight me at all as I force my way past her gag reflexes. I've trained her enough that she can endure a face-fuck like a pro. I'm huge, so she'll start struggling once I've rubbed her throat raw, but she can take me easily for a few minutes.

"Do you like that?" I ask, knowing she can't respond with me filling her mouth. I thrust deeper, loving the sound of her gagging on my length. "Do you like taking your master's cock where everyone can see you?" I pull out completely, a demanding arch of my brow signaling that I expect her to answer the question.

"Y-yes, sir," she admits, her eyes never leaving mine.

"Look around, Kara," I order. Hesitantly, she does as I ask, her eyes landing on all the people who have stopped to watch a beautiful girl get on her knees to serve her Dom. "They love watching you get all messy with cum and spit while you take my cock down your throat. Such a gorgeous fucking mess you are." I rub my cock over her lips, my pre-cum leaving a glossy trail of wetness.

"Eyes on me, love." She turns her attention back to me, her dark brown eyes hazy with lust. To my great surprise, I believe Kara Caine is an exhibitionist. "Spread your legs." I crouch down—my obscenely hard cock still out and very desperate for a hole to fuck—and slip my hand between Kara's parted thighs. I don't even need to pull aside her knickers to get the answer to my question. She's bloody soaked through them. "Oh love, letting all those people watch has you drenched."

I slip a finger beneath the thin scrap of lace keeping me from her cunt and dip into her slick entrance. I feel her clench around me, begging for more. I trail the wetness up to her clit and rub circles around her bundle of nerves. Kara moans at my touch, her cheeks flushing beautifully when she realizes everyone else in the club can hear her enjoying herself. She doesn't ask me to stop.

"Do you want me to make you come? Do you want all these people to hear what you sound like when you shatter with pleasure?"

Kara bites her lip, weighing whether her arousal or her humiliation is higher in this moment. Thankfully, she gets off on both. "Yes, please," she whispers, her lovely eyes locked on mine.

"Wrap your hands around my cock. I want to paint you with my cum so everyone in this goddamn club can see who you belong to."

Kara obeys and wraps her hands around my swollen shaft; she has to use both hands to fully encircle my girth. She squeezes hard just how I like it, and I have to force myself not to cum all over her right now. As a reward for being such a good girl, I want her to come first. My pleasure can wait.

"I'm not coming until you do, so you better watch those hands, Miss Caine," I chide, fisting her hair to keep my balance while I bend down on one knee to rub my thumb over her clit. When she melts into the rhythm of my strokes, I slip two fingers inside her. She pants in pleasure while stroking my cock, being careful not to go too fast or hard. She's merely teasing me at this point, but I like a bit of torture as much as the next person.

I feel her thighs tense and her cunt clench as she gets close to the edge. Now I just need to push her over. "Come on my hand, beautiful. Soak my fingers while all these fuckers watch, wishing it was them burying their fingers in your sweet cunt."

"Oh God," she moans, clamping down hard on my fingers as she starts to spasm with pleasure.

"Harder, Kara," I demand, giving her permission to send me over the edge with her. "Make me come. I want to see you fucking covered in me." Her hand moves faster, sliding slickly with the stickiness of my arousal. I curl my fingers inside her, massaging the sweet spot that makes her gush. I want her to drench the gilded floor so she can see how much she loves being my dirty girl.

"I'm—I'm coming," she whimpers as she surrenders to the pleasure.

"Good," I growl. "Take me with you." She practically strangles my cock, and I come without warning, spraying milky ribbons of cum all over her tits and thighs. And she's a gorgeous fucking sight when she's claimed as mine.

We're both panting when we come down from the high, our lungs laboring to catch up with our need for air. I slip my fingers from Kara's cunt and use them to smear my cum over her skin, rubbing it in. Holding her gaze, I reach my sticky fingers up to her lips and push them into her mouth. Without being told, Kara slides her tongue over them, sucking and licking them clean. I pull away with a wet pop and bring my fingers to my own lips. She moans when I drag my tongue up the length of my first two fingers, lapping at the lingering taste of her arousal and saliva.

"Mmm, you taste like sin," I purr, and she looks ready to let me fuck her in the middle of the club.

"Dammit, I missed the show," Finn calls loudly from the stairs as he stomps down them, dragging a very tear-stained slave behind him.

"Hardly," I scoff, staring down at Kara with sparks of mischief in my eyes. "We're just getting started."

I'm high on power. High on using Kara for everyone to see. And I want to do it over and over.

Chapter 3

KARA

Nothing cures an orgasm hangover like scones and a cup of tea. I'm sure Mrs. Hughes would agree with the way she's been plying me with pastries all morning to *help put the roses back in my cheeks*. It's her friendly way of saying I look like death after having spent nearly the whole night succumbing to Cade's mouth and cock. The strain in my neck and the soreness in my throat reminds me that there was a fair amount of reciprocation involved as well.

"So, how was it?" the motherly Scotswoman asks as she pulls yet another tray of scones out of the oven, adding to the already mountainous pile in front of me that I'll never be able to finish.

My eyes snap to hers in surprise. I hope it's merely the exhaustion making it seem as though there is a lurid insinuation in her words. As far as I know, Mrs. Hughes has no knowledge of the nature of mine and Cade's relationship, and that's how I would like to keep it. "How was what?" I ask, feigning innocence as I sip at my tea. It's too hot, burning my tongue. The burn is preferable to this conversation.

"Oh come now, I know the getting ons in this house. He took you to Mr. Holt's last night." She grins at me like she knows every depraved thing we did at Pandemonium.

Oh god. I try not to panic, thinking of a perfectly logical reason for us to have been at Finn's place. One that doesn't involve deviant sexcapades. "You—think we had dinner at Finn's house last night?" I guess, hoping the most scandalous idea she's entertaining at the moment is that we might have drunk white wine with our steak instead of red.

"Nay, I *know* he took you to that place out in the middle of nowhere. The one where people go to—play with their inner demons, if you like."

I choke on the tea in my mouth, nearly spitting it all over the kitchen. Oh. My. God. Mrs. Hughes is *not* making Hell jokes about Pandemonium right now. It's too early for this. Not that there will ever be a right time to discuss this with the person most resembling a maternal figure in my life.

"Have you got whisky in your tea this morning?" I ask, still reeling. "Because you're spouting nonsense."

"Psh, I've taken care of this house for near over a decade. I know what's hidden in the library, and I know what sorts of things you and Mr. Ashford get up to."

I spill my tea before it even makes it to my mouth this time. She knows about the hideaway. She knows about Cade and me. And I think I might die of humiliation if she says another word about either.

"Come now, stop gawking," Mrs. Hughes chides. "Ye'll get no shaming from me lass. I was young once too, ye ken?" She gives me a cheeky smile.

I groan, covering my face with my hand. "Mrs. Hughes, please stop."

She laughs, the sound of it warm and hearty. It makes me peek up at her in spite of my mortification. "All I'm asking is—did ye like it?" She has a twinkle in her eye, and I have the distinct feeling she just wants to make sure Cade and I are happy. That's all she's ever wanted as long as I've known her. And I don't know what we'd do without her looking after all of us. Starve at the very least.

"Yes, all right, I liked it," I admit with a defeated sigh. "Now get back to your baking, you filthy Scotswoman, and let me nurse my headache in peace."

"Aye, shagging until the wee hours of the night will leave ye wrecked in the morning. But it's nothing a good cup of tea can't fix." She fills my empty cup with more steaming tea.

Lovely, sex advice from Mrs. Hughes.

My humiliation is complete.

Chapter 4

CADEN

I've been hunting a shadow for six months. A wraith in the wind. A ghost who seems to walk the earth without footprints or trace of any kind.

There's been no sign of Jace or the first edition Chaucer he demanded as payment in exchange for our security. I gave him the text that Kara protected with her life without a second thought. I would give away a whole library of priceless books and an entire collection of rare artifacts to keep her safe.

Kara's academic integrity demands that she preserve historical literature at all costs. But I have no such scruples. The only thing I'm conditioned to protect at any cost is her.

I'd call the notion romantic; she'd no doubt call it heresy.

The only reason Jace walked away from our meeting in downtown Chicago that night was because I allowed it. But he still has a debt to pay. He took Kara and hurt her in ways that would have broken anyone weaker. But my girl is strong, and she used that pain to make her even stronger. And even though Jace didn't ruin her like he wanted, the cunt is still going to bleed for daring to try.

The only problem is—shadows don't bleed.

"I think you should tell her," Ortega says suddenly, ripping me from my murderous musings.

I gape at the over-muscled man looking too large for the steering wheel of the Escalade he's driving. "And *why* should I tell Kara that there's an unhinged psychopath stalking her, laying in wait for the moment I slip and he takes her right out from under me again?" I ask in a tone bordering on outrage. I'm pretty sure informing Kara that her nightmare is coming back to haunt her is the last bloody thing on my to-do list at the moment.

Ortega's calm expression doesn't change as he keeps his eyes on the road. "Because she deserves to know the very real *peligro* her life is in." He gives a small laugh. "I think vague warnings don't really work on her. She'll be reckless until you give her a logical reason not to be."

"I can't argue with you there," I reply, dragging my fingers through my hair. He's right. Kara is difficult any time I try to restrict her freedom to keep her safe, but I don't want her living in fear of what Jace might do to her. I want her living in fear of what *I* might do to her if she disobeys.

"She's tougher than you think, *jefe*." He turns his sharp, dark eyes on me. "She would want to know."

I scoff. "Yes, well what Kara wants and what's good for her are usually two entirely different things."

Sensing my blackening mood, Ortega decides not to press me any further. But I can read the tension in his body as he drives the car in silence. He thinks I'm making a mistake. And hell, maybe I am. But I would rather Kara hate me while keeping her safe then tell her the truth and have her looking over her shoulder the rest of her life. The bastard has already caused her enough grief as it is. Suffering the knowledge of Jace's intentions should be my burden alone to bear.

Two months ago, I received a message. A garbled bit of morbid poetry promising Kara's eventual death. But not just yet. First, the cunt promised to give us a show.

Since then, we've made finding Jace our number one priority. We don't bother with acquisitions or antiquities deals at the moment, not that there have been many this year to begin with. My righteous little librarian has an issue with fucking a man who profits from the occasional circumvention of the law. Needless to say, it gets boring as hell.

At first, it was just me, Ortega, and Braxton trying to track any of Jace's movements. Declan was eager to volunteer his assistance as well, but he's a better babysitter than investigator. Actually, he's fairly rubbish at that too. The boy is a good lackey, but he's failed to pick up any other useful skills yet. If it wasn't for his father, I never would have agreed to take on someone so green. But power is in his blood; sooner or later, he'll come into it.

We were quick to realize that the three of us weren't making any headway, so I hired mercenaries across the state too. They're a little easier to incentivize than standard private investigators, and I offered them an outrageous sum if they can lead me to whatever shit-hole Jace has stashed himself in. And after two goddamn months, we finally got a hit. Someone matching Jace's description was flagged in the outskirts of Chicago, a two hour drive from Ashford Manor. Ortega and I left as soon as we got the news. It could be nothing, but it's the first whisper of Jace's whereabouts we've had in six months, so we're going to bloody take it.

When we pull into a crumbling car park in front of the ring of dilapidated crackhouses moonlighting as motels, it's no wonder Jace stayed hidden for so long. Finding someone who doesn't want to be found in a place like this is like trying to find one specific rat amid the nighttime streets of London. It should be damned impossible. Which begs the question: if this is really him, how did we get him this time?

Ortega parks the car in front of a seedy motel that sits like a garish, teal blue beacon to anyone looking for a quick rut or something on the shady side. This is where my contact last saw the man who could be Jace. Ortega and I make our way to the rental office, trying to make as little contact with any of the surfaces as possible. Who knows what you can pick up in a place like this. The middle-aged woman at the front desk blows a puff of smoke from the cigarette between her lips as she eyes the two of us suspiciously. It doesn't take a scholar to see that we don't fit in here, and I'll not make any assumptions on the woman's level of education.

"You boys lost?" she asks in a gravelly voice, the cigarette never leaving her lips.

"Unfortunately not," I reply, trying not to let my eyes wander around the filthy room that reeks of smoke. I reach into my coat pocket, take out my wallet, and deposit a stack of hundreds on the desk. There's no sense in drawing things out. From experience, people who live life on the frays of society don't like to talk—about themselves or other people. Anyone sniffing around could be an officer, and handing out information to the police can be a deadly affair. However, money always has a way of loosening tight lips.

The woman's dull eyes brighten the moment she sees the notes on the table. She slides them off the counter, runs her thumb over the hundreds as she counts them, and then slides them into her bra for safekeeping.

"What do you need to know, honey?" she asks in a sweetened tone, taking the cigarette from her mouth and tapping it over the ashtray on her desk.

"We're looking for someone."

"We got a lot of *someones* coming through here. You got a name?"

I look at Ortega, and he shrugs with an arched brow. "Jace—but he might not have used it."

The woman nods her head. "Sure, sure, let me have a look." She grabs a large book and plops it on the desk. Clearly, nothing is computerized here. She thumbs through the pages, looking for recent customers.

"Uh-huh, here it is," she announces, jabbing her finger in the middle of the page. "Jacen Ashford. I remember him—pretty boy, like you two." She lets her eyes roam over Ortega and I, and I can't help cringing at being compared to Jace, even in something as shallow as looks. "He's paid up through next month. Not often you get people tryna stay. Usually it's just a night or two. Or a few hours if you're lucky." She shoots us a meaningful wink, and I have to mask my distaste at the insinuation.

"When was the last time you saw him?"

"Few days ago when he paid for the room, but not since. Most people don't come by the office unless they have a problem that needs fixin'."

"Do you mind if we have a look around the room?" I ask in a polite tone. I'm quite sure she's past caring about our intentions at this point.

"Sure, sure. I can take you up if you like," she offers, reaching for a large ring of keys.

"Just the key would be more than enough," I answer quickly, not wanting her to make any detours to give us a tour of the hourly rooms. "I wouldn't want to trouble you."

"It's no trouble."

I hope I've only imagined that she's pulled her tight-fitting blouse lower over her breasts when she stands from the desk. "Really," I reply, trying my damndest not to sound as frustrated as I feel. "I insist."

She frowns in disappointment. "Alright, if you say so." She drops the keys into my waiting hand. "It's number 6."

"Thank you so much for your assistance, Miss—?"

"Oh, Jolene," she answers, looking flushed and flustered.

"Thank you, Miss Jolene," I reply, falling even deeper into my usual accent because I know most of the women here find it charming.

She giggles, the sound a bit harsh coming from the throat of a smoker. "Not a problem, honey. Just make sure you bring those keys back when you're finished what you're doin'."

"Yes, ma'am," I answer with a salute before escaping the smoky room with Ortega right on my heels.

"Well, she likes you, *honey*," Ortega jabs as we make our way through the dark to the door marked number 6.

"Piss off," I bite back, trying to find which of the many keys on the ring unlocks the door. When the lock finally clicks open, I pause. What if Jace is actually in the room? Ortega is armed as usual, but we're not exactly prepared to handle the complications of a shoot out if it comes to that. "If he's in there, don't kill him," I whisper to Ortega.

He nods once. We both understand that whatever eventually kills Jace, it will be a lot slower and a lot more painful than a quick bullet to the head. Silently counting down from three on one hand, I get to zero and kick in the door.

A quick survey of the room suggests it's empty for the moment. I motion for Ortega to check the bathroom while I look behind curtains and under furniture. Nothing. The bed doesn't even look slept in. Jace may have paid for this room, but he didn't stay here. So why the elaborate farce? Why use my own last name on the registry just so we can be certain it's him? Why use the nickname Kara would occasionally bestow on him when she was feeling particularly put out? What the fuck is the point of all of this?

Feeling aimless, I open the drawer of the bedside table to see if Jace left anything of value. I gasp when I discover what's lying in place of the standard bible or notepad. I take it out, flipping through the pages to see if there are any notes or markings. There's a page that's been ripped out, but apart from that, there's nothing special or out of the ordinary. Other than the choice of book.

"What did you find?" Ortega asks, coming in and looking over my shoulder.

I toss him the book, and his reflexes are fast enough that he catches it against his chest.

"It's the goddamn Canterbury Tales."

Chapter 5

KARA

I'm following the devil into Hell for the second time in a row. Call me crazy, but eternal damnation is kind of growing on me.

The scent of sweat, sex, and leather hangs in the air like an intoxicating perfume as Cade leads me past the revelers at Pandemonium. I nearly trip over my own heels when a demanding tug of his hand drags me past the scene of a pretty sub pleasing her dominatrix that caught my attention. I feel so inexperienced compared to the intriguing displays of debauchery happening all around me.

And like the good student I am, I want to learn everything.

It's been two weeks since I made my submissive debut at Pandemonium. After I finally recovered from the number of orgasms Cade gave me in Hell in front of every member who cared to look over and see me writhing on his tongue or bouncing on his cock, I couldn't wait to go back. This time, I wanted a more private experience. But as Cade leads me up the winding staircase toward the level reserved for the demon Doms, I can't help the prickly swell of fear blossoming in my chest like rose vines rooting in my lungs and stifling my supply of air.

Cade pulls me toward his room, and I stare up at the ominous red door—the name *Beelzebub* emblazoned in shiny black letters at the top. All the blood red doors on the upper level have names—four demons, Eve, and Satan. It's all ridiculous and over-dramatic, but somehow terrifying at the same time.

There's a metallic scratch of a key as Cade unlocks his room. When the heavy wooden door swings open, I gasp. The sprawling room is a beautiful nightmare—equal parts gothic fantasy and macabre torture chamber. In fact, it's the perfect depiction of what you'd expect a high-end, hell-themed sex dungeon to look like. It's twisted and tasteful and it's got me tingling with excitement in all the right places.

Much like the lower level, hellfire plays a central role in the decor. There is a huge, open fireplace that is nearly my height and surrounded in a mantle of black stone carved to depict naked angels weeping above and fallen angels moaning in torment below. It's beautiful and grotesque at the same time. I'm mesmerized by the flames as they flicker and crackle, looking like the very mouth of Hell.

There is a large, four poster bed similar to the one in the hideaway, but with red sheets and drapes. Paneled mirrors line the entire wall opposite the bed, and I blush with the knowledge that I'll be able to watch every filthy thing Cade does to me in the reflection. There is a sex swing hanging from the ceiling in the corner, a St. Andrew's Cross in another, a leather spanking bench, and a metal contraption that looks disturbingly like a cage.

Great, he has an *actual* imprisonment kink. Fan-fucking-tastic.

There is a desk with a rack on the wall behind it lined with various instruments of corporal punishment. Apparently, Cade enjoys his schoolgirl fetish at the club as well. There are a few unfamiliar items that appear more befitting of a medieval dungeon than a sex room, and I'm hoping we steer clear of those—at least for my first time.

"What do you think?" Cade asks, disrupting the heavy silence hanging in the air.

"I think I better run while I still can," I answer with a nervous laugh. The subsequent scowl on Cade's face informs me that he doesn't appreciate my attempt at humor. "I think it's a little daunting," I admit.

"It can be overwhelming when it's your first time in here, but it isn't much different than the hideaway at home. What are you most apprehensive about?"

"Well, I would rather not go anywhere near the *cage*," I reply, trying not to sound too judgmental of his personal tastes, but it's a fucking cage. How is that even remotely sexy?

"Fine, no cage play for now," he answers, and I raise a brow at his addition of *for now*. "Anything else?"

"Just take it easy on me, please," I plead, shifting on my feet.

"Oh love, when have I ever done that?" Cade questions with a smug smile on his face. "I want to test some of your limits tonight. Are you brave enough to trust me?"

I nod in hesitant affirmation.

"Verbal responses in this room, Kara. I need you to voice your agreements and needs at all times, or we stop. Do you understand?"

"Yes, sir," I answer, feeling a flutter of excitement in my belly as he slips effortlessly into his Dom voice.

"Good. Now what is your safeword?"

"Thornfield," I respond without the need to think.

"And what will you say if you are at your limit and need to stop?"

"Thornfield."

"Will any word other than Thornfield end the scene once we've begun?" Cade asks, gripping my jaw in his hand and incinerating me with his smoldering gaze of green tinged gold.

"No, sir," I answer, looking up at him with trust in my eyes.

"Good girl." He chucks me under the chin before releasing me and walking toward one of the tall dark cabinets. I hold my breath as he opens it and pulls out several long lengths of natural fiber rope. He walks back toward me, twisting the rope in his hands as he eyes me with bright hunger in his eyes.

"I'm going to tie you—extensively. You'll have little to no range of movement, so you'll have to trust me. Have you ever heard of Shibari?"

I nod. "I read a book on it." After Cade took me to the hideaway for the first time, I read every notable source on BDSM practices I could find. "It's a Japanese style of rope bondage. It's meant to be more artful than standard bondage, and the knots and patterns can be quite intricate and beautiful."

"Very good," Cade answers in approval, and I feel a ridiculous sense of accomplishment as though I've just aced a test. "I'm rather fond of Shibari, and I happen to be one of the most experienced practitioners at the club. Since this is your first time, I'll start with some of the easier knot patterns, and we can eventually work up to more experienced ties and positions later."

Cade lays the rope on the bed, then walks back to me. "Take off your dress and shoes, but keep your bra and knickers on," he commands, settling into his strict Dom posture in front of me.

I obey quickly, taking off my things and laying them on the bed in a neat pile before returning to stand before him with my hands at my sides and my eyes on the floor as I have been taught. I'm thrown by his request that I keep my underwear on. Does the use of Shibari mean we won't be fucking? Surely tying me up won't be enough to get him off? It certainly won't be enough to get *me* off.

"Kneel," he orders, his expression impassive and his eyes dark.

I drop to my knees, sinking to the floor in one, lithe movement. I've come a long way from awkward kneeling stances and bruised knees from landing too hard. Now, the transition into Cade's favorite position feels like second nature. Under his command, I've adjusted to being rather comfortable on my knees. And the view from down here has certainly never given me any cause for complaint.

"Spread your legs wider, sit back on your heels, and arch your feet off the ground. I'm going to do a frog tie," Cade explains as he retrieves two lengths of rope. "Your thighs will be tied tightly to your lower legs right above your ankles. You will not be able to close your legs or stand after I've finished." I feel his fingers on my chin as he lifts my head up to look at him. "Are you ready?" he asks, his voice growing somewhat softer for just a moment.

"Yes, sir," I answer steadily. And I am. Of all the other items in the room, getting tied up feels like the safest option.

His face set in concentration, Cade bends down beside me and begins to wrap the rough rope around my upper thigh and lower leg, binding them together. The intricacies of his movements are lost on me, but soon he has firmly wrapped the rope around my leg three times and secured it with a knot at my inner thigh. I still feel steady—until he moves around to my other leg. This time, the knowledge that I won't be able to walk or stand or even squirm has my heart quickening with panic. Repeating the same motions, Cade expertly secures the other leg.

Somehow, knowing that I can't move from this position makes my muscles begin to ache far quicker than they usually do when I am left in a kneeling position, the tension of nervousness pulling too tightly on my stretched tendons. And the mental knowledge of being helpless is starting to psych me out.

"Does it feel okay?" Cade asks, standing before me to admire his work.

"It feels—strange. And a bit tight," I answer, not quite sure what to make of the sensations sending adrenaline coursing through my body. I can already feel the wetness soaking my panties, so I at least know I'm more aroused than anxious.

"It's meant to be tight. Can't have you escaping," Cade replies, the ghost of a malicious smile on his lips. "I'm going to tie your hands now. They are simple knots that will act as cuffs. Hands behind your back," he commands after retrieving a long length of rope from the bed.

Hesitantly, I obey, reaching both arms behind my back. I feel him kneel behind me, and he reaches for my left wrist—wrapping, twisting, and knotting the rope around it. He pulls tight, the rope biting into my skin as I wince a bit from the pain. Cade reaches for my other wrist, surprising me by leaving a bit of slack between my arms so that the strain on my shoulders isn't too great. Deftly, he threads the rope around my right wrist before securing it with a sharp jerk of his fingers. He then takes the remaining length of rope and wraps it around my waist before tying it off in the back.

"In standard rope play, I add an unchastity belt with these ties," Cade says with his lips against my ear. He's so close behind me I can feel the cool metal of his belt buckle digging into my spine. His hands glide over my hips before one slips down my belly and skims over my pussy. "You run rope from your waist down between the soft lips of your cunt and up between your arse. If you want extra stimulation, you can even add a knot right here," he says, pausing to press his fingers directly into my clit. My eyes roll in the back of my head at the first touch my neglected nub has gotten all night.

"That sounds—uncomfortable," I stammer, intensely focused on his touch. He removes his hand far too soon, and I whimper at the loss.

"I think you'll find it's quite stimulating. You can try it for yourself the next time we visit the club. I'm fairly certain what I have in mind for tonight will be more than enough stimulation for the evening."

I hear Cade walk away, and I can't help but test the strength of my bonds. The ties on my legs are brutal; I can't move an inch. I already know it will hurt like a bitch when he finally unties me. The rope on my wrists is looser—not the actual knots, which are also incredibly tight, but the space between them. I still have small movement in my hands, but I can't reach them past my hips on either side. And if I lose my balance at all, I'm fucked.

I startle when I hear the sound of the door opening. Is he leaving me here?

Instinctively, I pull against my bonds again, panic forcing me to search for an escape—just in case I need it.

Cade said he wants to test my limits tonight. In the hideaway, he is always careful to avoid anything that might push me too far. Considering the unorthodox start to our relationship, I would say quite a few boundaries were obliterated right at the beginning. Falling for the man who used to be my captor definitely demanded some dexterity in navigating relationship norms. Adding a healthy dose of kink to the mix took things from confusing to pure insanity. I've stopped trying to make sense of it and simply recognize that what we have—for whatever logic defying reason—works.

Suddenly, I can feel his presence, warmth radiating at my back and sending a wave of shivers over my exposed skin. He smells...*different*. Did he go put on cologne for some reason? I'm distracted from the thought when I finally feel his hands on me, rough fingertips tracing a pattern over my skin. Tantalizing and teasing, his hands travel along my shoulders, over my arms, and down the center of my back. I shudder as the soft touch sends my nerves running rampant, and I am desperate for more. I struggle to keep my balance as I instinctively lean into his caresses. The tickling stroke of fingers along the soles of my feet sends me into a fit of giggles, and I nearly fall on my face at the disruptive motion. The break in composure earns me a sharp *smack* on my ass.

"Sorry, sir," I apologize, teetering somewhat from the shock of the slap.

"I can think of another way you can use that mouth to beg my forgiveness, little sub," a deep voice answers from behind me. A voice that isn't Cade's.

"Cade!" I scream, startled by the presence of another man in our room. Another man who had his fucking hands all over me.

"I'm right here, Kara," Cade answers in an unbothered tone from somewhere in the room.

How can he be calm when there's some random stranger touching his half-naked girlfriend? That's basically grounds for murder. I've heard him threaten as much more times than I can count.

Cade comes into view from behind me, his hazel eyes dark with lust and a hint of sadism. He's joined by another man that I recognize from Hell, although I don't know his name. The man is immaculate perfection. He's sculpted in every sense of the word—his body, his face, his hair, even his damn eyebrows. His skin is alabaster—nearly vampiric—boldly contrasting his raven black hair. His eyes are the color of ice—crystalline blue, calculating, and cold. He's a bit taller than Cade, younger too, but he holds himself with the same sort of untouchable, unrelenting dominance. Clearly, he's a Dom.

"What the hell, Caden?" I demand once the shock wears off enough for me to find my voice again.

The other man's perfect eyebrows shoot up in surprise as he looks over at Cade. "This is *your* sub? No fucking way." The man looks me up and down, his eyes surveying the blatant scowl on my face with marked intrigue. "She's a brat," he concludes with a laugh.

"She's not," Cade retorts, fixing me with a glare of his own. "She's merely a work in progress."

"Can you kindly explain what the fuck is going on?" I ask, the honeyed sweetness of my voice masking pleasant thoughts of gruesome torture and murder.

"Mind your language, love, or Greyson will receive more of a show than he bargained for tonight," Cade reprimands in his stupid fucking Dom voice.

Suddenly, all my anger evaporates and turns to fear. What show? What the *fuck* sort of nonsense is spiraling around chaotically in Cade's head at the moment? Given our recent excursions in public, I know Cade enjoys having an audience. Hell, I've known that since the night Cade stripped me down in front of Finn. But I never expected that he would be willing to *share* me.

"You belong to me, do you not, Kara?" Cade asks, arching a brow as if challenging me to disagree with him.

"Yes, sir," I answer with a hint of tartness. This line of questioning never bodes well.

"You are mine?" he reiterates in a calm tone, as though we have all the time in the world to discuss the unequal balance of power in our relationship. Maybe *he* should have a little taste of being helpless, tied, and on his knees.

"Yes, sir," I agree, the admission not filling me with the usual thrill of excitement. Because I am currently scared shitless of what Cade is going to ask me to do.

"You see," Cade begins, bending until he is eye level with me. "Occasionally, Dominants find great satisfaction in lending the services of their sub to another. It proves that you are truly *mine* to use at my own pleasure—or someone else's if I so desire. And to that end, I have offered Greyson the use of your mouth."

"You did *fucking what*?" I balk. "You are gravely mistaken if you think I am going to allow you to whore me out to one of your fucked-up Dom playmates."

The British bastard is a fucking dead man. I don't care if he's got his claws buried deep in my traitorous heart. The misguided organ is what got me into this mess in the first place. I can rip him out one claw at a time, and my stupid heart can deal with the scars.

"I think that is exactly what I am going to do. And I'm going to enjoy it," Cade answers, gripping my jaw in his hand and squeezing his fingers tightly. I'm not acting the least bit submissive in front of the other Dom asshole, and it's starting to piss Cade off—I can see the need to punish me for it in his smoldering hazel eyes.

"I won't be passed around like a fuck for hire, Caden," I reply in a tone forged of ice. I feel my teeth cut into the inside of my cheeks where he's pressing too hard, but I don't react. I just swallow down the sickening taste of blood and stare at him defiantly. He can't break me. He never could.

"You will *do* whatever I *tell* you to do, whether it is fuck me, fuck yourself, or fuck ten guys in a line while I stand and watch because I own you, Kara. That is how this relationship works," Cade says with a touch of cruelty, his jaw working in anger. "Now, are you going to obey, or would you like to use your safeword and be escorted home?"

Fuck. Him.

Fuck him for finding the *one* thing that makes my resolve waver just the slightest bit. I've never used my safeword. I'm not even sure I can. One of my fatal flaws is that I don't like quitting or admitting weakness. And I realize how contrary that sounds to the fact that I am a literal submissive. But I genuinely enjoy submitting to Cade because, in a way, it shows the strength of what I can endure. It's not me giving up or me giving in, it's me withstanding whatever Cade can throw at me and coming out on the other end smiling—usually from an orgasm or five. Submission is different from using a safeword—where one feels like strength, the other feels like defeat.

And Kara Caine doesn't fucking lose.

From the triumphant look on Cade's face, he knows he has me. He releases his grip on my jaw and stands back, awaiting my decision—although he already knows the answer.

"Fine," I spit out as though the word leaves me with a bitter taste in my mouth.

"Try again, Kara," Cade rebukes with an expression of disapproval as he crosses his arms and looks down on me. The other man has a similar stance, and they both loom over me like dark clouds of destruction. Such big, bad men ganging up on a half-naked girl with her arms tied behind her back. My biggest fear is that the size of their cocks matches the size of their egos.

"Do your worst, *sir*," I answer, respectful enough that he can't chastise me further, but the hardness of my gaze does nothing to mask the challenge hidden in my words. It's probably a bad idea to taunt him, but this night is fucking full of bad ideas, so what's one more. Cade's expression turns fierce as he tries to think of ways to fulfill my request to the fullest.

"I think you need to apologize to Greyson for your behavior," Cade decides, a malicious smile playing upon his lips.

I grit my teeth in annoyance. He knows I hate groveling. Fucking bastard.

I turn my gaze to the other man who looks down on me with sadistic amusement. "I'm sorry for being disrespectful, sir," I choke out, making no effort to stall my humiliation. The past six months have taught me that the longer I wait, the longer Cade savors my discomfort. It's better to be quick and bear the sting, like ripping off a bandaid.

"You're lucky that Ashford seems to have gone soft in the discipline department lately. If you were my sub, questioning a direct order would have gotten you acquainted with my bullwhip, rather than at the receiving end of my cock," Greyson comments with a pointed look at Cade.

"Well, we don't all enjoy pain as much as you do, Greyson."

My gaze shoots to him in panic. Is Greyson a *sadist*? I've never even met a professed sadist at the club; most of the Doms I've seen enjoy inflicting a bit of pain, but none have made pain their sole focus. Instantly, the blood in my veins turns to ice.

Without warning, I feel a thumb being shoved into my mouth, the taste unfamiliar and the intrusion wholly unwelcome. I try to push against the foreign appendage with my tongue, but he only presses in deeper. He aims for the back of my throat, and I have to try not to gag. Giving up, I open my mouth wider and let him explore as he wants. This will be over quicker if he's satisfied, so let him do what he will.

"Suck it, little sub," Greyson orders in a voice that might be considered seductive. Personally, it makes me want to puke all over his hand.

Rolling my eyes, I do as he asks and suck hard, letting my teeth scrape over his skin just a little. Slowly, he fucks my mouth with his thumb. Although I doubt he gets any actual pleasure out of the sensation of having his finger sucked, I can see his dick hardening in his pants at my discomfort and humiliation. I swallow hard when I see him reach for the buckle of his belt with his other hand. Deftly, he undoes his belt, unzips his pants, and pulls everything just below his jutting cock.

I let out a small gasp when I see it. Not only is his shaft incredibly thick and long, but there are multiple silver piercings running down the length of it. It looks painful—for everyone involved. What does that even feel like when it's inside? Certainly not comfortable. I do not, under any circumstances, want that metal studded monster in my mouth. But, of course, that's exactly where he directs it.

He hooks his thumb behind my bottom teeth and pries my mouth open. "Open wide," Greyson instructs as he slaps the tip of his cock against my mouth. He's already leaking, and a drop of pre-cum smears over my bottom lip like lipgloss.

My eyes find Cade one final time, pleading with him to stop this. He's sitting on the edge of the bed in front of me, leaning over in anticipation with his elbows resting on his thighs. He's turned on—I can tell from the simmering heat in his golden eyes and the unmistakable erection in his pants. He won't save me; he wants to see me ruined for his pleasure.

So you know what? I'm going to give Greyson the best goddamn head he's ever gotten.

Cade sees the change in my demeanor. I'm no longer begging or frightened or avoiding. I'm *determined*. And it throws him for a second, his confident expression wavering for the briefest of moments. And that small flicker in his control breathes the fervor of defiance right into every fiber of my body. I open my mouth wide, welcoming Greyson to use me.

He pushes past my lips, filling most of my mouth with the sheer width of his shaft. The metal piercings feel strange as they drag along my tongue. I take him deep, opening my throat and allowing him to slip down as I try not to gag. He holds himself there, cutting off my air. I wait calmly as he toys with the back of my throat; I'm used to this with Cade, and I can handle it. I look over to see Cade shifting a little uncomfortably on the bed, but he says nothing.

At last, Greyson pulls out a little and lets me gasp for air. After a few quick breaths, he slams back into me. Realizing that I can take it hard, he grabs ahold of my hair and fucks my face with brutal thrusts. I move my head with his movements, hollowing out my cheeks as I suck hard and let him slide into my throat over and over. I look over at Cade and moan with Greyson deep down my throat, knowing how the vibration makes Cade go crazy when I blow him.

Cade scowls at me, clearly not liking the special attention I'm giving to his friend. The fucker should have thought of that before passing me off like a cheap whore. If he thought this was going to be some barbaric display of dominance where I submit and suffer another man's cock with tears in my eyes because he's commanded it, he was severely mistaken. The way I see it, they're both putting a lot of faith in my goodwill not to bite Greyson's dick clean off. They're the ones with sensitive little meat sticks that they like to use instead of their heads. I'm the one with teeth.

Greyson's grip on my hair grows tighter, and I feel him thicken in my mouth. Finally, he comes, shooting spurts of semen in the shallow part of my mouth rather than down my throat. Which means I can taste it and for some reason, I can't bring myself to swallow it down. So the disgusting, warm liquid sits in my mouth while I remain on my knees and wait for Cade's next command.

Greyson tucks himself back into his pants, apparently satisfied with the service. "Thanks for the great blow, little sub," Greyson says, not unkindly, as he pinches my full cheek. "See you in Hell, Ashford." A few footsteps, a shut door, and I am alone with the man I hate very much at the moment.

I keep my eyes on the floor, cowering with something resembling embarrassment. Even though I have no reason to be ashamed. And even though I taunted Cade the whole time his friend had his dick down my throat, I can't stomach facing him with my mouth full of another man's cum.

The only sign that Cade has made his way over to me is the dark brown leather tips of his shoes that appear on the floor beside my knees. Neither of us speak for a moment, and I still refuse to look at him. If he wants my attention, he'll have to force me. And that's exactly what he does, capturing my chin in one hand and tilting my head up. I try to look away but find myself ensnared by the disarming depths of his intense gaze. If I had the energy and the use of my hands, I'd likely claw his damn lovely eyes out of his damn pretty face.

"Did you swallow?" he asks, likely noticing that I've kept my mouth shut rather than spewing the string of expletives that are coursing through my head.

I shake my head, hating the nonchalance of his tone when inquiring if I've consumed the remnants of another man's assault on my mouth. An assault *he* fucking ordained. I entertain the idea of spiting Greyson's cum out on Cade's pristine shoes, but I doubt the momentary satisfaction would be worth whatever further torture I'd endure as punishment. So, I sit with my mouth full and wait.

"Here," Cade offers in a kind tone, surprising me by taking a handkerchief from his pocket and holding it out for me to spit. I do so with begrudging gratefulness, past caring about ladylike appearances at this point as I expel everything from my mouth.

With the latent instincts of a gentleman, Cade folds the handkerchief over and wipes at the corner of my mouth and over my chin, removing the humiliating drool left over from Greyson's blow job. The gesture would seem tender if it wasn't his fault that I was in such a state to begin with.

After he has somewhat cleaned me, Cade takes my face between both of his hands and searches my expression. Although I feel debased and abjectly hideous with tear stained cheeks and mascara rimmed eyes, he gazes at me with an overwhelming tidal-wave of adoration and lust. I ignore the tingling in my traitorous pussy that responds to his lust and cling to my fury. The bastard can go fuck himself.

"You're angry, Kara." The sound of his voice, so calm and placating, merely stokes the embers of hatred that burn within my heart.

"I am not *angry*, Caden," I answer, putting as much spite into the utterance of his name as possible. "I am *fucking infuriated*."

"I see," Cade replies, nodding his head in a way that is distinctly patronizing. "So you feel as though you've been mistreated? Or perhaps that my behavior as your Dom warrants reproach?"

"You lent me to another man!" I scream, my fury hard to maintain with my hands still tied behind my back. I would give anything to slap the smug look off his face. "You gave me to him like property to be used and borrowed at your pleasure." I feel the hot tears of anger fill my eyes and spill down my cheeks, and I hate that they make me look even weaker.

"You could have used your safeword at any moment if you found the situation so disagreeable," Cade answers in a steady voice as though managing an irrational toddler, and I want to kill him for it.

Because he's right, I could have used my safeword and ended the whole thing before it even began. But I couldn't give in, and he should have known that. He should have realized that what he was asking for was ridiculous and humiliating, even if it did fulfill some twisted fantasy of his. This is *his* fault, not mine, and I have no intention of allowing him to make me feel guilty.

Cade reads the stony resolve in my expression and frowns. "My actions were entirely justified given the nature of our arrangement. You could have stopped if you wanted to."

"So you enjoyed that? Giving me away to another man to be face fucked while you stood by and watched?"

"I did," Cade growls, his eyes flashing with arousal. "Immensely."

"You're a sick fuck, Caden Ashford," I spit out, trying and failing to pull myself from his hold. Cade merely digs his fingers deeper into the soft flesh of my cheeks.

"A fact I have never disputed," Cade replies, lowering his head to mine until we are nearly close enough to kiss. "And I'm about to make sure you never forget it."

I feel the sharp prickles of fear dance along my spine at the threat housed in his words. He's already trussed me up and gifted me to another man like a nicely wrapped present. What more could he ask of me tonight? When I see Cade reach down to unfasten his pants, my heart stops in panic for the briefest of moments before surging to life—an all-consuming rush of fury acting like a shot of adrenaline straight to the chest.

"You better be planning to service yourself," I advise, my tone sharp as knives aimed to maim. "Because all of *my* orifices have discontinued service for the foreseeable future."

"I think we've heard enough from that pert mouth," Cade retorts, waving his bare, engorged dick in front of my face. The sight of him pulsing with need at my degradation makes me even more livid. If he puts *that* anywhere near my mouth, I'll bite the damn thing off and watch him bleed out on the floor.

Cade must read my intentions because he scowls as he pushes my head down between his muscular thighs. "Open," he commands. "And if I feel the slightest scrape of teeth, I'll call Greyson back in, and we'll tag team your arse with a belt before we take turns claiming it with our cocks."

I shudder in spite of myself. We haven't even done *that* yet. Having something of his size shoved up my ass is currently a hard limit, and I have no intention of allowing him or anyone else to tear into me tonight. Begrudgingly, I sheath my teeth and lock my lips in a tight line. If he wants his dick sucked, he'll have to force me.

"Open. Your. *Fucking*. Mouth," Cade demands, his fingers digging deeper into my skin with every word.

I shake my head, lips pressed firm and unyielding. Exasperated by my lack of submission—which seems to be the running theme of the evening—he uses his fingers to pry open my clenched teeth. Unable to help myself, I bite down hard against the intrusive fingers when they slip past the barrier of my teeth.

"*Fuck*," he groans, ripping his hand from my mouth as though it's been seized by a rabid dog.

I taste copper on my tongue from having bitten him so hard. Before either of us can think, Cade raises his uninjured hand and slaps me across the face. It's not hard, I can barely feel the sting of it on my cheek, but the sharp act of reprimand twists at my pride in a painful way. The dam fortifying my emotions bursts, and I fracture, biting my lip to keep from sobbing as tears spill down my cheeks.

"Stop," I plead, my chest heaving as panic surges.

"That is not the appropriate word for this situation," Cade responds coldly. "Would you like to try again?"

Fuck, he's going to make me say it.

I *can't* say it.

"Please," I beg, already knowing that it won't save me. Try as I might, I can't get the word *Thornfield* past my lips.

"Wrong again, darling," Cade warns moments before shoving his cock into my mouth. I choke at the suddenness of the intrusion as he forces his way to the back of my throat. He holds himself there, allowing me to struggle frantically for oxygen, before he finally pulls back for a second and permits me to breathe. All too quickly, he slams into my throat again, his assault quick and merciless. I'll have bruises at the back of my throat to remind me with every swallow of who I *belong* to.

Cade nears his release quicker than usual, probably because he's been desperate to come since watching me with Greyson. He grabs my hair with both hands and pulls me against him, smothering me with his cock. I feel the warmth of his cum at the back of my throat, his length buried so deep I have no choice but to swallow him down and try not to gag.

"Swallow every drop," Cade commands as he continues to move in my mouth until his balls are fully emptied.

I choke down the cum in my mouth, struggling with the sickening feeling that what just happened between us wasn't exactly consensual. But as much as I tell myself I didn't want it, I'm left with the guilt of not ending the degradation before it began. All I had to do was say the word.

Thornfield.

It is such a simple out, but the idea of conceding and declaring that I'm not strong enough or skilled enough to take what Cade gives me goes against every facet of my nature.

Drowning in self-conflict, I don't notice that Cade has started untying the knots around my wrists. An almost painful rush of blood surges through my hands as they're loosened from the tight positioning of the ropes. Finally, I feel my arms fall freely to my sides, aching from being stretched for such a long period of time. Without waiting for his approval to move, I rub my tender wrists, willing life back into my hands as they prickle with pain. I'm strangely entranced by the deep imprint of the rope etched into my skin. In more pleasant circumstances, I might have even found the red, crisscrossed lines arousing.

Suddenly, Cade is in front of me, sinking to his knees to work at the knots by my inner thighs. Without warning, his fingers slip underneath the edge of my panties and inside me as he unwraps the rope. To my confusion, my entrance feels slick with need as he pulses in and out at a languid pace.

"You're wet," Cade informs me, his voice rough as crushed glass as he continues to fuck me with his fingers.

When he finally manages to untie both legs, I pull them closed, hating the sticky feeling of my panties. I'm not just wet. I'm *soaked*. But why? I hated what he did to me—what he *forced* me to do. But it seems that even when my mind rebels, my body is still a slave to Cade's commands. The thought makes me direct some of the fury overwhelming my body at myself for being so weak.

Cade offers his hand to help me stand. Having held a kneeling position for such a long period, I get to my feet with an awkward limp. I'm sullenly grateful for his assistance. He keeps my hand in his as we meet each other at eye level for the first time since entering the room. Unable to bear the scrutiny of his gaze, I look away. The act probably appears submissive, though it's the farthest thing from it.

"Are you okay?" Cade asks in concern, a small frown marring his features as he appraises my expression. I'm not sure what he sees in the dead eyes staring back at him.

I nod in answer to his question, lacking the energy to speak. And not entirely confident in my ability to form a summary of my state of mind at the moment.

"Verbal responses, Kara," Cade commands, his voice softer than it's been the rest of the evening. His thumb stokes my lower lip, and the tenderness of the gesture makes me want to fall to pieces right now. I need him to leave so that I can self-destruct in private.

"Yes, sir," I answer in a whisper, hoping he believes me. I wish I could believe it myself.

Cade seems conflicted in deciding how to deal with me after the events of the evening. No doubt most of the submissives he's been with will gladly take another man's cock and then beg for another. My reluctance to submit to his depravity is likely enigmatic. The thought of sharing being seen as a violation probably wouldn't even cross his mind.

"Get cleaned up," he says after an uncomfortable pause, reminding me that my face must be an absolute mess. Though his tone isn't unkind, I'm left trying *not* to feel like a whore being abandoned after the bill is paid. "I'll go get us some drinks. You need to hydrate after such an intensive session."

Cade kisses the inside of my wrist before releasing me, a loving act that contradicts his every other action tonight. Without another word, he leaves, shutting the door softly on his way out.

And I'm left alone with thoughts and emotions that weigh too heavy on my body and mind. Feeling drained to the point of exhaustion, I shuffle toward the bathroom at the far end of the suite.

Get cleaned up.

That was all he could say after everything he put me through. It's not like I expected an apology, but a little fucking aftercare would have been nice. When I reach the bathroom, I slam the door shut, turning the lock for a good measure. At the moment, I want as many fucking barriers between myself and Cade as possible.

Deliberately avoiding the mirror, I grab one of the toothbrushes from the vanity drawer and start scrubbing the events of the past hour from my mouth. The mundane task gives me something to focus on and keeps my mind from spiraling. After I've cleansed every inch of my mouth twice and rinsed thoroughly, the spit in the basin is red-tinged. I taste a faint hint of blood, but I feel nothing.

An involuntary shiver reminds me that I'm still standing nearly naked on the cold marble floor. I step into the large walk-in shower, turning on both shower heads. While I wait for the water to warm, I slip out of my bra and yank my soaked panties down to my ankles before stepping out of them. Steam has filled the room by the time I enter the shower, the blazing hot water searing my skin. The burn feels good, and I relish the sting of it, feeling myself melt beneath the heat that penetrates to my bones.

As my senses awake, the shame I've been trying to suppress ignites with a crippling force. Suddenly feeling as though I can't bear my own weight, I slide down the slick wall and land in a crumpled heap on the floor as the water beats down on me. I feel like a cheap whore after the things I did tonight, and the aftermath of self-loathing is stifling.

The concept of time seems to vanish entirely as I wallow beneath the hot stream of the shower. Sound dulls, sight grows hazy, searing droplets of water fall on desensitized skin. And I welcome the peace of oblivion with open arms.

Chapter 6

KARA

I'm confused when I hear the muffled sound of my name being called and discover the hands of a stranger on my arms, shaking me with a force that rattles my teeth.

"Kara!" the disjointed voice calls again. My eyes focus to find the perplexing sight of Cade kneeling before me in the middle of the shower. He's still wearing his clothes, the knees of his trousers darkening in the wetness of the tile floor, his white dress shirt turning translucent beneath the rain of water, and his expensive leather shoes drenched. His dark hair falls over his forehead as water drips into his striking hazel eyes. Eyes that are filled with a peculiar sort of terror as they stare back at me.

"You're wet," I comment blandly. It's an unnecessary observation, but I feel compelled to state the obvious all the same.

"I am," Cade answers as he runs his fingers through his damp hair in frustration. When he turns his attention back to me, his eyes are hard. "What the hell, Kara?" he asks through clenched teeth, his fingers digging into my upper arms. "I waited. I called. I knocked. You didn't fucking answer. Finally, I got so worried that I used the key to unlock the door."

In spite of his anger, I roll my eyes at the notion that he has a key for the bathroom. Not even the privilege of bathroom privacy is sacred when it comes to Doms and their fucking control issues. "No need to worry. I was just getting *cleaned up*," I answer, unable to keep the bitterness from my tone.

I try to pull myself from his grasp, but his fingers tighten almost to the point of pain

"It's been nearly an hour since I left, Kara," he informs me. His features are marred by an inexplicable anger. Why is he angry at *me*?

His response surprises me. By my count, it feels like mere minutes have passed. "Well, I suppose I was feeling particularly filthy after this evening's performances," I seethe, allowing the venom of hatred to drip into my voice.

Cade startles, his grip on my arms loosening as his eyes fill with horror. I'm mesmerized by the way the water collects in a single curl of dark hair on his temple and drips onto his nose one drop at a time. It's a momentary distraction from watching his composure fracture into minuscule pieces right in front of me.

"Did I push you past your limits tonight?" he gasps, his tone a mixture of shock and devastation. Good, now he knows how I've felt the entire evening.

"Well, I can't say getting face fucked by a stranger was at the top of my kink to-do list," I answer with a tart taste in my mouth. "Wouldn't even rank last."

"Answer my question, Kara," he demands. His eyes are rimmed in fury, but there's an unmistakable flicker of fear there too.

I bite my lip as I consider how to respond. Did he cross a line? *Fuck, yes.* Do I want to admit that I was too weak to handle his demands? *Fuck, no.* Ultimately, I decide honesty is best, as much as it pains me to confess my limitations. "Yes, tonight crossed a line," I whisper, unable to look him in the eye.

"*Fuck*, Kara," he groans in misery, pulling away from me and sitting against the glass wall of the shower. "Fuck!" he shouts as the grief turns to fury, banging his head against the glass.

I shrink back from his anger—though it's not directed at me in particular—pulling my knees up to my chest and hugging them tight against my chest. I thought Cade's guilt would satisfy my anger, but it only makes me feel more wretched.

"Why didn't you use your safeword?" he asks in accusation after taking a couple minutes to process what I confessed. His eyes burn with anger as he looks over at me. We're separated by a few feet of distance, but neither of us makes a move to close it.

"I don't know," I evade, too ashamed to give the real reason. The man gives me enough shit about my damned pride as it is.

"*Kara*," he scolds in a harsh tone, his eyes boring into mine and demanding answers.

"I didn't want to give up," I revise, making no move to conceal my resentment over being forced to have this conversation.

"So you think using your safeword when you've met your limit is a sign of weakness?" he questions, his tone suggesting that I'm about to be severely reprimanded regardless of how I answer.

"Yes," I reply with a shrug. Because it's true.

"You could not be more inaccurate if you tried," he retorts, and I grind my teeth at the insufferable arrogance housed in his deep voice. "Safewords exist *specifically* for that purpose. Playing without limits is far too dangerous a game, even with the most skilled participants."

"I didn't want to disappoint you," I mumble, nearly choking on the admission as it comes out of my mouth.

Cade's eyes soften, the fury in them cooling to embers. He moves toward me, not bothering with the fact that he's getting completely soaked. Sitting beside me, he pulls me into his arms. Starved for the tender contact, I bury my face in his chest as he tucks me under his chin.

"Love, I could never be anything but proud of you," he tells me, the unmistakable warmth of sincerity in his words. "And someone who admits weakness pleases me far more than someone with no limits at all. You should never be afraid to use your safeword. This relationship is meant to satisfy both of us, not enslave you to my needs alone."

He brushes the tears from my face, the gesture painstakingly delicate as he handles me as though I'm made of spun sugar that will dissolve at the slightest touch. Cade's softness is jarring in comparison to his earlier behavior, like two entirely different faces of the same coin. I've never thought of him as cruel, but tonight revealed a facet of his dominance that I'm not sure I'll ever feel comfortable exploring again.

I'll never forget the expression of pure satisfaction on his face as he shared and humiliated me. And yet, the same man—the one whom I recognize and care for deeply—sits beside me, soaked and on his knees, devastated that he may have caused me harm. I can forgive the man on his knees, but it will take time to efface the other version of him from my memory.

"Do you hate me?" he asks, his face contorted with the evidence of his own inner conflicts.

I'm fairly certain that his actions tonight hurt me just as much as my actions hurt him, and that knowledge crushes me all over again. He may have wanted to test me, but I allowed him to take it so much further than he would have gone had he known I was at my limit.

"Yes," I confess. "But I hate myself more."

"Don't," Cade commands, his voice turning harsh as he grabs my chin and forces my head up sharply. I have no choice but to look into his eyes, and they're brimmed with anger. "Don't fucking do that to yourself. You may hate me to your heart's content—I've known your hatred all too well—but *never* judge yourself so unkindly. That is an order."

I try to pull away, growing uncomfortable beneath the punishing heat of his gaze. Even if he commands it, I'm incapable of casting aside my feelings of guilt and self-loathing. Sensing my resistance, Cade digs his fingers into my skin even harder, forcing my focus back to him.

"Are you disobeying me?" he accuses.

"I'm trying not to." I *am* trying, but self-criticism is a tricky obstacle to overcome, and I've struggled against it for as long as I can remember.

"Kara Elizabeth Caine, do I need to punish you?" he asks, and there is a fire in his eyes that promises destruction.

I jolt at the scolding, startled at being called by my full name for the first time since I was eighteen. I didn't even know he knew my middle name, although I guess I shouldn't be surprised. His ability to obtain information is basically on the stalker level, and my registered name is public information. Still, it's jarringly intimate to hear my full name on his lips.

I pause for a moment to consider his question. I'm not a masochist—

I'm not. I don't *enjoy* pain on a sexual level. But sometimes I *need* it on an emotional level. I've learned that pain can help me cope, help me feel more in control when emotionally everything is spiraling. My relationship with Cade has allowed me to further explore that darker part of myself.

I've never asked him for punishment, my self-respect won't allow it. And when I actually earn a thorough punishment, I fight him tooth and nail—literally. But when I feel the need to hurt, to experience pain as a means of centering myself, I act out so that Cade is certain to give me the punishment I crave. He probably thinks I'm just an occasional brat, but it's the only way I know how to communicate my need in a way that doesn't demand a blow to my pride.

But in this moment, I don't want to fight it. Or him.

"Yes, sir," I answer softly, feeling as though I've peeled back skin and bone and laid bare my heart. The vulnerability I'm experiencing in this moment is more painful than anything Cade could physically do to my body.

"You *want* me to punish you?" Cade asks aghast, his expression almost angry. "After what I just did to you in there, you want me to hurt you *more*?"

"Yes, please," I plead, my voice barely even a whisper as I keep my eyes on the tile floor, watching the water slowly trickle down the drain.

His eyes search mine, and something about the brokenness that he finds there causes his own hazel eyes to soften, the fury in them dimming. "Alright," he answers at last, his voice calm and soothing. He pats the soaked material of his pants, the sound echoing in the enclosed space. "Over my knee."

Instantly, I obey, crawling over to him and laying my naked body over his thighs. I try not to choke as water rains down my mouth and nose from the partially upside down position. Cade reaches over to brush the wet hair from my face; he wants to see me when he does this. He wants to watch my reaction. I feel his hands on my bare ass, rubbing soft circles over my wet skin. It feels soothing, but I know it's only the calm before the storm.

In the swiftest of moments, I feel his hand pull away before slamming down hard against my ass. The pain of the slap is sharp, the sting amplified by the wetness of my skin. Before I have a chance to breathe, Cade spanks me again, the harsh *crack* of his palm ringing loudly. He adds another slap to each cheek, and my skin is already burning, the warmth of the water raining down turning searing when it meets the punished flesh of my backside. He's not taking it easy on me; these aren't playful smacks—they're hard and exacting. I think as much as he's doing this to alleviate my guilt, he's assuaging his own wounded feelings as well. Well, I'm happy to sacrifice my ass if it will bring us both back into balance.

Slowly, the hot sting of Cade's slaps builds into something sweeter—a warm, dizzying sort of high spreading over my whole body and encompassing me in a blanket pleasure. As he continues spanking me, Cade's other hand slides down from my waist and slips between my thighs. Instinctively, I open my legs wider for him, knowing that he'll discover water isn't the only wetness soaking my pussy. Without a word, Cade's fingers thrust into my entrance, slipping in smoothly with my arousal. He groans when I clench around his hand, desperate for more of him.

"Is my naughty girl enjoying her punishment?" he asks as he continues to spank my ass and finger fuck my pussy at the same time. The intoxicating mixture of pleasure and pain is driving me crazy with need.

"Yes, sir," I admit, my voice breathless and hoarse. At this point, the shame and anger over the earlier events of the night are completely forgotten.

"Do you want to come like this, dirty girl? Do you want to soak my fingers while I spank your naughty arse?"

"Yes, please," I plead, already desperate for release.

"Touch your clit," Cade orders. "Show me how badly you need it."

I'm more than happy to obey, lifting my hips slightly and sliding my hand down beneath my aching thighs to circle my clitoris. I'm already so close, my orgasm mounting with every stroke of my fingers. One little push, and I'll topple over the edge.

"Harder, please," I beg, wanting him to be the one that plunges me into ecstasy.

Happy to acquiesce, Cade thrusts three fingers deep inside me while he picks up his pace on my ass, spanking rapidly on alternating cheeks. My skin feels as though it's on fire even as the inner warmth builds higher and higher, threatening to explode. And I do—bursting into fragments of pleasure on a scream so loud it seems to shake the shower glass. Cade's fingers continue to plunge in and out of me, but his other hand leaves my ass and wraps around my stomach, pulling me close to his body while I writhe in bliss. When I finally emerge from the hazy cloud of orgasmphoria, I realize I'm crying, but all the sadness has melted away, leaving pure, overwhelming satiation in its wake.

He continues to hold me as I calm down, his fingers still inside me as though that is exactly where they belong. "Feel better, love?" He understands me well enough to tell when the inner darkness has dissipated. Even though I've never told him, he's probably intuited that sometimes I need his destruction just as much as I need his tender devotion.

"Yes, sir," I murmur against the soaked material of his pants, my head still buried in his thighs.

And once again, Caden Ashford has taken all my broken pieces and forged them anew with fire.

Chapter 7

KARA

Life has been heaven since our last trip to Hell. For some reason, our twisted relationship seems to thrive when dragged through darkness, like nightshades blossoming beneath the pale light of the moon. And even though that evening with Greyson started out as a nightmare, it ended up bringing Cade and I closer than ever. Our bond has never been stronger. Unfortunately, as fate seems unhappy with the tranquility of our current situation, that bond is about to be tested.

I'm elated and terrified as I look over at the beautiful bastard who holds a good deal more of my heart than I care to admit. Elated because of the letter currently weighing heavy in my pocket. Terrified because of how *he* will react to the news. My fear is almost enough to keep me from asking him at all. But the sparks of pure excitement flickering through my veins demand that I at least try.

I bite my lip, furtively glancing up at Cade from the heavy cover of my lashes. Our relationship started with me as his prisoner, and after all this time, he still hasn't managed to let me go. How will he react to my request of more freedom than I have been given in the last six months? Will he let me leave? Or will he convert the hideaway into an actual dungeon? Knowing the possessive bastard all too well, my money is on the latter.

"Is there a reason why your lovely eyes are boring a hole into my skull?" Cade asks as he adds a dollop of cream to his scone already smothered in raspberry jam.

"No," I answer too quickly, busying my hands with slathering clotted cream on my own scone before adding jam. Like a *heathen*, as I have been told by the local British dictator. Honestly, Mrs. Hughes scones are perfection no matter how you dress them. Or in what order.

"Kara," Cade chides, looking over at me with a disarming gaze that demands I spill all of my secrets on the spot. And as hard as I try, I can't resist the power of those captivating pools of green and gold.

"Okay, don't be mad," I warn, biting my lip to ease the nerves of my impending request.

"The fact that you've prefaced with *that* already has my sense of indignation tingling," Cade answers with a scowl.

"Please don't joke. This is important."

"Who said I was joking?" he answers, popping a piece of scone into his mouth. "I'm just winding up to deliver the spanking I'm sure you're about to earn."

"Cade! You can't just spank me every time I make you angry."

"Your arse begs to differ with that assessment," Cade retorts—accurately, I might add—before taking another bite of scone. I'm mesmerized by the small smear of red jam lingering on his full bottom lip. I am tempted to lick it off of him, but before I can, he swipes his thumb along his mouth and then slowly sucks it clean.

I choke a little on the pastry in my mouth. My god, the man is sex incarnate.

My thighs clench as my temperature rises, and I plead with common sense to rouse me from the ill-timed haze of lust. "*Caden,*" I scold with my best, severe librarian voice. I must say, I'm out of practice.

"Kara, just get on with it and tell me."

"Fine," I answer, sounding a smidge more exasperated than I would like. I don't think I've ever managed to keep my composure with Caden Ashford's innate ability to tug on all the right strings to unravel me completely. "But keep your trigger happy hands where I can see them."

Cade holds up his hands before interlacing his fingers and placing them primly on his lap. "My twitching palms are stowed until after you finish, you have my word."

Eyeing him warily, I clear my throat and jump right into it. "So, I recently published a journal exploring themes of sexual deviance in classical literature. Kinky classics, if you will." Cade raises his brows in piqued interest, but he allows me to continue without interruption. "It was only meant as a bit of fun research shining a light on the fact that sexual deviance in literature isn't a newfound phenomenon, but rather has been steadily present throughout centuries of academia."

Cade laughs, the warm sound of it melting my insides like butter. "It sounds as though I've thoroughly corrupted you, Dr. Caine."

My stomach flutters every time he uses my earned title. Which has happened a grand total of five times during our entire acquaintance. "It was actually your comment about Mr. Rochester being kinky that gave me the idea. Turns out, there are countless texts that can be interpreted through the lens of sexual deviance."

Cade leans back in his chair, a mixture of smugness and pride in his expression. "Well, I don't know why you thought I would be mad. I'm actually quite proud of your naughty academic endeavor."

"Well, I haven't gotten to the part you won't like," I caution as nerves threaten to drive me to madness. "I've been asked to do a full academic year of funded and assisted research and implement my findings for a course curriculum under Sex and Gender Lit Studies for the following fall semester."

"That's fantastic news, Kara. You should feel honored, and you have my full support if you want to accept. I know it means you'll be spending more time at the university, but I'm willing to sacrifice for the good of the academic community. Just as long as I still get to fuck my dirty little librarian every night."

My brows furrow with the weight of guilt. He is being way more amenable and supportive than I expected, which makes the next bit all the harder to confess. "That's the thing—the offer isn't in Chicago. It's at a top ranking university in New York."

"I see," Cade answers, his expression darkening as he considers all the personal consequences of me accepting the position. "Alright, bend over the table. You definitely deserve a thrashing."

"Cade!" I squeal at the absurdity, not quite sure if he's being serious. With Cade, you never can tell with these sorts of things.

"I'm kidding. Partially," he adds with a pointed look in my direction. "So, is this something you want to do?"

I pause, thinking over his question. Without a doubt, I want to do it. But I'm not sure where that leaves the two of us standing. "I think it would be a wonderful opportunity. My initial publication barely scratched the surface. It would be a chance to make new discoveries in the literary field, so of course I would love every minute of it."

"Well then, I think you should do it," Cade answers after a moment's consideration, his tone suggesting that the matter has already been settled.

"Really?" I thought I would have to fight and beg to win even the smallest hint of his approval. Instead, he is giving it freely.

"Of course—if it would make you happy." His eyes hold a lingering sadness that makes me very aware of how my selfish decision will deprive him of his own happiness.

"Wow, I never expected that you'd actually allow me to leave," I answer in a daze, still genuinely shocked that he isn't trying to punish me or lock me up for daring to leave him. Not that he ever would, but my imagination enjoys villainizing him on occasion, just to keep things interesting.

"You aren't my prisoner anymore, Kara," Cade replies, his voice deep with sincerity as he slides his hand over to my thigh. "I'd like to think we've come a long way from those initial roles of inequality. But," his hand squeezes my upper thigh, "don't think I won't spend every minute of every weekend ensuring that you pay for forcing me to endure days without fucking your cunt. I'm liable to go mad in the meantime."

"I happen to know your hands are very skilled, so I think you'll manage just fine."

"Hmm, maybe I should make you start paying now," Cade growls, his hand slipping between my thighs and traveling up until he reaches my pussy.

"What did you have in mind?" I throw my head back and close my eyes when I feel his fingers brush my center and pull aside my panties. I moan aloud when he thrusts two fingers inside of me; they slip in easily because I'm already fucking soaked. I spread my legs wide, giving him all the access he wants.

"Keen, aren't you?" he asks, chuckling softly at my wanton eagerness.

"Well, this isn't the reaction I was expecting," I confess, my eyes still closed as I focus on his touch.

"And what exactly were you expecting, love?" I can tell from his voice that he's smiling as he continues to thrust his fingers into me.

"I assumed you'd drag me down to the hideaway." I moan as he adds a third finger. "Maybe chain me up like I was your prisoner again." I gasp as he twists and spreads his fingers inside me. "Probably pull out your trusty cane and try to beat the idea of leaving out of me."

"Mmm, all excellent ideas for later tonight, but for now, stand up." He pulls his fingers out of me and I immediately feel empty.

Obediently, I push out my chair and stand. Cade is behind me in an instant, the firm contours of his body pressed against mine, the hardness of his erection thrusting impatiently into my ass. He grabs the back of my neck in a firm grip and forces me over the table, my face just nearly missing the jam as my cheek lands hard on the smooth, wooden surface. Cade doesn't bother with taking off my dress, choosing to unceremoniously flip the bottom of my light blue dress over my hips and rip my panties down to my ankles in two swift movements. Before I even have a moment to think or breathe, he's inside me, his hips forcing mine into the sharp edge of the table with every thrust. His grip is bruising and his pace is punishing and I am about to come on the fucking table from the delicious mixture of pleasure and pain.

A sharp slap on my ass distracts me from the edge of release that I was so close to going over. "Don't come yet," Cade commands in that dominant voice he uses to demand submission. "I want you sore." *Thrust.* "I want you to bear the imprint of my cock in your womb." *Thrust.* "I don't want you to be able to walk or sit or move without remembering how I took this cunt hard and made it mine." *Thrust.*

"Please, Cade," I whimper, my body trembling with the need to come.

"Please, *what?*" he asks with a bite of sternness.

"Please make your pussy come, sir."

"*Jesus Christ,*" he growls, his voice almost animalistic in nature. "Come on my fucking cock," he orders, slamming into me so fiercely and rapidly that the glasses on the table clatter. A cup of coffee is knocked over, but he doesn't bother with it, letting the dark liquid seep into the table. Mrs. Hughes might murder him later when she sees it.

Cade slaps my ass again when he notices I haven't obeyed his explicit order. "I said," Cade grips my hair and forces my head up at an uncomfortable angle to look at him, "*come on my fucking cock.*" As if his commands have a direct line to my pussy, I come. *Hard.* "That's my good girl," he praises as he thrusts inside me twice more before filling me with his cum.

He stays inside me, his cock still hard and pulsing against my sore and almost certainly bruised inner walls. His rough hands in my hair turn to gentle, stroking caresses. I feel the rough stubble of his cheek as he leans over me to place a kiss on my neck. "Congratulations on your new job, Dr. Caine."

Chapter 8

CADEN

This is fucking asinine. I should turn the car around right bloody now and introduce Kara to the metal cage I had custom made for her—on the off chance that I needed it at some point.

I can't believe I agreed to this. We're driving from JFK airport with everything Kara decided to take with her packed into two large suitcases in the backseat of the rental car. She'll be gone for eight months, minus any school holidays and the weekends I've demanded she spend visiting me in Chicago. She refused to let me have any say in her living arrangements, and she picked and paid for her own apartment. It's minimal and nothing special, but it came furnished and is in a good part of town. And it's right next door to an ex-special forces agent that I've hired to discreetly keep an eye on her. It sounds like I'm spying on her—and that's exactly what the fuck I'm doing.

There is a psycho on the loose vying for Kara's blood, and I'm allowing her to leave the safety and security of the manor. I've got to make allowances somewhere.

"Any chance I can get you to change your mind?" I ask, my hand slipping from her knee and up her thigh while my other hand rests on the steering wheel.

"Caden Ashford, don't you dare," she shrieks in outrage, slapping my hand away from her. "You promised."

Growling, I slap my hand back on her thigh and dig my fingers into her skin deep enough to bruise. She whimpers, but she's smart enough to leave my hand right where the fuck I put it this time.

"Please, Cade," she pleads, trying a different approach. One that she knows works far better on me than having a cheeky attitude. "You have to let me go. It's too late to back out now."

I sigh heavily. "Yes, I suppose it is."

That has her brightening right up. "So you'll let me stay?" she asks in excitement.

Though why the hell she's so eager to get *away* from me, I don't know. I feel as though I should be wounded by her lack of regard for my needs and company. In fact, I've decided that I am. "Can't wait to leave your Dom, can you, love?" I retort bitterly.

She bites her lip, her brow furrowing in distress. "I'm sorry, sir. I didn't mean it like that. Of course, I'll miss you." She looks up at me with baleful eyes, and I can see that she's sincere.

"Yes, I'll make sure of it." The words sound more like a threat than a promise. "Maybe I won't let you come unless you're with me. Then you'll really feel the pain of the separation you're forcing on me."

She pales at the severity of my suggestion, but she doesn't bite back with her usual ferocity. "If that would please you, sir, I am willing to try." She looks down at her hands, her eyes not meeting mine.

"And what would happen if you broke the rules?" I ask, my voice dropping low and rough as my hand inches up her thigh toward her bare pussy. I know it's bare because I got bored on the flight over and took off her knickers.

"I s-suppose," she moans as my knuckles brush across her wet center, "you could punish me."

She spreads her legs wider, welcoming me between them. I'm more than willing to please, thrusting my middle finger inside her. Her back arches at the intrusion. "Oh really?" I retort, fucking her with long, deep strokes. She keens when I stuff another finger inside her. "And how exactly am I supposed to punish you when you're all the way in New York?" I curl my fingers and feel her clench around me.

"I'm n-not sure..." Her eyes flutter shut.

"Eyes on me, love," I command in a soft tone. Her warm brown eyes turn to me, heavy and lust-filled. "Give me an idea on how I could punish you for touching this naughty cunt without me."

She licks her lips as her hips roll with the movement of my hand. I can see her eyes start to close again, but she forces them back open. "You could," she clears her throat, her mouth watering with arousal, "keep a tally of any mistakes I make. Take me to Pandemonium on Friday, and make me pay in your private room."

I growl with approval, twisting my hand so I can fit three fingers inside of her. She's already dripping all over the leather seat. At this point, we're definitely going to owe the rental company a cleaning fee.

"I like that idea," I agree. My cock is already hard with the talk of punishments and the things I could do to her in my private room in Pandemonium. So many fun toys to pick from—we've barely even had a chance to break any of them in. "Every Friday I can take you to Pandemonium?"

"Y-yes," she half cries out as I thrust three fingers deep inside her wet cunt. "Every Friday."

"And what if I don't want to wait until Friday? What if I want you to suffer as soon as you disobey me?"

She pauses, biting down hard on her lip as she considers my question. "You could...show me how."

"Show you how *to what?*" I ask, not appreciating the vagueness of her answer.

Heat blossoms on her cheeks. "You could show me how to punish myself for you," she whispers, her voice so low I can barely hear.

I groan, wishing I didn't need to keep my hand on the steering wheel so I could fist my cock. "You'd hurt yourself for me love?"

"Yes, sir." She nods her head listlessly, high on lust. "If you asked me to."

"Would you pinch these nipples hard if I told you to?" I ask, my wet fingers leaving her cunt and sliding up her ribs to her tits.

"Y-yes, sir."

"Do it now," I order. "Be my good girl and show me how much you can make it hurt."

"Now?" she asks, suddenly flustered as awareness spikes. "We're in the car."

I slap my hand against her bare pussy hard, a warning to obey. "You've been taking my hand up your cunt without complaint for the last twenty minutes while *in the car.*" I spank her pussy again. "So I don't really give a damn. Do as you're told."

Rolling her eyes, she slides her fingers up to her nipples and pinches them lightly through the fabric of her dress. I glare down at her. She's barely trying, and she knows it. Sighing with the drama of an unskilled actress, she grabs her nipples and properly twists at them.

"Better," I commend. It's a difficult task to split my attention between the traffic on the road and my girl's hands on her tits. "Pull down your top."

"Cade," she snaps. Her face is the perfect picture of Dr. Caine disapproval. It would look brilliant covered in my cum.

"This isn't a great recommendation for your ability to follow orders, Kara. I'm not even sure I can trust you on your own for eight months." I give her a knowing look that implies that her making it to her new job Monday morning is dependent on her obedience in this car. It would be damned easy to book us both flights back home before we even step foot in her new apartment building.

Groaning as though I've asked her to commit some heinous atrocity, Kara rips down the bodice of her lilac dress and her bra and pinches her bare nipples.

"Good," I hum with appreciation. "Now, keep doing it until we get there."

Chapter 9

KARA

My nipples are raw by the time we finally arrive at the apartment complex. Leave it to Cade to make sure my heart isn't the only thing that's bruised when he leaves tomorrow morning. Knowing him, I'll have a whole inventory of injuries before the night is out. The idea doesn't distress me nearly as much as it should.

After unpacking the small collection of clothes, books, and toiletries I brought with me from Chicago, Cade and I go shopping. He gets me trash bags, dish soap, paper towels—I'm fairly certain Mrs. Hughes gave him a list because there's no way Lord Ashford knows about shit like dishwasher tablets. He buys me mountains of groceries, loads up my fridge, and fills my pantry with far too many bags of salt and vinegar "crisps" because he knows I love them. It's been a sweet and paternal aspect of his dominant side that I've never experienced, him making sure that I'm taken care of even when he's gone.

Honestly, I feel more like a kid getting dropped off at college for their first semester than a professional about to start a job in a new city. I never got to experience this freshman year—parents helping you get settled in and fussing about whether you have enough food and laundry detergent. My mom and dad died the summer before college started. They'd toured the campus with me the year before, and we all loved how close I would be to home. In the end, I was left alone with no family to come home to.

I was eighteen at the time of the accident. My sister, Harper, was only seven. Legally, I could have become her guardian, but that was a lot to ask of an eighteen year old who just lost both parents. I didn't feel up to the task of raising a kid when I still felt like I was a kid myself. It took me a long time to get over the guilt of feeling like I abandoned my sister just so I could go off to college and have a life without her. Some days, the guilt still lingers, like a dark shadow at the back of my heart, knowing I'm not as close with Harper as I should be.

Thankfully, my aunt and uncle in California didn't have any kids, and they were happy to take her. They would have taken me too, but I was set on attending the university my parents helped me apply for. Staying in Chicago allowed me to feel closer to them, even though they were gone. And that meant more to me than anything else.

I get to see Harper once or twice a year, even though it's not nearly enough. After I graduated, she'd come spend the summers with me, but when she got to high school, she didn't want to be away from her friends for so long. She does great in school, she's smart as hell, and she would have made our parents just as proud as she's made me. She's graduating this year at the very top of her class. I've been contemplating inviting Cade to the graduation, but I'm not sure if I'm prepared to introduce my family to my Dom/boyfriend. I can't even imagine describing our relationship to my seventeen year old sister—she'd probably try to have me committed for enjoying Cade's control and discipline as much as I do.

I'm sure I'm a disappointment to feminists everywhere.

Thoughts of family and the future swirl about in my head as I look around at the furnishings that came with the apartment. It's all very standard, neutral and white furniture. White walls and beige carpets. Nothing like Cade's vibrant and ostentatious decor at the manor. Nothing like my own vintage, feminine style either. But there's a desk that's perfect for late nights spent researching, a bookshelf beside it—you can tell the complex caters to temporary teachers with how close it is to the university—and a pretty view of the park from the living room window. Cade has already made me promise to take a thirty minute walk in the park every day if the weather is permitting.

I sigh with contentment, happy with the feeling of being settled in. The apartment is starting to feel a bit like home. It's no Ashford Manor, but it's cozy and the perfect amount of space just for me. I ignore the growing ache in my heart that reminds me of the fact that it most feels like home because Cade is here beside me, holding me close to his chest on the couch. But he's not staying.

I wish more than anything that I could ask him to stay, but there's something holding me back. A small part of my stubborn, self-reliant self that demands I prove I still have what it takes to live on my own. That I've not become so wholly reliant on Cade's company and money and cock. I'll show the nagging bitch in my head that I can get on just fine without a man, *thank you very much*.

Even if it hurts my heart a bit in the process.

"What do you want for dinner?" Cade asks, startling me from my thoughts as his fingers stroke up and down my thigh. I'm still not wearing any underwear and could probably use a shower after coming all over the rental car.

"Hmm, not sure." I let my own hands trail over his muscular thighs. I can feel the hard length of him through his pants. "I could cook something? You bought enough food to feed the whole damn building."

"I don't want you slaving away in the kitchen. It's been a long day." His lips find their way to my neck, and he nips at the sensitive spot behind my ear. "Besides, I'd much rather you slave away in the bedroom."

"Is that so, Lord Ashford?" I ask coyly, reaching for the buckle of his belt. "Then maybe I should just eat you for dinner." I slide the leather out of his buckle with a loud *thwap*. Cade moves quickly, switching our position so that I'm straddling his hips and he's lying beneath me.

"You think I can fill you up, Miss Caine?" he growls, his voice deep and needy.

"Yes, sir." I unzip his pants and pull down his boxers, setting his hard cock free. It's heavy and pulsing in my hand as I bend down and lick my lips, hovering just above the tip of his length. "I think you can fill me up just right." Without any teasing or warning, I swallow him down, letting his warm shaft slide to the back of my throat and then further.

Cade groans, his hands digging into my hair and pulling me down hard against him. He thrusts his hips, forcing me to take more of him. It feels like I'm choking, but I try to remain calm and open my throat for him. I want him to use me; it's my way of saying thank you for being given a bit of freedom.

"Do you like choking on that cock, love?" he asks as his hands hold me down and keep me from coming up for air.

I nod my head, even as black spots dance in my vision and my head feels light.

"Do you like having your mouth and throat stuffed full?" he demands fiercely, his hands fisting even tighter in my hair.

I nod even slower as my consciousness fades. I have a drifting thought that I might pass out.

Just as everything starts to fade to black, Cade pulls out and grants me air. I gasp and heave, desperate for oxygen. I feel warm cum splash against my wide open mouth, Cade finding his release the exact same moment I reacquaint my lungs with air. Ribbons of white spray against my cheeks, lips, and throat. I'm pretty sure I feel the stickiness of his cum in my hair. It's a huge load, like he saved it all up for me to remember him by. I keep my mouth open, letting him see how he painted my tongue with his cum.

"Does your dinner taste good, love?" His eyes are burning with desire, his pupils blown and his iris dark. He looks as though he'd like to devour me too.

"Yss, srrr," I answer as best as I can with my tongue still sticking out.

"Swallow every drop. Let me see how much you love it," he orders.

Obeying, I close my mouth and savor the salty, earthy taste of his cum. As commanded, I swallow every drop.

"Mouth open," he demands, his hand grasping my jaw hard.

I open my mouth, letting him use his fingers to explore over my tongue and along the straight tops of my teeth. He slides two fingers down to the back of my throat and pushes them past my gag reflex. I hold out as long as

I can, but I eventually gag on his hand.

"Good girl," he praises, slipping his fingers out of my mouth and wiping the spit against my cheek. "Now," he pushes an open palm against my chest and forces me back until I'm lying down on the couch with my legs bent and spread, "it's my turn to eat."

I giggle when he slowly brushes his lips over my thighs, his stubbled jaw chafing and tickling at the same time. Cade takes his time, intentionally teasing me with slow kisses that are nowhere near where I want him to be. Where I *need* him to be. Finally, his warm mouth lands on my pussy, and I shiver with pleasure. Desperate for more, I wrap my legs around his back and drag him closer to me.

"This cunt is mine, isn't it?" Cade asks in between perfectly placed strokes of his tongue over my clit, and his mouth is the closest I'll ever get to heaven.

"Uh-huh," I mumble, more than used to making these declarations while Cade bestows his generosity upon my pussy.

"Naturally, I'll be implementing a few rules to ensure my property is protected while I'm gone." Cade's lips land on my clit, and I see stars the second he sucks the nub between his teeth.

"Naturally," I repeat, my voice breathless. Cade is so skilled with his mouth that I'm right at the edge already. But then he stops sucking, and the warmth that was starting to build in my core fizzles away to nothingness. I have to stifle a moan of discontent when I watch him stand up from the couch and hold out his hand. Groaning, I place my hand in his and allow him to hoist me off of the couch and onto shaky legs.

"First and foremost, no coming without permission," he orders with a tap on my nose. His hands reach for the hem of my dress, and I lift my arms so he can pull it over my head. He tosses it to the floor like an unwanted nuisance and reaches for my bra. I've never in my life known a man so adept at taking off a woman's bra, and mine is on the floor in less than two seconds.

"I would have thought that was obvious, sir," I snark back, standing on my tiptoes to nip at his bottom lip before he throws me against the nearest wall and takes his teeth to my neck.

"No wearing underwear inside this apartment," Cade breathes against my neck between bites.

"That's problematic. What if I have guests?" I shriek as he bites down hard on my collar bone. The bastard for sure left a bruise.

"No fucking guests," he adds. He wraps my hair around his hand and drags me into the bedroom. "No one except me is allowed in this apartment. Do you understand?" He throws me face down over the low bed, leaving my knees on the floor.

"Yes, sir," I answer, my voice muffled with my mouth pushed into the duvet.

He slaps my thighs apart and grabs my pussy from behind. "I want you to send me a picture of this cunt every *single* day. Just because you're here doesn't mean that I shouldn't get to see my property whenever I want." He bends and runs his tongue through my folds and up to my asshole. "Extra points if it's dripping wet when you do it."

"Yes, sir," I agree, pushing back my hips and begging for more. He gives it to me, spreading open my pussy from behind and piercing me with his tongue. I cry out, the pressure mounting low in my belly slowly driving me mad.

"No socializing after work," he continues, listing his rules in between thrusts of his tongue.

"Yes," I moan, more in answer to his tongue lashing at my clit than whatever nonsense he's spouting. I'd agree to anything at this point if he let me come.

"No drinking. It makes you far too horny, and I won't be here to take care of you."

"Okay," I reply breathlessly, my pussy clenching around his tongue and aching for something bigger. And harder.

"Greedy little thing, aren't you?" Cade asks with a laugh, moving his hand up to brush my hair out of my face so he can better watch my humiliating reactions. I writhe beneath him, my body screaming lustfully for more.

His tongue slips up to my puckered hole and rims the outside once.

Twice. My whole body convulses on the third rotation of his tongue over my asshole, an orgasm held off by the thinnest sliver of self-control. I won't be able to resist forever, and I can only imagine what he'll do to me if I come without his permission. I tighten all my muscles and force my body to resist the need to crash over the edge.

Cade's fingers slap against my back hole. "Don't clench," he chides. "Keep it open for me."

Inhaling a sharp breath through my teeth, I try my damndest to relax. And *not* come.

He dips into the center of my asshole, his tongue applying pressure as he tries to force his way past the tight ring of muscle. "You will fly to Chicago every single weekend." *Thrust*. "You will go to Pandemonium every Friday." *Thrust*. "And you will accept any punishment I deem appropriate if you've been a naughty girl and broken any of the rules." *Thrust*.

"And what if I've been a good girl?" I hazard asking, barely getting the words out between heaving sighs.

He laughs. "If you've been a good girl, you get to come with me inside you."

"Have I been good tonight, sir?" I hold my breath, hoping he gives me what I want. What I need.

"Yeah, love," he answers, his warm tone skating over my skin and giving me shivers. "You've been my best girl. Do you want to come, beautiful?" I feel his fingers slip into the wet entrance of my pussy, penetrating deep.

"Yes please, sir." As if it's even a question.

"Come on, then." His tongue continues to lave at my asshole while one hand strums my clit and the other thrusts inside me. "Come like a good little slut with my tongue in your arse."

Chapter 10

KARA

I cried when Cade left. I promised myself I wouldn't, but watching him walk out the door in the morning did crazy, stupid things to my heart. The mind may be fortified against any manner of threats, but the heart is a weak bitch that falters with even the smallest stirrings of love. If I could live without the damned organ, I would. As it is, I'm left with a nagging ache in my chest as I try to adjust to days that *don't* begin and end with Caden Ashford. It's harder than it bloody sounds.

Damnit, I can't even get his *voice* out of my head.

I shift uncomfortably in the unfamiliar chair, the leather crackling beneath me. Another rule that Cade failed to mention until the end of the night is that he wants me plugged. *Constantly.* The prick said it would keep me from feeling too empty while he's gone and that the never-ending pressure in my ass would be a daily reminder of him. Thus, I've got a large silicone plug chafing at the inside of my asshole at the moment. And the damn thing is already distracting me from my work.

A rap sounds on the closed door of my new office tucked away in the upper levels of the English department, interrupting my internal cursing of a certain British bastard with smoldering green and gold eyes. I take quick stock of the small room, although it's large compared to some at the university, and make sure I've not left too much of a mess—or any kink paraphernalia lying about with the books because my domineering Dom demanded I bring vibrators and a small paddle to work with me. To my great relief, everything seems to be in order.

"Come in," I answer at last as I smooth down my tousled hair and straighten my periwinkle blouse. I expect to see the kid that's agreed to be my research slave for the next two semesters. However, the dashing man with jade green eyes and faint silver streaks in his curly auburn hair and short beard is definitely *not* a student.

"Bloody fucking hell," I exclaim in surprise while gaping at the familiar form lounging nonchalantly against the doorframe. It's *not* my research assistant. It's Dr. Grant fucking Westford. Also known as—my previous mentor and doctoral advisor, the brilliant intellectual who helped shape me into the academic I am today, and the professor I fucked for three years while I was a grad student.

As a minor informative detail, he also took my *fucking virginity*. Those blowing skills Cade raves about? I learned them on Grant's damned cock.

He is literally the last person I ever expected to grace my office at this university. The last I heard from him, he'd accepted a teaching position at a university in Scotland. This was while we were together, and the day I heard of his move for the first time was the day he ended our relationship. Suffice to say, things ended badly—more for myself than him. I practically worshiped him, and suddenly losing my mentor and lover left me utterly devastated. It took me a long time to stitch the pieces of my heart into something that resembled wholeness once more.

So what the hell is he doing darkening my doorstep with that same mesmerizing smile on his damned face as though no time at all has passed between us?

"Dr. Westford," I greet with caution after a very long and very awkward pause.

"Dr. Caine," he answers, a trickle of amusement in his voice as he walks toward my desk. "I don't recall things being so formal between us."

"There are a great many things that happened between us that I would appreciate never recalling again," I reply coldly. I'm no longer that broken-hearted girl, but I can still hold a fucking grudge.

"Well, my memory of you does little justice. You're even more lovely than I remember. My little Karenina is all grown up."

"Do *not* call me that. You lost the right to silly endearments a long time ago," I rebuke, my face flushing with embarrassment at the things that ridiculous nickname used to do to me. Grant specializes in Russian literature and has a particular obsession with Tolstoy. I never understood why being compared to a female literary figure doomed to live an unhappy life and meet an unhappy end drove me mad with lust, but it did.

"What I'm trying to say is: I'm proud of you. Of everything you have accomplished and become." His warm tone tugs at something deep inside me—the ghost of a naive student who only ever sought his approval. I take that foolish girl by the hair and drown her in the river of the past where she belongs.

"Your pride is unnecessary and unwanted." I square my shoulders and sit straighter in my office chair. I'm no longer willing to beg for his esteem. If he wants to throw it at me now, I'll throw it right back.

"I'm sorry," Grant offers, and I know him well enough to know that the truest sincerity rings in his words. "I know I hurt you. I was selfish and arrogant and thoughtless."

"You were," I agree. "But it doesn't matter now. I've moved on. I'm happy and fulfilled now more than I ever was with you."

"I'm glad," he answers, but his voice holds a tinge of sadness. "You deserve it."

"Thank you," I respond, my initial bitterness at his presence slowly fading into a genuine happiness to see an old friend. "Well, now that we've gotten that awkwardness out of the way, what the hell are you doing in my office?" I ask, a mischievous smile pulling at my lips. Much like someone else I know, Dr. Westford doesn't take kindly to disrespect. He'll find me much changed from the adoring little schoolgirl who hung on his every word.

"That mouth always did get you into trouble," he answers with a small chuckle, his eyes glimmering with flirtation.

Yeah, Hell will open a ski resort before *that* fucking happens.

"Thankfully for both of us, my mouth is someone else's problem now."

We aren't traveling that road again. Ever.

"Lucky man," Grant replies, not looking the least bit dissuaded.

"He is indeed," I answer, and it's the fucking truth. "Back to my previous inquiry: what are you doing here? Did they run out of books in Scotland?"

"I heard about your study," Grant replies, passing over my jabs. "And I read your recent publication. It's good work—the best I've seen from you in fact."

I struggle to ignore the overwhelming fullness in my chest at his words. Grant is a man of many critiques and meager praise, so his compliment holds a lot of weight. I try to appreciate his words as coming from an esteemed colleague rather than a past lover, though the familiar warmth in his eyes makes it difficult to forget. "Thank you," I answer at last. "That means a lot coming from you."

"You know I wouldn't say it if it wasn't true. And your work is actually the reason for my interruption today. I've volunteered to be your research partner."

I stare at him dumbfounded, my recollection of the English language momentarily forgotten. He's here to work with me? Not only with me, but *for* me? He's a world-renowned literary expert. I've always excelled in my field, but I've never reached the level of notoriety that would explain having a multi-awarded Doctor of Literature work as my assistant. His suggestion simply isn't logical. "Why?" I ask after a very long pause, still entirely perplexed.

"Because I'm intrigued. You know I've never been a believer in the academic hierarchy; everyone is a learner—therefore everyone is equal. That's why I involved you with my research even before you received your PhD. *You* intrigued me, and I let the others in the department scoff all they wanted because I knew you would be brilliant. And you were. And you continue to be."

"That doesn't change the fact that you are far overqualified for this role," I answer, still hesitant about his suggestion of working together. Is that even ethical after we've been in a sexual relationship? Technically, it wasn't exactly *ethical* back then either.

"I'm not too proud to take orders or get my hands dirty, Kara," he says with a slight reprimand in his tone. He's clearly frustrated that I'm pushing back so hard. Well, he better get used to it because pushing back is now one of my fundamental qualities. One Cade tries to beat out of me every chance he gets.

"And you're resigned to take orders from *me*, Dr. Westford?"

He smiles, the act painting his expression in a familiar warmth. "It would be my honor, Dr. Caine."

"Fine, I accept," I reply, sticking out my hand to shake on it. He accepts my hand and shakes it firmly. Cade would be fucking murderous if he knew I just agreed to work closely with my ex on an eight month long project. Swallowing down my guilt, I make the self-preservative decision *not* to tell him unless the situation absolutely demands it.

And I hope for both our sakes it never fucking does.

"So what now, Dr. Westford?" I rise from my chair, feeling spurred into action and ready to conquer the literary world.

"I believe that is for you to decide. I am at your full disposal."

I bite my bottom lip anxiously as I adjust to taking the lead for the first time in ages. "I've heard the library here is excellent," I offer, though it sounds more like a question than a decision.

"You've heard correctly. Shall we get a coffee and then peruse the archival shelves?"

I look at the clock on my desk and realize it would be about time for tea at Ashford Manor. The soft reminder of Cade makes me wistful. "Actually, I'm rather fond of tea now."

He quirks a smile at me, his expression unreadable. "Tea it is, Dr. Caine."

Chapter 11

CADEN

"Do you think we'll actually catch him this time?" Declan asks, his tone tinged with excitement. This is the first time he's been allowed to join the big boys in the hunt.

Ortega and I had meant to bring along Brax, but the little prick has the flu and is currently being spoon fed broth by a very diligent Mrs. Hughes. He'd probably rather take his chances with the fever and be in on the action, but Mrs. H was very insistent, and we like to make her feel like she has some agency every once in a while. And I'm perfectly willing to let Braxton suffer some coddling for it. Actually, since Ortega and I are now on babysitting duty, I guess we'll suffer for it too.

"I wouldn't count on it, *niño*," Ortega says as he glances back in the rearview mirror before turning his eyes back to the road. "He's been a slippery *hijo de puta*. Even at our closest, the *cabrón* was still a week ahead of us."

"How the hell does he do it? I never thought of Jace as the smart one, so how does he keep slipping Ashford?" The reverence in the kid's voice is unmistakable. Sometimes he seems to think of me as a god, but right now, I'm feeling a whole lot more human than I would like.

"I don't know kid," I answer, tugging at my hair as I check how much longer until we reach the destination. Five more minutes of driving streets that seem to get more seedy the farther we get from Kara's old university in Chicago. Campus buildings turn to dorms, dorms turn to off-campus housing and cheap apartments, and finally we're in an area of run-down motels similar to the last one Jace used.

Every time we get close to Jace, my anxiety over Kara's distance grows. I'm grappling with the urge to either double the security I've secretly placed on her or remove her from New York altogether. Now that she's mine, she has no real need to work. Although, I have a feeling I'd be invoking her murderous side if I ever informed her that her daily treks to her beloved bloody bookshelves are financially superfluous. She doesn't work for the money. She works because she has more affection for those damn dusty books than she could ever have for me. So for the sake of my cock, I'll go with doubling Kara's security. For now.

We park beside the motel on the left whose red, flickering sign reads *Afternoon Delight* with about half of the letters burnt out. The shiny black Escalade sticks out like a sore thumb among dilapidated cars meant more for the junkyard than for driving. I'm tempted to ask Declan to stay back and make sure nothing gets stolen, but I'm not cruel enough to ask him to play lookout when he's practically giddy to be allowed the chance to play with the big kids. Let's just hope we have a getaway car to make it back to.

The man at the front desk looks at us suspiciously when we ask him about any rooms that have been leased for an extended period of time. From the disdain in his glare, he probably thinks we're cops, but that's fine; we can work with that. Since Ortega is the more physically intimidating of the three of us, I let him lead the interrogation. Sometimes a show of muscle is literally all it takes, and Ortega gets us the keys to two rooms that have extended rentals in less than a minute. We didn't even have to bribe the manager.

We go to the room on the first floor—87—and knock before letting ourselves in. Right away, I can tell this isn't the right one. There are little shoes on the floor, a few toys scattered along the dirty walls, the two double beds have been slept in but made, and there's a little stuffed bear tucked under the stained sheets with his head resting on the pillow. My heart twists a little at my first misjudgment of the kind of people who would frequent this motel. Not everyone living in squalor chooses to be there.

"Well, he's not in this one," Declan announces in disappointment as though he's just lost a game. As he is utterly miserable at chess, I know the sound of his defeat all too well.

"A fine observation, Declan," I congratulate with a heavy dose of sarcasm. "Head up to the next one." They both leave on my command and look for the room on the second level of the motel. Before I follow, I pull out my wallet and empty every note, tucking the stack of money beside the stuffie in the bed. It's not enough to change their life, but it will get them out of this shit-hole at least.

I find the boys waiting in the open hall in front of room 116. There's a tension in the air like a tingling static of anticipation. There is a very small chance that this could be our lucky break. If our past encounters are anything to go off, Jace is already long gone. But still, that lingering strand of hope stirs excitement like spiders crawling in my guts as I touch the key card to the door and hear the lock disengage.

The stench that hits my face is putrid—an unmistakable scent of death lurking in the air. I take quick stock of the room as I hear Declan gag beside me. Unlike every other time we've happened upon Jace's hideaways, this time the room isn't empty. Although, I wish it fucking were.

There's a body lying on the bed.

We're all in a state of shock, each of us silent as we absorb the horror staring us right in the face. I have to resist the overwhelming urge to spew my afternoon lunch all over the rancid carpet as I walk closer to the bed.

It's a girl in her mid to late twenties as far as I can tell. The first thing that stands out is her hair—it's a pale blonde, almost platinum, and an exact match for Kara's. My stomach roils at the sickening connection, and I have to steel myself before continuing my assessment. Her wide eyes have turned an unnatural grey, hazy with decay. From the scant state of her clothes and overdone makeup, I'd say she's a prostitute. Her bright red lipstick is smudged across her lips, as though she'd been snogged as she died.

There's no blood, no mess; everything is clean and precise and orderly. The only mark on the girl's body is the bruising covering the entirety of her neck. If I had to guess, she was strangled to death; there aren't any cuts or marks from a rope or cable, so the bastard probably used his bare hands. It wasn't a violent act of passion; it was organized and meditated.

The girl's hair has been smoothed and is lying over her shoulders, chastely covering her mostly bare tits. She's been positioned like a doll—her head resting on the pillow, her limbs all lined symmetrically on the bed, the points of her black heels touch as they rest primly side by side. Her hands are folded neatly in her lap, resting on top of something. I breathe into the crook of my arm to stifle the stench as I step closer to get a better look. My heart stops in my chest as icy shards of fear shoot through my veins.

It's a book. She's holding a book. Her dead, brittle hands are obscuring the title, but I can see the author's name at the bottom. *It's fucking Chaucer.* I choke on my own bile as I rush for the toilet, tripping over Declan who I hadn't noticed already spilling his guts all over the floor. I just barely make it, emptying my stomach into the unsanitary bowl, shaking and sweating with revulsion and nausea and fear. I wipe my mouth on my sleeve, lacking the dignity to be disgusted at the moment.

The whole revolting scene is a pantomime for what the sick fuck wants to do to Kara. He's always been a twisted piece of shit, but I didn't think he was capable of killing innocent girls just to taunt me. Who am I kidding, *of course* he's not against murdering innocents to satisfy his own needs. I always knew he was a killer; the detached humanity is what made him so good at his job. It's my own damn fault I never bothered about his methods until it affected someone I care about.

I guess that makes us both fucking psychos.

I flush my mess of bile down the toilet and douse my face with cold water, rubbing my wet hands over my hair and along the back of my neck until my head isn't pounding and my hands aren't shaking anymore. I've seen dead bodies before, but this staged cruelty—the unnerving casualty of using some poor girl's body like a mindless prop in a grotesque piece of art—it's fucking with my head.

Finally feeling less discomposed, I exit the bathroom and make my way back to the horrid scene. Declan is still on the floor by the pungent puddle of his own acidic fluids as he hugs his legs close to his chest. He tries to hide his face in the cover of his knees, but I still notice the tear tracks on his cheeks. Poor kid. Of all the days to let him into the fray, this was the worst. He saw his first corpse today, and that sort of thing stays with a man. That poor girl's gray, bloated face will likely haunt his dreams for the foreseeable future.

Ortega is stoic and composed, standing in the corner as he waits for my command. This sort of thing doesn't phase him. He's seen plenty of death before. Hell, being a harbinger of death was practically a hobby in his younger years. I've never felt the need to ask him about his cartel days. From the little he's told me, slaughter was merely another unholy Sunday. He's not scarred from the carnage; he's just desensitized. And it's that level head in the face of chaos that I really need at the moment.

"Get ahold of Taylor." I don't need to address Ortega specifically. We both know I'm not talking to Declan. Detective Taylor is one of our contacts in the Chicago PD. He's come in rather handy in a few difficult situations, and he's far more bribeable than his prick of a predecessor. And yes, I'm perfectly content in my morality, or lack thereof, to bribe members of law enforcement. A saint is one of the few things I've never professed to be.

"*Entiendo*," Ortega answers, pushing off of the wall to make his way to the door. "What should I tell him?"

"Fuck if I know. Tell him Jace left us a little present that requires a HU. He should get the gist from that. As usual, remind him that discretion is mandatory if he wants to get paid. I want the processed findings from evidence the same time the department gets it."

"What about the kid?" he asks, his eyes landing on Declan with a little more sympathy than judgment.

"Take him with you." I wave my hand in dismissal and attempt to soothe my current frustration by brushing my fingers through my hair. It doesn't help.

"Come on, *niño*. Let's get some fresh air." Ortega tugs on Declan's arm and pulls him toward the door.

When they're both gone, I take a deep breath, drawing the death tinged air into my lungs until my chest starts to hurt. I exhale sharply before walking over to the girl's side to look for any clues we might have missed. As has become expected from my current dealings with Jace, everything is meticulous, laid out exactly as he planned with not a thing out of place. I resist the urge to trail my fingers over the girl's hair as an offering of comfort; I'm not asinine enough to think that my sympathy does her any good at this point. She looks so much like Kara, I can't prevent myself from picturing Kara in her place, and the thought of leaving her alone in this dilapidated room makes my heart ache and my skin crawl. So I keep watch over her body as I wait for law enforcement to arrive, standing because I don't trust any of the disease ridden furniture in this hellish hole that reeks of death.

A sudden panic to make sure Kara is safe and accounted for claws at my sanity until I break and reach for my mobile. Without taking my eyes off the girl, I dial the only number listed in my favorites. It's Friday, so Kara is at the airport right now making the weekly trip that I demanded as the price of her freedom for two semesters. It's been four weeks, and I'm already contemplating kidnapping her again.

Honestly, I'm having serious misgivings about allowing her any more space than an actual leash. Maybe I'll just tie her to the bed and never let her out of my sight again. It's a soothing thought as I wait for Kara to pick up. She finally does on the fourth ring, and I can hear the loud blare of the airport announcements in the background and the din of planes taking off.

"Hello?" she answers, a note of nervousness in her tone. I don't usually call her when she's traveling; it tends to make her anxious when she feels she needs to cater to the needs of her Dom while also trying to navigate the chaotic JFK airport. But right now, staring at the body of a dead girl who's an eerie echo of her, I need to hear her voice.

"Hello, love." My voice sounds raw, and I try to clear my throat of the thickness of worry and dread.

"What's wrong? You sound weird." Damnit, I should have known this was a bad idea. No one's ever been able to read me like her, and I forgot how good she is at it.

"Nothing's wrong. I just wanted to make sure my sub is on time for her flight like a good girl." I detest the necessity of appearing blasé while staring at the body of someone who will never make their way home again.

"Of course I'm on time." Her typical sauciness quickly overtakes any of her previous worries. And instead of my usual annoyance, her attitude makes me smile. She's so vivacious and full of fire, and I will be forever grateful for that.

"Good. I would hate to punish you as soon as you make it home."

"Liar. You *love* punishing me." I can tell from her voice that she's pouting, and I picture her arms crossed over her chest and that cute little crinkle in her nose. The thought makes me desperate to have her home and safe in my arms.

"You're quite right; punishing you is one of my most beloved hobbies."

"Well then, I guess I better be on my best behavior," she answers primly. Of course, her highest motivation to be good is purely to torment me.

"Who knows, I might just punish you because I want to." My tone turns dark, and I can hear the blatant, burning need in my voice even if she can't.

"You can't do that." Her words are almost a whisper, and I wonder if I'm imagining the aroused huskiness of her voice. "That's cheating."

"When have I ever played fair?" There's a brief pause, and I start to think the call dropped.

"I miss you, Cade," she answers at last. She sounds tired; it makes me think that maybe these weeks apart are starting to weigh as heavily on her as they do on me.

"I miss you too, love." I scrub a hand over my face and try to rub away the tension of the day. "More than you can imagine."

"Are we still going to Pandemonium tonight?" *Shit*, I'd forgotten we made plans for the club.

"If you're up for it." I need to get the fuck home and take a scorching shower to rinse the scent of death and decay off me. And then go to a club and pretend I didn't spend the afternoon with a corpse who is a far sight too resembling of my girlfriend.

"I'm up for it," she answers eagerly. "I like going to the club with you. You're…different there. A bit more out of your own head. It's nice to see you in your element." Fuck, and there she goes seeing me too clearly again. But she's right, I could use the distraction that the club brings, especially after what I've dealt with today.

"Alright, I'll pick you up at the airport then. Is the flight on schedule?"

"Yes, I should be in Chicago right at six. I grabbed a sandwich from one of the stalls, so we can skip dinner and go straight to the club."

I frown at what she considers an appropriate dinner, but make no comment since I don't really have the ability or appetite to think of food at the moment. "I'll be there at six then."

"Oh, they're about to start boarding, so I need to go. I lo—" she abruptly stops mid sentence, "look forward to seeing you, sir."

"You too, love. Have a safe flight." The call goes silent, and I slip my mobile back into my coat pocket. A moment later, the room fills with the sound of heavy footsteps bounding down the hall. I know it's Ortega before he opens the door.

"CPD is here. Are you ready to leave this shithole yet?" He stands with his large body blocking the door, not caring to enter the rancid room any farther than necessary.

I take a final moment to look at the body of the poor, wasted girl who will never know anything more than these four filthy walls, the smell of sweat and piss, and the hateful eyes of a monster who wrapped his hands around her throat and squeezed until her lungs were permanently hollow. She didn't even know her last breath *was* her last breath.

I'm not a moral man—I do shady shit for twisted people with big bank accounts, and I've never lost a moment's sleep over it. I thought I knew villainy. To be honest, I thought I saw it in the mirror every day.

But *this*. This fucking display of evil is a variety of sinister malignancy that I have never encountered before. In truth, I don't know how the fuck to handle it. And I don't know how to stop him from escalating even further. Jace has always been just barely out of reach, like a phantom in the wind. But now, that phantom is leaving behind bodies.

Chapter 12

KARA

Cade has been acting *off* since the moment he picked me up from the airport. He sounded so eager to see me when he called at the airport, but now he can barely look me in the eye. And uneasiness has been growing like corpse flowers in my gut.

"Here," Cade says as he hands me a cold glass of bourbon on the rocks.

It's my second drink of the night, and there's a two drink limit at the club bar. Typically, I'm lucky if I even get a sip of alcohol on the nights we play at Pandemonium, but something has Cade feeling overly generous tonight. I take a steady gulp of the amber liquid, trying not to wince as it burns its way down my esophagus. While bourbon is my Dom's drink of choice, I much prefer something sweet and bubbly like a spritz.

He didn't seem inclined to ask for my opinion, so I suffer through as I take small sips and wait for the ice to melt and water down the sharp taste of straight alcohol. Cade hasn't had anything other than a glass of red wine, which makes me a little anxious. Why is he staying stone cold sober and helping me get smashed? Something tells me this won't bode well for me.

"Is everything okay?" I ask when I've finally gathered the bravery to address his foreboding mood.

"It will be." His tone is clipped and cryptic, and it doesn't make me feel any less uneasy. "Finish your drink." He takes two of his fingers and tips my glass toward my lips. I swallow obediently, trying not to fixate on the memory of how good those two fingers feel buried deep in my pussy. Cade doesn't release his pressure on my glass until I've drained it to the last drop. My throat burns, and I heave for air when Cade finally pulls away from my lips and sets the empty glass on the bar.

"Let's go," he orders, capturing my hand and dragging me toward his private room. We haven't even seen Finn yet or mingled with any of our acquaintances at the club. Tonight, Cade is all business. At this point, I'm not sure if that business is fucking me until I can't stand straight or torturing me until I scream. The tingly warmth of the bourbon unfurling in my belly whispers that I would be happy with either. My slick and eager pussy is inclined to agree.

I stand at Cade's side as I wait for him to unlock the door. A sharp *clink* disrupts my concentration. "Shit," he curses, seeming shaken as he bends down to pick the keys that he fumbled off the floor.

What the fuck?

Cade is always composed. Always. Even the few times I've seen him drink more than his share of liquor, he holds himself with the sturdy, sure footed certainty of a captain who has sailed safely through hurricanes dozens of times. And I was the only one getting hammered at the bar tonight. So what the hell has got Caden Ashford shaken?

When he gets the door open at last, I step in slowly, my feet dragging with wariness across the black marble floor. I hear the door close and lock behind me as I make my way toward the bed. As is customary, I strip out of my clothes and fold them neatly in a pile. Cade doesn't say anything, but I feel his eyes boring into me as I lay myself bare for him. When I'm naked apart from the ruby choker around my neck, I kneel beside the bed, feeling more exposed than ever as I hear Cade stalk toward my exposed back. I brace, expecting to feel a blow. I didn't hear him gather any implements, but there isn't always a sound of warning before the first lash falls.

The tension in my body melts instantly when I feel nothing more than the warmth of Cade's lips on my skin. I moan as I lean into his touch, the gentle caress so much more welcome than what I was expecting. He paints feather light kisses across my skin, covering every inch of my back from the small divots above my ass to the tips of my shoulders with the indulgent attention of his mouth.

I feel him nuzzle at my throat just below my collar, and I have to resist the urge to break position and wrap my hands around his neck to draw him down further. Tauntingly, Cade's lips trail over the sensitive curve of my neck, kissing, licking, nipping his way down my throat and over my collarbone. The stubble on his cheek tickles, and I squirm to get away even though my body begs and moans for him to keep going. All of a sudden, my moans turn into a yelp as Cade unexpectedly sinks his teeth into my shoulder. And it's not a love bite—it's a fucking assault of fangs in my flesh.

"What the fuck, Caden?" I accuse in a wounded tone as I instinctively lift my hand to rub the sting from my skin. I can detect the deep indent of his teeth etched into my shoulder, and I feel as though he's bruised me right down to the muscle. I'm thrown so off kilter that it takes me a moment to realize with dread that I've broken position, called him by his first name, and said *fuck*. Three damning sins all in one sentence. I brace as I wait for rebuke and punishment to follow. In this room, Cade takes submissive protocol very, very seriously, and I know I'm in for a sound spanking at the very least.

"Would you like to try that again, Kara?" Cade asks, his tone calm and surprisingly patient as he strokes his fingers over the hurt he inflicted on my shoulder.

Why is he being so reasonable? When his rules are broken, he typically likes to punish me first and ask questions after.

"I apologize, sir." My words are earnest, and I'm not merely groveling for mercy. I hate disappointing him when we're in this space because it's one of the few places that I allow myself to submit completely. Submission and I have a tumultuous relationship in the outside world, but here I feel like I can actually surrender myself without judgment or fear. Here—I belong completely to him.

"Do you need a moment before we continue?" His fingers dig into the bite mark he left, juxtaposing the tenderness of his tone with what seems to be an insatiable need to hurt. I whimper, but remember to hold still this time. He's not inclined toward outright sadism, at least not when I haven't misbehaved, but there's a violence in him right now that's simmering just beneath the surface. And ready to burst through.

"No, sir. I was just startled. You can—" I take a steadying breath. "You can keep going."

"Such a brave little love." His lips return to my skin, and I try not to flinch away. He moves his tongue over the impression of his teeth in my shoulder and laps at it before sucking my skin into his mouth. It doesn't necessarily hurt, but it's not comfortable as he sucks and drags all the blood to the surface right beneath my skin. He finally pulls off with a loud pop, and I know I'm going to be sporting a monstrous hickey there.

I take deep, calming breaths as I feel him move over to my left side. This time, I'm more prepared when I feel his teeth bite into the sensitive skin of my neck. Unbidden tears prick in my eyes, and a whimper forces its way out of my mouth as Cade tugs hard and grinds his teeth over my captured flesh. When he releases me at last, a little sob tears out of my throat.

Why the fuck does this hurt so much? I've taken canes, whips, floggers, and belts in this room, but Cade is practically unarmed, and I feel the strongest urge to fall to pieces already.

"How are you feeling, love?" I can't see his face, but there's genuine concern in his tone.

"I'm okay, sir." My breaths come out harsh and labored around the words.

"Lie down on the bed."

I stand on shaky legs to obey his command, taking his hand when he offers it to help me climb onto the high mattress. As usual, there are no blankets or pillows or fluff on the bed—because it's never served the purpose of sleep.

"On your back," he directs, and I lie down in the middle of the bed accordingly, widening my legs just a bit and placing my hands face down on my thighs.

I feel unbearably exposed with all of my soft and tender bits out in the open and unprotected. My nipples harden into stiff points as goosebumps of fear and anticipation raise along my body. I defer to his dominance, lowering my gaze as Cade joins me on the bed and straddles my hips. He's removed his shirt, but his trousers are still on, the hardened bulge of his cock chafing against my bare pussy. The sensation isn't pleasant, but somehow I want more of it. I'm unable to keep myself from lifting my hips just the slightest bit to get his dick to press into my clit. I feel a firm hand tug on my hair in reproach.

"No moving."

I'm not self-destructive enough to take that as a request, so I still beneath him even as my selfish cunt chants at me to keep going. Cade lowers himself over me, his hands planted right beneath my arms as he dips down to take a rosy nipple into his mouth. I melt at the sensation of his wet tongue rolling over the sensitive bud even as my body warns me to be prepared for the next assault. I'm tempted to dig my fingers into his silky strands and pull in that way that makes him moan. But I'm more intent on following his orders than my own satisfaction at the moment.

"You know how sometimes—" he pauses right before sucking hard on my nipple.

I groan loudly as I tip my head back and close my eyes to focus on the overwhelming feeling of him suckling at my breast. The delicious act seems to tug on an invisible thread that's connected right to my pussy, and I feel my arousal flood between my legs, my body instinctually preparing for Cade's cock.

"Sometimes you need the pain to take the edge off?" He nips at the nipple in his mouth, and I jolt both in panic at the sensation and surprise at this line of questioning.

I didn't think he'd noticed my occasional taste for pain. I thought I'd been subtle about acting out when I really just needed him to take control and hurt me for the sake of preserving my sanity. Apparently, he knows my hidden needs better than I thought.

I nod in agreement, not brave enough to allow this topic to turn into a conversation at the moment. I'm insecure about my sporadic tendency to use pain as a coping mechanism. It's not something that I understand, so it's not really something that I want to own up to. I'm not a masochist—at least, I don't *want* to be, but I can't rationalize why I sometimes like the pain so much that it feels like an incurable craving. It makes me feel broken, and I'd rather Cade only see me as whole.

"Well," Cade moves his mouth to my other nipple, biting down firmly before pulling away. "This is one of the rare moments where I need you to take the pain for me—to keep me from spiraling into a very dark place where I honestly don't see the light on the other side." Cade stills for a moment, his solemn gaze transfixed on something in the distance—he looks haunted, hollow. I'd do anything to vanquish the haze of darkness currently tormenting my indomitable Dom and making him appear almost human.

"I need to escape my own thoughts, love. Just for a moment." His voice is almost desperate, pulling at a protective need deep within my soul that leaves me determined to save him from whatever demons are currently stalking his mind. "Can you help me? Can you take what I give you?" His green-gold eyes are pleading as they bore into mine.

I don't even need to consider my response; it flows freely, instinctively, like the shore submitting to the waves as they crash in with invincible force. It is merely nature to submit to strength—you can see the examples of such a dynamic in nearly every living thing. It's humans who fight it the most, no matter how futile the effort. And I'm done fighting.

"Yes, sir. I can take it," I declare even as my whole body tenses at the feel of Cade's teeth biting into the tender flesh of my nipple. "Give me your pain." I whimper as he bites down even harder. "Do your worst," I gasp.

Cade's eyes darken to deep pools of green with only the smallest flecks of gold as he stares down at me with vicious need. I've given his beastly side permission to gorge and ravish, and I can tell Cade won't hold himself back. Not this time. I shiver with undeniable fear as he pulls away with my nipple between his teeth until the abused flesh finally pops free. I try to calm my trembling, knowing it will get worse when Cade surveys my naked body like a slab of meat ready to be devoured.

Without warning, his fingers dig into my thigh, raising my leg to rest on his shoulder. The feeling of vulnerability is instant and searing. I'm defenseless and spread open and Cade looks like he very much wants to take advantage of both. He brushes his cheek against my upper thigh; his stubble is coarse and feels like rug burn against the tender skin. His tongue flicks out, caressing my skin moments before his teeth sink into my thigh. The painful pressure grows harder and harder. There's no reprieve, nothing to stave off the sting of tears in my eyes as he clamps down until I feel my skin break beneath the violent force of it.

I sob. I can't help it; it feels like willingly being eaten alive. Cade doesn't flinch or pull back. My tears don't bother him like they usually would; in fact, I'm not even sure he can hear them. He looks down at my skin, seeming mesmerized by the angry red crescent branded into my thigh and the prominent trail of blood dripping down from his bite. If I'm honest, I'm captivated too as I watch him lap at the red stain until it's wiped clean from my skin. There's no reason why that should be sexy, but there's a primal spark of pleasure in my womb when I watch him feed from my body. I'll add it to the ever growing list of reasons why I should be in therapy.

There's a shriek that I eventually recognize as my own when Cade's teeth brutalize a spot higher up. A spot that is way too close to where I don't want his teeth. Preferably ever, but especially not when he's in a mood to literally exact a pound of flesh. My body instinctively tries to struggle against his assault, but the pain is even worse when Cade latches on like a possessive dog afraid to have their favorite toy ripped away. I will myself to relax and breathe into the pain. The deep breaths help, and soon the moment of agony passes. Looking down, I notice with relief that he hasn't broken the skin this time. Maybe his darkness is slowly starting to bleed out.

"Spread open your cunt," he commands with an abrupt harshness. Shit, the darkness is most assuredly still there, rippling in his eyes, swirling about him like an aura as black as clouds in a storm.

My fingers tremble as they move to obey, unwilling and leaden as they may be. I dip my middle fingers between my folds, embarrassed to find that they are slick with arousal. What sort of sick person is turned on by being bitten until they bleed? Even the fear of what Cade might do next has my skin prickling with lust-filled adrenaline. I'll be mortified if I end up getting off on this torture. As though Cade can sense my apprehension, he drags his warm tongue along my dripping slit and flicks the tip of it against my clit.

I cry out, the pleasure so sudden and jarring compared to the pain he's been meting out for the past half hour. I'm not sure that my strung out body can handle such contrasting extremes at the same time. Saving me from my internal crisis, Cade switches back to pain, nipping and tugging on my inner lips as I keep my outer lips spread open for him. It hurts, but I can tell he's trying to be more careful. It's not like he wants to permanently damage his favorite part of my body.

I whimper when he scrapes his teeth a little too hard against my inner labia, and he surprises me by pulling away. Before I have a chance to breathe, his mouth is suckling at my clit again, the pleasure setting fire to my core in the most delicious way. My body tenses against him, too afraid to forget that pain could come at any moment.

"Give in to it," Cade orders before sucking my clit into his mouth again. His lips and tongue are gentle as he coaxes pleasure from my aching bundle of nerves. He's in no rush; there's no sign that the torture will resume. He seems perfectly content to caress my clitoris while the need to come quickly builds inside me. "Let me give you this." His words are almost pleading, and in that moment, I realize what he's trying to do.

This is his apology. Giving me an orgasm is penance for wanting to give me pain. And he can't assuage his guilt unless I take the gift he's offering. I look down at the beautiful, complicated man between my thighs and wish I could hold and tell him it's okay. But he hasn't given me permission to take my hands off my pussy, and he's given me another way to show him I forgive him. Closing my eyes, I give in to the warmth growing in my belly, reveling in every searing lash of Cade's tongue as he drags me higher toward release.

When he feels me relax against him, Cade lifts my other leg and drapes it over his shoulder. With the full weight of my lower body resting against him and my ass hovering in the air, Cade buries his face between my spread thighs, devouring as though it's the last time he'll ever have a taste of his favorite dessert. I keen, savoring every single flick of his tongue expertly pushing me toward the edge of ecstasy. I just need the smallest spark to ignite the explosion.

I get it when Cade's teeth scrape against my clit, his need to hurt bleeding through the cracks. I fall over the edge with a scream, pleasure assaulting me like waves crashing over my head until all I can do is drown in bliss. I expect Cade's teeth to loosen when he makes me come, but they don't. They bite down harder. And harder. And suddenly my scream of pleasure morphs into a scream of pure, unfathomable agony. Blackness seeps into the edges of my vision, and I struggle for breath. But I don't pull away; I don't remove the hands that keep my pussy spread as he tears into me. I let him feed until the darkness is sated.

When he pulls away, I'm sobbing, my entire body wracked with tremors as my tense, overstrained muscles try to unclench. Hesitantly, I look up at Cade, anxious to see if there are any lingering hints of viciousness in his eyes. To my relief, whatever was troubling him seems to have melted away, his eyes a perfect mixture of green and gold as he stares down at me with adoration. His expression is so warm I barely even notice the tinge of red on his lips. When I do, I look down between my thighs in horror.

Sure enough, there is a red cut on each side of my clit from where his damn teeth broke through. He's brutalized what is arguably the most important square centimeter on my entire fucking body. Even the thought of going anywhere near my clit while it's basically split open is agonizing. I should be livid. I should be ready to slice Cade's cock with a thousand paper cuts in retribution, but when I look at him—that peace on his face that's such a startling difference from the broken man who walked into this room tonight—I realize that it's a sacrifice I'm willing to pay.

With my legs still wrapped around his neck, Cade leans down and kisses me, his lips warm and generous as they try to give rather than take. I can taste the earthy flavor of my arousal and the blood he's drawn from my clit on my tongue, but I don't pull away. I open my mouth wider and accept everything he wants to give me.

There's a smile on Cade's face when he gently untangles his lips from mine. It's the first smile he's worn today. He's quiet for a moment, his knuckles stroking along my cheek with reverent affection, only tenderness where there was ferocity moments before.

"Thank you," he says finally, his voice a soft rumble.

And I know, for him, I would do anything in my power to banish the darkness.

Chapter 13

CADEN

I feel like a fucking monster for using Kara to quell the futility slicing through my sanity like debris from a collision. To be honest, I am a monster. I'm no different from Jace, drawn to torturing the innocent to feed my own needs and weaknesses. I suppose the only difference is that my unfortunate victims are willing.

As I survey the empty motel room, an overwhelming sense of helplessness rips through my chest and threatens to uproot the peace Kara planted there at the steep price of her own suffering.

Nothing. Another dead fucking end. I suppose I should be grateful that this one wasn't accompanied by the body of a dead blonde. Jace's trail went cold at least a couple weeks ago. Somehow, that fucker is always two steps ahead. He was always good, but he was never *that* good. Certainly never as good as me at fading into the shadows when needed. Either the cunt was holding back the whole five years we worked together, or someone else is pulling the strings. I refuse to believe I'm being outsmarted by fucking Jace of all people.

Fuck, I need to find the bastard.

My fist finds its way through the wall of the abandoned motel room we'd been led to through my contacts. I flex my fingers before brushing the remnants of plaster onto my trousers. Even though my knuckles have split open from the force of the blow, rivulets of blood trailing down along the prominent veins of my now dirty hand, I don't feel a fucking thing. I could probably throw my fist twenty more times, making a bloody, mangled mess of the wall and my fingers, and still not feel a goddamned tingle.

"You okay, *jefe?*" Ortega asks from beside me. In my rage, I'd forgotten he was there at all.

"Fine," I answer, waving aside his concern with my uninjured hand. "Go to the desk and tell them we'll cover the damage," I order, still staring at the glaring hole in the wall. Without another word, Ortega leaves to find the motel manager. At this point, he's used to my moods, and he's not the type to begrudge a man his need to inflict violence and destruction. I just wish I could get my hands on flesh and bone rather than plaster.

As much as I don't like to admit it, I need Kara. I miss having her to come home to when the days have been shit. And lately, it has seemed like a very long string of shitty days. To make matters worse, my cock is in a constant state of denial. Usually a good fuck can purge the violence from my blood, but I don't even have that option at the moment.

I get glorified conjugal visits forty-eight hours out of the week, and the other five days I'm left to handle myself. Which I don't. After spending over six months burying myself in Kara's sweet cunt any time I chose, my own hand doesn't do it for me anymore. I don't wank—can't imagine I could even get off with only a lubed hand and some porn.

If I were a selfish man, I would have demanded a substitute cunt while Kara runs off and plays Dr. Caine a thousand miles away. If I were a weak man, I would have found a girl to feed the hunger without Kara knowing. If I were a wise man, I would have chained Kara to the bed in the hideaway and never let her leave. As it is, I'm an honorable fool with just enough strength to endure the suffering until Friday comes around every week.

It's only Monday, which means I still have four days of torture.

I'm feeling wired and aggressive, and there's nothing to take the goddamn edge off.

"All taken care of," Ortega says, popping his head into the stale, empty motel room once more. "Manger said the room's paid for through the next two months in cash, but no one has used it in at least a couple weeks."

Frustration gnaws at my nerves as Ortega confirms what I already knew. We're no closer to finding Jace. This bloody room is the same as every other we've discovered in connection to Jace. I fist the paperback Canterbury Tales that I found beneath one of the dingy pillows, a page torn out like the others. A cruel taunt. The glaring proof that we're mere participants in Jace's sick game. We're not hunting him—we're being led through a maze of his own devising with dead ends at every turn while he gets off on our futility from afar.

"*Listo?*" Ortega asks, clearly wondering why I'm still standing in a dead end motel room. I suppose he has a point.

"*Si, vamos,*" I answer, catching a faint hint of Jace's cologne as I pass the bed. I suppress a cringe at the familiarity, hating to have been so close to catching him, and yet really not close at all.

We're playing your little game, cunt. Man enough to stop skulking in the shadows and face us head on?

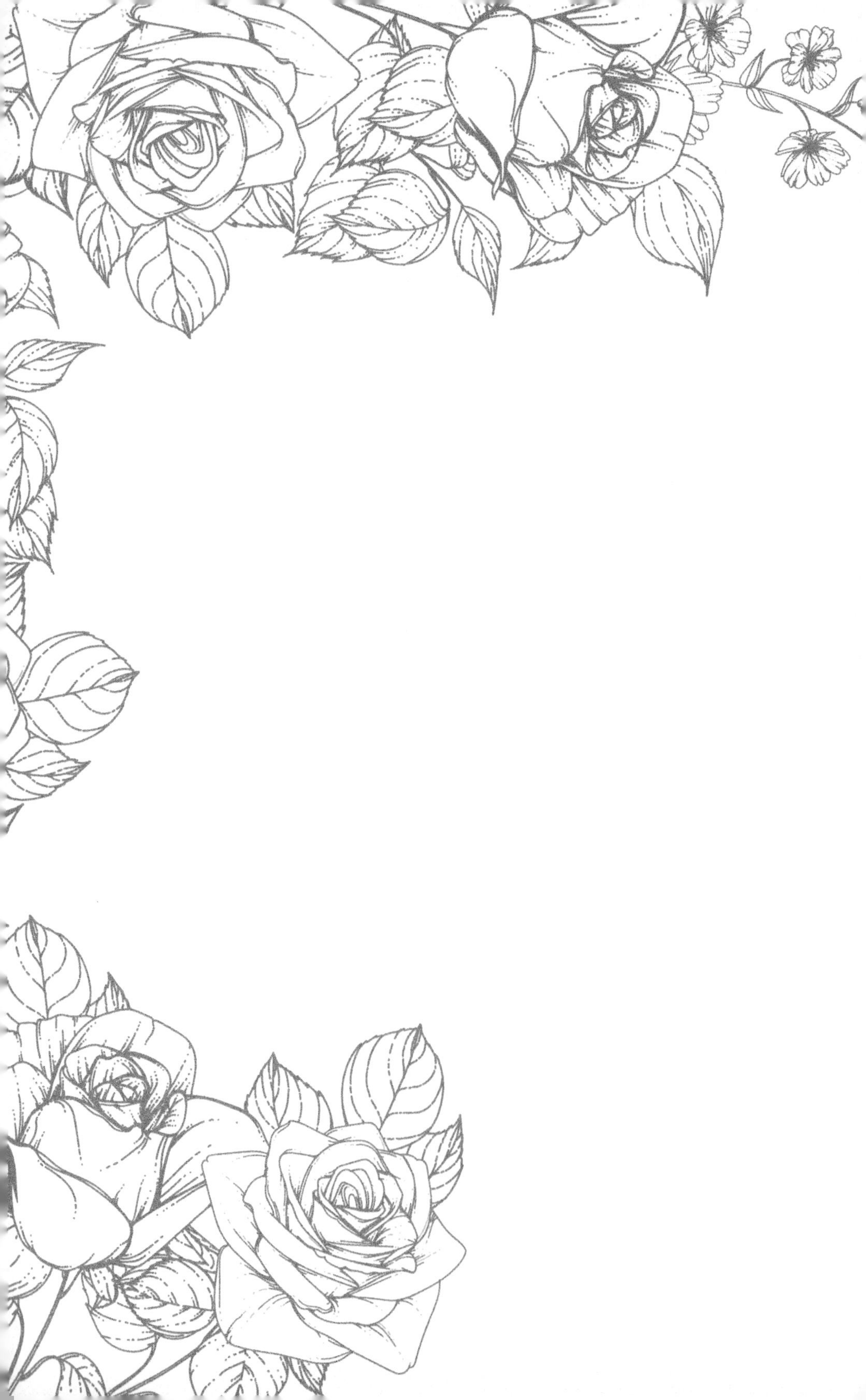

Chapter 14

KARA

There is a contagious feeling of merriment in the air. Prickly patterns of frost decorate the windows, fresh boughs of cedar are draped along the banisters, elegant wreaths intertwined with gold ribbons adorn every door, and mistletoe is strewn haphazardly about the manor. It's winter break, a few days before Christmas. I suspect because this is my first Christmas at the manor, Mrs. Hughes has gone all out, decorating the house to resemble the sort of perfect holiday cheer that belongs in a magazine. I helped where she allowed, and the boys helped begrudgingly when she demanded.

"Why do any of the heavy lifting when there are four more than adequately abled men skulking about this house at any given time?" she'd said in her usual brusque manner that I've grown to love.

This small break from work has been heavenly. I didn't realize how terribly homesick I'd grown. I've missed waking in Cade's arms every morning, hearing the boys' lively raucous at the dinner table, sharing gossip with Mrs. Hughes in the kitchen while she bustles around to feed us all. Work has kept me so busy that I didn't notice the subtle ache in my heart until being at Ashford Manor again has slowly soothed it.

I've been back for a week, and the days have been filled with making more gingerbread cookies than we could ever eat, drinks with charades and other silly games with all the boys in the library after dinner, trips to the stables to see Avalanche and Sugar Cubes and ride when the weather is nice, the occasional snowball fight, nighttime cuddles by the fireplace, slow dances to Christmas classics on the record player—which Cade insists is the only way to listen to them—and lots and lots of sex. It has been pure, unfathomable perfection, and I don't think I've ever been this happy. Cade and the others have invaded my heart with a tactical precision that I never expected, and I never thought I would feel this *whole* again. The only thing missing is my sister, but she chose to spend the holidays with my aunt and uncle this year.

I hum White Christmas on my way to the library. It's been stuck in my head since last night when it was playing while Cade used his tongue to reacquaint himself with every inch of my body—even the places you wouldn't expect a tongue to go. I feel my cheeks go warm as I remember the sight of him beneath me on the fur rug by the fireplace, his mouth between my legs as I reached back and spread my cheeks wide as he commanded. And then he decorated my face like a Christmas cookie in desperate need of icing. The holidays certainly put Cade in a slutty mood, and I have to say I'm catching a case of holiday whore too.

I take a deep breath when I enter the library, the scent of old ink and parchment mingling with the Christmasy smell of cedar and cinnamon that seems to pervade the entire manor. I've missed the library while I've been in New York; the library at the university is pristine and well-endowed, but Cade's library is welcoming and cozy, and it has an easily accessible, fully stocked sex dungeon right beneath it. So it's conducive to two of my favorite pastimes—reading and getting kinky with Caden Ashford.

As Christmas creeps its way closer, I still haven't picked out what to get a certain British lord who seems to have everything he could ever want or need right at his fingertips. At this point, I'm considering waking him up on Christmas morning wearing nothing but a big red bow and calling it a day. To my great personal embarrassment, Cade is already far ahead of me on the gift giving.

My last Friday on campus before coming home for the holidays, there was a small black box left on my desk on top of a half-annotated copy of *Lady Chatterley's Lover*. There was no name or note, but Cade is obviously the only person crazy enough to have someone sneak into my office and leave a surprise right before Christmas. Inside the box was a very gaudy pair of dangle earrings that seemed far more reminiscent of Cade's *eclectic* tastes than my own.

As much as I appreciated the thought, they were really too ugly for me to wear. I carefully placed them at the bottom of my drawer underneath some photocopied studies on sexual deviance from the early nineties. It gives me enough of an excuse to say I accidentally left them in my office if Cade asks about them. And for the sake of my sense of fashion, *I* have no intention of ever bringing them up. Thankfully, he hasn't mentioned the garish gold things, and I've been relieved of the burden of telling him I hate them. So it's a merry Christmas indeed.

I scan the bookshelves, feeling in the mood for something festive. Maybe a classic? A Christmas Carol seems fitting, so I run my fingers over the worn and new spines as I search for it. I've been begging Cade to let me sort the library properly for the better part of a year, but he always refuses. I think part of it is that he likes being a bossy bastard, and the other part is that he genuinely enjoys the chaos. It's not even fucking alphabetized. I've been trying to rearrange just a little in the hopes that he won't notice. I've got a small corner where I've organized based on genre, author, and title. And the little bit of academic rebellion makes me far happier than it should.

With a little gasp of excitement, I pluck the book I've been looking for from the shelf, feeling as though I've found the golden prize in a treasure hunt. I delicately open the book to discover that it's a second edition of Dickens' Christmas classic.

Guess Cade couldn't manage to steal a first edition.

The thought reminds me that this is right about the same spot where I stored The Canterbury Tales for safekeeping. The first edition is right where I left it, in between an Austen and a Brontë—the two of which had been thrust together as though someone had decided they should be companions purely because they were classic romances written by women.

Cade's sorting skills are abysmal at best.

I pull the Chaucer text from the shelf, loving the weight of it in my hands. Right away, something is off. It *smells* different. As an archivist, I can nearly date a book based on smell alone. The scent of this book isn't that of vellum that's been through centuries of wear; it's newer. Hesitantly, I open the book, horrified to find my suspicions are correct. This is *not* the Caxton first edition of the Canterbury Tales. The pages are too pristine and devoid of wear and blemish, and while the type looks nearly accurate, it could have never been done on a fifteenth century printing press. This is a fucking fake.

And I'm going to kill that motherfucking, thieving, British bastard.

I storm toward Cade's study, counterfeit Chaucer clutched angrily in my fist. At this point, I'm fully prepared to use it to bludgeon him to death as that is about the only thing a fake historic text is good for. There isn't a word in the entire English vocabulary to describe how fucking pissed I am. He knows how I feel about preserving the history of literature; it's my entire life's work. Ten months ago, I would have let him torture and kill me to protect that book. I thought I could trust him; I *told* where I'd stashed the fucking book so that he could appreciate my cleverness, and instead he used the information to stab me in the back.

Well, if I can find a knife, that phrase is going to lose its metaphorical charm right before I let Cade bleed out on the floor—my only regret being the mess that Mrs. Hughes will have to clean up.

My thoughts brimming with murder, I forgo knocking on Cade's door and let myself right into his inner sanctum. His deceptively warm hazel eyes jolt to mine in surprise, confusion marring his features as he catalogs the incandescent anger radiating from every molecule in my body.

"Kara," he greets in a cautious tone, sounding very much like someone trying not to antagonize a dangerous creature. "What's wrong?"

"What's wrong?" I reply with a scathing scoff as I stomp toward his desk and throw the offensive Chaucer decoy on top. The abomination lands on the smooth mahogany wood with a loud, satisfying *thud*. "That is *what's wrong*."

Cade drops the pen he was using and reaches for the text, his expression turning grim as he realizes exactly which book from his library I've thrown across his desk. As if I'd ever be so cavalier toward a real book. He scrubs his hand over his face as he seems to search for the words of an explanation, not that any assortment of words in any variety of combinations could ever make this travesty right. We've been living a lie this entire time; frankly, I shouldn't be surprised. I've known exactly who and what he is from the moment I met him.

I was the one stupid enough to believe he could be something more than a domineering bastard with a taste for thievery and kidnapping. He even promised me that all of his recent business ventures have been on the legal side of things—unethical perhaps, but legal. Now, I know that was probably a lie too. The fact that this entire situation is merely a byproduct of my own damned naivety makes me even angrier.

"I was hoping you wouldn't notice," Cade says softly, his tone guilty though nowhere near apologetic.

I realize instantly that this is because he regrets getting *caught* rather than the deed itself. And the sheer audacity has me seeing through a cloudy haze of red. In two steps, I close the distance between me and his desk, reach over, and slap him across the face as hard as I can. The two of us freeze in stunned silence, disbelieving what just happened even as the sound of my hand hitting his cheek is still ringing in my ears.

I can't believe I just did that. Even though I've done it before, that was ages ago, far before we'd established our relationship. And I just bitchslapped my Dom. My very unforgiving, delights in painful tortures and humiliations Dom. I'm terrified to imagine how he'll retaliate. But then I remember why I did it, and my meek subservience evaporates like water in a sauna as fury takes its place. I choke down the urge to get on my knees and beg his forgiveness and stand tall as I prepare to face his ire.

"I'll allow you that one because I know you're upset. And I probably deserve it," Cade says as he gets up from his chair and rubs the sting from his cheek that's now emblazoned with the red mark of my hand. "But hit me again," he continues, his eyes turning fierce and undeniably dominant as he stares down at me while resting a fist on each side of his desk, "and I will show you *exactly* what it feels like."

I raise my chin and stand firm, refusing to be intimidated by him, even though the muscles straining the material of his dress shirt make it frightfully clear how quickly he could destroy me if he so chose. I'll have to carefully tread the line that keeps me out of his reach—and free from his innate need to discipline. "Where is the real first edition, Caden?" I ask, my tone biting and spiteful. If this was any other day, I'd already be bent over his desk with my dress above my hips and his heavy hand spanking some submission into me. But today, I'm not the only one in trouble.

"I don't know," Cade answers simply and far too unbothered for my current state of indignation.

"What do you mean *you don't know*?"

"I've lost it," Cade says with a shrug of his shoulders, playing it cool.

Cool is not the fucking way to play it right now. Unable to stop myself, I lean over his desk and slap the blasé composure right off his stupid face. Cade goes deathly still, the soft brush of his hand leaving his desk the only warning before it connects with my cheek with a swift *smack*. I whimper at the sharp shock of it, bringing my trembling fingers to my face to soothe the burn of the blow.

He *slapped* me. And not just a little reprimanding tap, he fucking hit me like he meant it. I know he threatened to, but hearing it and feeling it are two completely different sensations. I cradle my aching cheek as I look up at him with judgment in my eyes and try to blink back the sting of tears.

"Don't look at me like that," he commands with a bitter bite to his tone, his index finger pointed at me as though he's scolding a naughty child. "You know I don't make empty threats."

I resist the urge to stomp my foot and show him exactly how a bratty child behaves. I settle for the mildly more mature stance of crossing my arms over my chest and glaring at him. "You hit me!"

"You're a feminist, love," he says smugly as he slips back into his chair. "You should be thanking me for establishing equality. And you shouldn't be afraid to take what you fucking give."

I scoff because he's a prick—not that he's entirely wrong. "You're barbaric," I spit back, knowing that insults are really my only weapon at the moment if he's going to play…fair.

"Yes, but that's why you like me," he replies with a laugh. I clasp my hands in front of me to keep from hitting him again. I'm not desperate to feel his hand across my cheek a second time.

"I don't like you. I *hate* you," I grit out of clenched teeth.

"Don't tell lies, Kara," he warns as he makes a tsking sound with his tongue. "Lies get you punished."

I roll my eyes, hating how powerless I feel in this moment. "Of course, you sold an invaluable piece of academic history, and you think *I* should be punished."

"I didn't sell it," Cade thunders at me, his eyes igniting with a burning fury I've only witnessed a handful of times. And each time it was scary as hell. "Do you truly think so goddamn little of me?" He runs his fingers through his hair in agitation. "I know what that bloody book meant to you." His tone is regretful, almost sad, and I wonder if my accusation actually pierced through that ironclad armor he constantly uses to protect himself.

But he's a criminal and a black market arts dealer; it's not like my first thought when I discovered The Canterbury Tales missing was very far from the truth as it is. "Then what happened to it?" I ask, trying to keep my voice calm and negotiating. "Why isn't it in your library where I put it ten months ago?"

"Jace," he answers as he avoids my gaze, his tone clipped like he had to force the name out of his mouth and it cut like glass along the way,

"W-what about Jace?" I ask as I feel the blood in my veins turn to ice. I haven't thought about Jace in months. I banished him from memory the moment Cade took the pain he left and crafted it into his own. The scars he imprinted on me are buried deep down, and I hoped they would never again come to light. But that's the thing about scars—they can fade, but they never truly disappear.

Cade sighs deeply before relaying a piece of information that he clearly never wanted to tell me in the first place. Now that I know Jace is involved, it was probably with good reason. "Jace demanded that I turn over the book or risk dismembered pieces of you being scattered about the country."

Cade looks at me, his eyes harsh as he silently relays that this wasn't some idle threat. Jace would have actually killed me if given a chance. And Cade saved me from that fate by bargaining with something I never would have traded.

"As you can imagine, I chose the option that kept you safe," he continues, seeming to read my thoughts. "I'm sorry if your self-sacrificial arse would have chosen differently."

"Do you…know where he is?" I ask, my eyes flicking around the room with the irrational fear that my personal monster could be hiding in the shadowy corners.

"Not a fucking clue. We've been tracking him for months." His eyes are distant, as though he's disappeared somewhere far removed from this room.

I allow Cade's words to sink in. This whole time I thought that we'd both decided to shove Jace into a tiny mental compartment never fit to see the light of day. This whole time, I thought we'd both moved on, like dusting off the rubble and simply rebuilding after a hurricane has come and wind-thrashed your world to pieces. Clearly, Cade hadn't moved on at all. I feel an enormous rush of guilt knowing that he was handling this alone. While I abandoned him to go off on my own and conduct self-satisfying literary studies, Cade has been off trying to fight my demons for me.

My very first thought when I found the counterfeit Chaucer was to accuse Cade of being a villain; turns out, he's trying to be an unlikely hero.

"I'm sorry," I whisper, my trembling voice full of remorse as I respectfully lower my gaze and stare down at my bare feet. I stormed into his personal space, thrust my unfounded accusations in his face, and physically attacked him even after being given a warning. Offering him my submission is an instinctual reaction to the guilt I feel like sharp pinpricks all over my skin; submitting soothes the sting. If he asked me to kneel and offer myself to him, I would do so in a heartbeat. If he asked me to accept punishment for my offenses, I would willingly accept atonement through his hand.

There is a charged silence in the air as I wait for Cade's response. Knowing him, he's not going to go easy now that I've accepted the blame; honestly, I don't know if I want him to. Without looking up, I hear him sigh, the sound filled with tension and resignation.

"It's okay, love," he says finally, and his tone has softened to sound almost doting. "As much as I would like to, I can't change the history that our relationship was built on. It's my fault for stealing you rather than earning your affections in fairness and honesty. And as much as it wounds me to hear that you still can't trust me, the reasons behind your distrust stem from a rational source. I hope that, one day, your trust is something that you'll give me freely."

I want to tell him that he's already earned that trust, but my current behavior disproves that assumption. Subconsciously, I still hold him at a distance even as my heart went straight over the edge for him ages ago. It is the constant battle of a reasonable woman to make peace between the warring factions of the heart and the mind. We are all likely to die trying.

Slowly, my attention returns to Cade's original statement regarding Jace, and I look up at him in confusion. "You said 'we've been tracking him.' Who are *we*?"

Cade laughs shortly—as though my sheer ignorance has startled the noise out of him. "Do you honestly think any of the boys would allow Jace to get away with what he did to you? I'll be lucky if Ortega lets me get in the first shot."

My mouth hangs open in surprise as I try to unwrap the idea of other people being willing to risk themselves to defend me. A tingling warmth of gratitude and affection stirs in my belly at the thought of these men treating me like one of their own rather than an outsider who regularly fucks their boss.

"I didn't know they felt that way—about me, I mean."

"Of course they do," Cade answers, his tone turning scolding because he knows I have a tendency to self-deprecate. "You're one of us—part of the family. A severely fucked up, dysfunctional family, but it's a far sight better than my *actual* family."

I can't help the ridiculously happy smile that stretches across my face at the thought of being accepted into the Ashford clan. "I like that—being part of your family."

"Aww, you want me to be your daddy, baby?" Cade asks in a teasing tone, knowing very well that this particular jab irritates me more than most.

"Fuck you, I do *not* have a daddy kink."

At least, not that I will admit to. Do I find it awkward and humiliating when he treats me like a little girl? Yes. Do I get turned the fuck on when he forces me to call him "daddy" while he does it? Also yes. What can I say, I spend my life in constant conflict with the things I want and the things my selfish pussy wants. Right now, she's winning.

"So," Cade says slowly, his smoldering gaze pinning me in place as he reaches for the buckle of his belt and loosens it, "if I told you to be a good girl and get on your knees and suck daddy's cock, your cunt wouldn't be dripping at the idea?"

My mouth waters instinctually at the sound of Cade unzipping his pants.

"N-nope, not a bit," I mumble, too transfixed by the sight of his hard cock pushing at the seams of his boxers, begging to be unleashed and allowed to ravage.

"Hmm, what did I say about telling lies, naughty girl? Maybe you need daddy to give you a spanking instead?"

"No, sir," I gulp out hastily. A spanking is not at all what I'm in the mood for at the moment.

"We'll see. Get on those knees," Cade commands, pointing to the floor beside him.

Without any hesitation, I scurry to his side and fall to the floor, slipping into the submissive position I'm so familiar with—my palms resting on my closed thighs. Kneeling at Cade's feet is surprisingly comfortable, the routine of the position soothing in a way. I already feel my mind emptying to surrender to Cade's will.

"Good girl," Cade praises as he pets my hair. "Now, open your mouth nice and wide."

I do as he asks, opening my mouth until my jaw hurts from the strain. Cade thrusts two fingers into my mouth, inspecting me as he runs them over my lips and teeth before pressing down on the back of my tongue. I try not to gag, but I can't help the tears that mist in my eyes as I try not to puke all over his hand. "So pretty," he comments as he hooks his fingers inside my cheeks and spreads until they're taut. I feel the farthest thing from pretty as he plays with me like some sort of perverse doll, but I can't staunch the arousal flooding down my legs at the degradation.

"Do you want daddy to fuck this pretty little mouth?"

"Yss plss, srrr," I plead around his intrusive fingers.

"What was that, baby?" he asks, removing his fingers so he can hear my humiliation more clearly.

At this point, I don't even have the self-respect to be ashamed of how needy I am to feel his cock literally anywhere inside me. "Please fuck my mouth, daddy," I gasp out, breathless and completely intoxicated with lust.

"*Fuck me*," he breathes as his eyes nearly roll back in his head. "Stick out your tongue."

I obey, obscenely sticking out my tongue. I watch him pull his boxers down to his hips. My mouth waters at the sight of his cock so thick and hard, pronounced veins jutting along his shaft until they reach the nearly purple swollen head already beaded with pre-cum. Cade digs his fingers into my hair and drags me toward him, rubbing his length back and forth over my waiting tongue, the side of his dick slapping into my cheeks as he moves.

Ever so slowly, Cade pushes the tip of his cock into my mouth, teasing me with the promise of more. My lips latch onto him hungrily, and I try to suck more of him into my mouth. "Eager little thing, aren't you?" he asks, making shallow thrusts into my mouth. "You want more, baby? You want me to stuff this greedy mouth full of cock?"

I nod, not really able to respond with his dick in my mouth.

Without another word, Cade grabs my hair with both hands and drags my open mouth onto his cock, spearing all the way to the back of my throat—and then forcing himself further down. I gag at the invasion, my poor throat struggling to take his width as he leaves no room for air to get through. Cade holds himself there, effectively suffocating me on his dick until he chooses to grant me air. When he first started choking me on his cock a few months into our relationship, I was terrified. For a person so adjusted to clutching onto control, giving up your ability to fucking breath is unfathomable.

The first time Cade did it, I nearly passed out from panic alone. Slowly, he's taught me to let go of the fear and embrace the high of submitting my breaths to him. Now, I actually love it, and it's my favorite type of breath play. I close my eyes as I feel my vision start to blur, welcoming the darkness even before it comes to take me. When Cade feels me relax completely, he pulls out halfway and allows me to gasp for air around his cock.

"Eyes on me, baby," he chastises. He doesn't like it when I take my focus off him, not that it's even possible while he impales my throat. I open my eyes and look at him, feeling wetness clinging to my lashes, and I'm sure my face is already a streaky mess of mascara. I know him well enough to know that making a mess of my face is half of his fun. He continues to fuck my mouth at a brutal pace. From the feel of it, he's working out some of the pent up aggression of having his sub slap him around and hurl insults at him. And I'm not complaining—being throat fucked is one of his kinder punishments.

"You take me so good, baby. You like daddy filling up that naughty mouth."

Even as I cringe, I feel arousal flood down my thighs. I'm so wet right now, I could probably take two cocks in my pussy, and they'd slide in easily. The thought has my neglected pussy clenching around nothing, and I wish my mouth wasn't the only one being filled. I need more. As discreetly as possible, I slip one hand between my thighs and try to reach my aching clit. To my dismay, I'm caught instantly.

"Kara Caine, you get that hand out of your cunt right now," he orders sharply, and I pull away my offending hand with a jolt. "You are not allowed to get off on this. And you won't be coming at all tonight. So that needy little cunt can keep you company tonight while you contemplate how to give your Dom some respect." Cade's thrusts still as he forces my head up to look at him. "And if you are *ever* so bold as to raise a hand to me again, you are going to get something a hell of a lot worse than my cock down your throat. A little friendly face-fuck is going to look like a dream compared to having your arse fucked dry and raw."

Cade hits a nerve with that one, the threat sending literal shivers down my spine. Of all the things we've tried, anal is *not* one of them. I am perfectly happy with being experimental with everything other than my asshole, which seems only sensible to be left exactly as it is. The very idea of allowing Cade inside *there* is mortifying. At this rate, the only way he's fucking my third and final hole is as punishment because there's no way in fuck I'm giving away that one short of being tied down and forced.

"Do you understand, little brat?" Cade asks with an arched brow.

"Yes, sir." And then he's back in my mouth, forcing his way down my throat at a relentless speed. I gag with every deep thrust, but he doesn't stop or slow, using me like an inanimate hole that exists purely for his pleasure. The brutality of it has tears flowing down my face even as my thighs clench together in need. I feel him swell even more in my mouth as he gets close to his climax. But instead of spilling down my throat, he pulls out.

"Stick your tongue out," Cade commands. He strokes himself up and down, his hand gliding smoothly with the help of my spit and his arousal.

Obediently, I open my mouth wide and stick out my tongue, prepared to accept his cum offering. Cade orgasms with a groan, his firm strokes sending ribbons of warm cum over my tongue and across my cheeks. Instinctually, I close my eyes right before a spurt of cum decorates my lashes. I'm technically supposed to keep my eyes on him when he comes, but it's hard not to flinch when your face is being used as a blank canvas for a mag*cum* opus.

When he's finished emptying himself on me, Cade uses his thumb to wipe the excess cum from my cheek and feeds it to me. I suck his thumb dry, and he repeats the gesture until I've essentially licked myself clean of him. It's disgusting and degrading, but the act of him feeding me his cum makes me want to climax on the spot.

"Now, what do you say?" Cade asks. He looks down at me with an adoring twinkle in his eyes that he only gets when I've survived him being particularly sadistic. The look of pride warms me to my very core.

"Thank you, daddy," I answer, not even having to choke out the words this time.

"Looks like daddy made a mess," he tsks as he swipes at a black smudge of mascara beneath my eye. Pushing back his chair, he stands and offers me his hand. I put my hand in his, loving the way his strong fingers dwarf mine. "Let's go give you a bath."

Chapter 15

CADEN

The manor is cold and empty now as silence fills the halls rather than the familiar click of patent heels. The holidays were too fleeting; I feel like I barely had a chance to hold my girl before she was gone. Back to that bloody university that receives more of her time than I do. I have half a mind to burn the whole goddamn place to the ground. Kara would be disappointed—and no doubt suspicious—but she'd get the fuck over it. I'd do everything in my power to make sure of it.

Violence and helplessness wage war on my mind as I sulk in the car and stare at the barren trees passing by. The snow has melted and turned to rain, leaving ugly, grayish puddles of slush along the road. It's the sort of bleak, dreary weather no one ventures into unless they have to. And, unfortunately, we have to.

We got another possible trace of Jace from one of our contacts. I have private investigators spread out over the whole state of Illinois. If necessary, I'll expand the search to be nation-wide. I'd pay off every mercenary in the bloody country if it meant we'd find the cunt. As far as we know, Jace hasn't left the state boundaries—which makes it even more frustrating that we haven't found him yet. He's as slippery as a rat in the sewers, and we can't seem to work out which dark corner he'll slither to next until it's too late.

Chicago PD is aware of Jace's presence, but they only have the resources to be reactive, not proactive. Taylor keeps me informed of any developments, but it's been radio silence. To our limited knowledge, Jace only has a body count of one. Chicago gets almost a thousand homicides a year. One dead prostitute with no known family isn't reason enough to start a manhunt. Not for the police, anyway.

The location we're headed to is different from the others—it's a residential area rather than a strip of seedy motels. That fact alone leaves me less than hopeful. Jace has been consistent in his methods and movements. He always uses an alias, books a motel in a rundown part of town, pays through a few weeks in cash. Apart from the dead girl, Jace keeps a strict routine. I don't see why he would change things up now—we haven't even been able to touch him.

Ellington Court. For some reason, the name of the street tugs at my memory, but I can't place it. Ortega parallel parks along the curb, and Declan and Brax jump out of the back seat. There's a tense mixture of anticipation and dread in the air. All the boys join me on these quests now. There's no point in pretending that we care about acquisitions when there's someone out there trying to hurt one of our own. Kara comes first—we can all agree on that.

The tip gave us the location of a house in this neighborhood. It's empty at the moment because the older couple who owns it is on holiday. It's not by any means an ideal location for Jace to hide away, but the investigator's information checked out. It did look like Jace was here at some point. But doing what?

We step up to the particular house as inconspicuously as a group of four men can in a family neighborhood. It's midday, so most people are at work or school. The house is yellow with hanging flower beds filled with blue, purple and yellow petunias lining the windows where the lace curtains are drawn. The rain has stopped, and the sun peeks out from behind the clouds. At least we don't have to do this in the middle of a downpour.

The front door is locked, as expected, but that's never stopped people in our line of work. Declan quickly pulls a small pick set out of his pocket. This is child's play, which is appropriate for him. In half a minute, he has the door open. We all step through one at a time, wary of our surroundings. Keeping the lights off to avoid unnecessary attention, we look around the space. It's cozy—exactly how you'd expect a grandparents' house to look with knick-knacks and doilies and far too many pictures cluttering the walls. Nothing seems amiss in the living area, so we split up and check bedrooms down the hall. There are three doors, all shut. I take the first, Ortega the second, Declan and Brax the last. Apart from a nightmarish display of stuffies lining the whole bed, floor, and shelves along the wall, there's nothing out of the ordinary in my room.

"*Jesus fucking Christ,*" I hear someone gasp from down the hall.

I think it's Braxton. I run that way and push them both aside as they block my view of the third room. I inhale sharply, my stomach twisting with sharp pangs of disgust and horror as I discover what caused the alarm. It's another girl.

Another *dead* girl.

This one is nothing like Jace's first work. This one is fresh—she was probably tortured and killed this morning while I was eating breakfast and drinking tea without a care. And unlike the first one, this scene isn't tidy and clean. The room looks like a massacre took place. There's blood everywhere, bright red seeping into the carpet, pooling on the bed, covering the poor girl's chest and face and arms.

Exactly like the first girl, this one is similar in age and build to Kara. Her hair is blonde, a startling contrast to the flecks of red splattered all over it. She's barefaced and clothed in modest sleepwear. The bastard might have snatched her right from her bed. She doesn't belong here—the couple lived alone. So why this girl and why this house?

My eyes rake over her injuries, trying to keep myself focused and clinical as bile claws its way up my throat. Her nails are manicured, but jagged and broken. She fought him. Unlike the last girl, there are no signs of strangulation. There are dark, fresh bruises on her arms. I study her mangled torso and count six stab wounds. There could be more—it's hard to tell with all the blood. So much violence, so much rage. Jace was methodical with the last body, leaving her neat and clean and unmarred aside from her neck. This time, he let himself play like the sadist I know he is. He's getting braver. Or he's finding his style one practice run at the time.

There's something shoved into the girl's right hand, and I already know what it is before I look. The Canterbury Tales. Jace's goddamned obsession with Kara. I curse myself every day for not killing the motherfucker when I had the chance. These girls' blood is on my hands just as much as it's on his.

When I finally glance behind me, I see that Ortega is already on the phone with Taylor; this is out of his district, but he'll know who to contact. Now that there are two bodies, they might consider the possibility that they have a serial killer running rampant. And he has a fucking specific type of victim.

With the situation being sorted, I walk away from the gruesome scene and escape down the hall. Apart from Ortega and I, the house is empty. Brax and Declan must have already walked back to the car. I don't blame them; no one wants to stay in a house where death hangs in the air. Standing in the living room, I pull out my mobile, my fingers trembling with emotions that my body seems to be processing even if my mind isn't at the moment. I can let myself go over every gory detail later when I have a bourbon in my hand to numb the shock.

More than anything, I need to know Kara is safe right now. I ring her, expecting her to pick up right away because it's lunch time. For her own sake, I commanded her to take a break and eat lunch every day at noon. If I didn't, she'd work right through the day without stopping. But the call rings on and on before going to voicemail. And no, I would *not* like to leave a message for Dr. Caine, thank you very fucking much. I try her again with no answer. If she's safe but ignoring me for her work, I'm going to bloody kill her. The third time I ring, someone picks up the call.

"Dr. Caine's phone," a distinctively male voice answers from the other line.

What. The. Fuck.

"Where is Kara?" I demand, my voice black and tinged with danger.

"She's in the library at the moment. May I ask who's calling?"

"Her D—," I remind myself I shouldn't use my title in case this is one of her colleagues. And it better be. If she's fucking around with someone, there will be hell to pay. I'll take it out of her fucking arse. "Her boyfriend," I finish lamely. The term sounds so juvenile as a description of what I am to her.

"Ahh, so you're Caden." I rile at the way he says my name. "She's mentioned you."

"And you are?" I spit back.

"Oh, I apologize. I'm Dr. Grant Westford, her research partner."

"Interesting, she's never mentioned *you*," I seethe. She has never said she's working with anyone, especially not a *male* partner.

"Oh, Kara and I go way back. I knew her when she was an undergrad."

My head is reeling with all of this new and entirely unwelcome information. If I have to handle any more jarring surprises today, I think I might explode.

"Indeed," I answer dismissively. "Well, I'll let you two get back to work."

"Of course. Shall I tell her you called?"

"No need," I retort in a clipped tone. "It was nothing important."

I end the call. Shoving my mobile into my pocket, I storm out of the house to find Braxton. He needs to get every last bit of information he can scour on the wanker.

Chapter 16

CADEN

Dr. Grant Westford. The name of the arsehole answering Kara's mobile as though he was her personal secretary. Except he's not some lowly intern at my little librarian's beck and call. He's her senior—both in years and in academic prestige. I ordered Brax to do the full write up on the pretentious bastard the instant we got back to the Manor. Brax's research uncovered a few unsavory surprises. Dr. Westford had been a tenured professor at Kara's university in Chicago for ten years before he left to pursue other academic opportunities abroad.

Not only had they been at the university at the same time, Dr. Dickhead had been Kara's advisor and eventually her personal mentor while she worked on her doctoral thesis. They were *close*. Brax found a published photo of them together while on a study abroad trip in Edinburgh. Though there were other students and faculty in the picture, my focus was immediately on the two of them. Dr. Westford's hand was on Kara's shoulder—it could have been a friendly gesture, but I read the possessiveness in his fingers clutching at her body as though she were his while she stared up at him as though he hung the goddamn moon. Brax was lucky to have made it out of the room unscathed after he showed me the damned photo. Say what you will, but shooting the messenger is always a nice way to take the edge off.

Grant Westford had a taste for predatory behavior that always seemed to hover just barely above the limitations of the law. Taking his *mentoring* role a little too seriously, Grant liked to fraternize with his students. A lot. From the records Brax could find, there were a few parental complaints. But the girls were always right about eighteen and a lack of consent could never be proven. So, the upstanding Dr. Westford got to continue playing with his toys to his heart's content.

From the little that Kara's told me of her past, I know that she had a relationship with a teacher that officially started when she was in grad school. She's never named any of her past lovers for fear that I would hunt them down and kill them—which isn't such an unlikely assumption—but I know in my gut that this is the prick. Clearly, the bastard had been grooming her since he was her advisor freshman year, and she was the tender age of eighteen. I clench my fists at the thought of how he might have abused her innocence. I have to resist putting a hole in the wall at the thought of how she's been working with *him* for months and hasn't mentioned a goddamn thing. Kara might not have lied directly to my face, but an omission of that magnitude is going to get her whipped. Literally.

It's Friday. Her lying arse is on a plane right now as she makes her way back to me for our weekend tryst before flitting back to her other life in New York. With him. I'm a relatively reasonable man. I'm not going to immediately accuse her of doing anything stupid to endanger our relationship, but she sure as fuck has some explaining to do. The new bartender at Pandemonium eyes me warily as he sets down my second drink in front of me. He's informed me *multiple* times that the club has a two drink limit, and his sideways glances are really starting to piss me the fuck off. I wonder if he'd be quite so stringent about doling out alcohol if he knew I was best friends with his fucking boss. I clench my glass in my fist as I raise it to my lips, begrudgingly reminding myself that the vigilant bartender isn't that one who deserves my anger. A dark fog of fury swirls around me, warning the club goers in my general vicinity to stay back if they value their personal safety. Most heed the violent ominousness in my expression, but there are a couple little club bunnies wandering unaccompanied who take it as an invitation.

One in particular is brave enough to approach me. I drain the bourbon from my glass as I take stock of the daring, foolish victim willing my inner monster to come out and play with her. She's cute—in an innocent and far too young sort of way—with full soft curves, creamy unmarked skin, a sprinkling of freckles across her slightly upturned nose, and hair that warm, autumnal mixture of burnt orange and burnished red that only natural red heads seem to possess. Her eyes are a mossy green, and they look up with me with a glimmer of a challenge.

"Is there something I can help you with, sir?" she asks, her voice sultry and far deeper than I expected. Against my better judgment, I find myself mildly intrigued in spite of my current state of irritation.

"Tempting, but I'm taken. And there's a certain librarian who would almost certainly scratch your lovely eyes out of your skull if she heard you propositioning her Dom."

The girl's cheeks blossom with warmth as she takes a small retreating step. "I'm sorry. You just looked like you could use someone to take the edge off."

"Oh you aren't wrong, but that edge isn't meant for you, and it's probably a little sharper than you can handle," I reply as I look her up and down. She barely looks fully grown, only coming up to my chest.

"You have no idea what I can handle," she bites back, offended by my insinuation.

"I have no doubt," I soothe with an easy smile. "What's your name, kid?"

She hesitates, looking around the club as though she's suddenly anxious to garner attention. I know the look. "Sinclaire," she answers finally, her voice nearly a whisper. "And I'm not a kid."

"An unusual name for such a pretty girl. How old are you, Sinclaire?" I ask, my tone turning scolding. Because I'm pretty sure she's not even legal—at least for the club entry limit of twenty one.

"Twenty four," she answers instantly, and I know I've caught her. I might have given her a pass if she said twenty one, but lying to me so blatantly is the biggest mistake she could make.

"Hasn't anyone ever told you not to tell lies, little girl? Especially to Doms who are guaranteed not to let the offense go unpunished?" She takes another step back, stumbling over her feet to get away from the threat in my glare. "Twenty four might be the age on the fake ID you used to sneak your way into an exclusive sex club, but there is not a chance in hell that you were even a baby sperm in your daddy's ballsack twenty years ago."

"Fuck you," she bites out bitterly, her bright eyes misting with unshed tears. I can't be sure if they're real, or if she's acting with the hopes of gaining a sympathy plea. Either way, tears don't fucking work on me.

"You're lucky that I've already got one brat to deal with tonight, or I'd have no reservations about putting you over my knee and giving you the well-earned spanking that daddy clearly never did. But I'm well acquainted with the owner of this club, and he doesn't take very kindly to trespassers *or* liars." I pause and allow a wicked smile of amusement to creep across my face. "Actually, now that I think about it, maybe you aren't so lucky. I'd let you off with a spanking, but who knows what *Satan* will do to you when he finds out you illegally infiltrated his hellish playground. Do you like whips, little girl?"

She whimpers as she backs further away, her face filled with the most pure expression of utter terror that I've beheld in ages. And I have to admit, her fear rouses my cock from its slumber. At this point, it's a toss up on whether Kara will get flogged or fucked the instant she walks through the doors.

"If you turn around right now and walk your cute little underage arse off the property, this indiscretion will be our little secret. If not, I'd be happy to go get Satan and let him handle you. Your choice, kid."

She bites her plump bottom lip, considering the ultimatum I've given her, not that it's much of a choice. With an irritated huff and a furtive last glance around the room, she turns and runs for the door.

Good decision.

In her rush to escape a fate in one of the dungeons with Finn's favorite toys, the girl runs right into someone entering the club. My blood simmers with devious anticipation when I see she's collided with the gorgeous, deceptive, very much in fucking trouble librarian that I've been waiting for all night. The little trespasser is knocked to her knees from the force of their run-in, and Kara immediately bends to help her up.

"Shit, sweetie, are you okay?" Kara asks in concern, and I'm thankful to be within earshot. Kara takes in the girl's teary mess of a face, and her expression grows even more worried. "Did somebody in the club hurt you?"

Kara has slipped into that *defender of the helpless* mode that I know oh so well by now. She looks about ready to murder whoever made the complete stranger on her knees in front of her cry. Kara's ferocious protectiveness is an admirable quality, but it can certainly get her into trouble as well. I wonder what she would do if she knew the culprit for little Sinclaire's tears was *me*?

"No, I'm okay," the kid answers with a sniffle, trying to brush off her knees as she stands up.

"Are you sure? You can tell me the truth. I know the owner of the club, and he doesn't allow anyone to knock around the girls. Unless the girl wants it, of course."

"I'm fine, really," the girl tries to convince Kara as she swipes her hair out of her eyes. I can make out a faint streak of blood across her left cheek. With a mild note of concern, I search the rest of her body for injuries. Sure enough, her knees are both scraped and bleeding from the roughness of being thrown to the hard floor. She must have smeared it on her hands when she haphazardly brushed herself off after the fall. Kara notices almost the same moment I do.

"Oh my god, you're bleeding!"

"It's just a scratch, really," the girl tries in an attempt to quell Kara's concern.

"That is *not* just a scratch. Come on, I know where they keep a first aid kit," Kara instructs as she tries to tug the girl toward Finn's office, unaware that his office is the literal last place the girl will want to go.

"Please, I need to go. I'm fine; I promise. I'll put a bandaid on it when I get home."

"Are you sure?" Kara asks, clearly considering holding the girl against her will until she gets her bandaged and taken care of.

"Yes, my car is already pulling up the drive, and I don't want to keep the driver waiting." Such a good little liar.

"Okay," Kara concedes hesitantly. "Be careful out there; it's raining pretty hard."

"Be careful in *here*; these guys are complete assholes," the girl warns, throwing me a deadly look from over her shoulder. Kara follows her line of sight and finds me smiling smugly back at her.

"Yes, they certainly can be," Kara agrees as she casts a glare just as dark as the other girl's. And what a pretty pair the two cheeky brats make with their dagger eyes and tiny kitten claws. I'm the slightest bit tempted to play with them both if I didn't already have plans. And if naughty little Sinclaire wasn't a damned infiltrator.

"Kara," I shout over the distance, my voice firm and dominant. She instantly recognizes the tone, her body already leaning toward me and eager to obey. "Come here," I order, snapping my fingers and pointing to the empty floor beside me. The snapping is unnecessary, but I love the humiliation that crosses her face when I call her like a dog.

"Good luck," Kara says as she parts with the girl and walks begrudgingly to my side. The kid watches her, a look of abject horror in her pretty eyes; like Kara's humiliation, the girl's complete disgust makes my cock bloody hard.

"Kneel," I command Kara, aware that the girl is still watching, not quite able to pry her eyes away from what must seem like an anti-feminist freak show. Kara hesitates, also aware that there's an audience and hating it. "You do not want to test me tonight, love. Get those knees on the fucking floor." Self-preservation winning out over pride, Kara drops to the floor like I've asked. I'm pleased that I've managed to train her quite so well. When we first met, I had very little hope of her submission, but now look at her—on her knees even though she hates it because that's what her master wants.

When I look toward the doors, the girl has vanished. I'm not sure how she's making it home because I know for a fact that she didn't have a chance to send for a car, but that's not my fucking problem. I have more pressing matters to deal with, like the damned deceptress at my feet.

"What happened with that girl?" Kara asks, looking up at me with a scolding expression that doesn't quite suit a woman on her knees. "Did you do something to her?"

"I don't see how that is any of your concern," I reply with intentional vagueness. "We're both allowed our little secrets, isn't that right, love?" She stares up at me with an adorable furrow of confusion between her brows. "You look perplexed, Kara," I comment in a tone of false concern. "Don't worry, you'll understand soon enough." I hook my fingers under Kara's collar, disregarding the fact that the pressure on her throat will be greatly uncomfortable. "Crawl," I demand as I drag her toward my private room.

Kara grunts as she struggles to keep up with my pace—not that my hold around her neck will allow her to lag behind. She should know that she's in for it at this point; we usually play in hell for a bit before taking things private. This is the first time since we've come to Pandemonium that I've led her directly to my dungeon. She should be grateful for the soundproofed walls of my private room that will keep her screams from providing entertainment for the entire club. No—tonight, those screams are just for me.

I drop her unceremoniously in front of the St. Andrew's Cross and turn back to bolt the door. According to my rules, Kara begins to take off her clothes and set them in a folded pile on the bed. Once we enter the privacy of my room, she's required to be naked—no exceptions. Slipping two sets of leather cuffs from a hanging rack on the wall, I walk toward where she is now kneeling naked on the floor and reach out my hand expectantly. "Wrists." She offers me her wrists one at a time, and I strap her into the cuffs, buckling them tightly—tighter than usual. This is the first time she might actually need them to keep her in place so that she doesn't hurt herself by flinching too hard.

Kara bites her lip, and I know she's scared even though she's followed the rules and remained silent while being prepared for her punishment. The thing is, she doesn't even *know* this is a punishment. The uncertainty has her tense and wary—and that's exactly how I want her. "Face the cross, Kara." She whimpers as she obeys; she doesn't like not knowing what is going on behind her. "Arms up." Trembling, she reaches her arms up toward the metal rings at the top of the cross, and I hook her in.

She yelps when I slap her thigh; I don't hit her too hard, but there's already a red handprint blossoming on her pale skin. "Spread your legs," I command. With a shudder, she obeys, spreading her legs wide and leaving herself open and vulnerable to my touch. Unable to resist, I trail my fingers between her arse cheeks and slide down to sink into her cunt. And she soaks my fingers. "All that fear is leaving you dripping, love," I taunt as I smear the wetness on the back of her leg before reaching down to grasp her ankle. I wrap a cuff around each of her ankles before securing her legs to the bottom of the cross.

I step back to admire the sight of her. She's all bare, milky white skin—exposed and practically begging to be marked. Her bruises from last week have faded, leaving me a perfectly blank canvas with which to create my masterpiece. Now, I just have to choose the perfect tool. I've borrowed a couple whips from Finn's collection; he's got the most extensive selection I've seen, and he really puts a bit of money into his leather toys.

I've never used a whip on Kara, and I'm not entirely sure how she'll respond to the sensation. Even though this is a punishment, I'll have to do her the courtesy of a warm up, or she'll never be able to take everything I want to give her.

Tonight, I want to test her limits. I've never played or punished with the intent of getting her to safeword. But right now, as I think of her spending all her time with Dr. Fucking Westford while I sleep in an empty bed, I'm feeling a little more sadistic than usual. When she says *Thornfield*, I'll stop. But the whipping will continue *until* she says Thornfield—no breaks, no pauses, no outs. It will be the harshest punishment she's ever endured at my hand, and I'm going to enjoy every bloody minute of it.

I go to one of the hanging racks and fetch a soft leather thronged flogger. Kara flinches when she hears the clatter of implements knocking together, no doubt trying to guess what my weapon of choice will be. She'll probably consider herself lucky when she feels the mild bite of the flogger she once told me was too soft for her. The poor thing has no idea this is just the practice run.

I walk up behind her and trail the soft strands of the flogger over the skin of her back; the light touch tickles, and I can see gooseflesh raise across her body. I've never concentrated on this area of her body, usually preferring to stick to her arse and thighs for punishment, so this will be a new sensation for her. Flicking my wrist, I bring the flogger down across her back gently. She flinches, scared by the hit, but her body relaxes when she realizes there isn't any pain. Yet.

"How has work been, Kara?" I ask, throwing the flogger against her back a little harder than before.

"G-good, sir," she answers, her tone confused and wary as I hit her again.

I'm merely desensitizing her skin so that when I whip her with the single tail she isn't in complete agony from the first lash. I tap the flogger against her back several times before drawing back my arm to hit her again. "Make any new friends at the university?" I throw a hit that wraps around her belly; again, this a soothing massage compared to what she has coming.

"A few," she answers, sounding a little relieved. She probably thinks I'm tormenting her a little out of jealousy over some flirtatious schoolboy interactions. She doesn't realize it's the Dr. Fucking Westfords I'm worried about, not the damned school boys who wouldn't know what to do with a cunt if it straddled their nearly pre-pubescent faces. But Dr. Westford sure as fuck would.

"I see." *Thwap.* "Run into any old ones?" I swing the flogger over her shoulder and it drapes over her chest to hit the top of her tit too.

"W-what?" The word stumbles out of her mouth as she tries to shift in her restraints, but she's got no room to move. I flog her again, this time making sure to put some of my weight into the throw. Kara cries out softly as her body goes rigid; clearly, this weekend reunion isn't going the way she expected.

"Oh, you're confused," I retort, my voice cold and merciless. "Let me see if I can help. Does the name Dr. Grant Westford ring any bells?" *Thwap, thwap.*

"Yes," she answers after a long pause, the word drawn out in a way that doesn't give me much confidence in her innocence. I hit her harder, about ready to fetch the bullwhip from where I hung it on the wall and really lay into her. "But it's not what you think," she protests, breathless from the last blow.

"It's not what I think? So you're *not* working with Dr. Westford, your dear old mentor from Chicago? And he's *not* the professor that you had a tumultuous relationship with for years while you were a graduate student? And he *didn't* take advantage of you and instigate a completely unethical sexual relationship with you when you were just barely legal?" I punctuate each question with a sharp flick of my wrist, throwing the leather throngs against her back over and over. Her skin isn't white and unblemished anymore; it's red and heated and just about ready for her *real* punishment.

While she tries to search for a response to my allegations, I head for the bullwhip, taking advantage of her turned back for an element of surprise. It'll hurt even worse when she expects the softness of the flogger and not the bite of the whip. I run the smooth thong across my hands, the flexible leather slipping through my fingers like a snake. There's quite a weight to it, and I know it has the potential to inflict serious damage if handled cruelly. I have no interest in harming Kara, but I need her to hurt. I need her to appreciate what the weight of her betrayal feels like. The moment she uses her safeword, I'll stop, but by God, I'll make sure she reaches her limit, and it'll burn like a motherfucker.

When I approach her bare, defenseless back, Kara tenses, seeming to sense the danger housed in my sudden silence.

"Nothing happened, Cade," she whispers, and I can hear tears in her voice melding with the thickness of guilt. Good, she has the dignity to recognize that she isn't innocent. "At least, not since I was a student." She takes a shaky breath. "And he didn't take advantage or take my virginity; I gave it to him. And in that moment, I regretted nothing."

It's all I can do not to choke to death on my own fucking shock. The whip drapes on the floor, momentarily forgotten in my hand as I process this new information that sure as fuck wasn't included in Braxton's little investigation into Dr. Westford. He took her goddamn virginity—no, she *gave* away something that should have belonged to me, like every other fucking piece of her. The short list of men who have been inside her are living on borrowed time, and Dr. Fucking Westford just shot up to second place right behind Jace. I hope Kara enjoyed her little reunion with the perverse professor because his time is nearly up.

"So, you've been spending every day with the man who got early access to *my* fucking cunt, and you kept it a secret? And now you want to tell me that nothing has happened between the two of you? How am I supposed to trust you after you've lied to my face for the past four months?"

"I didn't tell you because I knew you would overreact!" she practically shouts, her guilt turning to irritation and anger. And her lack of remorse and instant defensiveness does very, very bad things to my self-control.

That thin thread of restraint that was holding back my rage? It fucking snaps.

"You think *this* is overreacting?" I ask with deadly calm, giving her no warning before throwing the whip into the air and bringing it down across her back with punishing precision. She screams at the searing shock of it, but I don't think she could have concealed her anguish even if she tried. The bullwhip was originally intended for animals and not made for the softness of human flesh. It hurts like a fucking bitch—I would know.

"P-please," she cries, her entire body trembling. Even with the warm up, she wasn't mentally prepared to handle this level of pain. Since, *please* isn't her safeword, I hit her again, relishing the sound of the leather flicking against her skin with a *crack*.

"Please, what?" I ask, unable to control the venom in my voice because she's not begging for forgiveness. She's begging for mercy. "Please give you another?" I whip her again, watching as the tip of the whip slinks around her belly and she screams again.

"P-please, d-don't," she screeches, her words garbled through the wetness of tears.

"Tapping out of your punishment already?" She whimpers at the word *punishment* as if she didn't realize until this moment that I'm not fucking *playing* with her. She's broken my trust, and she'll pay in screams and tears until my temporary sadism is satiated. And my need for retribution won't be satisfied until she fucking shatters into pretty little pieces. I flick the whip at her back, and she flinches with a sob.

"*Please, Cade*. N-nothing happened." Her words are a broken mess as she tries to choke back her panic. "I would never hurt you like that."

I clench my jaw, hitting her again. I grind my teeth at the sheer stupidity of her thinking that she hasn't already hurt me. This is me fucking *broken* by her deception and using anger as a shield to piece myself back together—like a wounded animal lashing out.

"Of course, you didn't hurt me anymore than I'm hurting you right now." *Crack*. "Sorry, did that *hurt*?" I ask with a wry laugh.

"I'm s-sorry I didn't tell you."

I stay my hand, contemplating her apology as I wrap the whip around my palm. "Are you sorry you lied to me, or are you sorry you got caught?"

"I'm sorry I lied. You're right, that was a shitty move. I should have trusted you with the truth."

"So, you admit that you deserve punishment?" I ask, chivalrously handing her a shovel with which to dig her own grave.

"Y-yes," she answers, her body trembling with the knowledge of what that admission means when there's an angry man at her back with a whip in his hand.

"Are you sorry enough to take it like a good girl until I feel you've had enough?"

"Yes," she responds, her voice stronger in spite of the tears. I can tell from her body language that she's slipping into that place that allows her to withstand my harshest of demands. "Please whip me, sir."

"My wish is your command, love," I concede, intentionally twisting the words as I unfurl the whip and let it slither to the floor. And I give it to her hard, whipping the leather across her back and watching as a blazing red stripe raises on her back. Kara gasps, but that's the only sound I hear from her—no more pleas, no more excuses.

I work her over hard; I hit her until my arm grows sore. And I keep hitting her. Apart from a few whimpers and sobs, Kara is silent, taking her punishment with decorum and grace. Her complete submission is beautiful—her total surrender is a rare marvel that I usually only glimpse when she's subjected to pain. Kara likes to say that she isn't a masochist—it interferes with her image of herself as a sensible, self-respecting woman—but I know that pain and humiliation melt down her inhibitions like nothing else quite can.

If I'm honest, I can't really gauge how close she is to cracking. She's so strong-willed, and that character trait shows even stronger when she's dominated. She's not necessarily trying to beat *me*, but rather what she perceives to be her own weakness. With not a safeword in sight, I double my efforts; my anger is appeased, and now I just want to see her break on principle. I set out this evening to push her, to see where her limits truly lie, and I'm not giving in until she does.

As is unavoidable with this many blows, Kara's skin eventually splits beneath the whip, and my breath catches in my throat when I see the small trickle of red trail down her upper back and slip into the divot of her spine.

Christ, use your goddamn safeword.

I hadn't planned on whipping her to ribbons, I hadn't even planned on breaking her skin. The vicious monster inside me clamors for her surrender, not her blood, and even he grows squeamish at the sight. I need this to be over, but only *she* can make that call.

I draw back my arm to deliver yet another punishing blow, but the whip never makes contact. Something is wrong. Kara isn't standing in the restraints, she's hanging, her legs giving out beneath her as her knees buckle as much as they can with her ankles tied. And she is wordless—no sound, no motion. I realize with an obliterating rush of self-loathing and guilt: she isn't fucking *conscious*. She's blacked out under the stress of the blows.

FUCK.

I drop the damned whip to the floor and rush toward her, my heart thundering rampantly in my chest. This has never happened; I've never punished or fucked a sub into unconsciousness. I know it *happens*, but I'm more careful than that; typically, so are they. That anger that I'd soothed into slumber is back with a vengeance, black tendrils of fury latching onto every thought, feeling, and action like a malignant disease.

I make quick work of the restraints on Kara's ankles, thankful that my hands know these cuffs so well I could undo them in my sleep. Her body goes utterly slack as her legs are freed, and I support her weight with an arm around her waist as I loosen her wrists. Her eyes are closed and her head lolls with no sign of rousing.

Shit, what if she's actually hurt?

With her wrists finally free, I lift Kara into my arms and carry her to the bed. I hate having to set her on her raw back, but I don't have much choice. She's out cold. "Kara, wake up," I plead urgently. I brush the hair from her face and press two fingers to her neck to check her pulse. Her heartbeat is weak but steady. "Kara," I try again, patting her face firmly several times but getting no response. Frantic, I raise my hand and slap her across the face. *That* rouses her, and she winces as she opens her eyes and stares up at me in confusion.

She's okay, thank fucking God. Now I can kill her for letting me beat her half to death.

"What happened?" she whispers.

"You fainted," I bite back, taking out my frustration on my hair as I rake my fingers through it. "What the hell were you thinking?" I'm unable to resist grabbing her by the shoulders and shaking her until her bloody teeth clatter.

"What do you mean?" she asks, her tone cautious as she tries to shrink from my less than tender touch.

"You let me *whip* you until you *passed out*, and you didn't safeword."

"Did you—" she pauses as though trying to understand what I'm telling her, "did you want me to?" She sounds shocked and a little bit horrified, as though she can't believe I would want to push her that far.

Clearly, she hasn't seen enough of my darkness to know that it's always lingering in the shadows waiting for the opportune moment to strike.

"Yes, I wanted you to," I grit out. "I was angry and wanted to push you until you broke—to see where your fucking limit is. Turns out, you'd rather I *actually* broke you than allow yourself to give in and use your one out." Kara stares at me silently, tears shimmering in her eyes and making her look so much younger and more helpless than the fierce Dr. Caine I'm used to.

Maybe I did break her, just not in the way that I wanted.

"Christ, you'd let me fucking *kill* you before you used your safeword," I continue, my fury melting into frustration. "Perhaps I didn't make this clear enough the last time. You say 'Thornfield' when you hit your limit. No exceptions. I've played with countless people, and everyone has a varying level of tolerance. I can't be expected to guess when you've had too much, and I'd like a little more warning than you fucking blacking out."

"I'm sorry," she says, and the devastation in her tone twists at my guts like an iron hot poker.

I sigh as I look down at her; she hates to have disappointed me, but she doesn't know why the issue is so much more serious than merely upsetting her Dom. She doesn't comprehend why boundaries are such an integral element in the BDSM lifestyle, and she doesn't understand why limits are so important to me personally.

To make her understand, I'm going to have to submit to the most excruciating form of torture known to man—I'm going to have to gouge open the wounds of my past and scatter the blood and gore and rot out for her to poke and prod and *dissect*, looking for meanings as to why I am such a twisted fucking bastard.

"My last sub would have allowed me to do absolutely anything I wanted to her," I begin, trying not to choke on the words as I dredge up the memory. "She was naturally submissive, and I was drawn to it like carrion to a wounded animal sensing easy prey."

"Why are you telling me this?" Kara asks, hurt and panic mingling in her tone as she trembles like she's fit to burst into tears any second. I take my thumb and press her quivering bottom lip against her teeth hard enough that the sting shifts her attention to me instead of her spiraling fears.

"Just listen," I command in my dominant tone, and she calms right down, the familiarity and control in my voice soothing her. "I eventually discovered that her submission came from a darker source." I sigh sharply before continuing. "She was an extreme masochist. She never met a brand of pain that she didn't like—she consumed it as though it was the air that filled her lungs, and she always begged for more."

Vivid images of red flicker through my vision, but I chase them away, trying not to dwell on things that can't be changed. "It didn't end well. After that, I swore I would never undertake a relationship with someone who didn't have their limits sorted. I fully intend to uphold that vow, so if what we have is going to continue, you are going to have to find a way to prioritize your own health and safety because it is not my responsibility to save you from consensual destruction."

I dig my fingers into Kara's hair and jerk her head up to look at me. "I know why *she* wouldn't use a safeword. She honestly didn't have a limit. She craved the destruction; it was its own source of arousal, even more than the sex I think. But *you* don't suffer from the same affliction. You enjoy the pain, but you don't need it. You know I don't require suffering from others for pleasure, so you don't endure on my account. So what is it?" My grip on her hair turns harsh. "Certainly an educated woman such as yourself isn't too naive to consider herself exempt from human limitations? Maybe it's less about personal acceptance of weakness and more about admitting that weakness aloud? Is it a matter of pride, Dr. Caine?"

Kara remains silent, her face solemn as she allows me to pull her head back at a painfully unnatural angle. "That question was not rhetorical, Kara. Answer me."

"I don't like to fail," she confesses softly, having the good sense to look embarrassed at her utter irrationality.

"This isn't a fucking homework assignment, Kara. You don't pass if you let me beat you until you're unconscious, and you don't fail if you stop me before I get to that point. Christ, you're acting like a child trying to win a game. You can't win because the game is rigged." I release her with a frustrated shove and stand up, trying to give her space for fear that I'll give in to the urge to strangle her—and knowing that she'd probably fucking *let* me.

"Well, you did yield before I did," she retorts, a hint of victory in her tone.

She's being fucking smug about letting me whip her until she blacked out. How is that a win? It's like she wants me to fucking kill her.

"Would you like me to keep going?" I threaten. I walk over to the abandoned whip on the floor, pick it up, and flick it in the air with an ominous *snap*. The little brat is practically begging me to beat her arse and see how long it takes for her to pass out this time.

"No," Kara answers, her voice timid and small as she averts her gaze and stares down at the ground.

"Would you safeword if I did?"

She pauses before answering. "I'm not sure."

"Then I'm not sure you're ready to share this room with me," I fling back. I clench the leather handle in my fist, seriously considering forcing Kara to make an excruciating decision between her body and her pride. But I haven't the strength to force her to see reason; it's been a bloody long night, and I'm fucking tired. Throwing the whip at the wall in an admittedly immature display of exasperation, I stalk toward the door.

"Where are you going?" Kara asks in panic as she tries to rise from the bed to follow me.

"Sit your bloody arse down," I grit out through my teeth. She obeys, falling to the bed with a mixture of hurt and anger on her face. "Where I'm going or what I'm doing or who I'm doing it with are of no concern to you. Now, stop topping from the bottom, sit on that arse, and wait for me to come fetch you like a good little bitch."

Kara gasps as she stares at me in shock. I don't usually speak to her like that; she doesn't respond well to degradation outside of sex, and I'm respectful of her distastes. But in this moment—with her reckless behavior and her unflinching determination to cling to her pride—I don't really give a damn. I turn my back on her tears before they can claw into my heart and draw sympathy that she frankly doesn't deserve. Without another glance, I walk out the door, slamming it shut behind me and locking it for good measure. I don't want any misguided club lurkers walking in on her, and I need to give her some illusion of who is in control here.

And if Finn's new strait-laced fucking bartender doesn't give me another drink, I'm going to have *someone's* blood on my hands.

Chapter 17

KARA

It's been three days since Pandemonium, and I'm still seething. He left me. He fucking *locked me in the room* like I was his goddamn prisoner again, and he left me. As promised, he didn't tell me what he was doing or who he was with when he finally came to let me out of my prison a little after midnight. There was no coddling or apologies—not that I expected them. Cade was cold but not cruel as he wordlessly walked me out of the club, careful not to touch my back or irritate the welts that were chafing painfully, and led me to the car that Declan had pulled around.

With the partition up, the air was thick with tension. After his last words at Pandemonium, I didn't know where we stood, and he was even more brooding than his usual self—and that is saying a lot. I was terrified that he'd decide I wasn't worth keeping around. There was no reason for him to keep wasting his time on an untrained sub when he could have his pick of any of the beautiful girls at the club. And their submission would come so much more naturally than mine.

Like the sub who came before me. He said she was a natural, that she would have let him do anything to her. I'm sure it didn't escape Cade's notice that a comparison between the two of us is hardly in my favor.

Even though I desperately long to submit to Cade completely, there is always something holding me back, something I can't quite overcome. I've spent the last decade relying solely on myself—my *own* strength and determination—to survive and succeed. And I can't seem to eradicate that independence born of survival; it's fused with my being like a tumor on the brain—and fucking difficult to remove without killing me in the process.

Cade has been brutal since the blacking out incident. He is usually so skilled at blending his dominance with daily life, but as of late he's been all Dom and no Cade. And he's been treating me like a damn slave rather than his submissive girlfriend. I don't know how the lines got so blurred. Since the beginning of our relationship, there has always been this unspoken understanding that I will offer complete submission in the bedroom and give him as much submission as I can manage in other aspects of our life.

I know that Cade craves 24/7 control; anyone who looks at him can see the sheer dominance radiating off his body like a blazing aura of power. I love having a Dom in the bedroom, but this girl *cannot* be taking orders every moment of the day. I would murder his damned British ass if he didn't get mine first. Up until now, our arrangement has worked out pretty damn well. It's not always perfect, but I think we are very in tune with each other's needs and both try our best to accommodate them.

But since he whipped me right out of consciousness, things have shifted. Cade has been demanding more submission than usual. Actually, submission is an understatement. He's been demanding *perfection*. If I had expected Cade to be apologetic about going too hard on me Friday night, I would be sorely mistaken. In fact, it's been the exact fucking opposite. He's been harsh, exacting, almost cold in his demeanor toward me. I feel like I'm being perpetually punished for some grave sin that Cade has never even accused me of. At this rate, I wish he'd just come out with it, beat the shit out of me for whatever it is, and end the fucking purgatory.

Clearly, he's too much of a sadist to let me off the hook that easily.

According to Cade's rules, he gets my complete submission from dinner until morning. Sundays, my time belongs entirely to him to do with as he sees fit. The other days, I try to be on good behavior during the day—it helps when I'm at work and don't have to be constantly subjected to his demands—but I usually get a free pass when I want to be my usual "cheeky" self.

On Saturday, I forgot to call him *sir* during dinner. *Once*. Not a huge mistake, right? That's what I thought for the whole five seconds before he bent me over the table, yanked my panties down to my ankles, and spanked me until I sobbed. My ass is still covered in bruises that make me wince every time I sit down, which is why I've spent most of the past few days standing up. If Grant has noticed my recent distaste for chairs, he hasn't said anything.

Sunday, I was late. I was supposed to meet him in the hideaway at one, but I lost track of time reading in the garden and soaking up a rare moment of afternoon sun. I'd been lulled to sleep by the sound of the wind caressing the boughs of the weeping willow I'd perched beneath as the sunlight flickered back and forth between the branches. I startled from my light nap when a dark shadow cast itself over me, obliterating any trace of the sun's warmth. I opened my eyes to see Cade staring down at me with an expression of stern displeasure that I've grown far too familiar with. And I knew from the look on his perfectly brooding face that I was in trouble. I'd had the great misfortune of disobeying Cade on the one afternoon of the week that he could punish me to his heart's content.

Typically, Sunday disobedience would mean a trip to the hideaway and an education with one of Cade's implements of pain that I would pretend to hate but secretly enjoy. So I was confused when Cade marched me straight past the library doors and down toward his study. He dragged me toward a corner of the room facing away from his desk, grabbed my hair, and pushed my head down until I was forced onto my knees in front of the dark green wall. With his hand still fisting my hair, Cade shoved my head forward until my forehead was literally touching the wall in front of me. He then informed me that I would stay in the corner—in that exact position—while he worked at his desk and kept an eye on me. For *three hours*. Apparently: one hour for disobeying, one hour for making him come fetch me, and one hour to remember to be on time in the future.

And it was one of the most unpleasant punishments I've ever endured.

When I finally left yesterday to return to New York, things between Cade and I were tense. He's never *not* driven me to the airport in all the months we've been separated, but this time he got Declan to take me after dinner because he apparently had some *work* matters to handle. I tried to not see it as a rejection, but I couldn't hold back all the tears as Ashford Manor and its master faded into the distance.

There's an emptiness I can't seem to shake because no matter the trials and rough patches we've encountered over nearly a year of being together, sex has always managed to bring us back together. But Cade hasn't touched me—apart from the severe spanking—since the night we were at Pandemonium. And it hurts in a way I can't even begin to describe, like a hollowness in my chest that is somehow inexplicably heavy. There's an irony in how emptiness can feel less like nothingness and more like a ton of stones dead set on drowning you in your own sadness.

"Did you look through those chapters of de Sade, yet?" Grant asks from the other side of my desk as he holds *Justine* in one hand and jots something in his leather notebook with the other. His words unwrap me from the cozy blanket of melancholy, and I stifle a groan at the disruption.

"No, not yet," I mutter as I run my fingers through my hair and look at the mess that has become of my desk. The habitual gesture reminds me of the man I picked it up from, and a wave of despair washes over me again. Jesus, I need to pull myself the fuck together. So what if my boyfriend didn't fuck me this weekend and sent his errand boy to drop me off at the airport instead of taking me himself? Big fucking deal. I am a strong, intelligent, independent woman, and I don't need any man or his cock.

I rifle through the stacks of notes, papers, and books on my desk, trying to find my own copy of de Sade's heavily criticized narrative of sadism and lost innocence. Not finding the text I need amid the chaos, I start to throw open the desk drawers in the hope that I haven't left the literary material I needed for today at my apartment. Because that would be the goddamn sour cherry on top of today's sundae of shit.

Something slides to the back of the middle drawer when I angrily yank on the handle as though it's dealt me a personal injury. It's a black box. *Not* the one containing a pair of God-awful earrings that's hidden away in the very bottom drawer beneath a pile of papers. This one is new. I take it out of the drawer and turn it over in my hands feeling conflicted. No doubt this is Cade's way of apologizing for our disaster of a weekend without actually having to say the words *I'm sorry*. Damn coward.

Rolling my eyes, I flip the top off the box and wait to be astonished by what Cade thinks a good apology looks like. I'm confused when I see the plain gold bracelet. There aren't any charms or decorative elements, just a thin chain of gold. It's strikingly austere compared to the last gift Cade left in my office, but it's pretty.

"What's that?" Grant asks, looking up from his book and staring at the box in my hand.

"An underwhelming apology," I retort with a snarky smile. Grant knows me well enough to know I'm not *actually* being a bitch. "Help me put it on?" I push up the sleeve of my cardigan and give Grant the wrist that already has my lovely gps tracking bracelet courtesy of Caden Ashford. The man really does know how to spoil me.

Grant takes the bracelet out of the box and slides it under my wrist, deftly fastening the clasp. His fingers linger a touch too long on my arm before I pull away with a small nervous laugh. I hold up my hand and appraise the new jewelry. Begrudgingly, I like it. It's simple and understated with the smallest hint of sparkle in the light. I'm still too annoyed with Cade to say thank you for the gift, but I can compromise and wear the damn thing.

Grant clears his throat. "Now that you're finished with your presents, little Karenina. Can we please get back to our *actual* work?"

"Yes, yes. Perverse French novelists beckon," I acquiesce with a grand wave of my hand. I look back down at the open drawer and see *Justine* sitting on top. Suddenly, my mood is a little brighter. I look at the bracelets on my wrist, both of them small gestures that actually mean a good deal more coming from the man who gave them.

I suppose Caden Ashford is *almost* back in my good graces.

Chapter 18

CADEN

I'm in a pub, alleviating my irritations with alcohol like all the other burnt out wankers downing drinks right at five to escape the tedium of their day jobs. Finn is fidgeting on a barstool beside me because my misery decided it wanted company, and he was intrigued enough to indulge me. He suggested just going to Pandemonium, but the club is Finn's job; he can stand to get his head out of work every once in a while. Even Satan could use a break from Hell. And I didn't feel right going without Kara, especially after what happened the last time.

"Christ, I don't know what to do about her," I say more to myself than Finn as I reach for my glass. At this point I'm rambling, and he's being a good mate and taking it. "She let me whip her *unconscious*. I should hate myself for hurting her like that—and I do—but honestly, I'm more mad at her. Her bloody pride will get her killed if she doesn't figure out how to admit her limits."

"Kara just needs time. She's still new to all of this," Finn responds, making the same excuses for my sub that I've been making months. And they're getting damned old at this point.

"I can't keep being the one to judge where her lines of tolerance are drawn. I've had subs take twice what I gave Kara at Pandemonium that night. I've had subs I wouldn't even touch with a whip because they'd been clear about their low tolerance for pain. The problem with Kara is that there is no fucking boundary. No safeguards in place to keep you from falling right off the bloody cliff."

"Jesus, Ashford, she passed out. It happens. No one was harmed, so just let it go."

I rake my fingers through my hair, needing something to focus my anxious energy on. "It's not that fucking easy. Playing with Kara will always be dangerous because there aren't any rules. She doesn't have any hard limits. Don't get me wrong, she *has* limits, she just doesn't fucking voice them until after it's too goddamned late to do anything about it. I've been down this rocky path before, and I'm not sure if I have it in me to play such a high-stakes game again."

Bourbon burns my throat as I drink to find the bravery to admit the awful thought that's been lurking in the corners of my mind since Pandemonium. "I can't fathom letting her go, but I can't allow myself to be the source of her destruction either."

"You can't make this decision without her, Ash," Finn says after taking a drink of his Irish whiskey on the rocks, managing to *almost* keep the reproach out of his voice.

While he sympathizes with my situation, I'm beginning to sense that he's not entirely unbiased on the matter. He and Kara have grown close over the months of dinners and visits to the club, closer than I'd realized. And as much as I appreciate his investment in Kara's feelings, I'm a little pissed that he's not backing me purely on the principle of being my best mate.

"I really don't think her judgment on the matter can be trusted, Finn. Have you ever taken a sub so much farther than you should have because they didn't have the common sense to safeword?"

"Of course I have. It's one of the hazards of the lifestyle. Scenes don't always work perfectly every time. You just have to learn from it and move on." He takes a long draught, and I can read the tension in his body, like he's building up to something that I probably won't appreciate hearing. "She's not Évione. She's stronger than Ev ever was."

Christ, there it is. Finn knows not to bring up what happened; *everyone* knows not to mention her fucking name. I feel a shuddering chill as ghosts of the past pervade the air.

"I can't do it, Finn. I can't be the cause of destroying another life." I take a long drink, wishing the mistakes of earlier years could disappear as easily as the amber liquid in the glass. "What happened with her devastated me; you know how dark that period of my life was. If something were to ever happen to Kara because of me, I wouldn't make it back from that."

"That's not going to happen. The situation with Kara is entirely different, and you know that. Give her time. For someone who is still so new to this lifestyle, she has managed remarkably well."

"Don't you think I know that? She's bent to my corruption too fucking well, like a goddamn fallen angel without the smallest shadow of hope for salvation. The devil won't set her free now that she's in his grasp."

"Hey, sacrilege is *my* kink. Go find your fucking own. And what's with the demonization of deviance? Are you suddenly suffering guilt for not being some boring vanilla prick? You didn't force Kara to enjoy the things that she does; she's had those dark desires since before she met you. You were just the first person to give her the freedom to act on them. She chose this. Stop acting like she's a victim."

I grimace at his words, fully aware that I'm not innocent in the situation with Kara. A slow, bastardly smile crosses Finn's face the moment he realizes the goddamned irony of his statement. "Granted she *was* a victim when you kidnapped her and held her hostage in your house and fucked her under pretenses that could definitely be considered coercion. You've heard of Stockholm Syndrome, right?"

"Kara might have mentioned it a time or two when she was feeling particularly disgruntled," I admit. Of course I know what Stockholm Syndrome is. It's one of the reasons I was so reluctant to fuck Kara in the first place, but the damned woman insisted, and I'm fully susceptible to her powers of seduction. But what's the time frame for Stockholm Syndrome? I gave Kara her freedom almost a year ago. Certainly the psychological effects of being held in captivity would have worn off by now?

"Mate, I'm joking," Finn says brokenly through a bubbling of small laughs. Glad my goddamned guilty conscience amuses the prick. "I mean, you *did* all of those terrible things to her, but she clearly doesn't hold it against you. So nothing to worry about."

Fantastic. When a Dom who can't commit to a sub to save his life tells you that there is nothing to worry about in your own shaky relationship, definitely allow yourself a deep breath of reassurance. Before getting fucking smashed to forget how *not* fine things actually are. I roll my eyes before taking a long drink of my bourbon. It was a triple, and at this rate, I'm about to need another. I set down my empty glass on the counter a little louder than intended and motion to the bartender. "Another," I tell her, tapping on the rim of my glass. "Finn?"

"Why not? I've got no one to get home to tonight," he answers, swallowing the rest of his own drink.

I grimace as I'm reminded neither do I. This distance between Kara and me is killing me slowly, like a death of a thousand bloody cuts. It stings, it drags on endlessly, and most of all, it's fucking annoying. I shouldn't have let her go. I should have chained her to the goddamned bed if needed. As Finn so kindly reminded me, that's basically my forte. But she looked at me with those fucking sultry dark eyes so full of trust and desperation and lo—something I'd rather not name. And I was too weak a man to say no to letting my girl moving to the fucking edge of the country for some bloody academic fulfilment.

And now my cock and I are fucking paying for it.

I sigh in gratitude as the bartender sets an extra full glass of bourbon in front of me. She offers me a bold, seductive smile that I'm very familiar with. It's the kind of smile that says she'd gladly let me bend her over the filthy bar and fuck her until she screams for every customer to hear before continuing her shift with my cum dripping between her legs. She's not bad looking; I've already noticed Finn stealing lingering glances at her arse when her back is turned. But she's overdone. The tits spilling out of her too tight white tee are fake. The long, jet black hair that hangs down her back and nearly reaches the top of her arse is fake. Her too full eyelashes are fake and likely her lips are too. Everything about her seems to be perfectly sorted to project an image of what she thinks others want to see. Or perhaps what she wants to see of herself based on the level of distorted reality she observes around her every day.

But I want to see blemishes and scars and the things that make someone less than perfect. Because submission starts when you surrender the truest version of yourself.

I smear the condensation from my glass over the phone number that's been jotted in the far corner of the napkin beneath it. I won't be needing her or anyone else for that matter. The only thing I need is nearly a thousand miles away, likely sleeping with a stack of books while my goddamn bed is empty. I take another drink before pulling out my mobile and tapping on the contact that's been named *Sir's Good Girl*. She'd been cheeky and changed it when I'd been misguided enough to leave my phone unattended in her vicinity. Her contact details were originally under *Miss Caine*, which I'd done merely to torment her. Naturally.

I consider calling her, but the bar is too crowded and loud. I could just leave, but Finn has started talking to the bartender with the big tits, and I'm his ride home. Groaning at the inconvenience, I send Kara a text.

> **Me: Is my little sub behaving herself tonight?**

I can see that she reads it instantly, which means she was already on her mobile and not working like she usually is at this hour. Maybe my girl is missing me too.

> **Sir's Good Girl: Yes, sir. I'm laying in bed trying to annotate Jane Eyre.**

The message makes me smile as I picture her in bed. Naked, obviously.

> **Me: You're in bed early tonight, love.**

Three dots appear and disappear several times before she sends a reply.

> **Sir's Good Girl: I tried working at the table, but my ass is still sore. It's bad enough that I have to spend most of my day sitting at a desk. Although, I think I stood for about six hours straight on Monday.**

I laugh as I recall the cause of her discomfort. I did spank her arse pretty hard the other night during dinner. Not that the brat didn't deserve it.

> **Me: Send me a picture.**
> **Sir's Good Girl: Of what??**
> **Me: Your bruised arse, obviously.**

I smirk, knowing exactly how she'll react to that command.

> **Sir's Good Girl: Fuck. You.**

She's always far too cheeky when we're apart. God, if she were here right now, I'd let her have my belt and make sure she didn't sit for the rest of the month.

> **Me: I think you've spelt "Yes, sir" incorrectly.**
> **Sir's Good Girl: I think I know how to spell just fine, thank you very much.**
> **Me: Well, I did warn you. Kitchen or bathroom. Pick one.**
> **Sir's Good Girl: Why?**

I scoff out loud. She just can't help digging her grave even deeper, can she?

> **Me: I've given you a command. I don't need to tell you why.**
> **Sir's Good Girl: Okay...Kitchen.**

Her choice doesn't really matter in this scenario. Either way, she won't enjoy the outcome.

> **Me: Go to the drawer with the cooking utensils. Open it and take a picture of the inside.**

I take a sip of my drink feeling a smug smile of satisfaction tug at my lips. This is going to be fun.

A picture comes through in my notifications. Clearly learning from her earlier mistake, she doesn't question me before sending a picture of the kitchen drawer contents. She probably thinks she's gotten off easy with this picture instead of having to bare her bruised arse for the camera like

I'd previously requested. As is usual when my sweet little sub thinks she's gotten out of her punishments, she couldn't be more fucking wrong.

I eye my choice of weapons critically, deliberating the best implement for what I have in mind. It doesn't take long to pick out the perfect tool of punishment. Actually, it's rather a classic.

> **Me: Take out the large wooden spoon on the right side. Bend over the counter and use the spoon to spank yourself. Bare. Send me a picture when you're done.**

Her reply is instant.

> **Sir's Good Girl: You're fucking with me.**

And that's bloody typical. When is she going to realize I don't jest about punishments? Ever.

> **Me: I can assure you, I'm dreadfully serious.**
> **Sir's Good Girl: No.**

My god, she gouges holes into my sanity.

> **Me: Yes.**

I'm almost certain she can hear my tone of dominance in the single word. Daring her to either bend or break.

Shockingly, a picture pops up on my screen. It's her cute little arse still mostly covered in the green-yellow bruises from her weekend spanking. In the middle of her right arse cheek is a very faint pink splotch.

> **Sir's Good Girl: There. Happy, you sadistic pervert?**

Not even close.

> **Me: Harder.**

I can feel her rolling her eyes at my command. It makes my palms twitch with the need to spank her myself. To feel her skin turn hot and red beneath my hands as she begs me to stop. And I wouldn't stop.

Another picture. Another faint red mark overlapping the other on her arse cheek. Clearly, she isn't taking this assignment very seriously.

Me: Harder, Kara.

The chime of another picture coming in gets Finn's attention as he looks over my shoulder. I'd been so wrapped up in my Kara fantasies that I hadn't noticed the bartender walk away.

"Kinky bastard," he says with a laugh. "What did the poor girl do to earn those," Finn asks, gesturing to Kara's harsh bruising.

"She forgot to call me *sir*," I answer through gritted teeth. When her transgression is spoken aloud, it sounds like I overreacted. I don't like the guilt that settles in my gut at the thought. Because I was still reeling from her allowing me to whip her until she blacked out, I overcorrected on her mistake by being even more dominant. As if more rules and correction could save Kara from the folly of her pride.

"I didn't think you enforced high protocol?" Finn says with a look of confusion.

I typically don't whip my subs unconscious either. "I wasn't in a very forgiving mood," I answer, my tone swathed in darkness.

Finn knows me well enough to leave me to my brooding and makes a tasteful exit to fetch us more drinks. I make use of his distraction to finally look at the picture Kara sent. My cock turns hard as stone at the sight. My good little whore finally listened, and there is a bright red circle in the middle of her arse that is an exact impression of the wooden spoon.

Me: Better. Give yourself ten more.

A devious idea erupts in my mind, and I know how to make her humiliation even sweeter.

Me: Go set up your phone on the counter and film your spanking. You'll send me the video when you're done. If any of your spanks are too light, I'll make you do five more for each one.

That should put her in her place quite nicely.

Sir's Good Girl: You're a bastard, Caden Ashford.

I am, and she should be fucking used to it by now.

Me: And you're a brat. So go spank yourself like the naughty little girl you are before I make it 20.

Sir's Good Girl: Yes, sir.

I can't tell if she's being sarcastic. Knowing her, it's highly likely, but I'll give her the benefit of the doubt for the moment.

I look down to see another bourbon in front of me. It's a good thing I've been downing the finest Macallan in Lord Ashby Ashford's cabinet since I was twelve, or I would be completely pissed by now. My father would be horrified that I've developed a taste for the American stuff, which obviously makes me like it even more.

I throw back the drink, loving the smooth, smoky burn as it slides down my throat. Usually, I'd savor it rather than down it, but I'm eager to have some privacy to watch Kara's spanking film. "Drink up," I tell Finn as I set my empty glass on the bar. "I'm ready to call it for the night."

I check my phone for the tenth time as my driver makes his way to Finn's penthouse. Still no video. Thanks to the soothing effects of copious amounts of alcohol, I'm only mildly irritated at her delay. And I'm placated by the thought of wanking my cock into a pair of Kara's panties as I watch her spank her little arse red when I get home.

We pull up to the massive high rise invading Chicago's skyline. It's the most luxurious planned living space in Chicago, and Finn admittedly has the best view in the whole damned city. Because he has a chronic distaste for commitment, he rents the penthouse suite, even though he could afford to own the whole bloody building.

"This is me," Finn announces to no one in particular, his words a little slurred. "Thanks mate," he says as he pats me on the shoulder. "That was the best night I've had since…well, since the last night I spent drowning in pussy rather than getting hammered with my very attractive but not at all my type best friend."

"You think I'm attractive?" I ask with a teasing smile. Drunk Finnian Holt is always very loose-lipped. It's part of the fun of getting him smashed in the first place.

"You know you are, you beautiful bastard," he answers, moving his hand from my shoulder and patting my cheek a little firmer than he probably means too. It's almost a slap, and I would be offended he wasn't drunk off his arse. "Hey, I'd fuck you if it weren't for your damned dick getting in the way."

"Charming, but I'm afraid you're not my type either." I've been with men before, but I sure as fuck don't bottom. Ever.

"Bullshit, you love blondes," he accuses, sounding marginally offended as his fingers slip from my cheek and trail down my neck. He strokes his knuckles over my throat, and I can't be entirely sure if the gesture is platonic or if it's the alcohol in his blood telling him he needs to fuck something.

"*Submissive*, blondes," I correct, my tone more stern and less teasing than before. He needs to get out of the damned car and get his arse inside before he does something that he'll regret more than I will.

Even though there have been rare moments of *something* more than brotherly kinship between us, Finn has been strictly pussy for as long as I've known him. Not that I would allow him to try now. I've never been unfaithful in my life, and I certainly would never allow anything to jeopardize my relationship with Kara. But if *all* parties were willing at some point in the future, I wouldn't mind a little communal fun.

"Yeah, speaking of, I think I'll call Candice. I need a soaking wet cunt right now, and it's been a while since I gave her the privilege of sucking my magnificent cock," Finn changes the subject, naming one of at least five girls that he keeps on rotation at the club as he finally reaches for the car door and opens it.

"I'd give it an hour or two. Wouldn't want her taking advantage of you in your inebriated state," I say in a distinctly dominant voice to take the piss out of him, knowing full well he would never care what state he was in while getting off.

"It's not assault if I enjoy it," Finn says with a sloppy smile as he hangs his arm on top of the door.

"Legally speaking, I don't think that's true," I retort, my tone darkening with disapproval. It's a murky thing for people who engage in our specific lifestyles to joke about consent, and I know he never would if he were sober.

"Fine, I'll get her drunk too," he says, throwing his hands in the air as though I'm an impossible overlord to please.

"I think that's even worse, mate," I chastise.

"Fine, I'll go watch some porn and wank over the toilet. Happy, *sir*?"

"Yes," I rasp, ignoring the small bolt of electricity zapping through my blood with his words. Or rather, *word*. Fuck, I need Kara back in my goddamn bed every night. My cock is aching for even the smallest hint of dominance. "Off to bed with you, then," I command, waving him off.

"Fuck, you're boring," Finn complains with a pout before slamming the door. "*Godnat*," he says softly before turning to leave.

His words are low and muffled through the car door, but I still hear them. It's an unusual thing to hear him speak in his native tongue. Finn has a complicated history with his past. His father is Danish, and he hates his father. So, he has a tendency to hate most things relating to Denmark purely on principle. He hasn't been back home in longer than I have, which is certainly saying something.

So, he's either feeling inexplicably emotional, or he's even more pissed than I thought.

Chapter 19

CADEN

I've just barely sat down in my study when a familiar ding interrupts the silence. My cock springs to attention at the exact same time in anticipation. I look down at my mobile to see a video from Kara waiting for me to open. Took her bloody long enough.

I don't rush to watch it. I force myself to draw out the anticipation, making myself yet another drink before unfastening my belt and settling comfortably into the cool leather seat. After taking a long draught, I open the video. And there's my gorgeous girl setting up the camera for her punishment. Her movements are awkward and embarrassed as she tries to place the phone at the right angle on the counter. I knew this would be the perfect torture to put the cheeky girl in her place. Humiliation is so much more effective on her than pain, and this is a heady dose of both. Her face is burning red, a bright contrast between the rest of her pale skin; well, she should have an arse to match soon.

She finally makes it to the other end of the kitchen, gingerly bending over the counter and turning back to look at the camera and make sure she's fully in the frame. She pauses, seeming to gather the mental fortitude for what she's about to do. What I'm making her do. Nearly a thousand miles away, and she still bends to my will, no matter how much she fucking hates it. The sheer power she allows me to hold over her sends my dick pulsing in my trousers. I tug down my zipper and give my aching cock a little more room to breathe.

Kara grasps the hem of her dress and pulls it up over her hips to keep her lower half bare for her punishment. As requested, she's not wearing any knickers under her dress, but I'll admit I'm a little disappointed she didn't forgo the clothing all together. If I were there, she'd be naked, pulled over my lap and straddling my leg so that I can see the wetness of her arousal stain my trousers with every slap of my hand against her naughty arse.

Taking a deep breath, she grabs the large wooden spoon from the counter and aligns it with her arse. She flinches when it brushes against her skin. Poor love. How is she going to react when it does a far sight more than tickle her bare flesh? She lifts her right arm to deliver the first blow, but falters before bringing it down. The second time she raises her arm, she doesn't pussyfoot around. She goes all in, slamming the wooden spoon against her bare arse with a loud *crack*. *One.* My cock jolts at the familiar sound echoing through the room. Kara whimpers as though she didn't expect it to be so hard, even though *she* was the one dealing the blow.

She takes a moment to gather her nerve for the next hit. There's now a large red circle blooming in the middle of her arse cheek. *Good fucking girl.* Holding her breath, she spanks herself once more. *Two.* Again, a little whimper escapes her lips. Pain is even harder when it's self-inflicted; allowing someone else to dole it out takes some of the pressure off. This time, it's all on her.

Three. Four. She hits herself two more times before switching the spoon to her other hand, clearly already growing tender on her now very red right arse cheek. She holds the implement awkwardly, struggling with how to hit herself as hard as she has been commanded while using her non-dominant hand. She brings the spoon down on her left cheek, but it's a weak blow that barely leaves a mark. *Five.* Certainly not what I had asked for. Seeming to realize this, she switches the spoon to her right hand again, shifting on her feet as she prepares to take the rest of the spanks on one side for fear of getting more punishment for hitting too soft on the left.

She spanks herself again, flinching because it's impossible for her to find any bare skin on her arse that hasn't already been tenderized. *Six.* Seeming to get an idea, she lines up the wooden spoon with the unmarked flesh of her pale upper thigh. She hesitates for a moment, turning toward the camera as though asking permission. It's a perfectly admissible option; I told her that she would be getting ten spankings, but I didn't specify where. She could have spanked her fucking tits if she wanted. Actually, that's an excellent suggestion for next time.

"Fuck!" she screeches as the implement makes contact with the sensitive skin of her thigh. *Seven.*

With a grunt of irritation, she decides to simply get her punishment over with. She finds the thickest part of her arse and lays down three hard blows, sniffling and whimpering through each one. *Eight. Nine. Ten.* A shuddering sob leaves her body as she places the wooden spoon on the counter and buries her face in her arms. She's overwhelmed, abandoning all energy as she merely lies limp across the counter. I think she's even forgotten about the camera documenting her humiliation. As she succumbs to her emotions, I take stock of her marks. There are nine, lovely, red circles burned across her pale flesh. She did very well, all things considered. I wish I could stroke her arse and feel the softness of her skin and the warmth of her welts beneath my palms.

As I look closer, I see something I certainly didn't expect. She's fucking wet—dripping, actually—a trail of arousal slipping down the inside of her thigh beside the one mark beneath her arse. *Fuck me.* This girl will be my fucking undoing. My cock is weeping by this point, a dark stain of pre-cum seeping through my pants. Before even finishing the video, I click on *Sir's Good Girl* and ring her.

She picks up on the very first ring. "Hello?" she answers, her voice breathless and needy.

"Hello, naughty girl," I reply, my voice gravelly and just as desperate sounding as hers. "Did you enjoy your spanking?"

"No," she denies, but not confidently enough to cover her deception. Not that she could. I'm looking at the damning evidence on my phone this bloody second.

"That trail of cum leaking down your legs begs to differ, so why don't you try that again, hmm? Did you *enjoy* your spanking?"

"Yes, sir," she responds, her voice barely a whisper as though she's just admitted the most horrifying secret. When will she realize that I will never judge her for liking any of the twisted, delightfully kinky things that she does?

"Mmm, you needed that spanking didn't you?" I ask, adjusting my cock that suddenly feels like it's suffocating in my pants. "All this distance between us has you craving that discipline you know I'll give you when you act up. Is that why you're such a brat when we're apart? You want me to come punish you?"

Kara's breath heaves, and it sounds as though she can barely draw air into her lungs. "Y-yes, sir," she agrees, her voice raspy and raw.

Goddamnit, those two words coming from her lips get me harder than anything or anyone ever could. "Turn on your camera, baby. I want to see you," I command, finally giving in and pulling my pants all the way down my hips and letting my engorged cock spring free.

Kara turns on her camera at the same time I do my own. And *fuck me*, she's gorgeous all red-faced and tear-stained and needy for my dick. It's a goddamn sin that she's too far away for me to slam my swollen cock into her wet cunt this fucking instant. She deserves to be punished just for making me feel this burning desperation that can never be quenched.

"Hello, love," I say when I've finally swallowed enough of the desperation to form words.

"Hi," she answers shyly, looking up at me through her dark lashes. I don't know how she manages to sound so coy after nearly a year of doing the filthy things that we do. She could be naked on her knees sucking my cock like a dirty whore and still look exactly like a blushing virgin. Her appearance of innocence makes me even harder.

"As much as I like seeing your lovely face, it's your pretty pussy I want to look at right now. Put the camera between your legs, love. Let me see what that spanking did to your naughty cunt."

Without a word, she obeys, flipping the camera and moving her hand down between her legs so I can see her bare and spread wide open. She looks more delectable than I could have imagined, her wet folds swollen and red and just begging for someone to fuck her into a catatonic state.

"Oh baby, did I leave you all dripping and achy?" I taunt, my hand slipping down to grab my throbbing cock, my fingers sliding easily with the slickness of my own arousal.

"Yes," she breathes, the word a half sob on her lips. Her hips buck as she squirms with need, begging the very air to fuck her.

"Do you think naughty girls deserve to come?" I growl as I practically abuse my cock with my fist. I've been so busy that I haven't touched myself since I was with her last Friday, and I feel like I'm almost ready to blow right now at the mere sight of her.

"N-no, sir," she whimpers, and I can tell that it almost eviscerates her to say the words she knows I expect to hear.

"Did you give yourself ten hard spankings like you were supposed to?"

"Yes…" she answers hesitantly, her cheeky little fingers trailing down to her pussy and teasing her clit. I allow it simply because the sight of her hands on her cunt makes me fucking feral.

"Did you?" I reiterate with sternness. "Because I counted nine." Her fingers still over her clit as she considers my words. Maybe she didn't expect me to be quite so strict with the hardness of her spankings. Well, underestimating me would be her mistake.

"I tried to do ten," she explains as though it will save her. Which it won't.

"Do I seem like the sort of man to give an A for effort rather than complete obedience?"

"No, sir," she replies, her tone turning sullen rather than fearful. She has a self-destructive tendency to turn bratty when I'm being an arsehole.

"Correct. And what did I say would happen for every one you missed the mark on?"

"I'd get five more," she retorts with spite as she tries to pull the mobile away from her cunt.

"Put that camera back between your legs right fucking now," I command viciously. "I didn't say you could move." Without a word, the camera jerks back to her pussy; she's clearly pissed, but her anger has little effect on the arousal that continues to drip down her thighs. "Touch your clit," I order, knowing that having to do it by force will make her seethe even as her cunt gushes from my dominance.

Her fingers land on her clit without finesse, grinding along the sensitive bundle of nerves without trying to make herself come. The little brat is willing to deprive herself of pleasure purely to prove a point. Not on my fucking watch. "Not like that, Kara. Make it feel good."

She huffs in annoyance before rubbing soft circles around the side of her clit. Soon, the mobile starts to shake in her hand as her soft moans fill the emptiness of my study as though she's actually in the room with me. My hand stills on my cock; I don't want to come too quickly, and her adorable fucking whimpers are driving me mad.

"Are you getting close, love?" I ask, my voice steeped in sadism. She groans, knowing exactly what kind of game I'm playing at. It happens to be one of my favorite forms of torture, and she's well acquainted with edging by now.

"Yes," she spits out, knowing that her answer will bring frustration rather than the climax that hovers so closely.

"Spank your pussy."

"W-what?" she asks, her hand stilling once more. Clearly, that wasn't the response she was expecting.

"You owe me five more. So, spank that naughty little pussy."

She groans, the sound deep and guttural and filled with all of the hatred she currently feels for me. She pulls the camera slightly out of the way as her left hand hovers over her cunt, her fingers trembling a little. Recognizing the frivolity of fighting me, Kara doesn't argue before bringing the tips of her fingers down over her soft mound with a quick *tap*. My girl is pulling her fucking punches.

"Did I tell you to pat your pussy like it's been a good girl for me?" I snap in disapproval. "Spank your cunt like I would, or so help me I will get on a plane right now, beat down your fucking door, and punish you until you scream for me to stop. At this point, it's a toss up on whether I'll listen or keep going until you pass out. Because *that's* how you like it, isn't it?" I growl, unable to quell the venom seeping into my voice. Without intending to, I've gotten to the heart of why I've been so goddamn hard on her since last Friday.

Her whole body tremors as she raises her hand and brings it down heavily on the tender flesh between her legs. I hear her breath catch as she tries to stifle the pained sounds begging to be purged from her body. She contains her anguish, but barely.

"Again," I order. I won't go easy on her; she doesn't deserve my mercy, and frankly, I don't feel like fucking giving it. She obeys, the echo of her hand slapping against her cunt sounding sloppy and wet. As much as she hates this, she fucking loves it too. "Give me three more."

Smack, smack, smack. Her hand slaps against her swollen cunt just like I asked. I groan as I watch her skin turn a deep pink from the sting of it. *Christ,* I wish I could spread those velvety folds and run my tongue along the sopping wet length of her. "Such a good girl," I praise, strangling my shaft with my hand once more; my cock is dripping at the sight of her. "Let me see those fingers in your pussy. Show me how wet you are."

She dips two fingers into her slick entrance before pulling them out to show the camera. My growl of desperation is nearly feral as I see her digits covered in the creaminess of her cum. "Fuck your fingers. I want to see you come all over your hand wishing it was mine knuckles deep inside of you." Kara whimpers at the filth of my words as she shoves two fingers inside her cunt. "You can take more than that," I taunt, feeling my balls start to tighten as my own climax nears.

Quick to obey, Kara impales herself with three fingers, going as deep as she can and—judging from the heightened sound of her cries of pleasure—curling her fingers like I taught her to massage her g-spot. The video starts to shake violently in her hand as she gets herself so damn close; she's just waiting for me to give the word. And I wouldn't prolong her torture in this moment anymore than I would prolong my own.

"Come, Kara," I demand, waiting for the sharp cries of her release before I let go and come right alongside her, painting my abdomen and chest in thick ribbons of white as I groan and shudder with the pleasure rippling through my taut body.

"Goddamn, look at that mess you made," I say in awe as I notice the puddle of wetness that's soaked the sheets between her legs. "Let me see your face, love."

She's still breathing heavily as she flips the camera so that I can see her again. She's a beautiful fucking mess with her cheeks flushed, her pupils blown, her hair tousled, and a sheen of sweat layered over her brow and dripping down her neck. I wish I could suck the taste of her from her throat and lick the sweat away.

"So bloody gorgeous," I tell her, loving the way her cheeks redden even deeper with the compliment. "Look at the wreck you've made of me." I move the camera to show the obscene amount of cum decorating my torso like a Jackson Pollock painting. "If you were here, I'd make you lick me clean."

"I wish I was there," she whispers, the longing in her voice painfully apparent.

"I wish you were too, love. So much it fucking hurts." I run my fingers through my hair, hating how empty and raw I feel without her. "I was a goddamn idiot for letting you go. If I could go back, I would have chained you to the damned bed just like you expected."

"Don't, Cade," she begs, her voice wracked with guilt. "As difficult as things are at the moment, I'm where I need to be right now. You made the right decision letting me go. And in a few more months, I'll be back with you where I belong."

"Goddamn right, that's where you belong," I rumble, her words feeding a toxic possessiveness that has always lurked right beneath the surface but never fully bloomed until she came into my life. "But I'm not sure I can wait that long. I might have to resort to my original methods."

"Caden Ashford, you are *not* coming here to kidnap me. I won't allow it."

"Who said I needed permission?" I threaten. "I can take that chance; you forgave me the first time."

"Who says I forgave you?" she asks as her tone ignites with indignation.

"I don't recall there even being an *apology* the first time."

"I'm sorry," I profess out of obligation, knowing I would do it again in a bloody heartbeat.

Even though I've briefly considered setting her free for her own good, the truth is I'm a selfish man. There's nothing I wouldn't do to keep my fire-hearted librarian thoroughly ensnared in my arms. I would kidnap her from her fancy fucking university tonight if I thought I was in any danger of losing her. I would cuff her to the bed in the hideaway and leave her down there with regular fuckings and feedings until she saw bloody sense. I'm a brutal man, but my love seems kinder because she hasn't forced me to go to those extremes. Yet.

"Caden, why does that apology sound more like you're plotting something?" she asks with the chiding tone of a mum handling a toddler with stolen sweets. And the distinct sound of her topping from the bottom grates on my nerves.

"You had better watch that tone, Miss Caine. You seem to be misconstruing who is in charge here."

"Sorry, *sir*. I was just trying to dissuade you from committing another federal crime," she scoffs as she rolls her eyes.

"Well, being cheeky and rolling your eyes is not the way to do it," I scold as my latent temper starts to simmer in my veins.

She needs to get her damned arse back home. The longer she's away from me, the brattier she becomes, and I'm really starting to lose my patience. This weekend is going to be brutal. When I finally get my hands on her, she'll feel the full force of the frustration that's been building in my blood, like toxins begging to be purged. She is going to cry and scream and take orgasm after orgasm until she's shattered so many times she can't put herself back together. I'll use pain to edge her and pleasure to torture her, and I'll make sure she leaves with an unforgettable reminder of *who* she belongs to.

"I miss you, Cade," she whispers so softly I can barely hear, her eyes filled with a sadness I haven't noticed before. Maybe she needs this weekend just as much as I do.

"I miss you too, love. More than you can possibly fathom." My body feels hollow without her, and the emptiness leaves a lingering ache that I can feel in my very bones. "Go to bed and get some sleep. I'll see you in two days."

"I'll count the hours," she replies with a dramatic sigh that I've grown used to and missed hearing.

"I'll count the minutes," I retort with an indulgent smile.

"I'll count the seconds," she quips, sounding excited at the idea of having bested the vastness of my increments. Because she's a fucking swot.

"I'll count the heartbeats. Each one lonely and hollow without yours to beat in tune with." I'm waxing poetic to make her smile, but instead of amusement, her expression turns utterly startled, as though she's just realized she left the hob on.

"I—" she pauses, her face flushing as she searches for the words that seem to have escaped her. "I'm rather fond of you."

Christ, why do those words sound so much heavier than they should? Her eyes are glittering with a mixture of adoration and fear. Typically, I delight in both, but the combination of the two together is setting my nerves ablaze while simultaneously icing the blood in my veins. Intuitively, I can ascertain her meaning in the absence of the word she can't bring herself to say. If I valued honesty, I might admit I'd felt the intrinsic pull of that *word* for quite some time. However, for reasons unquestionably different from her own, I cannot bring myself to say it. So, I settle on the grandest understatement ever conjured since the invention of the English language.

"I'm fond of you, too." Like hers, my words bear the weight of a thousand oceans crashing violently against an unforgiving shore. And I can tell from the hopeful gleam in her eyes that I haven't fooled her any better than I've fooled myself.

Chapter 20

CADEN

Another body was found. Another ghost of Kara just like the others. This time, we didn't make it to her first. The police are actually starting to do their job. Taylor sent me the details as soon as he heard, along with all the crime scene photos. I'll admit, I'm glad I didn't find her first. When I saw the pictures, I choked on bile before swallowing it back down my throat.

Jace is escalating—each scene he leaves growing more and more chaotic. More frenzied. He got a little taste, and suddenly blood lust is driving him mad.

The girl was found at night, lying in the middle of the street. The person who called it in nearly wrecked themselves trying to swerve around the obstruction in the road. He thought it was deer. When he got out of his car to look, he saw that he was very, very wrong.

The blonde was stripped bare, her naked form dumped on the side of the road like rubbish. She'd been beaten, her body covered in traumatic injuries. There was no indication of a weapon. The bastard used his fists to bludgeon her to death. It wasn't a quick death—it was slow and painful. I grit my teeth to think of what she must have endured. Because of me.

The removal of clothing is new. He hadn't touched the clothes on either of the other two victims. There was no sign of sexual assault pre or postmortem this time or the others, so it's got nothing to do with sex or arousal. It's something darker than biological urges. It's like he tried to dehumanize her, defacing her body yet another level by stripping her. As if his violence wasn't enough of an assault.

Tucked beneath her body was an older edition of The Canterbury Tales, a documented page missing like all the rest. The first Chaucer we found had been brand new, the publication that's recommended for courses at Kara's university in Chicago. The second and third were used but nothing valuable. Same with the fourth book covered in the blood of the girl he skewered six times. This time, I'm pretty sure he threw a rarer edition of the book into the mud beneath the abused blonde. We tried tracing the purchases of the others with no such luck. I'm not hopeful it will be any easier this time.

I try to wrap my head around why Jace keeps changing his methods. Why he never kills in the same way, the same place, or even stages the bodies in the same manner. He's purposely sourced the same book from different places and different publications. There must be some meaning in all the madness, but I can't for the life of me figure out what it is.

I flip through the printed crime scene photos another time, ensuring that there's nothing I've missed. I stop on the one that's got a closer shot of the street sign. Arkady Lane. My heart stops. How did I not see it before?

Immediately, I ring Brax and ask him to look into a hunch I have.

I've not told the police of the connection to Kara. Not even Taylor knows. But I'm starting to think that this is all connected to her more than I thought.

Braxton calls back five minutes later, confirming my theory.

Darnell Road. The first girl was found in a seedy motel ten minutes away from Kara's old university.

Ellington Court. The second girl was murdered in a house directly facing the one Kara spent her whole life in until her parents died.

And the third girl? She was found lying in the same street where Kara lost her parents in a car accident and almost died herself.

Arkady Lane.

Jace is taking us on a macabre tour through Kara's life. The only question is: where does this all end?

I drain my glass to the dregs before pouring another. It's a bit early to be diving into the liquor, but I'm allowing myself some grace after the gruesome nightmare of Jace's artistry I witnessed this morning. Bourbon is a poor substitute for solace in Kara's absence; unfortunately, it's the best coping mechanism I have at the moment. Being a front row spectator to the gut-wrenching slaughter of innocent girls is turning me more toward my old vices than I would like, but I refuse to see Kara today without something to dull the sharp edges of those poor girls' bodies slicing their way into my memories until my mind and heart bleed in unison.

Fuck coping mechanisms. There's no way to *cope* with knowing these kinds of horrors are going to keep happening to girls who look like Kara until I find Jace and end his worthless existence. He won't stop. Not until he gets the real thing. All these girls are just a bit of playacting to him. His main endeavor is to make my girl bleed. But he won't get a fucking drop. Not while my goddamn heart still beats.

My mobile sounds with a message notification from Kara saying she's almost ready to board her flight. It's Friday—the only good goddamn day of the week lately. And like a right cunt, Jace has put a bit of a damper on this one.

I don't know if I have the fortitude to sit through a weekend with Kara and act like my world hasn't been wrecked by a deranged psycho stalking places of Kara's past and leaving mangled reflections of her as some sick prophesy of what is to come if I fail. I don't know how much longer I can keep chasing shadows with the faint hope of catching something corporeal. I need a fucking distraction, something to quiet the echos of my failure ricocheting violently through my thoughts.

And I need to hunt someone I can fucking catch.

A dark idea twists its way into my fantasies, offering a creative solution to satiate my craving to hunt, capture, and ruin and settle the frustrating feelings of helplessness clawing at my sanity. Kara is the one person who's able to leach out all the darkness and make me feel whole again.

I message her, knowing I only have about ten minutes before she's on her flight and out of reach.

> Me: Change of plans. Declan will fetch you from the airport.
>
> Sir's Good Girl: Why? Did something happen?
>
> Me: Nothing for you to be concerned about.

She doesn't need to know about the dead ringer for her lying naked and beaten in the streets. I can safeguard that nightmare on my own.

> Sir's Good Girl: Okay...
>
> Sir's Good Girl: Are we going to Pandemonium tonight?

I take a drink as I grapple with her question. It's not an unfair assumption given our previous agreement, but I can't take her back there after what happened last time. Not yet. The searing panic of seeing her unconscious body hanging from the St. Andrew's cross still hasn't left me, and I don't think I can handle any more daggers of guilt pointed in my direction at the moment.

> Me: Not tonight, love. Tonight I want you at the manor.

It will be the perfect playground for what I have planned.

> Sir's Good Girl: Okay.

I try to ignore the inferred disappointment in her one-worded reply. It's her own damn fault. If she wants to play at the club with the big kids, she needs to learn to be a little less childish with her safety. Plasters don't always fix the hurts that come with practicing unsafe kink, and I'm not taking that risk again. Until she can prove that I can trust her, she's bloody grounded.

But that doesn't mean we can't have some fun without all the toys. Tonight, we're going back to the basics. No whips, no ropes, no clubs or playrooms. Just me, my girl, and fifty kilometers of darkness surrounding Ashford Manor for her to hide in.

> Me: When you get to the manor, I want you to run.
>
> Sir's Good Girl: What do you mean?

> Sir's Good Girl: Run where?
>
> Me: Wherever you like, love. You may go anywhere on the grounds.

I smile as I recall giving her the exact same parameters when I kidnapped her and held her captive at the manor nearly a year ago. I never did get to catch her the last time she ran from me. This time, the privilege will be all mine.

> Sir's Good Girl: But why?
>
> Me: Because I'm going to fucking chase you.
>
> Me: I'll give you a thirty minute head start to make things sporting.

It could be thirty seconds or thirty hours—it wouldn't make a difference. I'll never let what's mine escape me.

> Sir's Good Girl: What happens if you catch me, Lord Ashford? Do you win a prize?

I can imagine the saucy smile on her beautiful face right now. My official title always comes out when she's feeling particularly cheeky. She's probably envisioning that I've challenged her to a playful game of hide and seek. But I'm not in the mood to play. Right now, I'm a predator looking for easy prey. And my sweet little sub is the perfect target.

> Me: If I catch you, I will strip you bare, take off my belt, strap you to a bloody tree, and completely destroy your pretty cunt while you scream for mercy.

There's a long pause before she begins typing a reply. There's an even chance that I've either scared the shit out of her or turned her the fuck on. Knowing my twisted girl, it's probably both.

> Sir's Good Girl: And what if you can't find me?

There's an unmistakable challenge in her words, and fuck if my cock doesn't rise to the bloody occasion. A challenge is exactly what I need, and I want her to put up a good fight. It will make it so much sweeter claiming victory when she doesn't want to give it.

Sir's Good Girl: What if I escape your plans for complete destruction?

I feel the familiar pulse of darkness swirling in my blood as a devil's smile tugs at my lips.

Me: You won't.

Chapter 21

KARA

Run. He wants me to run. I scour the black, spindly outlines of the winter-bare trees as their branches lurch from side to side, whipped about by the frosty wind shrieking through the night air. The grounds of Ashford Manor look eerie after dark, the rocky path in front of me lit only by faint moonlight and everything around me turned to shadows.

Whichever of Caden Ashford's kinks I'm playing into tonight as I shiver from the cold and trip over uneven ground in my heels looking for a good place to hide, I can safely say I'm *not* fucking into it.

I'm roughly half-way through the thirty minute head start my insane Dom so kindly allotted me. I made it as far as the stables, but picking a warm and welcoming hiding spot seemed like too obvious a choice, so I begrudgingly walked back into the cold after sparing a minute to pet Avalanche and Sugar Cubes. Now I'm walking along the moonlit river and damning Cade to hell with every shivery step.

I've firmly decided that the head start is actually just an extra little bit of torture. Cade's probably warming his British ass by the fire while I came all the way from New York to get frostbite rather than a good fuck. At least being pursued would make things a little more interesting. I check my watch for the time, and an unfortunate combination of poor multitasking, bad coordination, fucking darkness, and an insensible taste in shoes causes me to lose a battle with a large rock by the river bank. I fall to my knees, landing awkwardly as I throw out my hands to catch myself. And my nerves alight with pain.

My left wrist seemed to carry the weight of the fall, and it's agony to move it. With my clumsy luck, it's sprained. I can't see my knees in the darkness, but they feel wet and even colder in the winter air. The thin dress I'm wearing didn't protect much from the fall, so my knees are probably skinned at the very least. I can't wait for Cade to scold me for injuring myself even though it's *his* fault I'm traipsing about in the wilderness at night in the first place. He better get the fuck on with his chasing before I march back to the manor and—

A twig snaps in the distance, disrupting the silent stillness around me. Tingles trickle down my spine at the sudden sensation of not being the only one out in the night. And the small prick of fear at the very slim possibility that it might not be Cade stalking me from the trees sends adrenaline searing through my veins.

I run.

Panic sends all thought of scuffed knees and a hurt wrist out of my mind as survival instincts take over. There's a loud rush of movement from behind me, but I don't turn to discover the source. I run as fast as I can in damn heels, finally deciding to kick them off when the footsteps behind me start to sound closer. My rationality is turned off at the moment, and my body is telling me that cut feet are better than whatever happens if I get caught.

I can't get caught.

I start to weave through the trees, hoping to confuse the stalker in the shadows. I'm not athletic, and the sudden sprint is wreaking havoc on my lungs. I'm going to have to stop for air soon before I pass out. I duck behind one of the thicker trees, ignoring the protests of my knees as I crawl across the damp dirt to keep myself hidden.

Silence fills the air once more, making my heaving breaths feel so much louder. I try to still my raging heartbeat as I peek around the edge of the tree. There's nothing in my line of sight. No forms lurking amongst the trees. Nothing disturbing the quiet night but me.

Feeling as though I've imagined the whole thing, I drag myself up from the dirt and start to brush myself off. Without warning, a hand reaches out from behind me, grabs my sore wrist, and pulls me against a hard, muscular form. I shriek from the suddenness of the assault, throwing my other hand back behind me and hitting something that distinctly feels like a nose. There's a groan of pain, and I've created just enough of a distraction to slip out of my assailant's grasp.

I start to run like mad in the opposite direction, my nerves settling with the assurance that the bastard chasing me through the forest is *my* bastard. My wrist hurts like hell, but the need to beat Cade at his own game is even stronger. I make a quick turn and head back toward the manor. I don't like my odds of outrunning him here. He has the physical advantage, and he knows it. If I can make it to the manor, I might be able to tuck myself into a discreet corner and wait until he gives up. However long that takes.

My hopes are dashed when a familiar body crashes into me from behind and throws me to the ground. I cry out when the rough landing exacerbates my previous injuries of the evening. Against my will, tears fill my eyes, and I hate them even more than the pain. I hope the darkness hides my weakness as Cade turns me over onto my back and thrusts my arms up above my head. I whimper from the roughness of the motion.

"Come now, love," Cade growls as he bends to sink his teeth into my neck, the warmth of his mouth a welcome reprieve from the cold. "You weren't supposed to make this *easy* for me."

I bite my lip to keep from crying out as he captures both of my wrists in one hand and reaches for his belt. I haven't forgotten his promise of what would happen if he caught me. He takes his belt and secures it tightly around both wrists, pulling the strap firmly against the buckle so that there's no give at all. And I'm in absolute agony as the leather crushes my wrists together. I can only hope the threat of being strapped to a tree was an exaggeration on his part, but with him you never know.

"What happened to escaping destruction?" Cade asks, his rough voice scraping against his throat like sandpaper.

He reaches for my coat and rips open the buttons. Decimating my wardrobe has always been one of his kinks. The cold air rakes across my skin, and I shiver as goosebumps ripple over my body. Cade claws at my bodice before ripping down my dress and bra with one sharp tug. He runs his fingers over my pebbled nipples reverently. Since it's too dark to see much of my nakedness with his eyes, he uses his hands to appreciate my body, tracing over my slim curves with his fingers as though he's re-familiarizing himself with every inch of me.

"You were right," I whisper. I feel his hands slip down my hips, traveling along my legs until he captures the edge of my dress. "There's no escaping your destruction." He rucks my dress up to my waist and tears my panties off me with a savage rip of his fingers. "And I'm not sure I would ever really try if I could."

And it's true. I would choose Cade's destruction over salvation at the hands of anyone else.

Cade's expression darkens in the moonlight. "You're ruined for me, aren't you, love?" he asks in a tone of resignation, and I can't quite place the look in his eyes.

"Utterly ruined," I agree. I try to move my bound hands to draw him closer, but he slams them back against the hard ground with a force that has me whimpering. I feel tears spill down my cheeks, and I press my face against my arm to hide them.

Cade scoffs, the sound of it tinged with bitterness. "What a silly little whore you are, falling for the villain who stole you away. Don't you have any self-preservation at all?" His words are cruel, but his voice is filled with something deeper, something regretful.

"None," I admit. And as if fate chooses to revel in my apparent lack of sensibility, a quick pull of the belt around my wrists has me writhing in agony and flipped onto my stomach beneath Cade's raised thighs. I clench my fists to keep from screaming, but the movement just makes the pain in my wrist worse. I sob softly, letting the dirt muffle the sound of my cries.

Cade drags me up by my hips and puts me on all fours in front of him, and I try to balance on my elbows to keep the weight off my arms. Cade slaps my thighs further apart, the sting of his palm worse because my skin is chilled. I feel two fingers thrust inside me, twisting and spreading me open as the night air turns the wetness of my arousal tortuously cold.

"You're drenched," Cade growls while continuing to claw at my pussy. "Tell me, little slut, did you want to get caught?" I feel a third finger ram inside me, and I moan at the fullness of being stretched around his hand. "Did you want the brute in the woods to throw you in the dirt, ravage your filthy, wet holes, and make you scream into the night?"

Cade's finger curl inside me, and *fuck me* if that doesn't feel so good I can almost forget the innate need to crawl away from him and save myself from what comes next. A harsh thrust of his hand sends me toppling forward, and I whimper when I land hard on my arms. The faint embers of my survival instincts flicker to life, and I kick off with my feet and drag my elbows across the ground, trying to wriggle away from him like a worm squirming in the earth.

"Ah, ah, ah," Cade tuts, lunging for my ankle and dragging me back toward him. I shriek as the rough terrain scrapes against my exposed skin, small rocks and leaves digging in like knives. "The hunt is over, love." He jerks me back into position, his fingers sinking into my hips like claws to hold my steady against him. "You let the big, bad wolf catch you." I feel Cade unsheathe his cock, the hardness of it jutting into my thigh. "And now he's going to devour you."

He fills me with a thrust so deep I can't even hold position for the first two seconds. I fall down as Cade continues to slam into me, his cock reaching all the places that make me tingle and want to burst. Even though it hurts to be forced into the dirt with every thrust, I can feel the pleasure building in my core and spreading through my body like wildfire. The man has a talent for stretching my emotions in a hundred different directions at once, and I fear one day I'll snap like an elastic band pulled too tight.

Cade's fingers burrow into my hips with a force that is sure to leave instant bruises while he sheathes his cock inside of me over and over. My soft cries mingle with his groans of pleasure, and I could weep with joy when I feel his shaft thicken inside of me as he gets close. And for the first time in my life, I plead with the powers of the universe for this to be the quickest fuck ever. With a few more brutal rams of his hips, Cade holds me close against his chest and spurts his seed deep into my womb. I'm stuffed so full that I feel his cum start to leak down my thighs. Not wanting a drop to go to waste, Cade slides his still hard cock over my thigh to capture the overflow of cum. And then he fucks it back into me.

When he finally releases me to tuck his cock back into his pants, I'm so wrecked I can barely move an inch. Complete destruction fully delivered, though not exactly in the way I'd hoped. I suppose I have high heels and stupidity to thank if I can't move my left wrist in the morning. At the moment it feels as though fire is burning through the veins in my arm instead of blood, and I'm not even sure an orgasm would alleviate the sting.

Cade leans over my back to yank my wrists free from his belt. I scream without meaning to, and quickly bite down on my tongue until I taste blood to keep myself from sobbing out loud. Within an instant, I'm flipped onto my back and staring into a pair of frantic green-gold eyes.

"What the fuck happened?" Cade asks in alarm. "Are you hurt?" His eyes start to sweep my body for signs of injury, but it's difficult to see much in the darkness.

"I'm fine," I lie, putting on a brave face. I'm cold, covered in cum, and not in the mood to be scolded about my wrist while I lie half-naked in the dirt.

"Don't lie to me," Cade orders sharply. "You screamed."

"Just like you said I would," I quip, brushing off his concerns. I try to sit up, but he forces me back down with a firm hand against my chest.

"With my cock, yes," he retorts with a scowl. "But I wasn't fucking you. You screamed when I untied you."

"Did I? Must have been a latent reaction to the fucking."

"Kara Caine, if you aren't honest with me this instant, you are going to seriously regret it." In my responding silence, he starts to clinically brush his hands over my body, looking for something amiss. He pauses when he reaches my knees. "You're bleeding," he announces, showing me the smear of blood on his palm.

"I fell," I admit, feeling embarrassed over my encounter with the damn rock.

"Did I hurt you when I pushed you?" he asks, his expression turning guilty.

I'm half-tempted to let him think this is all his fault from our little scuffle on the ground, but I'm not that cruel. The suffering he'd inflict on himself over causing me to get hurt would be worse than anything I feel right now. And I'm not that selfish, even if it would save me a lecture from the self-righteous bastard.

"No, it was earlier," I confess. "Walking along the river in heels is inadvisable, in case you were wondering. I tripped in the dark."

"I'm sorry. I wouldn't have been so rough if I'd known you were hurt. And I certainly wouldn't have fucked you in the dirt on bloody knees." The sincere remorse in his voice makes the guilt weigh a little heavier in the pit of my stomach.

"It's okay." I try to sit up again, eager to make it back to the manor so I can tend to the other thing I have no intention of mentioning. He holds me down once more.

"One more minute and I'll have you bathed and in front of the fire, I promise," Cade soothes as he continues to run his hands over me. "I just want to make sure you're not hurt anywhere else." I wince and inhale sharply when his fingers reach my noticeably swollen wrist. "Kara," he gasps. "What the *fuck* happened?"

"I told you—I fell." Defensively, I jerk back my left arm and cradle it against my chest. "Are we done here? I'm fucking cold."

"We sure as fuck are *not* done here," Cade threatens as he reaches for my arm again to examine it. "Your wrist is so swollen it could be worse than a sprain. I should march you to the ER right now and let you explain to a doctor how you let me tie up your injured wrist and rut into you like an animal in the dirt. I'm sure a medical professional would have some choice things to say about *that*."

I blanche in mortification at the idea of having to explain a sex injury to a doctor. Or anyone, really. "Please don't take me to the hospital," I plead. "I'm sure it's just a sprain. A bit of ice and some sleep, and I'll be right as rain."

"Of course, because you're such an *authority* on your own health. Christ, you take more liberties with your personal safety than nearly anyone else I've ever met." Cade's brow furrows as he rakes his fingers through his dark hair. "Safe, sane, consensual. That is the *only* way to do kink. And you seem to always forget fucking one out of three. Those odds aren't great, Kara. For anyone involved."

Cade looks away from me, and I feel panic rise in my throat.

"You get injured—you safeword. The concept is incredibly simple, and you're a smart girl. So why is it so hard for you to understand?"

"I don't like showing weakness," I answer as I stare down at the ground.

Cade sighs deeply. "I'm afraid, one day, your strength won't be enough to save you." He gets to his feet and brushes the dirt from his pants. "As you currently look like a poster child for domestic abuse, I won't take you to the hospital. But I'll have a doctor come to the manor to look at your wrist."

"Thank you," I reply, grateful that I'll at least get to experience my impending humiliation in the comfort of our home.

Cade offers his hand to help me up, and I give him my right one. My expectations of walking back to the manor with a shred of my pride intact are shattered with a quick sweep of Cade's arms as I'm lifted into the air.

"I've got a sprained wrist, not a sprained ankle. I don't need you to carry me back to the house," I protest with as much authority as I can.

"You're barefoot and outside in the middle of winter. Of course I'm fucking carrying you. Shut the fuck up and deal with it," Cade growls before walking us toward the manor.

Chapter 22

CADEN

Guilt gnaws my insides like sharp-toothed piranhas set loose in my guts and hungry for flesh. Kara was injured, and she let me fuck her into the dirt like a beast. And she didn't say a *goddamn* word. Didn't end the scene. Didn't even tell me to take it easy on her. If she wasn't already injured, I would bend her over and beat her arse black and blue for lying to me and being so bloody stubborn.

Anguish hangs heavy on Kara's features; her eyes are tearful and red-rimmed as she sucks in pained breaths while the doctor carefully wraps a splint around her wrist. Although I allowed her to dress and move to the bed in my room before his arrival, she still met the good doctor covered in dirt, my cum, and my bruises.

Dr. Rosenthal is Finnian's on-call doctor for Pandemonium. He is a member of our community and has always been of the utmost discretion. And most importantly, he makes house calls.

The prognosis was very quick after an initial evaluation—Kara's wrist is fucking fractured. After the doctor finishes tending her and we're alone, she's fucking in for it. I'll make her say that goddamned safeword every fucking day until she learns her limits. Icy tendrils of fear swirl in my stomach, warning that even that might not be enough to keep her safe from herself. Safe from me.

"All finished," Dr. Rosenthal announces as he releases Kara's wrapped wrist. "I want you to come by my office first thing tomorrow to get this X-rayed. I need to make sure the fracture isn't any more extensive than I've determined. Understood?"

"Yes, sir," Kara answers as she nods her head. I'm not sure that she's noticed she's still in a submissive mindset. I suppose that's natural given that we had to break off in the middle of a scene. The fact reminds me that she hasn't come yet, and she's probably still aching for the release. After her behavior tonight, I'm resolved to ensure she learns the true meaning of *denial*.

"Thank you for coming," I say as I lead Dr. Rosenthal to the door. "I'm sorry we had to call you out so late," I add with a chastising glare at Kara. Embarrassed, she turns her gaze to the floor and studies it intently.

"Not a problem," he answers, patting me on the back. "It happens more often than you know. Although, I think someone is in need of a good hard spanking for being so careless with her health," Dr. Rosenthal suggests, looking over his shoulder at Kara. Her attention jerks toward us at *that*, her expression a mixture of horror and humiliation. I can't decipher if she's guessed the doctor's connection to the club, or if she merely thinks he's perverse to be suggesting that his naughty patients receive spankings. She's welcome to come to either conclusion as I don't really have a fuck to give at the moment.

"Don't worry, I'll make sure she gets what she deserves," I assure him before following him out of the room.

◆

When I walk back into my bedroom, Kara is right where I left her on the edge of the bed, her eyes downcast and her expression carefully composed in spite of the pain her wrist must be giving her. She's always been tough as fucking nails, but that's part of the goddamn problem. She needs to learn to bloody bend a little before she gets into a situation where she breaks entirely.

"Are you going to punish me?" she asks, her voice trembling with fear as she worries her bottom lip with her teeth.

Good, she should be scared. She should be fucking terrified after the stunt she just pulled.

"Yes, I'm going to *punish* you," I retort, my tone cold as the Thames in winter. She let me keep going. She let me continue ramming into her hard and rough without a single word of protest. She let me fucking *finish* while she had a broken wrist.

What the bloody hell was she thinking?

"But I'm not going to hurt you," I continue, frustration and latent fury turning my tone sharp and acrid. "As much as I would like to whip you for your unbelievable recklessness, you'd be getting off too easy. The bruises would fade eventually, and you'd have no reminder of how dangerous it is to play without limits."

I grab ahold of the wrist not wrapped in a fucking splint and drag her toward me. "So instead, you won't be getting off at all. *One month*. No coming. No touching. No *thinking* of your cunt. If you disobey, I will edge you *so* hard and *so* long that you won't be able to scream or see or breathe through the sobs of agony and need. And then I'll only push you harder—drive you to the very edge of release over and over until you break. Maybe then you'll finally learn your lesson, so you're welcome to fucking try it."

I have two more bloody days with Kara before she leaves for New York on Sunday, and I'm terrified to even go near her right now. It feels as though we're both standing at the edge of a precipice, and one of us is going to fall the fuck over.

"I'm sorry," she whispers, and I can feel her trembling in my hold.

Forcing myself to be as gentle as I can with rage coursing through my blood, I let go of her and stand back, placing distance between us. "Sorry doesn't mend broken bones, Kara."

Like a moth to a flame, she presses herself toward me, trying to fill the void I've intentionally drawn. She has a fatal flaw of clinging to her own destruction. I place my hands on her shoulders and push her back toward the bed. "Go to bed without me," I order. "I need some space right now."

Kara's warm brown eyes fill with grief, and she stares up at me as though I've taken a hammer to her delicate heart and shattered it to pieces like glass. I wish I could pick up those sharp pieces and mend them like I always do, but tonight I can't. I think I'm losing the knack for fixing the things I break. And I fear—one day—all the destruction will catch up with me.

Chapter 23

KARA

Starving someone of orgasms for thirty damn days is a torture so cruel that it should be considered inhumane. And Caden Ashford says he *isn't* a sadist? My neglected pussy would beg to fucking differ.

The week after the incident in the woods, another black box was waiting for me on my desk, discreetly tucked beneath the spread pages of *Venus in Furs* that I accidentally left face-down when I was in a rush to leave the night before. With Cade still unquestionably furious with me, I knew this present wasn't an apology. Inside was a lovely pair of diamond studs. And the tendrils of ice that had spread around my heart slowly started to melt at his unexpected thoughtfulness in spite of his anger.

That is, until I checked my phone to see several message notifications from Cade that I missed while my phone was on silent.

> Lord Ashford: I'm bloody hard, and I've got no one to take the edge off.
>
> Lord Ashford: Touch your cunt. I want you to edge because it's YOUR goddamn fault that I can't fuck you right now. Bring yourself close three times, but don't you dare come.
>
> Lord Ashford: Send me your picture after you've finished.

> **Lord Ashford:** I apologize for the poor choice of words. Send me your picture when you've obediently tortured your cunt and NOT finished.

And I immediately picked up the black box with the pretty earrings, opened the bottom drawer of my desk, and threw them into purgatory with the fucking ugly ones. He's lucky I didn't toss them in the bin just to spite him.

Because he is a petty bastard, Cade has forced me to edge myself every single day since then to remind me of the pleasure I haven't earned. My weekends have been filled with ruined orgasms and only things that will get Cade off. Because *he* still gets to come. Cade still hasn't taken me back to Pandemonium since I passed out in his private room. I'm not sure if it's because he doesn't trust me or doesn't trust himself. Or a bit of both.

Cade's been distant lately. Darker and a bit rougher around the edges. Our phone calls have gotten shorter. His responses to my daily pussy pictures have gotten less playful. When we meet on weekends, his mind seems elsewhere. It's as though a dark cloud has cast itself over us, and I can't remember the last time I saw the sun.

In the wake of Cade's distance this month, I've actually been able to focus more on my work. Grant and I have made great progress with our research, and we've put together about half a syllabus for an advanced studies literature course in the fall. I was asked by the head of the English department to stay on and teach for a semester or two, but I regretfully declined. Cade gave me eight months. If I asked for any more, I'd probably need to start preparing for captive life again.

And speaking of captivity, this day is significant for three reasons. One—it's been *thirty two* days since Cade's blasphemous orgasm ban. Two—it's Friday, which means I finally get to come on Cade's cock. And three—today marks one year since a beautiful brute of a man walked into a library with the intention of stealing a book and walked out with my heart instead. Cade and I have been together for three hundred and sixty five days. And sure, the date of abduction is an unusual choice for an anniversary—call me insane, but I'm sentimental about the whole kidnapping thing now—but it's *our day* just the same.

Some people have blind dates and fated airport run-ins as their meet cutes; Cade and I have attempted theft, abduction, and threats of murder. To each their own.

Obviously I don't expect Cade to remember the exact date we met—he's a different brand of psychotic than me—but when I get a message from him on my way to the teachers' lounge for a cup of tea, my heart nearly bursts with happiness.

> **Lord Ashford:** Happy Anniversary, love. We're going to Pandemonium tonight. Be sure to wear your collar.

He remembered. And he wants me back at Pandemonium. And tonight, I'm hoping for kinky presents in cock shaped boxes.

The day passes at the rate of Sisyphus taking an uphill stroll after Cade's text. I can't contain my excitement, and I'm bursting with so much energy that Grant tells me to fuck off with the sound of my knees bouncing against my desk. Eventually, I beg off of work early and rush home to get ready for a date in Hell.

◆

The car is quiet, heavy with a tension I can't describe. I'm tempted to call it anticipation, but that's not quite right. Anticipation is tinged with sweetness, but this tastes bitter. Foreboding. I'm beginning to think Cade has one last punishment planned before my suffering is over. I'm so ready for the chasm of mistrust to close between us that I'm prepared to handle anything he wants to dish out. And if he wants to hurt me a bit more? Fine. I get off on a little pain.

Cade holds my hand, our intertwined fingers resting against my bare thigh, but his touch doesn't roam. He doesn't taunt or tease like he usually does on our drives. At the moment, him holding my hand feels more like force of habit than affection. I squeeze my fingers against his, looking for some sign that the Cade I know is still inhabiting that far too enticing body of his. He looks over at me, his eyes dark with conflict and contemplation.

He doesn't squeeze my hand back.

I fidget with the jeweled collar around my neck, rubbing my thumb over the now familiar facets of the rubies. I always wear it when I'm with Cade, and there's a certain sort of comfort in knowing that he put it around my neck, that he's proud enough to own me. The upstanding feminist in my head scolds my pussy for just how soaked it gets at the thought of belonging to Caden Ashford; they're in constant disagreement these days.

The warm haze of torches blaze in the distance as a glimpse of the black stone fortress comes into view. We haven't been back to Pandemonium since I passed out in Cade's private room during a whipping session that went too far. I know he still holds resentment for how I handled that situation—how I let him go past my limits—but I'm hoping that our trip to the club tonight is a sign that he's willing to trust me again.

God, I'd give anything to go back to how our relationship was before the whipping incident—and the broken wrist. Both times, Cade scourged himself for allowing me to get injured, but he also knows that it wasn't his fault. Cade is a careful and meticulous Dom. I know the injuries are on me, and I know he still blames me in part for allowing them to happen. He needs to know that I'm strong enough to handle this lifestyle before he trusts me with the full extent of his dominance again.

If I had to guess, I would say tonight is a test. Lucky for me, I've never failed a test in my life.

Chapter 24

CADEN

Today is the day my heart dies. Or what's left of it anyway.

Kara looks stunning and fierce as I hold her hand in mine and lead her to the brass doors at the entrance of Pandemonium. Her determined expression is that of a warrior preparing to enter battle. If only I could tell her tonight isn't about victory. I want to kiss every ounce of damned strength from her body and beg her to sheath her weapons and discard her armor. Surrender is the only way I can keep her.

If she wins this battle, she'll lose the war.

We don't stop to mingle. With somber footsteps, I pull her toward the staircase that leads up to my private room. This is where things went to shit the last time we were here. I can only hope for a happier ending this time. But that hope is dim and bleak.

I've known this moment was coming from the instant I had to call a doctor to deal with another of Kara's severe misjudgments. I've allowed myself to overlook self-destruction in the past. I won't make the same mistake this time. Not with her.

I would rip out my beating heart if it meant saving her. And a sickening sense of dread in the pit of my stomach warns that's exactly what I'll be doing before the night is out.

Kara follows me without hesitation, her feet following exactly where mine tread with the greatest trust. At this point, it's the blind leading the blind. Her submission should bring me pride, but at the moment, all I have is emptiness as I contemplate what is about to happen. I say nothing as I deposit Kara in front of the St. Andrew's cross and tie her to the posts facing away from me.

In a sense, this is betrayal of the worst kind. Kara has given me one hard limit, and I'm breaking it. I can only hope she's strong enough to call me out on my bastardry before things go too far.

When I hear the door open behind me, I know they've gone too far already.

"Hello, little sub."

Kara jolts violently before going still as death, and guilt twists in my gut like shards of glass aimed to puncture and draw blood. *Fuck*, I don't even know if I can survive this. The temptation to untie Kara, take her into my arms, and tell Greyson to get the fuck out of my sight is strong. But something stronger draws me toward what is almost certainly imminent destruction for the both of us.

I would be more than willing to take the easy way out of this if I didn't fucking love her.

Shit. I shake my head viciously, desperate to evade the noxious word like a venomous snake slithering through my mind. I don't love her. I'm simply not hardwired to experience such an esoteric emotion. I indulge in all the baser layers of humanity: lust, greed, deception, selfishness, but my capacity for love is fully underdeveloped.

"Cade, please." Kara's tearful voice cuts through my chaotic inner turmoil, dragging me back into the painful present. Hearing my name on her lips makes me grit my teeth in self-loathing. For her to make a slip like calling me "Cade" while she's tied and at my mercy in the middle of a scene in my private suite—she must be terrified.

"Please," she repeats again, sheer devastation eroding any note of her usual submissive tone. I'm thankful that I blindfolded her. Seeing her tears would be yet another stab of anguish, but that doesn't mean I can't still hear them in her voice.

Steeling my resolve, I remain silent, clenching my fists at my sides with an unfulfilled need to unleash pent up anger and frustration in the form of violence. Tonight, my violence has a proxy.

"Did you miss me, little sub?" Greyson taunts as he trails his fingers down Kara's naked spine.

I swallow the instantaneous rise of bile at seeing his goddamn hands on her bare skin, but this is a fundamental part of the process. The need for her to feel violated is necessary. As much as it drives me bloody mad, he has my permission to touch her. And he'll do more than touch her before the night is out.

Kara shivers beneath Greyson's touch, struggling to pull away, but the restraints are too tight for her to find even a centimeter of escape from his advances. "Cade," she sobs, her breath coming in short heaves as panic begins to set in. "I can't do this again."

I harden my tone even as my heart fractures at her helpless plea. "You are going to do this because I demand it." I run my fingers through my hair to stave off the jittery frustration coursing through my body. "Who do you belong to, Kara?" My question is perfectly constructed cruelty, an echo of my words to her that last time I shared her—and inadvertently pushed her far past her limits. She knows what comes next. And she's going to fucking hate me when this is over.

"Y-you." Her voice breaks on a sob, and the daggers of self-hatred burrow deeper beneath my skin.

"And are you allowed to disobey me in this room?" I give a nod of acquiesce to Greyson, encouraging him to continue. His hands turn from gentle to harsh, his fingers arching as he claws his way down Kara's hips. She whimpers at the assault, and ten red scratches decorate her pale skin.

"No, s-sir." Her body shakes as she takes shuddering breaths, trying to stay still to please me. She always strives to stay so strong, when all I want her to do is bend just enough to save herself.

"Correct. Now, be a good sub and take it," I order in a stern tone, silently pleading with her to break for me. I *need* her to break. Or this is going to be the most painful night of my whole fucking life.

I move to the leather couch, watching with tension as Greyson stalks around her like a predator circling his prey. Prey that has been served bound, naked, and helpless.

"Last time, Ashford gave me your mouth," Greyson says as he drags his tongue along the curve of her neck. I feel nauseous at the wet trail of saliva lingering on her skin. Kara flinches when Greyson moves his attention to the opposite side, but she holds her body taut while his filthy mouth descends on her shoulder.

Why can't she put us both out of our misery and use her bloody safeword *now* like she's meant to? She told me that sharing was a hard limit. That she never wanted to experience that sort of degradation again. So why is she standing there silently while fucking Greyson licks and paws at what's mine? The spark of anger at her blatant refusal to admit her limitations fuels my need to continue with this insanity. For her own goddamned stubborn sake.

"Get on with it, Greyson," I order, my curt tone masking all the other emotions I don't want to give in to at the moment.

His attention snaps to me with a flash of fury—no doubt unappreciative of being bossed around—before turning back to Kara. I'm afraid she's the one who will feel the brunt of his irritation.

"This time," I hear him tell her in a lower voice, "he granted me something much sweeter. This time, he gave me your pain."

Neither of us have a chance to react before Greyson sinks his teeth into the flesh of Kara's shoulder. She shrieks in pain and surprise as she struggles beneath him, and I watch the knuckles of my clenched fists turn white in an effort to not walk over and rip the fucking bastard off her.

Kara gasps for breath when Greyson finally releases her and walks toward the racks of implements hanging along the wall. He takes his time, reveling in the delayed dread as he tests multiple implements as though he hasn't made up his mind on which method of torture he wants to inflict on his helpless victim. Although, from the malicious glint in his eyes, I'm almost certain the sadist knew exactly what he wanted to use when I offered him free reign of my sub.

"Please, please, please," Kara chants in soft, broken sobs, but that's not the word I want to hear on her lovely lips. That's not the word that gets her out of this, and she fucking knows it.

Greyson stalks toward her, nine knotted strands dangling from the whip in his hands. A cat o' nine tails to be precise. The man isn't one to disappoint. I've never used a cat on Kara, and it will hurt like the bloody devil. I've instructed him not to draw blood, but it will be a difficult feat to take Kara to the edge with such a harsh instrument without breaking the skin.

"Any final words, Kara?" I ask, trying to guide her toward salvation rather than impending destruction.

"Please, d-don't."

Her obstinance hardens my need to follow through with this, even knowing it will be more torture for me to watch another man whip her into submission than for her to be on the wrong side of the whip. I'm realistic enough to know that Kara Caine won't surrender with ease. If the night we met is any indication, even the threat of death doesn't endear her toward survival for fuck's sake. Kara needs to feel as though she's fought fiercely before allowing herself to surrender. And tonight, she's going to have to fight like hell.

"Begin," I announce, my voice cold and stoic.

Wasting no time, Greyson sends the leather strands soaring through the air. They land across Kara's upper back with a loud *crack*. Kara screams. The broken sound of it turns the blood in my veins to ice in a painful rush of panic. Suddenly, it's as though there's barbed wire in my lungs instead of air.

I can't breathe.

I jolt to my feet, desperate to escape the atrocities I'm condoning against the woman I care about more than anything else in this damned world. The angry red lashes on her back seems to stare back at me, condemning me for my cruelty. The air is tinged with the saltiness of tears and the sweat of fear—it's a suffocating mixture.

Another *crack*, another scream. I underestimated my own strength, underestimated my ability to sit back and watch Kara be scourged by another. But I don't doubt my resolve. This has to work; if it doesn't, we're both damned.

I catch Greyson's attention and wordlessly motion for him to follow me toward the door. With her blindfold in place, Kara can't follow our movements, and that's how I want it. "I'm leaving," I tell him, ensuring that my voice is low enough to be out of the reach of Kara's hearing.

"But I've barely gotten started," Greyson responds, his brows furrowed in confusion. "Don't you want to watch the show?"

"I'm not sadistic enough to consider something like *this* entertainment," I retort with a hint of murder in my tone.

"Then why the fuck are you letting me whip your sub?"

"I have my reasons," I growl back. "And they are entirely irrelevant to you. Your job isn't to ask questions; your job is to hit her until she taps out."

"Not that I'm complaining, but why don't you just do it yourself?" He swishes the whip in his hands with a bored expression, clearly eager to get back to his torture.

"I've tried." I stare at Kara's shivering form as she hangs there, awaiting more of Greyson's blows in silence. "I haven't the strength to break her. She takes everything I have to give her without offering that final piece of submission. She's never used her safeword."

"Isn't that a good thing?"

"Not when she's silently allowing me to violate her limits, no."

"I see," he comments as though he is contemplating an enticing challenge. He turns back to look at Kara, and I abhor the eager gleam in his icy blue eyes. "So how do I fit into this grand scheme?"

"After last time, she told me that being shared with you was crossing a line that she never wanted to cross again."

"So you're literally obliterating the one hard limit she's communicated to you?" His face twists into an expression of surprise mingled with distaste, and the judgment of it sets me on edge. "Even for me, that's fucked up."

"I'm grateful for the unsolicited opinion." I compartmentalize my urge to murder him as Kara shifts restlessly within her bonds. This delay is taking too long, and I'm sure her dread of what is coming is slowly overpowering her senses. "Does your sudden growth of conscience mean you don't want to continue?"

"Do you think I'm going to pass up the chance to whip a helpless little sub into submission?" He laughs in amusement, and I hate him even more. "I'm not that noble. She hasn't used her safeword, so as far as I'm concerned, she consents." Greyson flicks the whip into the air, and I see Kara flinch at the sound as she braces for impact. "Consider me impressed, though. You might give me a run for my money as top sadist at Pandemonium."

I scoff in disgust. "I'm pragmatic, not deranged. I need to know where the line is so that I don't cross it. Unlike you, I don't need to make girls scream and bleed to get off. So you'll understand if I don't appreciate the comparison. You and I are entirely different monsters."

"But a monster is still a monster," he comments, and the way in which he says it makes my skin crawl.

"Make her use her safeword," I order with a dismissive wave of my hand. That earns me a rather dark glare before he nods in agreement. We may both be Doms, but there's a hierarchy in this club, and Greyson is the lowest of Finn's demons. "I'll be at the bar. Message me when it's done."

I quietly open the door, turning back toward Greyson for a final time. "Oh and Greyson? Leave one lasting mark on her, and I'll fucking kill you." After one lingering glance at Kara, I turn and walk out the door.

She'll be fine; she has to be. If she isn't—if I've made the greatest misjudgment of my life and allowed her to be broken without repair—I'll happily let her kill me in whatever torturous manner she deems fit.

◆

I forcefully slam into the seat beside Finn at the bar, disrupting him enough that he spills a bit of his favorite Irish whiskey on his trousers.

"Jesus, Ashford, what the hell?" he exclaims as he gets a stack of napkins from the bartender and brushes himself off. "What the fuck's got you so riled up?"

"I'm suffering from a severely guilty conscience, sober, and not nearly masochistic enough to enjoy the misery of either." I wave down the bartender and order my usual before meeting Finn's dissecting stare.

"Where's Kara?" he asks with an arched brow. He knows she's here; he saw us walk in together. What he's really wondering is why she isn't with me.

"In my room, getting the shit whipped out of her by Gavin Greyson." Finn chokes on his drink at my blatant honesty. There's no sense in avoiding the truth with him, even if it makes me look like a right bastard.

"And may I ask: why the fuck did you hand your sub over to the most reckless sadist at the club?" Finn asks in disbelief after he finally regains his composure. "What could she possibly have done to warrant a punishment of that degree? And since when do you let other people touch Kara, let alone whip her?"

He and Kara have become close over the months, so I understand why he would be concerned, but at the moment he looks positively outraged. "She's not being punished," I answer evenly.

"Then why the fuck would you allow that twat to hurt her?"

I pick up my glass of bourbon from the counter and allow myself a long drag before answering. "Because sharing her with others is a hard limit." At my admission, Finn jolts from his chair, looking very much as though he's about to break down the door to my private suite and save the poor submissive in distress. To illustrate my overall lack of concern in his hysterics, I take another drink.

"You had better put down your damn drink, get off your fucking ass, and stop that cunt before he breaks her into pieces." Finn is simmering with rage, the source of which I can't quite place.

"But that's the whole bloody point, mate." I do a cheers gesture with my glass before draining the last of my bourbon and tapping the top of the bar for a refill. I'll hit my two drink limit in a record two minutes. I turn to Finn, allowing a little bit of my worry to shine through my blasé facade. "She needs to break, and I can't fucking do it myself. I need a cold bastard like Greyson to take her to the edge so that she can finally admit that there *is* a goddamn edge."

"Is this about the safeword?" Finn asks, his tone softening a little.

"She won't bloody use one. She let me fuck her while her broken wrist was pinned beneath her and didn't stop the scene. Didn't say a fucking word. It's not like she's a pain slut. She's just too goddamn stubborn to admit any weakness. And it will get her killed one day."

Finn seems to consider his words carefully before replying. "I keep telling you, she's not Évione."

"This has nothing to do with her," I retort, my tone acrid and bitter. I detest dredging up the past, and that name has been off limits for years.

"Caden, it has everything to do with her." I startle at his use of my first name. In our entire acquaintance, I don't think he's done it once.

"I can't allow myself to destroy Kara like that," I concede, admitting that my anxiety for Kara's wellbeing is borne of the catastrophic end to my last serious relationship. "Kara needs to recognize her limits. This lifestyle is too dangerous for people without limitations. I don't want to end up near killing her one day or breaking her beyond repair."

"And what if this little experiment fails?" Finn asks with seriousness, tapping into my own personal fears. "What if she still doesn't use her safeword after she's been taken past her breaking point?"

I swallow down the dread at that unthinkable outcome. "Then I let her go." Even speaking those words feels like crushed glass in my throat. "I can't dominate someone who refuses to trust me with their weakness. I can't dominate someone who negligently allows me to endanger their mental and physical health. After Évione, I refuse to be the source of someone else's destruction."

"That seems a bit drastic. Couldn't you try having a relationship without the kink?"

Of course I've thought of that. I've thought of everything at this point. It's not like giving her over to Greyson's abuse was my first choice. "I wouldn't do either of us the disservice of being forced to live half a life, repressing our desires for the sake of keeping a perishing relationship just barely alive."

"Jesus, Ashford, you're always so melancholic," Finn bemoans with a sigh of exasperation. "It's not as though it's life or death."

"Until it is," I retort, my tone black and unwavering. We sit in uncomfortable silence until the chime of a message alert ruptures the quiet with the grace of the Titanic navigating an iceberg. Another ding echoes with dreadful urgency as I drain the rest of my second drink. Unintentionally holding my breath, I pull my mobile from my pocket and look at the notifications on my screen.

> Maloch: I gave her as much as I dared without fearing you'd take liberties with my life. She's in pretty bad shape.

> Maloch: She didn't safeword.

I don't release the air in my lungs as I read the damning message over and over. My chest grows painful with the need to breathe, but I can't allow myself the privilege when my life is about to be wrecked to pieces.

Fuck.

Chapter 25

I can't stop shaking. My body is still riddled with the adrenaline of combating terror and agony at the same time. My knees ache from kneeling on the hard floor, but it's a distant whisper of pain compared to the searing burn of the lashes etched into my back. I never saw the weapon that Greyson employed with the most meticulous brutality, but it felt like a thousand talons dipped in fire, setting flame to my skin with every strike. And those are only the physical wounds.

I shift uncomfortably on the floor as I wait for either reprieve or the next round of torture. If there is a next, I'm not sure that I will survive it. I bite my lip anxiously, flinching when my teeth puncture the chafed skin. My throat feels bloodied from screaming; I wish I could say that I withstood Greyson's whip with dignity, but that would be a boldfaced lie. I screamed from the first, unexpected strike. I screamed for mercy, for Cade—neither of them came. I screamed for what felt like hours until all the energy and fight drained from my body—and then, when my voice vanished beneath the strain, I simply screamed on the inside.

The acrid scent of bile hangs heavy in the air, the bitter taste still lingering on my tongue. I should be grateful that my body's natural reaction to the pain gave me no choice but to spew my guts onto the floor. The whipping stopped after that. Without a word, Greyson wiped the acidic remnants from my lips and the mess from my body. Even though my blindfold was still firmly in place, I could tell it was him from the subtle scent of citrus. He released me from the cuffs, my nerves shrieking as the shift pulled against the raw skin of my back.

"Kneel," he commanded in a tone devoid of emotion, and I obeyed without delay. I felt so tired that I was grateful for permission to give in to the weakness in my legs. And that was the last time I was acknowledged.

Cade never said a word. Never checked on me. Never told Greyson to stop when he was whipping me within an inch of my life. The fact that he would give me over to another man so completely leaves my heart feeling shattered and useless within my chest. In the course of our relationship, I've only ever given Cade one hard limit: don't fucking share me. And tonight—when we should have been celebrating our first major milestone—he chose to break that limit.

I don't know how he did it. I don't know how he calmly sat there and didn't say a word or interfere while his sadistic friend whipped the hell out of me. And why? For his sick pleasure? Because he likes giving me to his friends to use and abuse? I'm livid that he would ever wish to degrade me in such a way. I'm furious that he and his friend probably got off on my suffering. But eclipsing that anger is a buzz of warmth—of pride—because I didn't bend beneath the pain. I didn't break, even as I felt my skin break beneath the endless lashes of the whip.

Was this the final test? The final expression of my submission to him? I had to go past my limits and survive to prove that I'm strong enough to handle him? If that's the case, I'll wear my marks proudly. I would happily be broken if it ensures that Cade will always be there to piece me back together. His love is worth suffering for, burning for, bleeding for. If he wants my pain and my degradation, he can have it.

Clearly, he can have my sanity as well. Goodness knows I lost that long ago when I so foolishly fell for my captor. And I haven't stopped plummeting. I ponder what awaits me at the end of the fall. Safe and level ground? Or perhaps destruction and death? At this point, I feel it could go either way.

"Kara," a strong, deeply accented voice calls, obliterating my resolute tranquility with a single word.

On instinct, I sit up straighter, my flayed back screaming in protest at the motion. I smell him before I see him, my other senses heightened by my lack of sight. I'm enveloped in the familiar, winter reminiscent mixture of cedar and mint as warm hands brush against my temples to remove the blindfold.

I emerge from the darkness, blinking against the blaring light before Cade's face comes into focus. He studies me as his fingers idly trace my jawline, soothing me with a repetitive cycle of stroking up and down. His expression is—well, it's unlike any composition of emotions that I've seen on his face before. His countenance borders on unrecognizable as he continues to stare down at me without a word. His eyes bore into me with an intensity that unravels my composition cell by cell.

Ignoring the instinctual urge to cower, I sit taller, allowing the strength of having overcome his test to flow through my body. I'm not broken. I'm stronger than ever because he and Greyson have shown me yet another torture I can survive in spite of my longing to escape.

"This wasn't supposed to happen," Cade says after a long moment of silence. His tone is…sad, heartbroken even. The jarring anguish of it sends chills down my spine. I don't know what he means, but I know it doesn't bode well.

"You are so strong, love." His hands move to my hair, and he pets me with gentle strokes, like he's consoling me for something terrible that has yet to happen. "Too fucking strong. But sometimes—even though I adore your fierce stubbornness with every fragment of my soul—sometimes your strength isn't all I need. Sometimes I need you to entrust me with something as precious as your weakness and fragility too."

My exhausted mind aches with the effort of trying to decipher Cade's words. He thinks I'm strong. That's a good thing, right? So why does the sadness in his voice and the pain in his eyes and the consoling repetition of his caresses on my head make me feel like it's a bad thing?

Abruptly, Cade pulls away from me. His distance feels like a frost coating my skin in icy dread. He drags his fingers through his hair, an obvious sign that he's troubled. Trepidation fills my gut, and I feel so heavy that I couldn't move even if he commanded it. Somehow, I know his next words will break me more than any whip ever could.

"I can't do this anymore." His voice has turned from sad to cold, and the metamorphosis is startling. When I glance back up at him, his eyes are hard. Any glimpses of the broken man before are gone—this is Lord Caden Ashford, the punishing master who dominates with an iron fist as though it was his God-given right. I've not met this version of Cade often, and when I have, it hurts like hell.

"I refuse to waste any more time training a novice sub who doesn't know how to submit. You aren't pliant enough to fulfill my needs. And you're simply not cut out for this lifestyle."

I blink stupidly, waiting for him to tell me this is all a very misguided joke. I've been his sub for a year, and he's never once suggested that I'm not enough to satisfy him. Or that my submission is insufficient. On the contrary, he's always called my submission a beautiful gift, one that he knows I've never bestowed upon anyone else. Even though I'm almost certain of Cade's feelings toward me, that certainty wavers as he remains silent, staring down at me with a superiority that suggests he has better places to be.

"What do you mean?" I ask after a very long pause. The answer to my question seems implicit in his sudden disdain, but it's the only question that seems to form on my lips amid the shock.

"I gave you a year, Kara. A year to see if you could truly become the submissive I deserve. But your time is up, and you've fallen a far sight short of the objective. I will not squander any more of my efforts on a disobedient, willful, stubborn girl who is nothing more than a B-grade fuck."

Jesus, he managed to pack so many insults into a single, succinct sentence that a punch to the gut would hurt less. Revise that: a blow to the gut would feel like a welcome reprieve compared to having my character, submission, and sex skills desecrated in the same breath. And I do not make fucking B's. Ever. My pussy is an A+, and the British bastard bloody well knows it.

"I call bullshit." I shoot him a scathing glare even as I remain on my knees before him. It's a contradiction, I know.

"Excuse me?" Cade inches closer, darkness simmering in his eyes as his fists clench. He's not used to being challenged in his private room at the club; this is one of the few places that we have an unflinching adherence to the D/s roles. My momentary boldness shocks him, further illustrating my usual, exemplary submission, in spite of his accusations. In my opinion, it proves that he's lying about our relationship not working, but I can't fathom why.

And his misplaced anger merely stokes the fire of my rebellion.

"Bull. Shit," I repeat, forcing the words out of clenched teeth.

"Call it whatever the *fuck* you want." Cade's hand lashes out, capturing my jaw and squeezing to the point of pain. I whimper, but his grip doesn't loosen. In fact, he doesn't bat an eye as he attempts to crush my bones beneath his strong fingers. My eyes brim with tears, but I don't try to pull away. I allow him to take what he wants from me because I belong to him. And I trust him.

There's a flicker of something in Cade's eyes—a small ripple in the darkness—but it vanishes before I can attempt to draw it out. Ice fills the beautiful hazel spheres that usually remind me of cozy, autumn warmth, snuffing out any hint of humanity or light. Without warning, he shoves me away, and I fall back on my elbows before demurely getting back into my kneeling position. I refuse to be pushed away or shaken, and Cade marks my resilience with a discouraged crease between his brows.

Taking a deep breath, I bow my head before him, offering him my complete submission. The submission he apparently so disdains. I hear Cade groan in response, and I can only imagine that he's taking out his frustration on his dark, wavy hair. There's a heavy silence, and I wait patiently, never moving or raising my eyes.

"I'm bored, and I'm done." His cold words are venom tipped daggers, and I shudder as they strike. I feel lightheaded, doubtless from the internal bleeding of a heart that's been wrecked and mangled without any hope of repair. I whimper without meaning to—the guttural sound is broken, agonized, and almost animalistic in nature. I lift my hand to my mouth to stifle the next sob, biting into the flesh of my knuckles so deeply that the skin breaks.

The metallic tang on my tongue heightens the nausea of my despair, and I fall onto my hands and knees dry heaving. Thankfully, I already relieved my stomach of its contents with Greyson, so I don't have to fear the embarrassment of puking on my Dom's Italian leather shoes as he dumps me. Because that's what this is. He's breaking up with me. Although smashing my soul into slivers of black shards would be an apt description as well.

"As you will no longer be my sub, any further involvement with the club or its patrons is forbidden," he continues, driving the daggers in deeper as though I haven't bled enough to satisfy him. It doesn't escape my notice that he both deprives me of my position as his submissive and gives me a firm command in the same sentence. The bastard thinks he can have it both ways.

"You, of course, will have no further need to reside at Ashford Manor. Although, you did already take steps to make our living situation a less permanent arrangement. I suppose that was a preemptive decision on your part."

Is that what this is about? Is he punishing me for taking the job in New York? Did I kill our relationship by putting too much space between us?

"I'll have Declan clear out your things and send them to your New York apartment." The twist of that dagger stings a bit more sharply.

"C-can I at least say goodbye?" My heart shatters all over again at the thought of not getting another chance to see the people who have become family to me.

"I don't think that's necessary. A clean break is probably best for everyone involved." His tone is emotionless, and somehow, that's worse than the darkness.

"So that's it?" I ask, somehow managing to hold back the tears. "Everything we've built together over the past year is just over and done because you've decreed it?"

"Not quite done." The smallest flicker of hope sparks in my chest at his hesitation. "I'm going to need your collar back. Now that you no longer belong to me, my mark of ownership shouldn't be wrapped around your neck." That small hope dies a gruesome death right in its infancy, never being allowed to grow.

I don't belong to him. *I don't belong to him.* The terrible truth chants in my head with a frenzy as I reach back to unlock the clasp of the necklace he put on me when he called me his. It feels like an unspeakable crime for my fingers to remove it. And as my fingers tremble uncontrollably, I can't.

"I'm s-sorry, sir." I bite my lip to stifle a sob at the fact that I no longer have the right to call him that. "I c-can't undo it." I brace, expecting to be met with anger and impatience, but he doesn't reprimand or ridicule as he walks behind me to help unfasten the clasp on the ruby choker. I flinch when I feel his hands on my neck, not because they're harsh, but because the gentleness of his hands is so stark in comparison to his cruelty.

"Give me your hand," he commands with a soothing voice. At the familiar rumble of his accent, I melt immediately, leaning into the back of his legs like a pet desperate for attention. I lift my left hand, and he takes it, bringing it up to my head. "Hold your hair up so I can see what I'm doing." His fingers trail down my neck like a caress, and I shiver at the tender touch. He takes his time, his hands lingering on my skin for much longer than necessary as he works on the clasp. It feels like he's saying goodbye, and tragedy tinges the warmth of his touch. Suddenly, the weight of the necklace is gone.

Even though I've been naked the whole evening, I never felt bare until the moment Cade's collar left my neck. I feel empty—completely devoid of any emotion or sensation. My ribs are a hollow prison caging nothing—merely an empty void where my heart used to be. At the same time, my limbs are lead, fusing me to the floor. It's like there's an invisible force pushing me down, trying to crush me into nothingness. How is it possible to feel heavy and hollow at the same time?

Cade walks back to face me, dropping the ruby necklace into his pocket. Distantly, I wonder if such a priceless piece of jewelry should be shoved unceremoniously into a pocket without a case to protect it. I suppose that's a problem for his next sub to worry about. The thought brings a faint echo of pain, but it's lessened by the cloying haze of apathy—my depression's current flavor of choice.

"Are you alright?" His concerned question is so wholly incongruous with our current situation that I have to stifle an unhinged giggle.

"Yes, sir." If he actually cared, he wouldn't be asking because he'd *know*

I'm not alright. So I give him the lie he's looking for to placate his conscience.

"You don't need to call me that, Kara. You aren't my sub anymore. Caden is fine."

A subtle flicker of pain ripples through my body, but it's faint—more like a mosquito bite than the usual stab of daggers. "Yes, Caden," I correct. His given name feels funny on my tongue. I never call him that. Unless I'm angry. But I'm not angry. Right now, I'm nothing. Nothingness is nice.

"I booked you a hotel for tonight and tomorrow night before your flight back on Sunday. Of course, you can arrange an earlier flight home. The hotel is already paid for, so it won't matter either way."

Another little nip of pain. He pre-planned this enough to purchase a hotel room. He knew I wasn't going home with him.

"Thank you, Caden." I have the verbal fervor of a zombie.

"You don't need to thank me," he bites back. I peek up at him quizzically. He's angry; my current lack of emotional processing leaves me wondering why.

"Yes, Caden," I acquiesce, my voice lifeless.

"*Goddamnit*," he growls under his breath, and I just barely catch it. "I've arranged for a driver to take you to the hotel in an hour. Will that be enough time for you to compose yourself and gather your things?"

Compose myself? What needs composing? I'm dead inside, but my motor skills are fully functional, and my thought processes are firing perfectly without the added bother of emotions. "Yes, Caden."

He mutters something that sounds like another string of curses. "Get up off your knees. You don't belong beneath me anymore." Small fissures erupt along the torn shreds of my heart, but it doesn't really hurt. You don't notice a paper cut when you're already bleeding out.

Don't belong. Don't belong.

I get to my feet with more ease than usual, unhindered by any pain or stiffness in my legs from kneeling for such a long time. Seems like having your heart broken is the cure for many ailments; it should be highly recommended. I stand quietly with my hands clasped behind my back, my eyes lowered. Even though I'm not Cade's sub anymore, the posture of submission feels comforting.

Cade shifts, seeming unsure of how to proceed. Maybe he expected more of a fight? But why expend the energy? In the end, he'd still leave. He steps toward me with caution, as one would a wounded animal. Gentle hands reach for my cheeks—they're dry; somehow, I've managed to die on the inside and not shed a single tear. I'm not sure whether I should be proud of my strength or worried that I'm truly broken.

I flinch when he draws my mouth to his, the warmth of his lips the last thing I expect. He doesn't hold back, passionately invading my mouth with the slick heat of his tongue as though I were still his. I open myself to him as if by unspoken command, welcoming the taste of him, drinking down everything he gives me like it's holy wine.

Cade's kisses are always wrapped in violence, and this one is no different. His teeth tear into my bottom lip with unhinged aggression, and I welcome the sting of it—because it actually allows me to feel something for the briefest of moments. I offer him my bleeding lip, willing him to take from me, to feed from me. He does so with a growl, pulling my lip between his teeth and sucking the metallic essence from the wound. Groaning against my mouth, Cade uses his tongue to thrust the taste of myself back into my mouth, and I moan at the twisted perversion of being forced to swallow my blood mingled with his saliva.

Slowly, the kiss turns from brutal to bittersweet, and my body trembles with the intuited knowledge that this is him letting go. This is him saying goodbye for the last time. I will my mind to ignore the instinct to beg him to stay. I order the emotions that stirred during his unexpected kiss to return to their slumber. I long for the numbing shroud of indifference like one would a warm blanket to keep out the cold. Instead, I feel my heart beat firmly in my chest—the traitorous bitch of an organ proving that I still live, that I still feel.

One bloody kiss, and Cade awakes every weak, inane, useless emotion I've been trying to bury six feet under since the moment he told me this was over. I feel as though I'm searching in the dark for an apathy that simply doesn't exist anymore. And that heart that suddenly beats again? Yeah, it hurts like a motherfucker.

Cade pulls away to search my face, his expression warming a bit when he brushes his thumb against the furrowed crease between my brows. "There you are," he breathes with a small smile, his words so soft that I barely hear. Something about my destroyed state seems to give him comfort, though I can't imagine why. Did he intend to wake me from my blankness? To make me experience the pain of him leaving in full effect? I suppose he really is a sadist.

"The driver will be ready when you are." He brushes his knuckles over my cheekbones once before stepping away. "I'm sorry." His words are genuine—searing with truth—and it's the last thing he says before turning and walking out the door.

Wait.

Don't leave.

Come back.

I love you.

But not a single word slips past my lips as I watch my whole existence walk out the door.

Cade's words play over and over in my head, like hearing your least favorite song stuck on repeat for an eternity in hell.

You no longer belong to me.

Chapter 26

CADEN

Christ, it fucking hurts. Being kicked in the chest by a bloody horse would hurt less than the ache I'm currently sporting in my heart. I rub at my sternum, trying to soothe the pain, but it doesn't help. Nothing can. There's no medication that can heal a broken heart. But that doesn't stop me from heading to the bar with every intention of trying as hard as possible anyway.

No drink limits tonight. If anyone refuses, I'll buy the whole damn club and throw everyone out so I can look for oblivion at the bottom of a bottle in peace.

When I get to the circular bar in the far corner of Hell, Lief slides a glass of bourbon in front of me without a word, his expression wary. Finn must have warned the bartender to be *accommodating*. Brilliant, I won't need to threaten anyone tonight.

"Ashford," a low and angry voice calls from behind me.

Fuck, except for *this* twat.

I ignore Greyson and keep drinking.

"Ashford," he shouts again, this time grabbing my shoulder and forcing me to acknowledge him.

"Get your goddamn hands off me if you want to keep them, Greyson," I seethe, just barely managing not to slosh alcohol all over my trousers.

"Where the hell is Kara?" he asks, his bright eyes livid.

"As she is no longer my sub, her whereabouts are no longer my concern," I reply with feigned disinterest. I can't imagine a time where I'm *not* worried about Kara, even if she is no longer mine. And I certainly didn't remind her to return the bracelet I gave her with a tracking device inside. If I get too concerned, Braxton can track her movements in an instant. With Jace still on the loose, I'm not completely mental.

"You can't just leave her after a session like that, you asshole," Greyson protests with a chaotic gesture of his hand toward the upper level of the club that I just left a bit of my soul in. "She needs aftercare. Even an unfeeling prick like you should know that."

"I've set her free." I glare at the bastard, reminding him to know his fucking place. "That's the best aftercare anyone could offer her. Kara needs a clean break so she can find her place in normal life again."

"That's insane," Greyson replies through gritted teeth. "She's not made for *normal* life. And she shouldn't be alone."

"That's none of your concern. I've made my decision." I cringe at how coarse I sound to my own ears. I must be acting like a right prick if fucking Greyson is playing the defender of morality. The nagging possibility that he might be right paired with the latent guilt curdling in my gut turns every atom in my body towards viciousness. "Run along and find a warm hole to fuck, Greyson. Playing white knight doesn't suit a black-hearted cunt like yourself."

"Fuck you, Ashford." His eyes are blazing, and he looks as though he is about to start throwing punches. As it is, I could use a good fight.

I look him up and down as though appraising what I see—and finding it lacking. "Hmm, enticing offer. But you're not my type. That is, unless you want to try being on the receiving end of a little torture tonight?"

Greyson's blue eyes simmer with murder, but to my great disappointment, he backs down. "You don't deserve her," he spits in my face before turning around and storming off in the opposite direction.

"Yeah, mate, that's the whole fucking point," I reply to the empty spot where Greyson was standing before lifting my glass and throwing my drink back. On the way down my throat, it doesn't burn nearly as much as I would like. I ask Lief for another and try to drown out the expression on Kara's face when I flayed my own soul to set her free. She looked as though her soul had been slaughtered right alongside me.

Chapter 27

KARA

I am shell-shocked. Cade's words still ring in my ears like the after-effect of an explosion. With the way my heart has been obliterated to mere rubble, it might as well have been.

God, it hurts. *Everything* hurts. The hole in my fucking chest, my goddamn back that's been ripped to shreds, my head that's been trying to comprehend what the fuck just happened. It's a miracle I'm even standing with the sheer weight of devastation pulling me down as though it was stones in my pockets, hell-bent on dragging me down to drown. As if my body is in agreement, the strength of my legs gives way, and I fall to my knees. Exactly where Cade likes me. Except Cade isn't here.

Tonight, I was going to tell the damned bastard I *love* him. Instead, I'm left alone on the floor trying not to give in to the tears that threaten to spill. I cover my face with my hands to discover that tears have already fallen, my cheeks damp and burning with heat. My chest rattles with soft sobs as I draw my knees up to my chin and bury my face in my arms. The movement stretches the raw skin of my back, and I can't help but cry out in anguish.

"Kara?" a concerned voice calls from the direction of the door Cade walked out of minutes ago. Without much interest, I note the sound of footsteps drawing toward me. "Are you okay?" I feel a warm hand touch my shoulder, and I flinch from the contact.

Greyson.

I completely forgot about his involvement in this fiasco of a night. "I'm s-sorry," I apologize through the sobs, not daring to look up at him. I just need a minute to compose myself, then I can run away with what little remains of my dignity and never look back.

Hopefully.

"J-just give me a moment, and I'll be gone," I plead with heaving breaths. Cade or Finn must have sent him to evict me from the premises since I no longer *belong* here. I wrap my arms tighter around my legs, trying to make myself as small as possible—as little an inconvenience to him as possible. With what I know of Doms, he might take it upon himself to beat me a little more for the inconvenience.

"Look at me, little sub," Greyson orders, his voice kind but firm as he pulls my arms away from my face.

I cringe, knowing what he must be seeing: an absolute mess of a girl with mascara and tears staining her cheeks, snot running from her nose, and blood on her lips from biting down so hard. But his eyes don't fill with disgust or disappointment. He looks down on me with a kindness I know I don't deserve. Because I failed. Whatever Cade's test was tonight, however he was measuring my strength and submission, I know I didn't pass. The shame makes me try to pull away, but Greyson only holds on to me tighter.

"*Little sub*," he reprimands, and I turn my eyes back to his. "Are you okay?"

"Y-yes." Clearly, I'm fucking *not*, but that's not his problem.

"Don't lie to me, Kara," he answers, his tone growing angry as he fists my hair and pulls my head back to look up at him. His grip on my tender scalp is painful, but I don't mind. At least it allows me to feel something other than emptiness.

"No," I whisper. I hate admitting it just as much as I hate using my safeword, and the single syllable word tastes exactly like ash in my mouth.

"Good," Greyson replies, his feature softening as his hold on my hair turns from harsh to tender, his fingers gently stroking my head as though I'm a kitten at his feet.

"*Good?*" I'm confused as to why my fractured state of mind could possibly be seen as a good thing. Inadvertently, I lean into Greyson's touch, craving tenderness from any hand at the moment. Even the hand that was whipping me senseless a half hour earlier.

"Yes, good that you're finally able to recognize your limitations—and when you've exceeded them." Greyson removes his other hand from my arm and brushes away my tears with the back of his knuckles. "Brokenness is just as beautiful as strength. In fact, I like your brokenness most of all."

"That's depraved," I scoff.

"I'm a sadist, little sub." Greyson smiles as though the admission is something to be proud of. "It comes with the territory. Now, get on the bed and lay on your stomach."

His command sends any momentary comfort scurrying away as panic flares in my veins. "Greyson," I begin carefully, now quite aware that I'm naked and alone with him in a private room. "I can't do this right now. I am not at all in the headspace for that." I look pointedly at the unused bed.

"Jesus, Kara, I'm not trying to fuck you," Greyson retorts, mortification written across his well-sculpted features.

Not that I *wanted* to fuck him, but for some reason his rejection makes me feel worse. Clearly, I'm a goddamn basket case at this point.

"You took a thirty minute whipping before puking from the pain. Your back is raw, your skin is split, and you need fucking aftercare. And since Ashford just walked his ass out the door, *someone* has to do it." Greyson crosses his arms over his chest in annoyance, though I can't be sure if it's at me or Cade. "So please, lie on the bed and let me do my fucking job."

I stare up at him from my spot on the floor, still making no move to obey his command. "You're a *sadist*, so why are you offering to take care of me?" I ask warily, not understanding the logic of his intentions. "Shouldn't you want to rub salt into my wounds or something?"

"At the moment, I'm seriously considering it," Greyson answers with a dark expression as he again directs his attention to the bed as though I'll follow his silent request. Which I definitely will not. "Jesus, has Ashford trained you at all?" he finally asks in exasperation.

"Apparently not. According to him, I'm *untrainable*," I bite back. My attitude is a problem. I know it, Greyson knows it, Cade sure as hell knows it, but I can't fucking help it. Being stubborn is one of my core attributes.

"Well, maybe he was too soft on you. But trust me, little sub, I won't have that problem. Now get your ass on that bed before I give you another taste of the whip."

Not wasting any time with *that* threat hanging in the air, I struggle to pick myself up off the floor and scurry to the bed, keenly aware that Greyson is getting an eyeful in the process. With as much modesty as possible, I crawl onto the bed and lay on my stomach as requested.

"Look, you're behaving better for me already," he says in a patronizing tone.

I roll my eyes in response, thankful that he can't see it with my face pressed into the mattress. He leaves me there for a few minutes on my own. He doesn't tell me what he's doing, and I don't bother asking. I jolt when I feel something cool and wet on my back.

"Easy, little sub, I've got to clean you. Your skin is broken in some areas, and I don't want it to get infected."

The sadistic bastard drew blood. Lovely. I don't know who I should hate more—Greyson or *him*.

I hiss in a breath at the more tender spots, but Greyson is surprisingly gentle as he cleans me. Afterward, he applies a cream that is cool and soothing. In no time at all, my back is feeling much better with only the slightest echo of pain. Now, if only my heart was so easily mended.

"There you are, all done," Greyson announces with satisfaction as he steps back. "I would advise not sleeping on your back for a week until the cuts are more healed. The scabs could reopen and that might damage your skin. As long as you're careful, there won't be any permanent marks, and you'll be fully healed in two weeks tops."

"*Two weeks?*" I gasp. "Fuck, how do your subs survive you? You must not get to play very often with that kind of recovery time."

He laughs at the horror that must be written plainly on my face. "One, I stick to masochists and pain-sluts. The kind who can take everything I gave you today, get off on it, and beg me for fucking more. Two, I don't keep a regular submissive. I have a rotation with the masochists at Pandemonium, and I switch them out often."

"All of the masochists?" I ask in surprise.

"All of the ones who aren't in committed relationships with other Doms, yes," he answers with a shrug as though he isn't admitting to keeping a rotation of over twenty different sexual partners.

"Why don't you have a permanent sub?" I'm aware that it's a personal question, but I don't really give a damn after the breaches of privacy I've experienced with him in our short acquaintance.

"I haven't met a girl who could handle me," he says with a wink.

Makes sense. If he likes to beat girls this hard on a regular basis, they wouldn't last long.

"Well, I should get going." I try to wrap the sheets around me as I climb off the bed, keenly aware that I'm still fully nude.

"You shouldn't be alone right now," he rebukes with a scowl.

"You shouldn't be giving me orders. I'm not your sub. In case you hadn't heard, I don't belong to anyone." I turn away from him and try to search for my damn clothes.

He grabs my arm and pulls me back toward him, careful not to touch me anywhere else. "I'm a Dom—and I don't give a fuck if you're my sub or not—ordering people around is my speciality."

"Then what would you suggest, *sir*? I can't stay here; Cade's already told me to be gone within the hour."

Greyson's eyes darken at the mention of Cade's order, but then they slowly spark with mischief. "I know a place," he answers with a smirk that I'm tempted to call charming. "Do you trust me?" He holds out his hand, beckoning me to take it.

I've already made a deal with the devil once. This one can't be any worse. "Not in the least," I answer, shocked to find that I'm actually smiling back. "But what the hell do I have to lose now?"

I put my hand in his, and Greyson squeezes it firmly before walking to the other side of the bed and tossing me my clothes. He turns his back to allow me to dress, giving me the first bit of privacy I've been granted all night. Maybe chivalry isn't quite yet dead.

"So, how exactly do you plan on us getting out of the club without being spotted?" I ask while shimmying into my tight dress. When I'm fully dressed, I look myself over with the nagging feeling that I'm forgetting something.

"Afraid to be seen with me, little sub? My feelings are hurt."

"Well, we'll both be hurting if Cade catches me disobeying his orders and you escorting his sub—ex-sub—out of the club." Out of habit, I reach a hand up to my neck, and that's when I realize what's missing. My neck is bare. It's the first time I've been at the club without the comforting weight of a ruby choker around my throat. And the loss of Cade's collar makes me feel naked all over again.

"Do you honestly think I'm scared of someone like *Lord Ashford*?" he scoffs, adding a perfect touch of Cade's British accent to the last words. I can't help but laugh at how spot-on the impression is, wincing when the movement pulls on my sore back. Greyson notices, and the humor in his eyes dies a little. "I don't give a fuck what Ashford or the other pretentious assholes running this club think. You no longer belong to anyone, and you're free to do whatever the hell you want. Besides, Cade left the club before I came to check on you."

I feel two stabs of pain to my heart at Greyson's words. He doesn't mean to be cruel; he's merely speaking the truth. And the truth hurts like a bitch. Cade didn't even wait to see if I made it to the car he ordered. It's like I'm already forgotten. Well, the least I can do is return the bloody favor. "Okay, let's get the fuck out of this hellhole."

Chapter 28

KARA

Gavin Greyson drives a blood-red Maserati. And if that isn't a completely accurate depiction of his character, I don't know what is.

We've been driving for nearly an hour, and he still won't tell me where we're going. The only detail he's mentioned is that it "sure as fuck isn't the pity hotel Ashford booked." We're almost in the downtown district of Chicago; even though it's past midnight, the streets are busy and cacophonous from people enjoying their Friday night. Lucky bastards.

We made it out of Pandemonium without a hitch. I suppose I was imagining that everyone's attention would be on me as I made the walk of shame to the front door. When Cade and I are at the club together, we always seem to be in the spotlight. But I guess that's the difference. When we're together, all eyes are on him. Alone, I'm nothing; I'm practically invisible. I should be used to anonymity. Before Cade, it was something I actually strived for. But he's taught me how to come out of the shadows and be comfortable with being seen and admired.

For the briefest of moments, I was Caden Ashford's shiny thing—his pretty little possession. Without him, the sparkle is gone.

Greyson drives toward the wealthiest sector of the city. It's more tranquil and quite lovely with historic buildings and perfectly manicured streets alongside warmly lit lamp posts. I've rarely ventured to this part of town aside from a few holiday parties at board members' mansions. They like to include some of the younger faculty members to spice things up, not that I was proficient in that regard.

"Are you going to tell me where we're going now?" I ask, feeling a mixture of irritated, hungry, and tired. Probably more hangry than anything.

"Hush. We're almost there." He doesn't even look at me as he brushes aside my concerns. Stupid Doms and their stupid pretentiousness.

True to his word, a few minutes later we pull into a reserved parking spot along a street lined with upscale restaurants and shops. Everything is closed, the windows darkened and unwelcoming.

"What are we doing here?" I question, almost keeping the tremor from my voice. And how do I keep getting myself into precarious situations with men? Judging from previous experience, Greyson is probably either a thief, kidnapper, rapist, or an unsavory combination of multiple vices.

"Christ, do you ever shut up?" Greyson snaps, finally looking over at me. "If I had to deal with that mouth on a regular basis, you would have an intimate acquaintance with the back of my hand."

Jesus, remind me not to piss of Pandemonium's number one sadist. His rebuke is enough to keep me silent as we exit the Maserati and start walking down the empty street. He stops in front of a three story, historic brick building with a glass rooftop that looks like a conservatory. The facade is familiar. I check the name on the gold Art Deco style sign above the intricate doors.

GREY'S.

I know this restaurant; it was rated Chicago's best new eatery when it opened a few years ago. Now, it's got three Michelin stars. And a waiting list that's at least thirteen months long. I could never afford to eat here on a librarian's salary. I suppose Cade could, but he's never brought me here. In fact, I'm kind of surprised that he hasn't. Either way, a closed restaurant won't do anything to satiate the gnawing hunger in my belly that's suddenly come to life standing before one of the most renowned restaurants in the city.

I look over to see Greyson pulling a set of keys from his pocket. Does he know the owner or something? These rich bastards always seem to know each other. They've probably got their own little kinky and filthy rich clubs. Cheers to fucking them.

Still keeping my less than becoming thoughts to myself—definitely not trying to get smacked for smart-mouthing tonight—I watch Greyson unlock and open the double doors. He motions for me to follow him inside, flipping on the lights so that I'm not being beckoned into complete darkness. Without pausing, he passes the reception area and bare tables, looking very much like he knows his way around. Finally, we enter a huge open kitchen with marble countertops and large copper pots and pans hanging from racks on the ceiling. It looks like any of the fanciest kitchens you'd see in Paris.

Still not bothering to tell me what we're doing here, Greyson starts toward the pantry. "So, any particular reason why we're visiting a three Michelin star restaurant in the middle of the night? And how do you even have a key to get in?" I call across the kitchen.

Greyson turns back to look at me, that endearing mischievousness from earlier gleaming in his bright blue eyes. "You're a smart girl, Kara. Give it a think."

I bristle at the implication that I am not, in fact, a smart girl, and do as he says. Suddenly, it hits me like a stack of Tolstoys falling off the shelf. "Oh my God, *you're* the Grey from *GREY'S*?" I'm stunned that he actually has a talent other than beating girls black and blue.

"Of course," he confirms with a smug shrug of his shoulders. "Though I do appreciate you knowing my Michelin star count. Are you a fan?"

I scoff. "I can't afford to be a fan. But I've heard of the restaurant; it would be hard not to. The wealthy and elite seem to appreciate your food."

"Why does that compliment sound more like an insult coming from your mouth?" There's a reprimand in his tone, but it's slight. "I'll have you know everyone appreciates my food, but it's the rich and elite that pay to keep the lights on."

"Yes, you really look like you're struggling in that regard," I bite back, looking around at the grandeur of the cooking space.

"Keep it up, little sub, and I'll spank you instead of feed you. Which would you prefer?" He looks at me with a stern expression on his face, his muscular arms crossed over his chest.

"Food, please," I answer, keeping my tone respectful and submissive. As I've been taught.

"Good choice." He walks into the standing refrigerator, collecting various things as puffs of cold air fill the room.

"Aren't you going to ask what I like?" I scoff as he grabs a heavy copper pot from the hanging hook and places it on the huge gas stovetop. He hasn't even asked what I'm in the mood for. I could have a food allergy for all he knows.

"I'm the chef. I tell you what you like, and you say *yes, chef* and eat it like a good girl."

"Yes, chef?" I ask with a laugh, jumping up onto the counter as though I have every right to. "Is that some sort of a weird kink for you?" I kick my legs back and forth with the bored energy of a child, intentionally trying to annoy him. I can't explain the instinct—it's like I'm made to frustrate the hell out of stern Doms with control issues.

His stark blue eyes fixate on me with an unnerving intensity as he rolls up the sleeves of his black shirt, revealing intricate tattoos covering practically every inch of real-estate on his forearms. I'm entranced by the inked narrative woven into his skin. The beauty of it makes me wonder if there's more to the self-inflated sadist than I thought.

"You're in my kitchen, little sub," he answers, his tone dark. His hand reaches out and grabs my calf mid-swing before pinning it to the back of the kitchen island. "Chef is the only thing you call me. *Comprenez vous?*"

"Y-yes, chef," I stutter back, thrown off by his overwhelming Dom energy, his sudden closeness, and his smoldering use of French—which I don't speak a word of, yet somehow contextually understand in this instance.

"*Très bien.*" With a warning glare, he lets go of my leg and directs his attention to a very sharp and somewhat threatening collection of knives, running his fingers over the handles intimately. If I had to guess, Greyson has a closer relationship with those knives than any of the women in his life.

"So, why the French?" I ask, still stumped on how someone from the same area as me is able to perfect an authentic Parisian accent.

"I studied culinary in France. And cooked at three of the best restaurants in Paris before opening my own restaurant here. It's rare for someone of my age to already have their own successful restaurant, let alone one that's received the level of accolades I have. I guess you could say I'm a bit of a prodigy."

"That sounds rather pretentious," I retort with a scoff.

"Yes, it's meant to," he answers, his tone serious. He makes his choice of knife and moves right on to the chopping aspect of *mise en place*—dicing onions, mincing garlic and fresh herbs, and roughly cutting up a variety of different sized tomatoes in mottled autumnal colors.

The sharpness of the onion makes my eyes water and sting, and I wipe at the wetness in annoyance.

"Those are the last tears you're allowed to cry tonight," Greyson warns, pointing the knife in my direction before continuing to chop so quickly that I'm surprised he doesn't lose a finger. The kitchen already smells wonderful, and he hasn't even started cooking yet.

He lights the fire on the stove before adding a more than healthy portion of butter to the pot. The butter sizzles as it melts, and my mouth waters as I watch him scrape in the onions and give them a quick stir.

"Can I help with anything?" I'm more than used to meal prep laziness after being spoiled by Mrs. Hughes's cooking, but I feel silly sitting in the kitchen with no purpose. I could at least stir the pot or something unimportant that won't ruin the Master Chef's dish.

"Absolutely not," he tuts. "Only professionals have run of this kitchen, and even then I'm picky. There is only one thing you're good for in my kitchen."

"And what, may I ask, is that?" I inquire, expecting nothing more than an innuendo.

"Sitting there and looking like a gorgeous mess." His smile is surprisingly artless as he looks over at me from the heat of the stove. I'm touched by the unexpected sweetness. "Of course, you'd look even better without the clothes." Ah, and there it is.

"I think you've seen enough of me for one night, thank you very much."

His comment is a reminder that he *has* seen me without my clothes. Twice. I'm shocked to find that I'm quite comfortable around someone who witnessed me naked and vulnerable in some of the most traumatic moments of my life. Guess I don't hate Masterchef Greyson as much as I thought I did.

"Worth a try," he answers with a smirk before adding the rest of the vegetables to the pot.

The smell filling the kitchen is heavenly, and I can't resist hopping down to take a peek at his concoction. Pasta sauce maybe? He swats me away with his wooden spoon before I can get close enough. "Ah, ah, ah. No crowding the master at work. Sit your ass down."

Sulking, I do as he says. "I'm bored." I just barely resist the urge to start kicking my legs again. Apparently, free time with no commands or preoccupation for my hands is too difficult for me to adjust to.

"Boredom is good for you."

"I'm hungry."

"I'm sorry, are you five?"

"I'm sorry, does Master Chef Greyson take five *hours* to make spaghetti?"

"It's not spaghetti. And yes, it should take at *least* that long if done right."

"Well, I'm not one of your rich and elite clientele. Just make me a sandwich, and I'm good."

"Did you just order me to make you a sandwich?" He holds the spoon in his hand threateningly, as though he might use it to beat me for insubordination. Which would be ridiculous because it would get tomato everywhere and make an absolute mess.

I take an educated guess that I'm safe from the cooking utensil and push a bit more. "I did. Is that in your repertoire, chef, or is it too advanced for you?"

"Jesus, Ashford wasn't kidding about you. Do you ever shut your pretty fucking mouth? Or do you like being punished that much?"

I freeze, the air vanishing from my lungs as I fixate on that one, sanity-obliterating word. For a short, blissful moment, I'd forgotten about Cade and the absolute destruction he rained down on my life tonight. Hell, I'd even forgotten about the whipping. But now, with full consciousness fully restored, everything hurts like fresh wounds.

"Shit, sorry," Greyson apologizes when he looks up from pouring some sort of broth into the pot. "Sometimes I forget that other people actually feel things. I have an underdeveloped capacity to process other people's emotions, which is usually an asset because I'm not constantly bothered by the weight of people's feelings, but I believe this is one of the rare instances in which having a heart might actually be helpful."

"It's okay," I answer with a sniffle. "I'm quite used to men who are careless of other people's feelings."

"And how are you...feeling?" The words sound awkward coming from his mouth, but I appreciate the effort.

I pause, searching for the most concise expression of how I feel at the moment. "Broken. But I'll mend. I always do."

"Is it a common occurrence for you? Brokenness, I mean."

Memories flood my senses, sharp and searing, each one highlighting a fracture—in my body, in my heart, in my mind, in my soul. The car accident. The loss of my parents. Jace's assault. Cade removing my collar. Each one felt like agony. But each one, even the most brutal, mended with time. I can only hope that time is enough to heal the most recent fissure of my heart.

"No more than most," I answer once the painful ruminations clear my head like a fog lifting. "And far less than some. By all accounts, I consider myself lucky."

"I'm sorry Ashford was just another asshole to break your heart." The concern on Greyson's face is genuine, and I can't help but feel gratitude for the one person who's shown me kindness and understanding tonight. Who'd have thought it would be Gavin Greyson?

"Well, does heartbreak earn me a sandwich?" I look up at him with the most pitiful expression I can concoct, playing up the dampness of tears that already cling to my lashes. I probably look like a half-drowned cat, but hell, that will work too.

He holds strong for about twenty seconds, but I've always been told stubbornness is my specialty. He caves with a gruff expression that I know probably masks a touch of indulgence as he throws his hands into the air in surrender. "Fine. You get the damn sandwich, but you'll eat what I give you without complaint. *Oui?*"

"Yes, chef," I respond with a cheerful eagerness, my eyes shining with victory. I forgot how nice it is to actually win a challenge. Cade likes to deny my demands just to spite me. It's usually for my own good, but it's still a dick move.

"You're lucky I don't mind a little topping from the bottom. Usually because I'll make my subs suffer for it later. I enjoy pain, but pain as a punishment is as delectable as the first truffles of winter foraged straight from the cold earth."

He walks into the refrigerator and comes back with something wrapped in white paper. Unwrapping it, he reveals a black lump that I can tell is a truffle from smell alone. Apparently, his illustration was rather on the nose.

"I don't particularly like truffles." I scrunch up my nose at the musky, earthy fragrance filling the kitchen and mingling with the scent of tomato, garlic and herbs. The smell of the fungi is quickly overpowering. "They're too pungent."

"Blasphemy," Greyson snaps, his expression so irate I shrink back a little. "You will not disgrace the truffle in my kitchen. It's one of earth's greatest tributes to the human palate. And you will eat it and enjoy it."

His stern gaze leaves little room for argument, so I give in without a fight. "Yes, chef."

"Good girl."

I can't help the warm tingle that courses through my body and the slickness that erupts between my thighs at those two innocent words. I'm afraid the response is ingrained, and my praise-minded pussy can never be untaught.

Greyson laughs, and my cheeks redden with mortification, knowing I've been caught. "You aren't going to make a wet mess on my counter are you, little sub? Pussy juices in the food definitely wouldn't be up to code."

"Oh my God," I squeak, covering my face with my arm in humiliation.

"I can't help it. It's a Pavlovian thing. I hear those words and expect…well, a reward."

"I see," he responds. His voice is gravelly and seductive and smug, and I hate it to my clenching, aching core. "Should I *reward* you, little sub? I would hate to deviate from what you're used to. And you have been very obedient so far. I think a treat for the good little sub could be arranged."

He puts his hands on my spread thighs, and the blood in my veins incinerates at the feel of his coarse fingers on my bare skin, the calluses on his well-worked hands tickling my nerves. And I'm tempted. For the briefest, infinitesimal, sliver of a millisecond, I consider letting his hands slide further up my thighs. It would feel good; his reputation at the club is enough to know that I wouldn't leave unsatisfied in any regard. And, in a very irrational sense, the thought of screwing around with him to get back at Cade is enticing. But all of that pales in comparison to the betrayal I would feel in my heart if I ever let another person touch what belongs to Cade. Because in my heart, I'm still his.

Gently, I take Greyson's hands in mine and move them to either side of the counter. "I think getting fed by a Michelin star chef is all the reward I need." I plead with my eyes for Greyson not to take the rejection personally. It's too soon, not that any amount of time would be enough for me to seriously consider sleeping with Greyson. He is gorgeous and sexy and far more human than I expected of a hardened sadist, but he's not Cade. No one will ever be Cade. Which leaves me in quite a pickle in the pussy department.

Greyson looks unfazed by my denial as he starts slicing a large loaf of house-baked bread. "I agree. It will be the best reward your dirty, cocksucking mouth has ever received."

Fuck, me. I'm fairly certain that sadistic streak of his manifests in more ways than the physical. And his humiliating retort reminds me that I have, in fact, sucked his cock. And it was *not* one of my top ten greatest moments.

"Was that too much?" he asks, looking up at me in mild concern before starting to cut long strips of cheese from a few different white wedges that all smell delicious.

"I've had worse," I answer with a shrug. "But that's your one low blow. No more mention of my oral escapades unless you want to lose your favorite appendage."

"I have several favorite appendages. Can you be more specific?"

"The pierced, seven inch appendage."

"It's eight inches," he scoffs. "I've measured."

Of course he has. "Sorry, my throat isn't well equipped to measure such things accurately. It was a rough estimate."

"Do you want me to give you another rough estimate?" His threat might be unnerving if his bright blue eyes didn't glitter with amusement.

"The only thing going in my mouth tonight is food. Speaking of, are we recreating the Mona Lisa over there or something?" I arch an eyebrow at his current task. "Just how long does it take a professional chef to make a sandwich?"

I shriek when an unexpected smack lands on the thigh closest to Greyson.

"You're pushing your luck, little sub. Keep running your mouth, and there's plenty more where that came from. Last warning. I might seem like a fun Dom compared to Lord Tea and Scones, but I'm not afraid to make you bleed. In fact, I'd get a fucking kick out of it."

I giggle at the jab at Cade, but amend my amusement when I see that the expression on Greyson's face is serious. "Sorry. Best behavior from now on. Promise." I hold out my pinky as a sign of good faith. Much to my surprise, he wraps his own pinky finger around mine, sealing the oath. He's so unlike what I expected, I have to suppress another urge to giggle.

"I'll have you know, I take pinky promises very seriously. I have a five year old niece, and she informs me they are of the highest standard."

Now I can't help but laugh at the image of Greyson swapping pinky promises with a little girl while they wear matching pink tutus. It's probably not a realistic comparison, but it's more than enough to lift my spirits for the moment. It's such a change to be around someone who willingly shares intimate details about their life and family. Cade is always so tight-lipped about anything having to do with the past or his family. The only reason I know his parents' names is because I googled it. Getting Cade to talk about himself is like trying to draw blood from a rock.

A loud, mechanical whirring sounds in the distance, drawing me back from the haze of contemplation as I realize I've been staring off into the distance for a minute or two. Greyson is using an immersion blender on the tomato mixture while an open sandwich layered with cheese and thin shavings of truffle sizzles in a frying pan beside it.

"Where did you run off to?" he asks, his face contorted with the same mild concern he wore earlier.

"Nowhere worth staying," I brush off. "That smells divine. Don't suppose you make deliveries to New York?"

He laughs, the sound warm and inviting like a winter fire. "We don't deliver anywhere, but I suppose we could make an exception for a very special acquaintance of the executive chef." He stirs some cream into the pot and uses a spatula to join the two halves of the sandwich, pressing down on the top lightly to get the pieces to meld.

I'm content to watch him work, appreciating his level of balance and concentration. Even making something as simple as a grilled cheese, there's a sort of art to his movements, like he pours a bit of himself into everything he creates. My stomach growls in eager anticipation as I watch Greyson gather a bowl and plate from a shelf of pristine, white dishes, a cloth napkin, and handful of utensils. He sets a place on a clean bit of counter, meticulously laying the emerald green napkin and setting out the sleek gold silverware. It looks like a proper restaurant place setting on the kitchen counter.

"Sit," he orders, grabbing a stepping stool that's almost counter height and dragging it toward the end of the counter.

I obey, watching as he ladles tomato soup into the wide, shallow bowl, garnishing it with a circular drizzle of garlic oil and a single basil leaf. He slides the sandwich onto the oblong plate and cuts it diagonally, standing the two halves against each other. I try not to drool as I watch the melted cheese start the drip down the middle. I wait as patiently as possible as Greyson puts the finishing touches on both dishes before carrying them over. There are so many ways in which this night hasn't turned out as expected, but being personally served by an award-winning chef in his own kitchen is definitely up there.

"*Bon appétit*," he says grandly as he places the food before me.

He's only dished enough for me, so I guess he's not hungry. I pick up my spoon, starting on the soup, and—my God—I don't think I've ever really tasted food until this exact moment. The depth of flavor is indescribable, and it is not from a lack of vocabulary. I moan involuntarily on the next bite, and Greyson chuckles with a smugness that suggests my orgasmic reaction is exactly what he expected.

"Good?" he asks with an arched brow and a smirk on his lips.

"I'm speechless." And it's the truth.

"Kara Caine speechless? What a novel idea. I should feed you more often," he taunts, leaning back against the counter as he watches me eat in a studious manner that somehow isn't creepy. Much.

"Yes, please. I'd take a fucking vow of silence for this food." At this point I've practically scarfed down half the bowl before moving to the grilled cheese. I take one bite, and it's perfect. Complete, utter, perfection. "Jesus, are you even human?" I ask with a groan of appreciation as I inhale the entire half. I spent my entire adult life thinking I hated truffles, but now I'm pretty certain I'm in love with them.

Having tasted each element on their own, I go to dunk the second half of my sandwich in the soup.

"What the fuck are you doing?" comes a growl from beside me as a hand grabs ahold of my wrist and pulls it back from the bowl.

"Dunking?" I try to pull my hand back, but he won't loosen his grip.

"You are in a five star restaurant. You do not *dunk*." He plucks the uneaten half of grilled cheese from my hand and takes a bite. "You've lost sandwich privileges for the foreseeable future."

"That's just cruel," I pout before scarfing down the rest of the soup before he takes that too. By the time I've scraped the bowl clean, I'm surprisingly full. I'm just missing a little something sweet before feeling fully satisfied. "I don't suppose this five star restaurant has any dessert on hand?"

"Greedy little thing," he tuts, licking the remnants of butter off his fingers. "I think I can scrounge something up."

He goes to the freezer, bringing back something that looks promisingly like chocolate. He grabs another couple things from the pantry, along with two small bowls and a couple spoons. I'm giddy when a lifted lid reveals the darkest, richest looking chocolate ice cream I've ever seen.

"Bitter, dark chocolate gelato," he announces as he molds the soft gelato into smooth balls and puts two in each bowl. "Raspberry balsamic reduction." He drizzles ribbons of dark red syrup over the chocolate spheres. "And a sprinkle of sea salt and caramel pralines." He dusts the tops with amber colored granules. Honestly, it almost looks too pretty to eat. Almost.

Having no care for lady-like manners when it comes to dessert, I dig in. The flavors are an exquisite combination of sweetness, bitterness, and salt—perfectly melded, perfectly balanced. I could eat this single dish for breakfast, lunch, and dinner for the rest of my life and be perfectly content.

"This is amazing." It feels as though I'm stating the obvious at this point.

"Well, I can't take the credit for this one. Confectionery is my weakness. Chef Flores is testing this one out for our spring menu, but it's not perfect yet."

"Tastes perfect to me. You should give him a raise."

"Her," he corrects. "And I think she'd much rather I give her a promotion than a raise. She's just a *commis* chef, but she's got a fair amount of potential."

"In that case, I think you should give her a promotion *and* a raise."

"I will take your very knowledgeable opinion into consideration, little sub," Greyson answers with a smirk.

Chapter 29

KARA

By the time I finish, I'm so full and satisfied that the emptiness I was feeling earlier in the evening is merely a distant memory. If Gavin Greyson has only one talent, it's conquering emptiness with style.

"So, now what?" Greyson asks after we've both sated ourselves with dessert.

"I suppose it's time to make my way to the pity room he booked." I don't say his name. I don't think I have the strength to even think it yet. "I think the hotel was actually on this side of town, so it shouldn't be too hard to get an Uber."

"You can't possibly think I'll let you leave at this hour and stay alone at a hotel. That pitiful end to the night would be a disgrace to the five star meal you just ate." He gathers all the dishes and puts them in the huge sink.

"Here, I can at least clean up after you cooked," I offer, making my way toward the sink to wash the dishes.

"Don't bother. They'll be here early enough to do it in the morning." He walks toward the opposite end of the kitchen, the side we didn't come through. "Follow me."

I've followed him this far tonight, no sense in turning back now. We walk in near darkness past storage rooms and utility closets until we reach an elevator at the back of the building. Given the seclusion of its location,

I don't think it's for restaurant patrons. Greyson pulls a key card from his wallet and scans it on the elevator panel. The doors open on a space that's probably only built to hold four people at maximum.

Greyson steps in, but I linger in front of the doors. Do my anxieties from past encounters with strange men blare like warning bells not to get in the confined space of the elevator? Yes. Am I still going to do it anyway? Probably. My common sense likes to take a vacation at pivotal moments like this. "Greyson?" The single note of hesitation is the minimal amount of due diligence I feel like participating in at the moment.

"It's okay, little sub. You can trust me."

And somehow, I truly think I can. He offers me his hand, and this time I walk in to take it. He presses level two, and we start to ascend. There's also a level three, but I'm not sure I'm ready to ask what lies above at the moment. I'm not in the mood for a secret sex dungeon surprise.

The elevator doors open, and I'm met with a huge, luxurious apartment entirely swathed in black. The walls, ceilings, and floors are black. Twin, spindly black chandeliers decorated with hundreds of tiny light drops give the illusion of abstract spider webs dripping with dew as they dangle above elegant velvet couches. It feels like a mixture of modern and macabre at the same time—the perfect sanctuary for a twenty-first century Dracula.

Looking back at Greyson, I realize he fits the part rather well. I've always been under duress when we've interacted, so I've never actually taken the time to study him closely. Now that I do, I'm struck by how lovely he is, his features exquisite in an entirely different sense than Cade.

Everything about his appearance feels sharp, angular. His eyes are bright, crystalline blue—piercing and cold. When he smiles, they warm slightly, but when he's stern, they're glacial. His cheekbones could cut glass, and his jaw has a razor edge that's trimmed in the faintest shadow of stubble. His black hair is long, wavy layers falling just above his shoulders. His skin is practically alabaster, perhaps paler than mine. The contrast makes his hair look even darker, and I absently wonder if he dyes it, or if he's naturally the perfect goth stereotype. I expect that he must tie it up when he's working in the kitchen.

He towers over me, which is easily done, but he's far taller than six feet. He's lean, rather than broad, but perfectly toned from what I can tell from his well-tailored dress shirt and trousers. The purely black tattoos wrapped fully around his sculpted arms look far more detailed up close. Everything represents a twisted sort of beauty. Delicate flowers whose thorns draw blood from the hand holding them. Snakes hidden amongst twisted berry brambles. Butterflies with their wings pulled off. Flies trapped in honey. Skulls—because deep down he's just your typical bad boy.

"Find something you like?" Greyson asks with an exaggerated cough to disrupt my perusal of his body. My entirely detached, purely documentative perusal of his body—which is beautiful, and I can admit that with complete objectivity.

"Shit, sorry," I apologize when I finally manage to retract my gaze. "I've just never really gotten a good look at you."

"And what is your consensus?" he asks with an amused smirk as he settles onto one of the couches. The length of his body takes up most of it.

"You're very well-constructed."

"Well, that's hardly the most glowing compliment I've ever received, but I'll take it." He pats the seat of the couch adjoining his, and I am more than happy to take it. "Now, what are we going to do about you?"

"What do you mean?" Does he want me to leave?

"While you're more than welcome to spend the rest of your Chicago trip here, I'm not sure that you want to shack up with another Dom after what you just went through."

Oh yeah, that. "I don't want to inconvenience you. My flight leaves Sunday night. I can just stay at the hotel until then."

"Like hell you will. As long as you're in town, I demand you stay here. You deserve more than some empty, lifeless hotel room. But wouldn't you rather get back home to New York sooner?"

"My home is here…or it was. I'm not really sure what to call home at the moment. I could try to change my flight, but it's not really worth the effort. I'll just rough it at the hotel for a couple days."

Greyson makes a low sound that resembles a growl. An angry one at that. "You really suck at doing what's good for you, don't you? So damn stubborn. If you were mine…" He trails off, shaking his head at the idea.

"If I were yours…what?" I'm curious—not necessarily interested, but curious.

"You'd be screaming for mercy at the bite of a cane by now. And you would be *very* obedient afterward."

A shiver ripples over my skin at the thought of Greyson's brutality. It's merely a biological response. My body occasionally uses pain as a coping mechanism. And at the moment, I have a very valid reason to want to escape reality for a bit.

"That doesn't scare you though, does it?" he asks, his voice turning harsh and rough. "No, you're just twisted enough that the idea excites you. Does the idea of me hurting you turn you on, little sub?"

"A-a little." The humiliation of that admission has my face burning.

"Ashford didn't say you were a masochist." He looks at me with ravenous eyes, as though he's just discovered that his favorite dessert has been sitting before him on a silver platter the entire time.

"I'm not," I respond with an edge to my voice. I sound defensive—and perhaps I am. I've just never appreciated having my sexual preferences confined to a small box with a label on it.

"Kara, if you get off on pain, you're a masochist. Like it or not, it's in the definition. If it offends you, take it up with a dictionary." He pauses to look at me, his expression contemplative as he takes in the full force of my scowl. "Why does that bother you?"

"It doesn't." I cross my arms over my chest, and I can just feel the moody teenager vibes emanating from my body.

"Don't lie to me." Greyson grips my elbow and drags me between his open thighs, locking me in place. "Why does being called a masochist bother you?"

I don't want to flesh out my weaknesses with anyone, least of all him. I try pulling away, but he digs his damn knees into my legs until it hurts so much that I go still. Since escape eludes me, I turn to silence instead, jutting out my chin and challenging his stern stare with a glare of my own.

"Answer me, Kara." He's using his Dom voice, and as though dragged forth through dark magic, the words start flowing from my mouth.

"People shouldn't want pain." The explanation comes out in a rush, as though my traitorous tongue couldn't wait to do *Master Greyson's* bidding.

"Why not?" He keeps his expression blank, allowing me to form my own defense without any hint of his own opinions.

"It's not normal," I choke out as embarrassment heats my cheeks. God, having these feelings forced out of me feels like physical contortion, and I am *not* flexible.

Greyson laughs, and I don't know if it should make me feel better or worse. "Little sub, nothing about what we like is normal. That's basically the point. Why would you want to be ordinary when you can be extraordinary?"

"It's more than just being kinky, though." Suddenly, this feels much more complicated as my thoughts leave the perfectly sensible space of my own head. "People shouldn't romanticize pain. It's an insult to every person who has no choice but to endure actual pain in their lives."

"So…you feel guilty for enjoying pain because some people would choose not to feel it?"

"I guess," I answer with a shrug. When he puts it like that, I can't deny that it sounds a bit stupid.

Greyson shakes his head as his knees slacken around my thighs. "Kara, if you think you're a bad person for enjoying a bit of pain, then I must be an absolute villain for the things I like to do."

Now it's my turn to laugh. I suppose if we're two evils, he would be considered the worst of the two. "You make a good point." I take a step back in faux horror. "I should probably go now. Wouldn't want to fall prey to your perverse desires."

"But why bother running when we both know you like it?" he asks, a raptorial gleam in his eyes. His hands wrap around my back, his sudden touch setting fire to the lashes he left across my skin. I whimper in agony, and he flinches back before understanding fills his features. "*Shit*, I forgot about earlier. Sorry."

Somehow, I know his apology is for forgetting to handle me like fragile glass and not for actually whipping me. Because Gavin Greyson would never apologize for gifting someone his pain; he wields his sadism like an artist with a paintbrush, crafting his own masterpiece in flesh and blood. And I can't help but respect his unabashed acceptance of himself in spite of what some might consider flaws. And—it's unfathomable that I'm even considering this— I might be able to learn something from him.

"So, do you always play with masochists at the club? Or sometimes submissives too?" I bite my lip as I try to look nonchalant about his reply.

"Starting out, I played with both. But I quickly realized it took someone interested in pain to withstand the activities I enjoy. If a girl uses her safeword the first time we do a scene—which is completely acceptable when you've reached a limit you're not comfortable with—I know we aren't going to be compatible. Of course, submission and masochism is the best combination. Why, did you want to put in an application?"

He chuckles at the idea before realizing that he's laughing alone while I stare back with determination. "Wait, you can't be serious? Ashford would kill me. So would Satan. Hell, they'd probably do it together and jerk each other off with my blood on their hands." I shoot him a confused look at *that*. "All I'm saying is: do you want me to die? Because that would be the result if you and I went anywhere near Pandemonium together."

"We wouldn't have to do it at the club." My voice is tinged with shame, and I cringe as I realize I've just admitted to wanting to do something with him. Even though it's probably not what he has in mind, I still feel dirty for considering being with another man in any capacity. It feels like betrayal.

"Not at the club, huh?" He sounds angry, and I have no idea why. He stands up from the couch with a force and moves toward me with the pent up energy of a caged predator. Without thinking, I take a couple steps back, spurred by an irrational sense of fear. Or maybe it's rational. At this point, my mind is very confused by how it should react to approaching men with aggression in their gaze. My misguided pussy, to my great dismay, has no conflict at all, and I feel the instant slickness of arousal between my thighs.

In a dance of advance and retreat, Greyson pushes toward me until my back crashes painfully against the firm panes of the floor length window.

I gasp as the ache of pain steals the breath from my lungs, but it doesn't hinder Greyson for a moment. He presses the firmness of his body against me, placing his hands on the glass on either side of my head, effectively trapping me as an unwilling window display for whatever onlookers are walking the streets at two in the morning.

"So is this what you want? You want to keep me as some dirty little secret to fill the hole Cade left in your heart and your cunt?"

"W-what do you mean?" I ask, flustered by his proximity and sudden anger.

Instead of explaining what the hell is going on in his head, Greyson bends down, and I have a split second of warning before his lips are on mine. I shriek against his mouth, protesting as loudly as possible without a voice that I don't want this. His mouth captures my protests, swallowing them down and replacing them with his own tongue. He tastes like chocolate and raspberries, a lingering remnant of the sweet moments we shared less than an hour ago; it's pleasant and welcoming, but its wrong. Because he's not *him*. And no one will ever be him.

I don't want this. I don't want this.

There's no anger to draw on to save me from this situation. No aggression or fight. I'm just exhausted and devastated. The struggle leaves my body, a tear rolls down my cheek, and I wait for the storm to pass. Greyson stills suddenly, his body growing tense before he pulls away. He holds me at a distance, his searing blue eyes studying my face with bafflement.

"Why the fuck are you crying?" he asks finally, his tone cross.

"Because you shoved your tongue down my throat," I snap, finding a little spark of that anger that tends to be my salvation and my curse. I push him away, heading for the elevator as I brush the stupid tears from my face. I take two steps before I feel Greyson's hands on me again, spinning me around to look at him.

"But you wanted me." He sounds confused, as though any contradiction of that fact is impossible.

"No, Greyson, I didn't. Which I would have told you if you had let me come up for air."

"But—you talked about doing things outside of the club."

"If you hadn't decided that tongue fucking was an appropriate substitute for conversation, I would have explained." Jesus, men. Queue eye roll.

"Shit, sorry. Clearly, I misread the room." He lets go of me and starts pacing the room to work off some of his unfulfilled energy. When he's finally calm, he sits back on the couch and looks up at me with the darkness of guilt in his eyes.

"Again, I apologize. I have a complicated history with someone who chose to play in the dark in private while denying and defaming any such interests in public. When you suggested doing something out of sight, I let my imagination get the best of me. I take full responsibility and willingly admit to being a complete dick. You can knee me in the balls or something if it will make you feel better."

"That's an enticing offer. I just might take you up on it one day."

"You've got a sadistic streak tucked inside that tiny little body," he says in a cheerful way that suggests he's giving me a compliment.

"I'm not tiny!" I wear heels for a reason, damnit. "You're just freakishly huge."

"In more ways than one, little sub." He shoots me a wink, which promptly earns him an eye roll. "Sorry, that's enough sexual harassment for one night." He pats the spot beside him. "Come tell me what you were trying to say before thrusting my tongue down your throat cut you off."

I plop down on the couch, and my God it's so soft I could fall asleep. And I am tired, so I better make this quick before I pass out. "I want you to teach me how to be a good submissive." I avoid his gaze, the shame of Cade's words tonight coming back at full force.

"Kara," Greyson gently nudges my chin up so that I'm looking at him, "you are a good submissive."

"No, I'm not." Thankfully, there are no tears this time, just stubbornness and anger.

"*Ma douce*, whatever he told you tonight, he said it because he thought it was for your own good. He was so afraid that you would get hurt beyond repair, that he chose to be the one to hurt you just enough to get you to leave.

He wanted you to be so angry that you would run away from this life and never look back. He wanted you to hate him."

"I could never hate him."

"Then he failed, and he's a complete idiot on top of that."

Well, that I can agree with. "Can you help me?"

"Can I help you *what*? Find pleasure? Find pain? Find a way to make that pompous bastard wish he'd never let you go?"

I pause before answering, not sure how to put this overwhelming feeling of disjointedness into words. The most painful blow Cade dealt before walking out the door. The emptiness that can't be filled. "Can you help me find where I belong?"

Without a word, he pulls me against his chest, his touch tender and soothing. I surrender to the warmth of his embrace, my eyes closing as his hand brushes against my hair softly. He doesn't feel like home—not like Cade—but he feels like sanctuary. And for the moment, it's enough to give in to the lulling call of slumber. Just before my consciousness fades, I hear Greyson's answer against my ear.

"*Oui*, little sub, I can do that."

Chapter 30

CADEN

Jace might have made another move, and I have to deal with the goddamn guilt of being excited by the possibility of having another dead body to deal with. At the moment, I'm grateful for any distraction from thoughts of Kara, even if they come in grim and gory wrappings. And I know I'm a black-hearted bastard for it.

Kara Caine is like an open wound in my chest that I refuse to tend to. I'd rather let it fester and rot on its own so I don't have to handle the finality of it healing over for good and leaving me with nothing but a scar to remember her by. Besides, the pain is comforting in a way.

We got another possible sighting. Two days ago, one of my contacts followed a man fitting Jace's description, tailing his car across four state lines before losing him close to the border of New York. I've been anticipating Kara's university being a potential target. The sick fuck has tied every kill to Kara—it only makes sense that he would try to wreak havoc on her present as well as her past.

As a precaution, I've had the university watched. This morning, we got a sighting on campus. A girls dormitory on Dillon Drive. If it's Jace, then a dead girl is certain to follow soon after.

Finn and I got on the next flight out. He didn't exactly come willingly to help me investigate another potential murder, but I can be rather persuasive when I want to be. Ortega hates flying, so he volunteered to keep things locked down at the manor. Declan and Brax are useless when it comes to gore, so Finn gets to play my knight in shining armor.

"Remind me again why I'm here?" Finn grumbles as I drive the rental Audi to the university. We're ten minutes out from the girls dormitory.

"Because you love me," I goad, swearing when a car pulls out in front of me. This city is too bloody crowded.

"I'm fairly certain my love is conditioned on not being dragged out to creepy murder sights that will give me nightmares."

"Don't worry, I can chase the nightmares away," I coddle with a pat on his leg.

"Fuck off," he bites back, shoving my hand away. "I'm being serious. I can't handle this shit."

"I don't recall you ever being one to shy away from a bit of blood."

"Well it's different if I'm the one drawing it," he answers with a scowl. "I don't have the stomach for murder. I can't even watch scary movies."

It's true—he hates scary movies. His brother Cillian and I would always take the piss out of him for it.

"There's a good chance we won't find anything, so don't get your knickers in a twist."

Finn doesn't look convinced. "If there's a body, you fucking owe me."

"Fair enough," I agree. I pull into the lot in front of the dormitory and try to find a spot to park. It's crowded, and it takes several turns before we get a free space.

Finn gets out of the car, slams his door, and storms toward the building. "Let's get this shit over with," he mutters from ahead of me.

We're so close to Kara's office that I could probably catch a glimpse of her through the window if I tried. I tamper down the weakness in my heart that begs me to try. I added more security to her building on campus and her apartment. We've got cameras on both, not that I would use them to spy on her now that she's no longer mine. Well, probably not. I've always been deficient in my appreciation of ethics. At least I know she's safe, and that's all that matters at the moment.

We go to the front desk and are greeted by a girl in her very early twenties with blue and black hair and a nose ring. Her black nails tap loudly on the desk as she looks us up and down. Clearly, no one ever taught this generation that it's rude to stare. "Can I help you," she asks finally, her voice low and flirtatious.

"Yes, I'm...here to see my niece." Shit, am I even old enough to have a college-age niece?

"Cool," she answers, not batting an eye. I'm assuming anyone over thirty looks old to a twenty year old. "What's her name? I just need to verify."

Bloody hell. In my head, I start rifling through basic girl names. "Brittany," I answer, my voice smooth and compelling. I hear Finn chuckle from behind me.

"Oh my god, you're Brittany's uncle?" The girl brightens immediately. "I'm Isla; me and Brittany roomed together freshman year."

"Isla—of course, Brittany has mentioned you a few times," I lie through my teeth. This is already taking longer than expected.

"She never said her uncle was British and so..." she lets her gaze slide over me, "hot." Her eyes drift to Finn, and her overt interest suddenly turns to disappointment. "Wait, are you gay?" she asks with a pout on her black lips, looking between the two of us.

Given the look of things, it's a fair accusation. Finn denies with a too quick "no" at the same time I answer "sometimes" with a shrug.

"Awesome," the girl replies with a sultry lick of her lips while she focuses her gaze very obviously on the lower half of my body. Apparently, being bi wins me bonus points.

"Britt is expecting us, so if you could key us in?" I gesture toward the locked doors, trying to cut things short.

"Oh yeah, sorry." She rips the lanyard with a key card from around her neck and hands it to me. "Here, take mine. Just make sure you give it back to me later," she adds with a wink.

"Perfect. Thank you, Isla." I give her a warm smile before motioning for Finn to follow me toward the doors. She could be an unexpected problem. If there *is* a body somewhere in this dormitory, the girl on desk duty is definitely going to be able to give an accurate description of two unusual men turning up for visitation. Especially if sodding Brittany doesn't get a visit from her uncle.

"Jesus," Finn swears when we've made it beyond the closed doors and start searching the halls for anything unusual. "Do you always cause such a stir amongst the youth of tomorrow?" he asks with a scoff.

"I wouldn't know," I bite back, checking the doors as I pass. "I generally try to avoid them."

The first floor is clear. So is the second. When we get to the third floor, I can see a door left slightly ajar at the end of the hall. Finn and I exchange a loaded glance. It could be anything. Speaking from experience, college kids are lazy wankers. Anyone could have forgotten to shut their door as they popped out for their morning classes. But I have a gnawing feeling in the pit of my stomach that this is something much more sinister than forgetfulness.

I lead the way down the hall, Finn following close behind. When I get to the open door, Finn takes a step back. "I'm not going in there," he declares with his hands raised. "It's either a fucking murder scene—which is terrifying. Or it's a just barely *not*-teenage girl's bedroom—which is also terrifying. I'll wait in the damn hall."

"Suit yourself, coward," I call over my shoulder as I reach for the door.

"And if this fucks me up for life, you're paying for my therapy, you bastard."

"I can afford it," I answer back with a grim smirk. It must seem terribly morbid to be making light in a situation like this, but having a go at Finn is the only thing keeping me from spiraling at the moment. I'm so goddamn sick of being forced to witness what my stupidity has caused another girl who never had a fighting chance. I feel guilty enough that if they tried to lock *me* up for these murders, I'd probably let them.

Taking a deep breath, I open the door. Any false hope that had been burgeoning dies a cruel death in my chest as I take in the sight on the bed.

It's another girl. Another dead ringer for Kara. She looks barely eighteen. The youngest one yet.

I step closer to the bed, covering my mouth with the back of my hand to keep from getting sick on the dormitory tile. The cause of death is nauseating and obvious. The blonde's head has nearly been severed from her neck. The fact that there are still ligaments and bits of skin just barely stringing her body together is somehow even more gruesome than finding a fully decapitated head beside a body.

Like the last girl, her clothes have been removed. I'm overwhelmed with the urge to cover her nakedness with the blanket on the bed to keep her from the cold. I know it won't do her any good now. I scan her body for any clues, any details that might be new. There don't seem to be any injuries other than the gaping hole in her neck, the only blood stemming from the spray of her sliced carotid arteries. There is a sparkly, pink sign with the name ASTRID taped to the wall that's covered in blood. It's probably *Astrid's* blood. Somehow, knowing her name makes it worse.

Beside her body is what appears to be a very old edition of The Canterbury Tales. I can't inspect it further here, but I'll scan the police report later for more details. Depending on how rare the edition is, I might be able to find a purchase trail.

I pull out my mobile and ring Taylor. He's probably come to dread seeing my name come up on his screen. "It's Ashford," I answer unnecessarily when the call picks up after the first ring. "We've got another girl. The bastard crossed state lines. This one is in New York. I'll send you the details. This one is…" I stare at what remains of the young girl on the bed, "fucking sick."

I shut the door on my way out; I don't want any of the students to walk in on their classmate in such a state. That sort of thing will never leave them.

"Well?" Finn asks anxiously, jumping to his feet as I walk over to him.

"Good call on staying in the hall," I answer, keeping any details intentionally vague. It's enough for him to get the point.

"*Christ*," he swears, looking ill just at the thought of it. "What a sick piece of shit. How did you not know you had a psycho working for you for half a decade?"

I shrug. "It wasn't relevant information at the time."

"That's pretty goddamn cold, Ashford." He glares at me, and I scowl right back. We're both unfeeling bastards on the gray side of morality, but I'll admit I'm the worst of us two.

"Yes, I'm well-aware," I sigh, backing down from the challenge in his eyes. I don't need a fight right now when I already feel like shit.

I didn't question Jace's methods until they put my girl in danger. And I know that makes me just as despicable as him.

The desk is thankfully empty when we exit the doors. I leave Isla's key on the desk, and Finn and I make a run for the car, both of us more than eager to get the fuck out of here.

A somber silence hangs in the air on the drive back to the airport. There aren't really any great conversation topics for post-witnessing a murder, but the silence suits us both just fine. It gives me a moment to work through what the fuck to do about Jace.

He's evolving—that much is obvious. He's no longer bound by state lines, so who knows where or whom his next target will be. Or when he'll finally get bold enough to make a play for Kara. We have to be sure we're ready for when he does.

It's sheer luck that Kara hates to watch the news and is adverse to technology. It's the only way I've managed to keep her in the dark about the murders. But this—this will be all over campus. Probably all over the goddamn country. People get antsy when pretty, young girls are found decapitated on college campuses.

Kara will find out. I just have to make sure she doesn't discover this whole production is a sick pantomime of her own murder. If they release the information about The Canterbury Tales, she'll know. Without a doubt, she'll know. I just have to pray the NYPD chooses to keep some details out of the press.

It's all connected to her.

Darnell Road.

Ellington Court.

Arkady Lane.

Dillon Drive.

Four girls. Four murders. Four Chaucers with a missing page accompanying the bodies. Four periods of Kara's life. Will there be more? Will we ever catch him before it's too late? When will it end? I'm left only with questions. Questions with no answers.

But I know this—more death will come.

Chapter 31

CADEN

Finn and I turn to our usual solace to keep from dealing with the shitty mess of reality. It's a talent that we both learned from our fathers, though mine was infinitely more skilled in the art of drinking himself into oblivion.

"You better stop now if you don't want me to have to carry your drunk ass to bed," Finn scolds as I pour another tall glass of bourbon. The bottle is almost empty by the looks of it, although to be fair, I am seeing double of the bottle, so my sight isn't much to go off at the moment.

"Don't be a twat," I mutter as I bring the glass to my lips, savoring the slight burn. Given the carnage I witnessed this afternoon, I think a little overindulgence is allowed.

This has become a nightly ritual since Kara left. Or I left her. Either way—she's gone, and bourbon is my medication of choice to soothe the perpetual pain in my chest. Unfortunately, the numbing effects of the alcohol are only temporary. In the morning, I wake up with the same heavy ache in my rib cage and an even worse ache in my head. Finn is a good mate and keeps my misery company most nights.

"I apologize for trying to keep you semi-conscious. Remind me to leave you on the damn floor when you pass out from being so hammered." He storms toward my desk, snatches up my very expensive bottle of Willet's and throws it in the bin with a jarring clatter.

"What the fuck Finnian?" I seethe as I reach for the bottle.

"I thought you weren't going to do this shit after Alister?" he asks with an arched brow, his face marked with disappointment.

The sobering mention of my brother is enough to have me pull away from the bin and lean back heavily in my chair. I did promise myself I would stop overindulging after my brother succumbed to his addiction. My father will too eventually, though his demise seems regrettably slower. I suppose you could say alcoholism runs in the family. If nothing else, it's a side effect of being wealthy and without an occupation or purpose to keep your hands busy. The English aristocracy has born and bred at least a thousand years worth of alcoholics, not all of them nearly as closeted as they are today.

I try to temper the urges as much as possible—a drink or two at most—but with Kara gone, I find myself giving in to my own weaknesses more than I should. Old habits die hard, I suppose.

"Thanks for the reminder," I respond through gritted teeth, not sounding nearly as grateful as I actually am. "Since the subject of family is apparently on the table this evening, how's *your brother*? Still alive, so presumably better than mine."

Finn scowls at me. He hates talking about his family; there are wounds there that will never quite heal. "Cillian's great," he answers, the sarcasm in his voice obvious. "*More* than great, apparently. He's getting married."

I can't hide my surprise. The four of us were close more than a decade ago—Finn, Alister, Cillian, and me. After Alister died four years ago, Finn and I grew even closer, but his twin brother drifted away. Cillian's always had his own shit to deal with; when he lost his best mate, he went off the deep end. We didn't hear from him for over a year. Not even his mum, and both twins have a soft spot for Talulah. We all thought Cillian had been dead too. He turned up eventually, but he was different. Sharper. Edgy. Now, he and Finn can't be in the same room without fighting unless they're putting on a good show for their mum.

I never expected Cillian to be the marrying sort. I didn't expect it of any of us really. We've all been damaged by the less than happy marriages of our parents that all ended in divorce. As most do these days. I didn't think any of us saw the point in tying ourselves down to someone we might hate in a few years. Somehow bloody *Cillian* is the first one to turn conventional.

"That's a shock," I retort finally. "Did they ask you to officiate?" I smirk up at him, appreciating the opportunity to give him grief over his failed attempt at joining the priesthood.

Finn did one year at seminary before deciding God wasn't worth giving up pussy for the rest of his life. It's a fair choice, but we still like to take the piss out of him every now and then for nearly becoming a priest. Now that he's used his love of theology to create an elaborate sex club and calls himself Satan, the whole thing feels very full circle.

Finn laughs loudly, tipsy enough that the dig doesn't smart too badly. "Haven't heard that one in a while," he says as he plops into the leather chair beside me. "And it's even worse—he's asked me to be his best man."

"How is that worse than having to wear a dress over your celibate cock as you join together two people who promise to only fuck each other for the rest of their miserable lives?" I scoff.

"True. They're equal, I suppose." Finn has worse commitment issues than anyone I know. It would be a miracle for anyone to get him to attend a wedding, even his brother.

I shake my head and pour myself a glass of water because that's apparently the only thing I'm allowed to drink for the rest of tonight. "So, have you met the girl?"

"I have." Finn takes a drink of his *bourbon* because double standards are clearly in fashion. "She's nice, a little bland though. She looks at Cillian like he's hung the goddamn moon; it's a bit sickening to watch. She was married before, but her husband died in some freak accident. She's got a little brat too—kid acts like the marriage is the end of the goddamn world. Cil is gonna have his hands full playing the new daddy." Finn takes another drink. "Oh, and speaking of, father dearest is going to be in attendance at the blessed nuptials."

I wince at the new information. Finn hates his dad as much as any neglected, passive-aggressively abused son could. Now that Finn is old enough to stand up for himself, things quickly turn atomic anytime he and

Magnus Holt share breathing space.

"I'm sorry," I commiserate. "Is your mum going too?"

"Of course," he answers with a short laugh. "She wouldn't miss her precious boy's first wedding. But she's better at dealing with Magnus than I am."

It's true. Talulah is as close to a saint as a mother could be. Some days I wish she were mine, although I'm sure she'd be happy to call me hers already. She's known me a third of my life.

"I'm sure it will be a riotous affair," I retort, raising my glass of water in a mock cheer.

"Don't celebrate yet, you bastard, you're invited too. I'm sure he would have tried to make you stand up at the altar with him too, but his soon to be wife doesn't have many close friends, and he wanted to keep the bridal party even."

"Brilliant," I quip with an eye roll. "When's the happy day so I can mark my calendar?"

Finn throws back his glass. "Sometime in June. I think they're trying to be as traditional as fucking possible. Black tie. Wear a damn tux."

"I'll see what I have in my closet," I answer with a smirk.

"Jesus, who'd have thought Cil would be the first one to bite the marriage bullet?"

"And which of us would you have picked? Certainly not yourself?"

"*Fuck*, no. I can barely commit to an apartment, let alone a woman. And for the rest of your life? That shit is terrifying." He sets his glass on the desk and looks at me thoughtfully. "No, I expected it to be you."

I down the rest of my glass, hating the fact that it's damned water and not something stronger. I slam my glass down beside his.

"Yeah," I reply with a heavy sigh, thinking of Kara and all the ways our futures will never intertwine. I feel as though I've been robbed of something I never truly knew I wanted until I had to let it go. "For the briefest, fleeting moment, I thought it might be me too."

Chapter 32

KARA

I'm fine. Really, I am. I get up every morning. I go to work. I eat. I write. I read. I sleep. I survive.

But they're just motions—socially determined gestures that constitute a healthy human life. I go through the empty cycles of daily routine because I know it's what is expected of me. If living is determined as having a beating heart, lungs that breathe, and a brain that processes thought, then I am in perfect order. But everything else beyond that is missing.

I'm being over-dramatic, I suppose. Greyson helps. A lot. After we spent the night together on his couch—platonically—we sorted out the details of our unusual relationship. There's no sex. At all. I can't contemplate giving that part of myself to anyone other than Cade.

I was shocked that Greyson actually accepted my no-sex clause, but I guess he has enough submissives at the club who can get him off. There's no jealousy on my part because I've never needed Greyson in a sexual capacity. What he does offer is stability—order through dominance.

If it wasn't for him telling me to eat at the appropriate times, get out of the house for a short walk every afternoon, take a moment to do something enjoyable, I would have a much harder time forcing myself to do it. He's the one thread of sanity keeping me from falling into a sandpit of depression.

It seems I've forgotten how to function without a demanding Dom breathing down my neck every second of the day. Really, I should be in therapy dealing with whatever codependent shit that is, but Greyson's methods will have to do for the moment.

It's Friday. An unassuming day by all accounts. A welcome day for most as it signals the end of another work week. But for me, Friday is the day I gave to Cade when I accepted this job. And it's the day I've most looked forward to every week for the past five months.

But today, for the first time, there won't be any Cade.

I try to focus on my annotations, but I can't seem to form a useful thought today. My concentration has been in shambles since I walked into my office this morning and found a goddamn black box lying on top of my comfort read of Jane Eyre as though it belonged there. Which it *fucking* didn't. I was fully resolved not to open it purely on principle, but that only lasted until lunchtime when my damn curiosity got the better of me.

When I opened the lid of the box, I laughed out loud at the twisted irony, not entirely sure whether Cade meant the gift to be kind or cruel. It was a necklace. A dainty, silver necklace with a little star in the middle. And a glaring reminder that my neck is bare without Cade's collar. It took me a few minutes to decide whether I should shove it in the drawer with the others or put it on just for a moment to see if it would help ease the hollowness in my chest just a little bit to have the last thing Cade ever gave me close to my heart.

In the end, I fastened the necklace around my neck, but the hollowness never faded.

A drop of wetness lands on a page of Bram Stoker's Dracula, turning a few of the words into an ugly, blurred blob. *Shit.* I realize I'm crying as I try to read through the sudden blurriness of my vision. I hate crying, and I've already wasted too many damn tears on the sorry bastard.

A bit of white waves in the corner of my vision, and I turn to see Grant holding out a handkerchief. I can't help but laugh when I see the blue W embroidered in the middle. I used to hide one exactly like it under my pillow when I was a starry-eyed eighteen year old who thought she was in love for the first time. I gratefully accept it and dab at my eyes and wipe the embarrassing trail of snot running out of my nose.

The soft material still smells like clary sage and tobacco, just like I remember. Nostalgia floods my senses as I remember what it felt like to be an innocent girl who thought a man would pull stars from the sky just to fill her world with light. Now I'm jaded enough to know that the only stars men bring are supernovas that disrupt the entire order of the universe.

"Still keeping hankies in your pocket in case a girl needs a shoulder to cry on, I see," I tease as I hand the tear and snot soaked cloth back to him. To my surprise, he takes the filthy thing and tucks it back into his top coat pocket. "Your tricks are getting as old as you are, Dr. Grant."

"I think you'll find I've aged as well as a barrel of good, Kentucky bourbon, Miss Caine," Grant quips, speaking as a proud descendant of Lexington.

Fuck, my heart hurts. I can't escape the memory of Cade attached to that name. It was one of his favorite torments. Grant must read the sudden devastation in my eyes, so he pulls his chair around to the other side of my desk and sits beside me.

"What's wrong, little Karenina?" he asks, resting his hand on my knee. "What's made my strong girl cry?"

The comfort of his words and his touch are so familiar to the recesses of my memory that if I closed my eyes, we could be sitting in his office in Chicago ten years earlier, rather than in my office in New York. The unexpected intimacy of the moment makes me spill more of my personal troubles than I usually would.

"Remember that British lord I told you about? The one I said made me believe in happy ever afters for the first time?"

"I do," Grant responds, his expression thoughtful. "I spoke to him once when he called and you were out of the office. He was a touch on the taciturn side, if I'm honest."

Well there's one mystery solved. Grant's the fucking tattle-tale who got me whipped until I passed out at Pandemonium. If he'd done me the favor of mentioning that he spoke to Cade from my phone that day, I could have at least confessed my sins and pleaded for mercy *before* Cade brought out the damn whip.

"Yes, he can be a little harsh." Understatement of the century. "Anyway, he's gone. And I currently have as much faith in happy endings as Juliet searching for something sharp and deadly."

"I'm sorry," Grant says, his thumb rubbing against my inner thigh as his hand moves a little further up my leg. I allow it because *saying* it makes me uncomfortable would actually be even more uncomfortable than just letting him keep stroking me. It's probably just a force of habit anyway. A reflex of having spent many years confiding in each other while sitting in his office just like this.

"You always were a secret romantic, you know," he continues, his thumb brushing across the thin material of my dress.

"I was not," I scoff, shifting in my seat. "I've always loved tragedy."

He laughs sardonically. "You've always *professed* to love tragedy. But in your heart, you've always been too optimistic regarding love."

I swallow hard, the reference to *that* word haunting me. The word I felt with the depth of a thousand oceans but never had the bravery to put into words. And now it's too late. The weight of that missed opportunity weighs heavy on my chest until I struggle for breath. "And what do you know of my heart?" I ask, hoping that continuing to talk will ease some of the sadness poisoning my bloodstream.

He smiles, the same dazzling smile that would turn me into a lump of malleable clay as an undergrad. "I used to know a great deal about it," he responds in a deep voice that seems taut with expectation. Or anticipation.

And it is in this exact moment that I realize our conversation has distracted me from his hand resting right below the junction of my thighs. "Yes, the operative word being *used*. I'm certainly not that girl anymore." I reach down to remove his presumptuous damn hand, but I'm stopped with a firm grip on my arm. I look up at him in shock. "What exactly are you doing?" I gasp, trying to jerk my hand away.

He holds my arm back with one hand while his other slips up a few more inches to palm my pussy. "Nothing that I haven't done to you a hundred times before," he says in a voice dripping with salacious intent, and I think I might gag on my own disgust.

I struggle uselessly against him, my body telling me to fight even as my mind warns I won't be able to win in a battle of brute strength. So I go for the least ladylike attack in my disposal. I spit in his fucking eyes.

"Fuck," he seethes, momentarily removing both of his hands so he can wipe my spit from his face. What a shame I've already dirtied his handkerchief.

Taking advantage of the distraction, I shove back my chair and bolt upright. If I'm going to be dealing with handsy dickheads who think they can touch whatever they want, I'm not going to take it while sitting on my ass. "Do not think because you were my first over a decade ago that it somehow entitles you to a lifetime of privileges. Because it doesn't," I snarl as I inch toward the closed door of my office, anxiously waiting for him to pounce before I get there.

Grant lunges toward me, his handsome features twisted with fury as his green eyes glitter with vengeance. "If you take one step closer, I'll scream and bring the whole English department running," I warn, continuing to creep toward the door.

"And what would you tell them?" Grant asks with a cruel sneer. "It was an accidental brush of my hand. And you're a lowly, limited-contract librarian trying to get some attention by crying wolf and accusing an esteemed and world-renowned member of the academic community." He takes a half-step forward, and I take a half-step back. "You'd be metaphorically burned at the stake like the seductive little witch you are."

Rage simmers beneath my skin at his fucking audacity. "I don't give a *shit* about how well-known you are. *Sexual assault* isn't permissible under any circumstances. If I were to report what you just did, you'd be finished."

I can see the confidence in Grant's eyes waver ever so slightly. He thought he could exert his power and influence to manipulate his way out of the mess he created with his own arrogance. Unfortunately for him, I have an intimate acquaintance with power-play courtesy of Caden Ashford. And it's not about who's strongest. It's about knowing and exploiting someone's weak points.

"Public opinion has a low tolerance for men with groping hands at the moment," I declare as I keep moving backward. "If you touch me again, I will destroy you."

Grant glares at me with murder in his eyes as his mouth twists into an expression that is ugly and cruel. He's no longer the attentive professor who fed my need for love as a young student who just lost both of her parents. This is the monster that has always lurked beneath his skin. Since he's a predator, it's only fitting that he look the part.

"I'd advise you not to make an enemy of me, little Karenina. If you do, things won't end any better for you than they did for her," he threatens with a sharp sting of venom in his voice as he stalks toward me. "Didn't you ever wonder about why I chose to endear you as Tolstoy's most tragic heroine?"

Of course, I pondered the nickname countless occasions over the years, but this is hardly the time for endearments or Tolstoy, so I remain silent.

Like a proper narcissist obsessed with the sound of his own voice, Grant continues without my participation. "It's because your heart is drawn to chaos just like hers was. And one day, the violent consequences of your lust for ruin will trample your fiery spirit with the force of a freight train on a collision course. And then you'll be nothing."

His words are cruel, and they sink into my heart just as deep as he intends them to. But this isn't the moment to be focusing on my gravitation toward all the things that are sure to wreck me. This is about getting Grant's depraved ass out of my personal space.

"I'd advise *you* not to insult me with thinly veiled threats masquerading as allusions and allegory," I retort. The door is almost within reach. "I'm used to big, bad men making threats they intend to deliver on, but you're not one of them. You're just a small, pathetic excuse for a man who likes to prey on the innocence and naivety of others to make yourself feel important."

Grant opens his mouth to hurl his own insults, but I cut him off with a warning wave of my hand. "I've seen Cade's file on you. A little bit of skilled hacking revealed that I wasn't the first student you seduced. I wasn't even your last. I was simply your *type*—barely legal, lonely, astute but desperate for affirmation—and a name on an extensive list of girls you used for your own ego."

I consider whether gaining some sort of closure is worth exposing this piece of my heart that used to belong to him. And finally decide that it is. "I used to look up to you like a damn god. You were fucking Apollo, and all I wanted to do was sit at your feet and bask in your light when you chose to give it." I close my eyes at the painful memory of what it felt like to lose such an influencing, all-consuming presence from my life.

When I open my eyes, the pain I held onto for Dr. Grant Westford fades away for good. "Now, I just see a flawed mortal of flesh and blood and an unremarkably average-sized cock. So if anyone is *nothing* in this situation, it's you."

Grant's fists clench at his sides as he struggles to come to terms with being in a situation where he can't force his own, preferred outcome. "Watch yourself, Kara," he says finally, his voice disturbingly calm. "You're on your own now, remember? He left you. So no hero is going to come save you if I choose to take what used to be mine."

I reach behind my back until my hand lands on the handle of my office door. With a small burst of victory, I turn the handle and fling the door open. "I don't need a fucking hero, you chauvinist twat. I can save my goddamn self. Now get the fuck out of my office before I have security throw you out."

"Careful, little Karenina. Ruin might come sooner than you think." The ominous threat hangs heavy in the air as Grant turns and walks out the door.

Fuck, I hate men.

Chapter 33

KARA

Non-consensual pussy grabbing seems like a reasonable excuse to take a break from work, so I leave my office early. I'm still left with the complications of today being Friday, Cade being gone, and my mental fortitude being on the brink of collapse, but at least I don't have to sit in a small room that reeks of clary sage and near assault.

The weather is brisk but dry as I take a third lap around the woody park beside the university. The exercise has given me plenty of time to think, but I'm not sure that being left alone with my thoughts is exactly what I want at the moment. In fact, having no thoughts at all would be far preferable.

I'm terrified to go back to my apartment. A few boxes of my things were sent from the manor this week, but I haven't unpacked them. I can't bear the finality of what they represent. I've never spent the weekend alone at my apartment. It feels lonely enough when I come home late, cook a quick meal, and crawl into bed. I've never been forced to bask in the emptiness. If I'm left to the solitude of my thoughts, I might drown beneath the flood of emotions I've spent the whole week barricading against with work.

The tickets to Chicago are still booked; Cade had Declan purchase flights for every weekend through the end of the semester. I guess he overestimated how long his attachment to me would last.

Contrary to Grant's accusations, I am not a happily ever after kind of girl. Give me *Tess of the D'Urbervilles* or *Madame Bovary* over *Pride and*

Prejudice any day. I prefer stories that have a little more depth than the fairytale endings, and I expected nothing more from my real life experiences. But there was something about Cade that had foreign concepts like *forever* flitting around in my head.

I bite my lip as I pick up my phone and contemplate calling the one person I know can make the emptiness go away. At least for a little bit. We've talked every day since the night Cade left. Well, *talked* is perhaps a stretch. He sends me orders throughout the day—which I obey. And the occasional, "Do any high ledges look dangerously appealing at the moment?" To which I reply, "Not yet, although I do prefer to take my suicidal strolls at the bottom of rivers rather than rooftops. Scared of heights." I was thoroughly scolded for that one, but a Woolf reference is always worth it.

Greyson can give me the distraction I need, but I have to ask for it. And there is very little I detest more than having to ask for help. Deciding my dignity can't possibly be any more decimated, I type a quick message and hit send.

> **Me: Hey...Are you free tonight?**

No going back now. I worry my bottom lip as I watch those three little dots appear on the screen far quicker than I expected. Maybe he'll turn me down, and I won't have to follow through.

> **Master Chef: I think I can make some time for you, little sub.**
>
> **Master Chef: What did you have in mind?**

Shit. I expected to at least have to beg a little or something. The fact that he's so eager leaves me suspicious. The sadist has probably been planning some unique form of torture this entire week. I take a deep breath and offer myself up like a lamb for slaughter. Because for some reason, this kinky little lamb likes to play with things that are sharp and dangerous.

> **Me: Pain play? I need to get out of my own head for a little. Hurt me, please.**

I don't want to think about what happened with Grant today. I don't want to bring it up to Greyson, even though I'm pretty sure he'd be more than happy to march over to Grant's apartment and beat his ass in the name of my honor. I just want to feel something that clears the darkness from my head and lets me have some peace for a moment.

Greyson's response is instant, as I knew it would be. He's like a shark smelling blood in the water.

> **Master Chef:** My three favorite words…
>
> **Master Chef:** When and where?

I have to take a moment to consider his question. My heart twists a little as I realize Pandemonium will no longer be an option. Cade explicitly stated that I wouldn't be welcome at the kink club—a place where I had finally started to feel comfortable and accepted. Not that I would want to chance running into Cade playing with someone else. The thought sends ice water shooting through my veins, leaving me with a sharp pain in my chest.

No, Pandemonium definitely isn't an option. Would it be too forward to suggest his place? I know he's got the appropriate equipment stashed away somewhere in his apartment. Maybe I just need to find his library. Shit, and there's another paper cut to my already bandaged heart. I need to stop fucking thinking.

> **Me:** I'm flying into Chicago at 6:00, and I booked a hotel downtown. Maybe meet around 8:00?

That's open ended. Leave the location deciding up to him.

> **Master Chef:** I'll pick you up from your hotel at 7pm.
>
> **Master Chef:** Don't eat anything before.

The inherent bossiness of his tone sounds incredibly familiar. Are all Doms like this?

> **Me:** It's okay; I can just take an Uber.

I don't want him thinking that he has to take care of me. It's bad enough that I've dragged him into becoming my deranged form of break-up therapy.

> **Master Chef:** Not up for discussion, Kara.

Uh-oh, he used my actual name. I must be in trouble. The thought sends an unwanted rush of heat straight to my core. Jesus, Cade did a number on me.

> Master Chef: I'm taking you to dinner. And I'm driving. Send me the hotel address.

Lashing out against my stupid pussy and its ill-timed lubrication, I shut Greyson down with cold precision.

> Me: You don't need to do the whole wine and dine thing. This isn't a date. It's a mutually beneficial exchange.
>
> Master Chef: Call it what you will, you're still going to dinner.

Why is he trying so hard? He knows that he's a rebound at worst and a friend with kinky benefits at best. And neither of those require taking a girl to dinner.

> Me: I'm not going to sleep with you, Grey. No sex. Just pain.
>
> Master Chef: Okay.

He's fucking with me.

> Me: I mean it. That's my only offer. So you don't need to try so hard with the romantic nonsense.
>
> Master Chef: Trust me, there will be nothing romantic about tonight.
>
> Master Chef: Send me the address and be ready at 7pm.

You'd think I would have learned by now that you can't negotiate with a Dom.

> Me: Fine.

That's the most cooperation he's getting out of me.

> Master Chef: Watch the attitude, or your ass will pay for it later.

Ha, I've heard that one before. And most definitely felt it afterward.

> **Me:** Yes, sir.

I hope he can hear the sarcasm ringing in my words as I send him the hotel address.

> **Master Chef:** I prefer Master Greyson.

I choke a little when I read his reply. Apparently, Cade's pompous bastardry has been topped.

> **Me:** ...you must be joking...

> **Master Chef:** Does that sound like the sort of thing I'd joke about, Kara?

> **Me:** One can only hope...

I ignore the incoming dings from my phone and head back to start packing up my desk. It's early, but everyone in the department seems to head out early when the weekend is calling. I might as well join them. And I need to pack a few things before I leave for the flight I had no intention of taking when I got up this morning.

Leaving early *and* making impromptu visits to someone who is not my Dom or my boyfriend. My, I'm full of surprises today. I check my phone one more time before turning on the car to let it warm and let the windshield defrost.

Shit. I swallow thickly as I look down at Greyson's texts. I'm going to need a fresh pair of panties by the time I get home.

> **Master Chef:** Well, why don't you test me and find out? This is all in good fun. But if you disobey me, I will punish you. And I'll make sure you don't enjoy a second of it.

> **Master Chef:** Self-destructive enough to earn a punishment from a sadist, Kara?

The sensible part of me is terrified and wants to do anything to avoid incurring the wrath of a well-known sadist. The danger-drawn part of me wants to see how far I can push him. Surprisingly, common sense wins the day.

Me: No, Master Greyson.

Master Chef: Good girl.

As usual, those two words obliterate my insides. I suppose it doesn't really matter who says them. I've basically had a praise kink my whole life.

Master Chef: I'll see you tonight.

Master Chef: Wear red.

Chapter 34

KARA

I don't have anything red. The wardrobe I brought with me from the manor consists of sensible, professional layers in neutral colors with the occasional floral print thrown in for the fun of it. I didn't feel the need to bring anything seductive. And I certainly didn't bring the slutty red number that I know is one of Cade's favorites.

With an hour to spare before needing to leave for the airport, I make the very rash decision of going on a shopping spree, purely because I'm too much of a coward to risk a punishment from Greyson over dress code. Thankfully, there are plenty of shops by the university, even if they are out of my price range. I'm a little embarrassed to say that I've gotten used to such luxuries after spending a year as Lord Caden Ashford's submissive. In fact, his black Amex is still sitting in my purse. I wonder if he remembered to have Declan cancel it.

To my surprise, I find the perfect dress in the very first store. It's stunning—deep red silk that drapes down to the floor, backless and sleeveless with a high, braided neckline, a braided band at the waist, and the bodice is made of three vertical panels that split in the middle to show a glimpse of skin. It feels very romantic, but in a Romeo and Juliet sort of way. It fits perfectly, apart from being too long, but that's nothing that my highest pair of heels can't fix.

I have a small crisis of conscience when I slide the black card with Cade's name on it across the counter at the register. But my petty need for a little revenge wins out. If the card doesn't work, then there's no harm done. If it does—well, the bastard should have remembered to be more diligent when breaking up with someone who has access to his bank account.

The card goes through. And I have a new, very expensive dress courtesy of Caden Ashford. It's a shame he'll never get to see it on. I know money isn't supposed to buy happiness, but when it's your ex's money, it can get you pretty damn close.

◆

Shivers wrack my body as I wait by the hotel's revolving doors and watch for Greyson's unmistakable red eyesore of a car. One little detail I'd forgotten when picking out the "perfect dress" was that it was winter—and it's sleeveless. I didn't want to ruin the elegance of the dress with my everyday winter coat, so I went without. Clearly, my body is protesting my decision to sacrifice comfort for the sake of being fashionable.

To my great relief, I am saved at exactly 7:02 when Greyson's Maserati pulls up. Rather than texting or getting out of the car and greeting me like a gentleman, he revs the engine twice as a signal for me to get my ass outside. Rolling my eyes, I wince against the sting of the winter air as I head toward the door he's reached over and opened. I slide in, reveling in the warmth of the heated leather seat against my skin. As soon as my door is shut, Greyson is flying down the drive.

"Where's your coat?" he asks without taking his eyes off of the road, his tone clearly disapproving.

"I—forgot it," I fib, fidgeting with my nails and hoping he doesn't press any further. Which, of course, he does.

"You *forgot* your coat?" His hands clench against the leather of the steering wheel. "In winter? I thought you were supposed to be smart."

"I *am* smart, thank you very much."

He scoffs. "Clearly. You're so smart that if I kicked you out of the car and made you walk back, you'd freeze to death in the first ten minutes."

"That's a highly unrealistic scenario," I retort back with a scowl.

"Keep talking back, and I can make it very realistic."

I settle into angry silence because I don't know him well enough to tell if he's serious.

He smiles in victory. "Good girl. Maybe I'll let you off with a spanking instead of abandoning you to the elements."

I bite back the snarky comments that instantly blaze to the surface and glare at the side of his head. I'm startled when he turns toward me for the first time tonight and catches me mid death stare. I look away as heat floods my cheeks. I guess I'm probably getting that spanking.

"You look stunning," he says, his tone warm and doting. I look up at his bright blue eyes, and realize he means it. His praise sets my insides twirling with chaotic glee.

"Thank you," I answer, blushing even deeper. "You don't look so bad yourself." As usual, he's dressed in full black, looking very much like the goth kid in school if they grew up to be absurdly wealthy with high-end fashion tastes. Even if it is a touch too severe, the black suits him, highlighting the startling icy-blue of his eyes.

"Glad you approve," he says with a laugh. Silence fills the car as Greyson studies the road and I study him, absentmindedly looking for flaws. I find none.

"So, why the red?" I ask in an effort to break the silence. I twist the fabric of my dress around my fingers, feeling self-conscious of having to make small talk with a man for the first time in a while. It's starting to feel like a date, and after a year of being in a committed relationship, I hate the strangeness of this unfamiliar territory.

"It's my favorite color." He says it like it should be obvious.

"I would have thought it was black," I scoff, pointedly looking him up and down.

"Red is my favorite color on subs," he clarifies. "It gives me a reference to match your skin to later."

I blanch as he reminds me of who I'm dealing with. And I most definitely do *not* want my skin to match this dress. "I think I'm regretting this decision."

"No backing out now." He glances over at me, and the grin on his face is pure wickedness. "You're my sweet little victim for the whole night." There's a primal glint in his eyes as he roves over my exposed skin. It's not sexual; it's something darker and even more insatiable.

"Okay, now I'm definitely regretting this decision," I respond with a nervous laugh, wrapping my bare arms around my sides and trying to make myself as small and un-tempting as possible. "Do sadists allow safe words?"

Greyson scoffs. "If they're not fucking idiots they do." He turns the car sharply around a corner. The streets are starting to look familiar.

I bite my lip and look up at him. "May I assume you're not of the idiot variety?"

The leather of the steering wheel cracks as his grip on it turns deadly. "I'll pretend you didn't just ask me that." He flies around another corner and down a street I know I recognize. We're going to GREY'S. Or more likely whatever torture den he keeps locked away in his apartment above it.

"Safeword all you want," he continues, his tone biting. "Although, I was under the impression that *you* don't use safe words. Even when you need them. So who is the real idiot here, little sub?"

My cheeks flush, and I'm not sure whether it's with embarrassment or anger or a combination of the two. "Maybe I haven't used a safeword because no one has been strong enough to break me yet." I can't dissuade my eyes from finding his and glaring up at his smug face. The undisguised antagonization probably isn't the best move on my part, but self-preservation often evades me in these situations.

"Is that a challenge?" he asks, his blue eyes cold and his voice low and dangerous.

I resist the urge to cower and sit even taller in my seat. "It's an observation."

"You're not invincible, Kara. Your body has limits, even if your mind won't admit them. Going through life like you're made of iron rather than flesh and blood will get you hurt."

"I want to hurt," I whisper.

His eyes leave the road as he turns to me, dissecting me like a dead frog in biology class. "You're not a pain-slut, so why are you acting like one? I'm all for a little experimentation, but I'd like to know why."

His question is fair, and I take some time to consider before answering. My relationship with pain is always something I have a difficult time explaining, even to myself. "Pain gives me something to feel that I can control," I reply after a long pause.

His face twists with an emotion that I can't quite place before his eyes are back on the road. "You're a submissive; you shouldn't want control."

We spend the next seven minutes in silence. I know because I watched the time tick away on the dashboard to keep from looking at him. Greyson's last words throw me, and I don't really know how to respond. He's right—by nature, I shouldn't want control. But I can't think of another way to describe why I sometimes like to hurt. When I already hate the idea of being a masochist, not having a reasonable explanation for the urge is leaving me on-edge and insecure. I hear my stomach rumble and acknowledge that being hungry probably isn't helping things either.

The bastard better feed me at least before the torture ensues.

Greyson pulls into the same parking spot as last time and unbuckles his seatbelt. He looks at me expectantly, but makes no move to turn off the car or get out. I undo my seatbelt at a languid speed, uneasy under his heavy gaze. When I reach for the door, he grabs my arm and pulls me back.

"Ah ah ah, not so fast," he chides, an unmistakable streak of sadism in his voice. He pats his thigh and looks at me as though I should understand the signal. I just stare back at him in confusion. "Did His Lordship discipline you at all?" Greyson asks, his voice heavy with derision. "Lay across my lap."

I choke a little at the insinuation. "W-why?" I ask, keeping my body glued to the door with my hand still on the handle in case of needed escape.

"Are you out of sorts today, or do you usually need everything spelled out for you?"

Grinding my teeth at the attack on my intelligence, I respond with as much composure as possible, "I'm not used to playing with you, and I'm unsure of what the rules and expectations are. Can you please be more specific at the beginning, and I will try to learn as quickly as possible?"

Greyson sighs. "I apologize. I forget that you've only ever been with Ashford." He takes my hand and gently pulls me toward him until I'm splayed across his lap. "I am going to spank you for going out without a coat in the middle of winter. I require that you keep yourself healthy, and hazarding frostbite so you can show off your pretty dress is against the rules." He lifts the long skirt of my dress up until I can feel the cold air on the almost bare skin of my ass. Thankfully, he leaves my red panties on. "When I'm done, I'll take you inside and feed you. Do you understand and consent?"

"Yes, sir," I answer with a short nod.

A slap lands on my ass with a mild sting that feels more like a chastisement than a punishment. "What do you call me, Kara?"

Shit, force of habit. "Yes, Master Greyson," I correct with a small plea for mercy in my tone.

"Good." Then the real punishment begins.

Smack. There's no warm up, and his slaps are brutal. I clench my fists and try to take the blows in silence. He focuses most of his attention on the tender sit spots at the junction of my ass and thighs. *Smack. Smack, smack.* He's probably trying to make sure I really feel sorry when I sit on a sore ass at dinner. Damn sadist.

When he's set fire to my entire ass, he pulls the edges of my panties up into the crack of my ass and continues to hammer down on the new exposed skin. *Smack. Smack. Smack, smack, smack.* I squirm beneath the pain, my legs kicking out and knocking into the gear shift as I try to pull away from his slaps.

"Hey," he barks, fisting my underwear in his hand and jerking it up painfully. I stop kicking. "If you damage my car, I'll make sure you're *really* hurting. Now sit still and take ten more, and we'll be done. Keep fucking squirming, and I'll leave you tied up in the trunk and go eat dinner without you. What's it going to be?"

I will myself to stop struggling and go still beneath. "P-please give me ten more."

"Good girl," he answers, and I can hear the smile in his voice. Without another pause, the slaps continue. Two on my left cheek. Two on my right cheek. Four across my stinging sit spots. And the last two rain down hard as hell in the center of my ass.

I flinch when he tugs my panties out of my crack and drags them back in place over my scorched ass. He pats my butt lightly. "There, perfect match," he comments, and I can only assume he's admiring the shade of my abused skin in comparison to the red of the panties. "Can I take a picture?"

I scoff. "Not a chance in hell."

"Suit yourself," he answers, not sounding too displeased. He pulls my dress back down and helps disentangle me from his legs. Running his fingers over my head, he smooths down my hair so I can look presentable enough for his posh restaurant. His fingers trail down to my cheeks, and he brushes his knuckles against my flushed skin. "No tears?" he asks, a note of disappointment in the question.

I sit up a little taller, proud to have been stronger than he expected. "It's going to take a little more than a spanking to earn those, Grey." Without waiting for a reply, I reach for the door and leave him sitting a bit stunned in the car.

◆

We walk into the restaurant, and I'm floored by how stunning the place looks when it's lit up and filled to capacity with diners dressed to the nines. I'm glad that I decided to get a new dress, and I'm happy to feel like I blend in rather than standing out.

Unlike last time, Greyson doesn't walk us through the kitchens and up to his apartment. This time, he takes my arm and walks up to the *maître d'* with his dominant expression fixed in place. "Violet," he greets, his tone direct and a little cold. Clearly, he is not the type to make friends with his employees.

"Good evening, chef." Her smile is warm, and she's not the least bit put-off by his brusqueness. The perfect hostess.

"The usual table." It's not a request; it's a demand. Even if it is his restaurant, I find myself wanting to apologize for him. I suppose I'm not the only one at the mercy of Gavin Greyson's power. He acts like God when he enters his restaurant, and everyone else is a lowly worshiper.

Before we've even taken our seats at the secluded table surrounded by large windows looking out on downtown Chicago, a waiter appears to take our order. "What will it be today, chef?" a lithe girl with porcelain skin and a sleek black bob asks. It doesn't escape my notice that the restaurant is mostly staffed by very attractive women. I guess a man of Greyson's talents will never fail to draw feminine interest.

"I'll have a bottle of the *Sancerre*," Greyson starts to order without referencing a menu or asking me what I want. Bloody typical. "The porcini mushrooms. The duck Niçoise salad. The truffle scallops. And the Chilean sea bass. *Merci*, Collette."

"*Oui*, chef," she answers, quickly inputting everything into her tablet. She turns to look at me for the first time, giving me a speculative once-over. She has an unkind smirk on her face when she spins around toward the kitchens.

"So, do you bring girls here often?" Maybe Collette was comparing me to all the other dates Greyson drags in. Not that this is a date.

"No, I don't," he answers in disinterest. He scans the room, no doubt looking for things to critique and berate his staff over later.

"Not often?" I try to clarify his vague statement.

"Not at all," he replies, letting his full attention fall on me. His gaze is so intense it makes me want to look away, but I don't.

"But you date a lot," I guess. Judging from the number of women he keeps on rotation at the club, he would have to.

"I don't date. I play at Pandemonium, and I work here. There's nothing in between, really."

Well that's surprising. "Why don't you date anyone from the club? I'm sure there's a line of girls trying to belong to the famous Chef Greyson."

"Probably," he says with a shrug. "I don't like having to take my problems home. And having a full-time sub would definitely fall into the annoyance category."

"Well, you've taken me home twice now, so what am I?" I ask, trying to figure out why I'm apparently getting special treatment.

"You are, without a fucking doubt, a problem and an annoyance. But it would weigh too heavy on my conscience to get rid of you, so I'll just have to suffer through." He doesn't smile or give any indication that he's joking. Much to my wounded pride, he's probably serious.

"You're a true saint, Gavin Greyson," I retort, rolling my eyes.

"That I am," he agrees with a smug smirk.

Thankfully, the wine arrives to distract me from feeling like Greyson's kinky charity case. The starters and appetizers follow soon after, and everything is delicious. I scrunch up my nose when I'm forced to eat the scallops. I'm not very fond of scallops, but I give them a try to appease him when he levels me with a Dom glare. To my great surprise, they're buttery and sweet and practically melt in my mouth. I have to fight Greyson for the last one, but he concedes like a gentleman and shoves the last scallop into my mouth. The sea bass is the star of the night—simple and perfectly cooked with a hint of citrus and sides of pumpkin polenta and winter greens.

Because the portions are decidedly smaller the more expensive a restaurant is, I'm just barely satisfied by the time we've finished all of the food and most of the bottle of wine. When Collette comes around again to ask if we want any dessert, I answer with a gleeful, "yes," before Greyson even has a chance to respond. He fixes me with a stern look, but lets it slide and turns to our waitress.

"Have Flores prepare the dessert she's been working on this week for the spring menu," Greyson orders. "Just one," he arches an eyebrow at me, "this greedy girl can share."

I almost give in to the urge to stick my tongue out at him, but I don't trust that I'm safe from his vindictive side, even if we are in a public place. We'll see how well sharing works out for him; I'm feral when it comes to sugar.

In ten minutes, Collette comes back with the most beautifully plated dessert I've ever seen. It's a delicate, almost romantic composition of dollops of color and different textures with raspberries and lychees interspersed with edible flowers. The center of the dish is a luscious panna cotta with a wisp of pink spun sugar on top. If I have it my way, Greyson's not getting a damn bite.

I break from my awe to see Greyson judging the dish with a frown, his eyes full of criticism. What could he possibly find fault with?

"This is lovely," I compliment, even though I know it's not his work. He told me pastry wasn't his strong suit and mentioned Chef Flores when he was feeding me in his kitchen the last time I was here.

"It's acceptable," he answers with a curt nod.

Without waiting for his permission, I grab my spoon and dig in, feeling a touch guilty to be ruining the edible art. I moan when the panna cotta hits my tongue; it's so creamy and there's a hint of rose mingling with the taste of vanilla. Greyson picks up his spoon and scoops a small amount of each element into one bite. He lingers on the taste as he rolls it around in his mouth. When he swallows, his eyes turn hard. He's mad if he thinks there's any flaw with this food. It's the best non-chocolate dessert I've ever had.

He snaps to catch Collette's attention, and she rushes over. "Yes, chef?"

"Bring Flores out here," he commands, his voice stern. I feel a slight unease with what he plans to do, but that doesn't stop me from trying to eat anyway. He grabs my wrist as it hovers over the plate. "Do not eat that." I pout, but put my spoon to the side.

Collette escorts toward our table a beautiful girl with deep brown eyes, warm bronzed skin, and a luscious set of curves hiding under her white chef uniform. Unlike the rest of Greyson's fawning employees, this girl is glaring daggers at her glorified head chef.

"Chef," she greets, her tone sharp as a knife.

"Flores, would you like to explain what this is?" Greyson gestures to the beautiful dessert in front of us. The one I'm not allowed to eat.

"It's my sample for the spring menu, chef," her words are respectful, but they're laced with venom.

"I see." Greyson prods at the panna cotta on the plate. "And *this* is what you expect to serve to our patrons? You've used too much gelatin; it's got the texture of a rubber ball. And what exactly is this?" He picks at the spun sugar and tosses it to the side.

"It's—" she shifts nervously, the disapproval of Greyson's glare getting to her even as she tries to stand up to him. "I wanted to add a bit of fun, chef." She swallows like she knows that's not the answer he's looking for.

"It's fanciful and superfluous, and Grey's offers neither of those things on their menu. Take it away," he orders, shoving the plate toward her.

"Yes, chef," she answers, reaching for the plate. I can't tell if it's a trick of the light, or if her eyes are glistening.

"Collette," he addresses without another glance toward the chef he just publicly tore apart. "Bring me the chocolate tart, a glass of milk, and a double of Macallan neat." He looks over at me, and there's a dangerous shift in his stark blue eyes. For someone who's just finished a multi-course meal, he looks positively ravenous. "And a vial of cinnamon oil."

"*Oui*, chef," she answers with a bright smile, and both girls depart. I wish Greyson had allowed them to leave the damn dessert.

"So what was that about?" I ask after they've left.

"What?" he answers, sounding oblivious to the scene he's just made.

"The public flogging you just gave that poor girl," I retort, arching a brow.

"Nonsense, a public flogging would have been much more enjoyable."

"*Grey*," I chide.

"I expect perfection to come out of that kitchen. Perfection and nothing less. Chef Flores disappointed me."

I consider him for a moment. He was uncharacteristically harsh with the pastry chef, even for him. "She's very pretty," I suggest, gauging his reaction.

"What?" Greyson answers, looking startled.

"She's gorgeous." Definitely too gorgeous to be slaving away in a kitchen for a torturous bastard like Greyson. And I would personally kill for her tits.

"I hadn't noticed." There's a strange note in his tone that makes me think he definitely *has*.

It's another couple minutes before Collette comes back with Greyson's order. The chocolate tart looks tasty, but it's lacking the artistry that Chef Flores put into her plating. Her dish was clearly made with a dash of love, while this one is clean and elegant—much like Greyson. I pick up a fork to dig in because I'm starving for sugar at this point, but I glance over to see Greyson staring down on me with disapproval from the rim of his whisky glass.

"May I eat?" I ask, wondering if maybe I'm meant to ask for permission before starting.

"No, you may not," he answers. He takes a long draught of his drink, his steel blue eyes never leaving mine.

"No?" The single word is full of devastation. Is he going to deprive me of two desserts tonight? That's a pretty fucked up idea of sadism. When I asked him to play tonight, I didn't mean *literal* torture.

"No," he reaffirms, his tone unbothered as he takes another drink. "You've got to earn the right to eat that chocolate tart. What did you ask me for this afternoon?"

"I—" I pause, and he arches a brow, watching me fidget and worry my bottom lip under his searing gaze. "I asked for pain."

"And I've yet to deliver," he continues, his grin devious.

"But in the car—"

"That was a punishment that you earned," he cuts me off. "The spanking doesn't count. You said you wanted to play. So let's play." He swirls around the whisky in his glass.

"O-okay," I agree with a shaky breath. I have the sudden urge to declare that I've been cured of my need for pain to fill the emptiness. Chocolate can fill the hole in my heart just fine. It would be easier, but it wouldn't be true.

"Good." He leans back in his chair, getting comfortable for whatever sadism he's about to demand. "Take off your panties, slut."

"W-what?" I couldn't have been more surprised if he'd asked me to run naked down Main Street. "Why?"

"Do I need to explain myself, little sub? Or are you going to obey?"

Feeling properly shamed and hearing Cade's accusations that I'm a terrible submissive ring in my head, I reach down and try to shimmy out of my panties with as much discretion as possible. Greyson seems to enjoy my discomfort, his eyes bright with hunger. After a minute of struggling, I get the panties off and dangle them on one finger in front of him. He snatches them from my hand and drops the bright red lace in his lap. I hope he hasn't noticed the damp spot in the center because I certainly did.

"It seems someone's enjoying their evening." He shoots me a playful smirk, and I know he noticed. I say nothing, clenching my bare thighs together as if that will save me from his humiliation. Spoiler alert: it won't. "Touch yourself," he orders.

"We said no sex," I half-whisper, my voice furious.

"This has nothing to do with sex. This is about humiliating you and making you suffer. I don't give a fuck if you get off in the process."

Gritting my teeth, I slip my hand underneath my dress and slide my fingers through my wet folds. My head snaps up in horror as I try to gauge if anyone can hear the sound of my arousal as I rub my hand up and down my pussy. Somehow, the fact that anyone could see heightens the pleasure even as I'm drowning in embarrassment.

"*Fuck*," I let out with a startled gasp when Collette pops by our table again. My cheeks are burning crimson, but a sharp glare from Greyson tells me that I'm not allowed to stop masturbating beneath the table.

"Did you not like the tart either?" Collette asks with a frown. "Should I get you something else, chef?"

"I'm sure it's suitable. Unlike Flores, Chef Henley is always very precise in the kitchen." I cringe for the sake of the poor girl who obviously bears the brunt of Greyson's cruelty amongst his staff. "Kara is just having a little lesson in delayed gratification." Bloody hell, I'm going to die of mortification. "*C'est tout*." With a catty little grin at me, Collette bounces off.

"I hate this," I groan. My fingers continue to strum at my clit beneath the table.

"Are you wet?"

"Yes," I grumble.

"Then don't tell lies. And I can assure you, you're going to hate this even more." Greyson's pupils are blown, and he looks high on the thought of whatever torture he's about to inflict. "Push your dress up to your hips. I don't want it getting ruined."

Why would it get ruined? is on the tip of my tongue, but I remember that he prefers submission to questions, and I move to obey. I feel very exposed in the middle of a luxurious restaurant with my expensive dress rucked up like a whore and my bare pussy hanging out for anyone to see if they happened to glance. And my arousal has already dripped down to my thighs.

"Hold out your hand," he commands and reaches for the small bottle of oil on the table. The order seems like a tame one, so I reach out my hand willingly. Greyson uncaps the bottle and pours three drops onto my fingertips. It smells spiced and sweet. *Cinnamon oil*, I remember. "Rub it on your cunt."

I do as he asks, spreading the oil over my clit and down to my entrance. It feels like lube—at least, it does for a few seconds before it starts to burn like the fires of hell. "What the fuck?" I shriek, trying to rub it off, but only managing to smear it more into my skin. It feels like acid against my tender flesh, searing my engorged clit. "Greyson, what the fuck!" I try to keep my voice down, but I'm panicking.

"It's cinnamon oil," he answers, sounding amused. I look to see that he's smiling and casually sipping his drink. He's not bothered by my suffering—he's getting off on it.

"I'm aware of that, you sadistic prick. How do I get it off?" There are tears in my eyes that I can't hold back because the sting is so strong.

"If you can be a good girl and suffer until I finish my whisky, I'll tell you. And I'll let you have that chocolate tart all to yourself."

I fucking hate sadists. "A-and if I'm not good?" I ask, barely remaining coherent beneath the agony.

"Then I'll tell you how now, and you can sit there with your sore cunt and watch me eat the tart myself. And I'll ban you from sugar for the rest of the week."

"That's not fair," I sob, very tempted to crawl under the table and hide so no one can see me falling apart.

"Little sub, when—at any moment—did I say you'd be treated fairly? I want to see you suffer. It's one of the few things in life that gives me unadulterated pleasure."

"It hurts," I whimper. I want to rise to Greyson's challenge, but I'm not sure if I have the strength to endure much longer.

"I know it hurts. That's what you asked for. Now, can you be a good girl and take it?"

I bite down on my bottom lip to distract myself from the pain and nod. "Yes, Master Greyson."

He drinks his drink slowly, savoring every sip as I writhe in agony and try not to scream. But there's a warmth growing in my belly each second I submit to the pain. And when I look over at the glowing admiration on Greyson's face, the warmth in my core swells into something that resembles pleasure. It's then that I realize the sexual satisfaction Greyson derives from delivering pain is a mirror of the gratification I feel while enduring his pain. We're two sides of the same fucked up coin.

I don't even notice that Greyson has finished until he sets his glass down on the table with a loud *thud*. "Would you like me to save you now?" he asks, his tone light and a little bit teasing.

"If it would please you, Master Greyson." I've gone so deep into submitting to the pain that the burning between my thighs is a mere nuisance now.

"Good answer," he purrs, his blue eyes pooling with need. "Milk." He gestures toward the glass of milk that seems out of place on the table.

"Milk?" I question, not quite sure what he's suggesting I do.

"Cinnamon oil isn't water soluble. You need something to neutralize it. There are a few other things that will work, but I've found milk is the simplest."

"And what exactly am I supposed to do with it? Pour a glass of milk over my pussy?"

He laughs, and for the first time tonight, it's not a cruel sound. "No need to get dramatic. Dipping a napkin in milk and wiping away the oil will suffice."

All too quick to listen, I grab my napkin from the table and dunk it in the glass of milk. Well past preserving any dignity at this point, I slide the napkin under the table and wipe it over my burning skin. I moan in relief as the milk starts to cool the heat of the oil. I dip the cloth back in the glass and rub it between my folds, using delicate care on my clit to neutralize any remnants of spice. When the burning stops at last after what feels like an hour, I use the dry side of the napkin to wipe away any dampness left between my thighs. If I'm being honest, it's more than just milk.

I throw the napkin on the table when I'm finished, thankful to be able to relax in my chair once more without feeling fire between my thighs. Greyson slides the glass of milk toward me. "Now drink it," he orders with a mischievous smirk.

I stare at him in slack-jawed disbelief. There is no way in hell I'm drinking a glass of room temperature milk that's mixed with pussy juices and cinnamon oil collected straight from the bowels of hell. No damn way.

"I'm joking," he says with a laugh, and I heave a sigh of relief. "Here." He pushes the plate with the chocolate tart toward me. "You've earned it, little sub."

Feeling quite pleased with myself for enduring the great Gavin Greyson's cruel and unusual torture, I scoop a huge bite of chocolate and enjoy my fucking just desserts.

Chapter 35

CADEN

"You're buying another kink club?" I stare at Finn in surprise. Owning one kinky sex club is a niche market as it is. Owning two practically makes Finnian Holt the king of the Chicago kink scene. "I had no idea you were so entrepreneurial."

"It wasn't my idea. The owner of The Sanctuary came to me. He's drowning in debt, made some bad investments, and he thought making a sale with someone in the business would be a better move than waiting for the mafia to come in and take it. Rest assured, I got it at a killer price."

"What about Pandemonium?"

"The waitlist for membership at Pandemonium is a mile long. You know we have clients from all over the country salivating to enjoy the unique experiences we offer in kink. Pandemonium is luxurious and exclusive—a perfect playground for experienced professionals; I want to make The Sanctuary the opposite. An inclusive, inviting space where anyone, even beginners, can practice kink safely. We can do workshops and help people understand what it's like to be part of the lifestyle. I want to keep the clientele local rather than appealing to a broader audience—a haven for all the misfits right in the heart of Chicago."

"And when did you develop such a bleeding heart for the misfits of Chicago?" I retort with a bite of sarcasm. "You've never had an issue making a fortune off the rich and privileged before."

"Yes, yourself included, Lord Ashford," he answers with a laugh. "And I am very happy to continue doing so. But the wealthy have always had their proclivities catered to; I want to show the normal, everyday people that kink isn't a luxury. That having a safe place to play and act out your fantasies can be just as accessible as signing up for—I don't know, yoga or something."

"A kink club that appeals to desperate housewives and men who don't know how to come without thinking about or fucking someone other than their wife. Sounds brilliant," I scoff.

Finn groans. "Don't be such a stuck up prick, Ashford."

"I'm part of the aristocracy—it's in my blood." He glares at me, but he also knows that I'm right.

"So will you come tonight?"

"My best mate is forcing me to go to a bottom tier kink club that he wants to turn into a playground for frustrated mommies and daddies—it sounds like the last thing I'll be doing tonight is coming." I fix him with a deprecating stare, but it has no effect because the only thing he heard is that I'll tag along on his silly little escape tonight.

"Perfect," he cheers, slapping me on the back a little firmer than necessary before jolting to his feet. "I'll get my car."

"The fuck you will." I push him back down on the sofa, and he falls hard on his arse. "If I'm being forced to endure torture on your behalf, I'm bloody driving."

◆

The Sanctuary looks the same as the last time I was here, signing away my soul to the devil by way of a first edition Chaucer. And I still haven't caught the damn devil sending pretty blondes to their deaths. My fists clench at the reminder of my failure as Finn and I climb the stairs toward the old Lutheran church, its facade bathed in red from tinted spotlights on the spires. The dark stone building seems to tremble and pulse beneath the heavy bass of club music coming from inside. A long time ago, for a young and naive boy adjusting to life in a new country, this den of revelry was home.

The inside looks nothing like how I remember; although, it has been over a decade since I've stepped foot in The Sanctuary. What used to be a dark, moody space for social outliers to get together and test out their limits has turned into a trendy night club. The artsy, postmodern vibe has been tastelessly covered up with strobing lights, metal dance cages, stripper poles, and fucking smoke machines. And—I am not taking the piss—Rihanna's S&M is playing in the background. The whole thing feels like a vanilla fantasy of what being hardcore and kinky would look like.

As Finn and I make our way to the bar, I nearly bump into a gyrating couple dressed in cheap latex and matching studded collars and realize they're dancing. Lots of people around us are dancing to the beat of pop music blaring from the speakers in the ceiling. Who the fuck dances at a kink club? That's vanilla shit if I've ever seen it.

Thank Christ, the bar is just as mainstream as the rest of the place. There's no drink limit—and I have every intention of burning through Finnian Holt's fortune to make sure I forget this hellhole by morning. I order a double; there's no real top shelf here, so I'm drinking the common people's bourbon tonight. I suppose, since there's really no need to savor the taste of it, I can get pissed quickly.

Finn goes to meet with the owner, Luca something or other, signing some papers to make everything official. Although, who the hell knows why Finn would want to buy this place. He'd have to raze it to the ground just to sanitize it. My eyes wander over the crowd, more out of boredom than interest. It's a writhing sea of black clothes, bodies crashing into each with carnal lust, though not violently enough to be appealing. They got the color right at least, even if there are far more sequins and denims than I've ever encountered at a kink club. I don't bother looking at the faces. They hold no interest for me. Nothing does since…her.

I slip my hand into the pocket of my dinner jacket and clutch the remains of Kara's collar, fisting the mangled jewels until they bite into my skin. I've done it every time I've allowed thoughts of her to enter my head since she left. Well, since I left. My left palm bears the cuts of my weakness almost constantly. I grip the necklace harder, relishing the sting of it until images of Kara slowly start to dissipate. I drain my bourbon and ask for another double.

Past the throng of dancers, there are leather sofas. I can see a few subs kneeling at the feet of their masters, one with a leash and collar. There's a St. Andrew's cross along the back wall where a dominatrix is using a crop on the testicles of an older, fully nude man. I look away quickly—dominant women are not my kink. I look back over to the sofas; clearly, that's where the small population of true kinksters actually is.

In spite of myself, a girl captures my interest. She's one of the few not wearing black. She's wearing a short, red dress that hugs her slim curves and shows off the perfect tightness of her arse. My cock stirs in my trouser, and a barrage of guilt instantly overtakes me. I shouldn't be admiring another girl's arse, and my unfaithful dick definitely shouldn't be standing at attention at the sight of someone who isn't Kara.

I haven't been with anyone since Kara. I haven't even played with anyone at Pandemonium since the night I left her. It's been thirty six days, and although common sense suggests that I can't go celibate for the rest of my life, I've never for a moment entertained the thought of replacing her. Still, my traitorous eyes roam back over the girl across the room, drawn to her as if by some supernatural force. She's not on her knees, so maybe she's not submissive. She's straddling the hips of a man sitting on the sofa. I can't see his face, but his hands are on her hips, helping her grind against his body. For some reason, I want to rip his fucking hands off and break his fingers at every first knuckle—or every second knuckle I revise as his hands slip lower.

She turns her head to the side as the man buries his face in her neck, and my heart freezes over in my chest. It can't be. It's impossible. There's no fucking reason for Kara Caine to be giving a lap dance to some wanker in the middle of a very second rate kink club. And yet, when the man pulls away from her throat and looks up, I realize that this club is an even better representation of Hell than Pandemonium. Because the man that my girl is rubbing her barely clothed cunt up against is none other than Gavin fucking Greyson.

Greyson's steel blue eyes lock on mine, and if looks could kill, that man would be murdered so gruesomely that there wouldn't be a scrap of blood, guts, or bone left to bury. I watch the bastard say something to her, and her hips stop rolling instantly. Her head whips back to search the crowd, terror filling her eyes as though she's been told the club has been overrun by zombies desperate for warm bodies to feed from. Nothing so severe really, just her Dom quite ready to slaughter the fucking both of them.

When she finally finds me standing at the bar, the look of pure devastation in her deep brown eyes guts me. Momentarily deprived of motor function, my glass falls to the ground, shattering. "Shit." I shake the bourbon from my ruined leather shoes and apologize to the waitress when she makes it over with a broom to sweep up the glass. When I look back up, Kara is gone and the bastard is sitting alone on the lounge.

Blood boiling in my veins, I push through the crowd of sweaty, half-clothed bodies, my usual good-manners well-exhausted at this point as I shove strangers out the way without a care. My body is working on instinct, propelling me forward as though my life depends on it. The need to find Kara is as fundamental as the need to fill my lungs with air, and I won't survive unless I have both.

It takes too bloody long for me to navigate the crowded club and find the exact spot Kara vanished from. Sodding Greyson is still sitting there, looking bored without my girl rubbing up against his cock. It takes all my self-control not to gut him on the fucking spot, but I have more important things to sort at the moment. I need to find Kara. Torture and murder will have to bide their time.

"Greyson," I spit out, the word tasting like acid as it rolls off my tongue. "Where is she?"

"Fancy seeing you here, Ashford. I didn't know you sported amongst the commoners. You should have let them know you were coming—they could have rolled out the red carpet."

"I don't have time for your droll attempts at wit," I growl. "Where the bloody hell is she?"

"Who?" Greyson asks, feigning stupidity—not that it requires any acting on his part. He takes a nonchalant draught from the glass in his hand, and I want to punch his damned teeth in.

"Kara," I answer through gritted teeth. "My fucking sub. Where is she?"

"Last I checked, you didn't have a sub, *mate*."

"Last I checked, your heart was still beating. If you would like it to continue to do so, answer my bloody question."

The desire to snap Greyson's worthless neck is tingling in my fingertips. I ball my hands into fists in the hopes that they won't do something of their own accord without the consent of my thinly tethered reason. Greyson shoves off the lounge angrily, invading my personal space within the span of an instant. With a barbarous growl, he throws his fists into my chest, and I think I can hear the distinct sound of that thin tether snapping.

"If you think I am going to let you go anywhere *near* Kara after the shit you pulled at Pandemonium—"

"If you think I give a *fuck* about what you want, you are gravely goddamn mistaken," I thunder back, cutting off whatever asinine demands he was about to make. "If Kara had wanted to turn me away, she would have stayed and watched you defend her honor like the good little foot soldier that you are." I take a step closer, our chests nearly touching as I glower at him. "But she didn't. She *ran*. And that's because she knows I will always catch her." I shove against him, unable to refuse the call for violence singing in my blood like a battle cry. "So, step the *fuck* away and let me *find my fucking girl*."

Greyson glares at me, conflict flickering in his too blue eyes. As much as he hates me, he knows I know my sub better than he does. "If she says *no*, you better get your sorry ass the fuck out of here," he spits out as though the words are poison in his mouth. With a look of pure loathing, he steps out of the way and allows me room to pass.

"Don't worry. If she says no, you'll never see me again," I reply before shoving past him to head toward the dimly lit corridor beyond the lounge area. I look back to give him a final, friendly warning. "And Greyson, if you value your worthless cock at all, don't be here when I get back." Without waiting for a retort, I turn on my heel and walk away.

◆

Just as I remember from a decade before, there is a secluded hall of private rooms beyond the leather lounge area. If Kara is looking for a place to hide, this is the perfect choice. For security reasons, the doors don't lock, but a red sash is left on the door handle if the room is in use. Not expecting Kara to be familiar with the protocol, I look for the empty doors first. If I don't find her in one of those, I'll start barging through the ones with red sashes too, their privacy be damned.

The first two rooms yield no such luck as I glance around the familiar furnishings, being thorough enough to check under the beds and in the adjoining bathrooms. But the third room—the third room has me transfixed in the doorway, the blood in my veins turned to lead as I stand immobilized and helpless. My hand fists at the jewels in my left pocket, the slight sting as the bits of broken metal cut into my palm reminding me that what I see before me is truly real.

Kara sits on the floor, her back against the bed and her knees pulled up to her chest. Her head is buried in her crossed arms, and she doesn't look up when I open the door, even though I know she heard me enter. As it turns out, she didn't try very hard to hide from me. Maybe she knows I will always find her. Or maybe—my heart starts to thaw from the icy clutches in my chest—she wanted to be found.

"Kara," I call, my voice raw. I sound like a man at the brink of death. Depending on her answer, perhaps I am.

She startles at the sound of my voice, her frail body flinching even as she holds herself in a tight embrace of her own arms. There's nothing about her stance that suggests that she's pleased to see me, and there's a gnawing ache in my stomach that reminds me she probably hates me. She *should* hate me. I'm torn between begging her to stay and fleeing the country so I never have to see her face again.

"Cade," she answers at last. I expect emptiness or anger, but the warm burst of emotion in that single word from her lovely lips gives me hope for something more.

"Kara, look at me." I'm not asking, I'm ordering, and her body instinctively knows the difference. She obeys and glances up from the cover of her arms, her dark lashes wet with tears and dark shadows smudged against the pale skin beneath her wide, brown eyes. She looks like a doll—a beautiful, broken doll. My heart fractures at the sight, and I want nothing more than to piece her back together.

She watches me warily as I take hesitant steps toward her until I'm standing in front of her. With her at my feet, I can almost pretend that nothing has changed, but the mistrust in her eyes reminds me that everything has changed.

"Why are you here?" I ask, unable to squelch the burning need to know why I saw her rubbing up on Gavin Greyson five minutes ago. The jealousy curdles my tone, turning it bitter.

Her brown eyes flash, and I can detect the exact moment that Kara's brokenness disappears as anger takes its place. "I could ask you the same question. Were none of the subs at Pandemonium up to your standards? You must be desperate if you've come downtown to adequately fulfill the needs of your cock." Her expression is haughty, and she somehow seems to be looking down on me even though she's the one on the floor.

My dominant side riles at her disrespectful tone even as another part of me swells to see her looking so alive with fire in her eyes and fury in her belly. This is not a girl who is broken. This is a girl begging for a fight. And I will bloody well give her one.

"Tread very carefully, Kara," I warn, my voice tight as I take another step closer. My body radiates with the need to remind her of who the fuck she's dealing with; Greyson might allow that kind of behavior, but I sure as hell don't. "That damn mouth is going to get you into trouble." I reach for her jaw and jerk her head toward me. "I'm not the slag who was dry fucking Gavin Greyson in the middle of this club," I whisper against her ear as though pouring poison.

She looks like a rabid dog who might bite as she rips herself from my grasp. I'm met with daggers glared in silence. As I've spoken truth, she has no retort to offer, and I can see her seething with the need to spar. Much to my satisfaction, the playing field is in my favor.

"Tell me, how long did you do me the honor of waiting before thrusting yourself onto Greyson's shaft? A week? A day? Or were you truly cruel and went to him the moment I set you free?"

"Fuck you," she spits back, her words dripping with venom and her eyes dark with fury.

"Am I wrong?" I stare down at her with a brow arched in challenge. My vicious girl didn't even let the crocodile tears dry on her face before stuffing herself with the next available cock. The knowledge cuts at my heart a little deeper than it should, and I instinctively rub at my chest in a hopeless attempt to soothe the ache.

"I don't think it's any of your damn business what I did after you broke me and left me bleeding on the goddamn floor."

Her evasion is doing nothing to quell the violence pulsing through my blood, begging to be set free. "Oh, so you *didn't* run right into Greyson's waiting arms the minute I walked out the door?"

"Yes," she bites out. "I went to Greyson. You want to know why? Because he was fucking there to pick up the pieces!" There are tears in her eyes, but they glitter with anger. "Grey tended to my lashes—the ones *you* asked him to put there. He fed me. He made sure I went to bed without hating myself."

I feel prickles of guilt trickle down my spine as she reminds me of every way I've failed her, but they drown in a torrent of jealousy as I fixate on a singular part of her declaration that twists at my black heart. *Him* taking her to bed.

"And how is *Grey* in bed, love? Is he the sadist of your goddamn dreams?"

Kara glares at me. "Not that it is any of your fucking business, but I've never slept with him."

I scoff, the sound bitter and harsh. "Come now, darling, you can't expect me to believe that. You were practically shagging right there on the lounge." She looks insulted at the insinuation, not that it's even an insinuation. It's a goddamn fact that she was rubbing up on him like a cat in heat for everyone in the club to see.

"It was nothing," she answers with a roll of her eyes. "I was teasing him about something."

I give her a long, criticizing glare. "I see. So, do you usually *tease* people with your cunt against their cock?"

"I don't know, Caden. Do I?" she retorts with a suggestive smirk, and I have to resist the urge to slap the tarty smile right off her face.

"The only time you ever teased me with your cunt was when you wanted me to stuff it full and use it extra hard. Does that apply to Greyson too? The git you're supposedly *not* fucking?"

"I'm done having this conversation," she spits as she rises in a rush to get up.

"Get the fuck back on the floor," I command, fisting her hair and dragging her back down. "I didn't give you permission to stand."

Her eyes flutter shut as a brief flash of emotion softens her face. Then it's gone—and her eyes are open and blazing. "I'm not your sub, remember? So you can shove your permission up your ass." She pulls against my hand in her hair even as I grip her tighter. As usual, she'd rather give herself pain than give in.

"If you don't get on those knees, Kara Caine, you are not going to like what happens next," I growl, my face mere inches from hers as I hold her suspended in the air before dropping her down with a harsh release of my hand.

The air in the room is thick with the threat of violence, teetering on the razor edge of destruction. I heave a breath, and there's an acrid taste on the tip of my tongue, like the promise of blood being spilled before the night is out. Even in silence, the small space crackles with an energy that's almost audible.

I wait.

She waits.

Neither of us breaks. By definition, it's a stalemate.

But then, in defiance of the very laws of nature, Kara bends. She shifts—tucking her legs underneath her, settling gracefully onto her knees with her hands on her thighs, and lowering her eyes in submission.

My blood singes with elation a split second before I fall to my knees right alongside her. With a need as desperate and intrinsic as the necessity for oxygen, my mouth is on hers, devouring the sweet taste I've deprived myself of for far too long. Kara moans against my tongue as it tangles with hers, her defenses completely obliterated. She kisses me back with a frenzy that matches my own, and I force myself deeper, devouring more than caressing.

"Is this okay?" I ask breathlessly against her lips before trailing kisses down her throat.

"Y-yes," she gasps, her chest heaving because I've half-drowned her with my mouth. "More—please."

At her invitation, I tangle my fingers in her hair and sink my teeth into the soft flesh of her neck. She keens, melting into my vicious embrace as she tilts her chin up and offers more of herself to me. I bite my way up her neck and over her jaw—I'm not gentle, and she'll look like she was mauled by a wild animal come morning. Not far from the truth, in all honesty.

When I feel Kara reach for my belt, I freeze, reality shocking my system like ice water in my veins. I'm not meant to be fucking her. I'm not meant to be kissing her. I'm not even meant to be in the same room as her. I thought I was gallant. I thought I was strong enough to save her from herself—from me. But I'm not. I'm a selfish cunt, and I aim to keep her.

At the end of this, there are only two options. Either Kara will hate me. Or she'll be mine.

Chapter 36

CADEN

"I'm going to tell you a story."

I know there's no way around it. Kara has to know the truth. And she has to decide for herself if staying is worth the risk. She looks up at me with a trust I know I don't deserve, and I have to clutch at the necklace in my pocket to distract myself from the stab of self-loathing in my gut.

"It's not a pretty, fanciful tale. It's dark and brutal and there's no happy end. Not for her." I drag my trembling fingers through my hair as I swallow down the thickness of dread. "I want you to listen. And in the end, if you still want to leave, I'll let you go. But if you decide to stay, it's with the knowledge that you are mine completely, and I am never letting you go again. Do you understand?"

"Y-yes." There's no *sir* following her agreement, and I have to tamper down the ache of disappointment in my chest. Maybe she's already decided that I'm not worth the destruction that comes alongside me. She'd be right, but that doesn't make it hurt any less.

"There once was a girl called Évione."

Understanding flashes in Kara's eyes, and I know she must have already guessed part of this story. She knows that someone came before her. I've told her that things ended badly. She knows that I'm to blame for another woman's death. Perhaps she already knows who the villain is in this story.

"Évione was a French art student on a summer study abroad trip to New York. We met at the Metropolitan while she was sketching a Pollock painting and I was doing…something less artistically inclined." I scrub my hand over my face as the memory tugs at my heart with a nostalgic twinge that is more bitter than sweet. "She was breathtaking—intoxicating—a perfect combination of light tempered with darkness. At the time, I didn't know how deep the darkness ran, but it called to me, and my demons answered that fucking call."

"She never made it back to her home in Calais. She never had a fucking chance. I plucked her from her life, from her studies, desperate to make her mine like some precious jewel I wanted to hoard away with the rest of my treasures. She was naturally submissive, and she suffered pain exquisitely—the masochism came as easily as breathing, or a chronic illness you can never purge from your blood. I made her mine in every sense of the word. I kept her in the manor, lavished her with anything she asked for, shielded her from the need to ever venture into the outside world. Due to my particular line of work, I lived my life in the shadows, and she was perfectly happy to live in the darkness alongside me."

"However, her artistic soul was drawn to chaos, and her emotions constantly vacillated from one extreme to the next. She needed anger to warm the coldness. She needed pain to satiate the numbness. She fed the monsters inside me, and they grew. I fed the appetite for destruction inside of her, and it grew. I whipped her, and she loved it. I cut her, and she begged for more. She pushed harder, each time edging me farther. I could have commanded that she crawl to me through a maze of broken glass, and she would have done it with a smile. She could have begged that I beat her bloody, and I would have done it and gotten off with the stain of her blood still on my hands."

I pause, near heaving with disgust at the damning truth pouring from my mouth. I'm horrified to peel back the façade of humanity and reveal the insatiable monster lurking beneath. I brave a glance over at Kara, expecting to be met with her repulsion. But it's not judgment filling her eyes, it's empathy. Timidly, she stands and inches toward me until she's close enough to touch. I jolt when I feel her hand on mine, tugging me toward the leather settee in front of the bed.

Without a word, she gestures for me to sit. I listen, expecting her to follow. My breath catches when she lowers herself, not to the couch, but to the floor, kneeling at my feet as naturally as she would have done a month ago. With heartbreaking tenderness, she lays her head across my lap, instantly banishing the sharp fangs of self-hatred looking to feed from my guilt. I second-guess myself for the briefest of moments before placing my hand on top of her head and stroking the soft waves of her hair. This moment is the closest I've felt to peace since I left her thirty six days ago.

But the peace is undeserved, and I still have a story to finish.

"It was a constant cycle of toxicity, the rot of it spreading and breeding more infection as time went on." I continue to run my fingers over Kara's hair, the touch providing me with enough calm to relive the awful anguish of those moments. "Finn was the one who finally pulled me from the haze of lust and dependency to show me the truth of what was happening. Évione and I were killing each other. Slowly. Painfully. And if I didn't cut out the rot, we would both end in destruction."

"I pulled away bit by bit, not strong enough to completely remove the first person I'd ever loved from my heart. Évione latched on even tighter. She told me she loved me, I told her that our brand of love was doing more harm than good. Finally, in a drastic move, I took away the pain that she craved so badly, and she fractured. Like a cracked mirror—still reflecting some semblance of the person you recognize, but it's distorted and deformed. In the absence of pain, the numbness was too great, and she became desperate to feel anything."

I brace myself for the worst of it. Kara must feel me tense because she looks up at me, her deep brown eyes warm and full of trust. Is she even hearing what I'm telling her? Lashing out against Kara's unwarranted compassion, my tone turns cynical as I brace for her hatred.

"One night, when I was out working on an acquisition, Évione rolled out a white canvas. It was huge—bigger than her; she was going to use it for a painting to hang in the hideaway. She lay the canvas on the floor of my bedroom, lighting candles in the windows like beacons for me to see on my drive home. She removed her clothes, folding them neatly as she would any time before a scene. She took the whalebone knife that we used for play from my bedside drawer, and she gouged her arms open."

I pause before I'm able to force the next words from my lips, the horror of the memory still giving me chills. "And then she painted. *Painted.* As though it was perfectly rational to use her lifeblood to compose a masterpiece. And perhaps in her twisted mind, it was. She painted as her blood flowed over the canvas, her life draining out in streaks and splatters of grotesque red against the bright white. She staged her own death as a fucking piece of art."

Kara is inhumanly still, her body tense with horror, but she never looks down, never shies away from the horrible truth. And I love her so much that my heart could rupture with the fullness of it.

"I walked into my room that night to find the candles burning low, her body spread out on that damned canvas like an offering—like a sacrifice. She had a ghost of a smile on her face, her long dark hair fanned out perfectly beneath her shoulders, her body decorated in flecks and smears of dried blood. The strokes she'd left on the canvas had turned from bright red to a ruddy brown, the sight ugly and macabre. A tarnished fantasy. An atrocious waste of life." I force back the tremble of anger and frustration at the loss.

"I was implicated in the homicide investigation, of course. And with good reason—I was the catalyst for the violence if not the exact cause. And with the way things had been staged, it looked ritualistic, like a sick, rich bastard getting caught in his perversions. Again, not exactly wrong, even if those weren't my precise deviances. In the end, there wasn't enough evidence to pin on me, and I had enough money and connections in the department to make the implications disappear. It was ruled a suicide, and Évione's ashes were shipped back to her family in France who hadn't seen her in two years. By that point, they might have assumed she was dead already."

I look down to see tears have spilled down Kara's cheeks as she mourns the tragedy of the girl she never knew. The girl who was diminished to a mere flicker of life in this world before the light was snuffed out. Because of me. Kara should save her tears for herself; I'm begging her to risk the same fate.

"I had the canvas framed. I keep it in the attic like some twisted version of Dorian Gray, hiding away my inner monstrosity from the prying eyes of others. But every time I feel myself slipping out of control, I look at that grotesque painting and remind myself of what happens when we let the monsters inside roam free." I allow my fingers to trail down Kara's jaw, tracing the distinct edges I know by heart.

"In the past year, I've made more trips to that dreadful attic than I can count. Because there's something inside you—a glimmer of self-destruction that shines like a beacon, calling to the darkness in my soul just like she did. You're reckless enough to disregard limits, you're stubborn enough to risk your own safety constantly. It's like blood in the fucking water, and the darkness just wants to feed."

I grasp Kara's shoulders, hard enough that she winces. Pain is a signal to her brain that she needs to be cautious, and I need her to heed my words with the utmost care and understanding. "That is why I am so hard on you. That is why recklessness with your health or safety is punished so extremely. That is why your refusal to safeword was enough for me to leave, even though it goddamn killed me to do it. Because I *fucking love you*, and I can't lose you like that."

I press my fingers harder into her shoulders, feeling the fragile bones shift beneath my touch as she gasps. I could crush her so easily, and there's no denying that the impulse is there. The darkness isn't always malicious, sometimes it's just curious—entranced by the idea of what the bones would sound like if they snapped. I repress the urge like I do every other day, prying my fingers from her skin, but it's undeniably harder when she makes no move to stop me. She never does. One day I fear my self-control won't be enough to stop me. That's why I left. And yet, here we are again, our fates forever intertwined and almost certainly doomed. Because I haven't the strength to leave again. If she stays, there will be no escape. Ever. Till death do us fucking part.

"Y-you love me?" Kara asks finally, glossing over every other gritty detail of my statement. Very bloody typical.

"Yes, I love you." I shove off the couch, unable to remain stationary and contain the frustration boiling inside me. "But that's not a good thing, Kara. My love is poison. My love means never being safe, never being free."

"But…you love me?" She's still kneeling beside the couch, looking up at me with dark, wide eyes.

It's like she can't believe it, although how could she not? She is everything to me. She has been since the moment I demanded that damned book and she told me no without a tremble of fear. Since she was brave enough to give me her body when I was still her captor. Since she gave me her submission on her knees in the dining hall. Since she came back from Jace even stronger than ever. Since she demanded my dominance in my office even after I scorned her and ignored her. Since she offered me her pain in the hideaway in spite of her fear. Since she promised to be mine. Since the moment I told her she no longer was.

"Of course I love you," I retort, the warmth of adoration and the sharpness of fear twisting in my voice to make my declaration equal parts fire and ice. "Every hour, every minute, every second, every heartbeat, it's only ever been you."

I look down to find Kara's lovely eyes filled with the glossy sheen of unshed tears. But these aren't tears of devastation or fear as she stares up at her own destruction. These are tears of happiness, and they are startlingly misplaced for the object of my dark affection. "Don't act as though I'm offering you a gift, Kara. My love is a death sentence." The truth of the statement feels like thorny vines wrapping around my heart and squeezing until blood bursts.

"You didn't cause her death, Cade. She was troubled. You couldn't have saved her. Apart from psychological or medical intervention, I'm not sure anything could have."

"Why do you sound so fucking calm?" I feel the anger rising, threatening to overtake my senses. "You should hate me."

"Don't expect impossible things. I could never hate you. I love you, Caden Ashford. Call it my natural inclination toward disaster if you like, but I love you just the same."

My heart stops in my chest, utterly stunned into silence. Those three words are more than I could have ever hoped for. They're certainly more than I could ever deserve. And she said them on her knees. It's like she's *trying* to be the death of the self-control keeping me from ripping into her cunt this very moment.

"You're playing with fire, love." My words are deep and guttural, like a growl clawing its way up my throat as my fists clench at my sides.

"I enjoy a little burn," she taunts, her lips spreading into the most devious of smiles.

"You're beckoning ruin with open arms," I caution with a stern glare. And it's the last warning she'll receive. If she tempts me one more time, I'm done for. To hell with the consequences.

"Then come ruin me, Caden Ashford. I'm begging. Ruin me, please."

The darkness bursts, spilling into my veins and flooding my body with aching, pulsing need. I can't resist her call any more than I could tear my own heart from my chest. I storm toward her, wrapping my hand around her throat and lifting her to her feet. My mouth is on hers instantly, devouring her, but it's not enough. It will never be enough. I need her blood. I need her body. I need her soul. I suck her tongue into my mouth before biting down hard. I relish the sound of her choked whimper as I lap at the coppery tang, continuing to irritate the cut with my teeth as she struggles beneath me.

"That's it love, fight me," I rasp against her ear, barely giving her a chance for breath before my lips are on hers again. Fuck, I want to bleed her. I want to *break* her. And if this is going to work, I need her to deny me the chance.

I pull away, viciously grabbing her hair by the roots and jerking her head back. "Did you let Greyson have this mouth? Did you let him taste you?"

"N-no, sir." There it is. *Sir* on her trembling, blood-smeared lips. It's enough to make my cock jolt painfully, begging to be seated deep inside her hot cunt. But I need to deny myself a little bit longer. Kara and I still have unfinished business, and it's time for her to pay up.

"And what about this?" I ask, my tone sharp and cutting. I drag my fingers down the exposed skin of her breasts, digging my nails in deep until I feel the skin break beneath the force. Kara is so overcome with lust that she barely even flinches at the violence of it. Not satisfied with her reaction, I move my hands to her thighs and brutally claw my way up. This time she whimpers, and it's music to my fucking ears. "Did you give that bastard your pain?"

"Y-yes, I let him hurt me."

I slap her across the face. I'm not gentle, and she cries out from the shock and sting of it. "Your pain belongs to me, Kara. *Only me.* Do you understand?"

"Yes, s-sir." Her lips are trembling as she stumbles over the words. Her fear drives me higher, pushing me toward the edge. It's delicious and decadent, and I just want to gorge myself on it. I remind myself that she needs to stop me *before* I go over. Or this is the end for both of us.

Fueled by pure, animalistic instinct, I reach for the straps of her flimsy red dress and rip it off her body in a single jerk. Sure enough, Greyson's faded marks mar her skin; the abhorrent sight of them causes a black mist of rage to cloud my vision. "Strip," I bite out. She obeys instantly, unhooking her bra and tossing it on the floor before sliding her panties down and stepping out of them. "Shoes," I order. She kicks off her black stilettos, standing with her bare feet side by side as she waits in submission for my next command.

"So, what to do about your sins, hmm?" I lower my voice as I wrap my hand around the back of her neck. My touch isn't harsh, but my fingers tremble with a violence that begs to be set loose. "What should I do with the naughty whore who let another man take what's mine?"

"Punish me." Her tone is heavy with need, her pupils blown in her dark eyes as she stares up at me with pure, instinctive need. Her darkness calls to mine, and fuck if I don't want to embrace it with every fragment of my twisted soul.

"Are you sure? I won't take it easy on you, Kara. This isn't playtime; this will hurt. I'll make you scream."

"I know." She doesn't take her eyes off me, willing me to see her readiness and submission. "I deserve it. I need it. Punish me please, sir." Even after everything I've told her, everything I've done, she's offering to sign another deal with the devil in blood. This time, there will be no breaking the ungodly pact. This time, if she can earn it, she's mine for eternity.

"Grab the bedpost," I order, tendrils of violence bleeding into my tone as I stare down at her. After a moment's doubt, Kara turns to fulfill my command, walking to the side of the bed and gingerly placing her hands on either side of the wooden post. Her fear is so thick that it permeates the air, filling my lungs with an intoxicating scent of bruised berries and wilted violets. It smells like her but darker, twisted. I drink in her fear like a gulp of red wine, reveling in the bitter fruitiness bursting on my tongue. I've always craved her pleasure, but in this moment, after a month of starvation and torment without her, my body demands something darker—I want her pain just as much as I need her surrender.

"I'm not going to restrain you," I tell her as I press my body against hers, my hard cock digging into the cleft between her naked arse cheeks. I'm tempted to forgo this whole display and simply take out my frustration on her cunt, but that would leave us right back where we started. If she's going to insist on this lifestyle, if she's going to submerge herself in *this* world, she needs to learn how to ensure her own safety. Tonight, I'm setting the beast free; if she's going to survive, she needs to learn how to bring him to heel.

"You are going to hold on to this post," I continue, taking her hands and wrapping them tightly around the smooth wood so that she's hugging it close to her body. "You will not let go. If you do, we'll start over. And I'll hit you twice as hard. Do you understand?"

"Yes, sir," she whispers, her face buried in her arms as she braces for the storm.

"This doesn't stop until you say *Thornfield*," I explain, grabbing her by the jaw and forcing her to look at me. "I. Will. Not. Stop. I'm no longer going to be the safety net that keeps you from falling into the abyss of self-destruction. I will hit you until you safeword. If you pass out, I will wait for you to come-to, and then I will keep hitting you. No breaks, no pauses, no outs. The only way this night ends is with you using your safeword."

I dig my fingers into Kara's cheeks until she winces, warning her that her only options tonight are pain or submission. "Do I make myself perfectly clear?"

"Y-yes sir," she answers, her body trembling beneath me. She's terrified. And she should be; I'm going to tear her apart before I piece her back together.

"Good," I reply darkly, shoving away her face and pushing myself off her body.

I reach for my belt, unbuckling it and whipping it off with a loud slap of leather. I hear Kara whimper with dread; she knows what's coming. The last time I gave her a thorough belt whipping was when she escaped the manor for the first time—breaking her promise and endangering her own safety in the process. Since that punishment, she has begged me not to use the belt again, and I have tried to respect her wishes. However, since tonight is all about testing her limits, I think using my belt has a poetic symmetry.

Although, I doubt my little librarian would agree with my idea of poetry.

I give Kara a moment to resign herself to her fate. This can end right now if she uses her safeword, but she won't. She's testing me just as much as I'm testing her, trying to see who will break first. Unfortunately for her, tonight my will is wrought in steel, and she'll get no bend or break from me.

I test the weight of the belt briefly, adjusting my grip before drawing back and throwing it across Kara's arse. She flinches hard at the stinging impact, and I can hear a strangled cry in her throat, begging to be released. This isn't a warm up, I'm going in blazing from the very first strike.

I hit her again, leather slicing across her shoulders. This time, she does cry out, caught off guard by the placement of the blow. If she thought she was only getting an arse warming tonight, she's sorely mistaken. I swing the belt against the middle of her back, and she twists to the side in an effort to escape the next strike.

"Get back in position, Kara," I reprimand with a bite of harshness. "Remember what happens if you let go of that post." I give her a moment to straighten her body and present herself for my continued infliction of pain. The submission of the act makes my already hard cock throb in my pants, desperate to be unleashed.

I allow the lust to feed into blood lust, and I double my efforts, hitting her hard and fast. *Slap. Slap. Slap.* She trembles as the leather of the belt bites into her skin, leaving angry, red streaks across her pale skin. I've missed having her body as a canvass, her skin coloring beautifully when subjected to sadistic artistry. The thought reminds me of Greyson bearing witness to a masterpiece he didn't have the right to see. Gritting my teeth, I take out my anger on Kara, bringing the belt down across her arse over and over. *Slap. Slap. Slap. Slap. Slap.*

She sobs loudly, her chest heaving with the effort of drawing air into her lungs. Still, she makes no attempt to use her safeword, choosing rather to burn than to bend. Her stubbornness makes me clench the belt in my hands in frustration, desperate to make her admit her own weakness. For this relationship to work, she has to show me her limits. Without those boundaries, we're on a collision course with no detour from destruction.

I harden my heart to her cries and strengthen my resolve. I tried leaving to save her, but that only pushed her further toward the flames. For this to work, I need to let her burn until she chooses to pull herself from the fire. "Spread your legs," I command, my tone infused with indifference even as my conscience roils in my body at having to keep hitting her. She cries softly as she obeys, her legs shaking as she spreads them apart. *Slap. Slap. Slap.* I aim the belt between her legs, whipping upward to sting the tender flesh between her thighs. She whimpers and cries wordless pleas for mercy as she takes the beating right on her pussy, but she still doesn't give in.

Mindless with frustration, I abandon strategizing and strike out at every unscathed scrap of skin I can find. *Slap.* I whip her hips, the belt wrapping around to hit the tender softness of her stomach as well. *Slap.* I aim for her tits, slamming the belt against the exposed sides of her breasts. *Slap.* The leather bites into her upper arms wrapped tightly around the bedpost as though holding on for dear life. *Slap.* I whip her lower, the belt snapping against her calves as she jumps from foot to foot to escape the torture.

"Lift your left foot," I command, her little dance of discomfort giving me a wicked idea.

"W-why?" As I didn't give her permission to speak, let alone question me, I deal an especially brutal slap across her arse.

"Because I *fucking* said so. Now get that foot up."

She stills, and I wait with bated breath to see if this is the moment she uses her safeword. Instead, she lifts her trembling leg and offers me her foot as requested. Without giving her a moment to suffer the anticipation, I slam the belt against her upturned foot. She screeches in pain, and I give her another. And another. Five slaps in total on her delicate little foot that's now turned red as she shakes with the effort of keeping it held in the air as I whip her.

"You may put your foot down." She does so gratefully before hissing when she realizes that it hurts to stand on the abused flesh. She shifts before putting all of her weight onto her other foot and keeping the punished appendage on point.

I come to terms with the fact that I am a cruel man before my next command leaves my mouth. "Now, lift your right foot."

Kara sags against the bedpost, exhausted from the scourging I've given her. Her mind may hold firm in her stubbornness, but her body is about to surrender, even without her permission. I meant what I said earlier. Only she can decide when this stops. Even if she collapses, I'll revive her and keep going until she gives in. It's the only way for her to unlearn the recklessness she's clung to as though it was the sustenance of life. Sobbing softly, Kara balances on her whipped foot and offers me the other.

She's still fighting. Always *fucking* fighting. *Slap. Slap.* I give her two savage strikes, one right on top of the other against her sensitive arch. She lets her foot slip as she tries to contain the agony of the assault. "Get your fucking foot up," I growl, close to madness with her incessant obstinance.

In response, she whispers something I can't quite hear.

"Speak up," I order, in no mood to handle whatever mouthy retort she's thrown at me.

"Th-thornfield," she calls out a little louder, her voice broken and anguished. And my heart stills in my chest for the slightest of moments, its mundane task forgotten amid the wake of sheer awe.

Bloody fucking hell, she actually said it.

For the first time in her goddamn life, she's actually used a safeword.

Within a fraction of a second, my hands are on her as I draw her against my chest. Kara cries out when the material of my clothes rubs against her raw skin, and I pull away for just the amount of time it takes to rip my shirt free and throw it to the floor. Bending down, I sweep her up into my arms and cradle her against my bare chest, letting her cry against me as I offer comfort in the only way I can. Her whipped skin burns hot against mine, but I hold no guilt or regret over my unorthodox methods. My chest constricts, unable to contain the overwhelming pride that erupts in my heart like a nuclear explosion decimating every other thought and emotion in its path.

"I'm so fucking proud of you," I praise with my lips against her hair, planting soft kisses as I hold her tight and carry her to the bed. "So goddamn proud." I settle down on the side of the bed with Kara still nestled in my arms. She clings to me as though I'm her salvation rather than the man who just pushed her until she broke.

I kiss her. I kiss the woman who means more to me than the entire world and everything in it. The woman I *love*. And that is the most terrifying thing I've ever encountered. Holding something so precious and fragile in my arms and somehow trusting myself not to break it. I pour everything into our kiss, all my fear, all my uncertainty, all my anger and guilt. I offer her every sharp and jagged piece of my soul, daring her to take it and hold it in spite of the pain it can cause.

I feel her vie for dominance as our tongues twist together sensually, and I allow her to take control. She pushes me to my back, straddling my hips with her bare thighs as she attacks my mouth with hers, infusing the kiss with an aggression that I restrained from using against her. I sated my need to mark her and claim her with my belt, but it seems she too needs to stake her ownership in violence. I'm her willing victim as she drags her teeth over my lips, biting and sucking as though she's in a frenzy. When she can't get enough from my mouth, she skates her teeth down my throat, nipping and leaving hickeys over my skin.

I grab her by the hips and lift her a little bit higher, trying to reach around to my trousers so I can set my damned cock free. The small adjustment leaves her slick, hot cunt spread bare over my abdomen, her clit grinding against the ridges of my muscles. I can't resist bucking up to give her a little bit of friction. She moans, and the desperate desire of that tiny sound is even more enticing than her screams.

"Do you like that love?" I continue to thrust my hips at inconsistent intervals, catching her by surprise each time I stimulate her achy little clit. "Do you like feeling yourself drip all over me? Christ, you're so fucking soaked." I swirl my fingers around her entrance, teasing her, but never dipping them inside her. Her moans grow louder as she pushes back against me, trying to fill her pussy with something, anything.

"Uh-uh," I tsk, tapping my hand against her pussy with a wet smack. "You don't get to stuff this cunt until I allow it. And right now, I like watching you wiggle that cute little arse in the air."

"Cade, please." God, she's desperate, the scent of her arousal hanging heavy and sweet in the air.

"Oh, I think you can do better than that. How much do you want it, love?" I go back to tracing the edge of her hole, running my index finger in a circle and watching it get all sticky with her cum.

"Please fill my cunt with your cock. Fucking tear me open, I don't care, I just need to feel you inside me. Please." Her eyes mist over as she pleads with me. "Please fill the gaping whole you ripped inside of me when you walked out of that door and left me. When you said I wasn't yours." She fights back tears. "I-I need you to make me yours again."

"Oh, love," I answer softly, my need to torture replaced with an instant need to soothe over the hurt I caused. I'd been so obsessed and angry about Greyson that I forgot I was the one who sent her running into his bloody arms in the first place. "The night I left you at Pandemonium, I was heartless and cruel, and you didn't deserve either. I thought I could save you from my darkness by playing God, but it seems the devil has already claimed us both for himself."

I make quick work of my trousers and pants, ripping them down my legs and throwing them on the floor. I'm completely naked beneath her. I don't usually offer anyone this much vulnerability; I always keep some of my clothes on during sex to maintain a level of control. But for her, for her I can offer this. My whole body and whole self—because she owns every piece of me anyway.

"Take it, love," I command, guiding her toward my swollen shaft. "I'm yours to use. Show me how much you need me."

With frantic urgency, Kara reaches between her legs and slides my cock into her slick entrance. She pushes up on her knees before dropping down, trying to impale herself in one thrust. I hear her whimper when she only gets half-way seated. There's no denying that I'm far bigger than your average dick, and her poor little pussy has been empty and out of practice for over a month. Without taking it slow, this is going to hurt like her first fucking time. I smile wickedly at the thought of getting to tear into her again and make her mine.

"It seems your cunt has forgotten me. Would you like help remembering?" Kara nods as she hovers above me, not quite prepared to rip herself open on my cock. But she'll let me do the honors.

Not giving her a moment to hesitate, I grab her by the hips and slam her down on my cock until I'm seated to the root. She cries out, covering her face with her arm to keep me from seeing her fall apart. But she isn't allowed to hide. Not from me.

I take her hand in mine and pull her arm away. "None of that. Let me see you." Her body heaves as she looks up at me, tears clinging to her dark lashes. "There you are, beautiful." I brush the back of my knuckles over her damp cheeks. "So fucking pretty when you come undone for me." Her eyes flutter shut as she leans into my touch eagerly, as though she's been starved of any love or attention in her life until this exact moment.

"Take what you need, love," I urge her. "Use me to make you feel good."

She rocks her hips, still whimpering as I stretch out her insides. She has to get used to the pain again before it can bring her pleasure. Slowly, she pulls herself up a few centimeters before sliding back down, the slickness of her arousal making it an easier fit this time. She lifts off higher this time, her whimpers turning into moans as my cock massages her sensitive inner walls. Feeling braver, she pulls out almost to the tip before dropping her full weight down.

This time, it's my turn to groan. She feels so fucking good wrapped around my dick like a vise. As much as I want to dig my fingers into her hips and fuck the living daylights out of her, I don't. I let her decide the pace; for this one, finite moment, she is in control. It is my penance as much as it is her just reward for everything I put her through. Leaving her was a mistake, and it had the potential to be a fatal one. And though I don't think I'll ever be able to put into words the depth of my regret, this is my apology.

Kara's movements turn harsher as she chases her pleasure, her hands changing from caressing to clawing as she drags them down my exposed abdomen. I suck in a sharp intake of breath, but make no move to stop her. "That's it, love. Show me how you feel." She continues to ride my cock as she leans down to sink her teeth into the flesh of my chest. And *bloody hell* it hurts, but I keep my hands calmly at my sides.

"You left me." She says it like a curse, her tone full of bitterness and venom. Those damned claws find their way into my skin again as Kara rotates her hips above me. There are tears in her eyes, but they mingle with fire rather than sadness. She's furious, and it's a gorgeous thing to behold. Pure, effervescent fury.

"I did," I agree, egging her on. "Make me pay." I don't expect the sharp backhanded slap that comes an instant later. *Damn*, I forget how much strength she can house in that tiny little body when she's angry. The darkness in me attempts to rouse, longing to join her in violence, but I just barely ignore the urge. This is for Kara. My own little sacrifice of pain after she gave me everything she could of her own.

"You *left me*!" It's a scream and a sob blended into one, encompassing every ounce of suffering she must have felt over the past month of emptiness. I felt the cruel agony of her absence just as heavily as she did, but I had the comfort of knowing it was self-inflicted misery. I had only my arrogant sense of self-righteousness to blame. For the past thirty six days, the villain in *her* story bore my face.

I feel another slap land on my cheek, and I grit my teeth and take it. It's not the pain that bothers me—I can take as good as I give—it's the humiliation of allowing someone else to control my body, pain and pleasure. I never bottom. Ever. And this is the closest I've come to willingly giving my submission to another.

She shrieks in frustration as she digs her nails into the skin right above my heart. "*You left me.*" The tempo of her thrusts picks up with the mounting of her anger, and I feel close to coming already. Her hands claw their way up to my throat and wrap around as tightly as she can. Her fingers are so small that she can't even fully encircle my neck. Even if she wanted to strangle me, she'd never be able to manage the job on her own.

"You will never leave me again, Caden Ashford. Do you hear me?" Her demonically beautiful face hovers just above mine, her dark eyes vicious and haunting, her full lips so close I could brush them with my tongue if I wanted to. And I desperately want to. Catching her off guard, I lick along the seam of her delicious, red mouth. Rather than melting into the caress, Kara takes my tongue between her teeth and bites.

"*Christ,*" I swear as blood trickles down my lips, warm and metallic. Viperous little monster. She's made me bleed—my debt is paid.

"Promise me," she demands, her voice powerful and fierce as she keeps her hands locked around my throat. "Promise that you'll never leave. Promise that, no matter what happens, we'll face it together."

No longer able to resist the urge to touch her, I grab her hip in one hand and help her ride me faster, her pace instinctively picking up to fulfill my unspoken command. With my other hand, I capture her throat and drag her closer to me. "Darling, the next time I let you get away from me, they'll be putting you in the ground. And I'll be right there, waiting in the dirt beside you. You and me? We're fucking forever."

Neither of us relinquishes our hold on the other's pulse as our lips crash together, combusting with a mixture of rage and devastation and a sheer resignation to fate. Reclaiming my dominance, I thrust into her violently, desperately, and she meets me each time with an unhinged need of her own. The room fills with the wet sound of skin slapping together as we attack, claw, bite, and suck our way toward release.

I could have come from the first moment I felt her tight cunt choke my cock after a month of abstinence, but I'm waiting for her. I don't want to go over the edge until she comes with me. As she continues to ride me hard,

I slip my hand between her spread thighs and find her swollen clit. She cries out when I brush my thumb over her clit, her poor neglected nerves practically set to ignite already.

"That's it, love. Ride my fucking cock while I play with your pretty pussy." I run my fingers around her clit; she is so damned wet I can barely get any traction on the tiny nub. Thinking of a good use for all that cum, I wrap my arm around the back of her and slip two lubed fingers into her arsehole. Kara shrieks at the unexpected intrusion even as her cunt clamps down hard on my cock. "Mmm, you like that, dirty girl." Too far gone with arousal to even be embarrassed, she bounces up and down on top of me, fucking herself in both holes. It's so tight, I barely have room to fit inside of her.

"Come on, love. Fuck both of your slutty holes. You just can't get enough, can you?" I get her closer, thrusting my hips at an angle that I know will rub against her g-spot. "My filthy little girl likes to be stuffed full, doesn't she?" I thrust again, and her legs tremble at my sides.

"Yes. God, *yes*," she breathes in ecstasy as she edges closer to release. Her eyes flutter shut while she focuses on the building pleasure.

"Say it. Tell me how much you love it," I order, twisting my fingers inside her as she starts to spasm on top of me.

"I love it when you stuff my slutty holes. Please can I come?" She's sweating and shaking as she waits for my permission. She can barely keep herself from toppling over the edge, but she denies herself the release for me. Her perfect submission makes the love in my heart swell even greater, the ache in my chest a strange mixture of pleasure and pain.

"Come on my cock. Let me feel you strangle me with that tight little cunt."

"Cade," she cries out as she fractures into fragments of bliss, like she knows I need to hear my name on her lips as she orgasms.

Her cunt clenches so tightly around me that I have no choice but to come right alongside her. I'm going to stuff her so full of cum that she won't even remember what it felt like to be empty—what it felt like to be without me. And I'll make sure she never knows that feeling again. I'll be her past, present, and future, and that's all she fucking needs.

I stay inside her for long after we've both climaxed and calmed down, savoring the feeling of finally being where I belong. I briefly entertain the idea of ripping out her IUD, filling her with my cum again, and using my cock to plug her up after so not a drop of it escapes. I've resigned myself to the fact that I love her, now I just have to make sure I keep her forever. Fucking my baby into her seems like a pretty good way to tie her to me permanently.

Kara shifts on top of me, rousing me from the daydream of her riding me while her belly is heavy with my child, her tits swollen and milky. And goddamnit, I'm already sporting a hard-on again. We've never talked about kids, but now that I've gotten over the hurdle of admitting I love her, I realize that I want everything with Kara. A collar on her neck and her finger, a certificate that officially says I own her, a brood of heirs to carry on the Ashford name, a home that we can share and raise a family in.

As soon as we get back to the manor, I'm calling my lawyer and the family jeweler.

It will never be enough until I have her to touch and fuck and hold every second of every day. I'm a greedy man, and I won't be satisfied with anything less than everything. I'm shackling her to me and never letting her out of my sight again. Kara started as my captive, and I am more than willing to play the captor again.

"Caden Ashford, what are you plotting?" Kara asks, looking at me with a scathing glare.

"Nothing." I help her off me, wincing when I lose the warm comfort of her pussy.

"It's not nothing." Her expression is chiding as she settles in beside me on her stomach and sits up on her elbows. "That look usually means I'm in for an unpleasant surprise, and I don't think I can handle anything that isn't sleep at the moment."

"Well, nothing for you to worry your pretty little head about right now," I amend, placing a kiss on her forehead.

"That sounds…ominous." She has a worried crease between her

eyebrows, and I can't help leaning down and kissing that too. I could kiss every inch of her skin, and it still wouldn't be enough. I want to devour her just so I can always keep her inside of me. Metaphorically, not literally. I'm not that brand of psychopath.

"You trust me, don't you?"

"Loving you and trusting you are two entirely different things. I love you, but do I trust you not to fuck with my mind and body? Absolutely not."

"Shut up before I spank you for being cheeky," I order, giving her arse a light swat.

"Ow, you've already wrecked my ass with your bloody belt." She rubs at her welted backside, and I can't help but smile at the marks I left. "I'm going to be bruised for weeks because of you."

"And I am going to think about how strong you are and how much I love you every time I see them." And it's true. Those marks represent her willingness to save herself. Her willingness to give us a fighting chance. I'll cherish them until they fade, and then I'll put new ones on her.

"Deranged bastard," she mutters, but she can't keep the smile from her face.

"You love me, so which one of us is really deranged?"

"You've skirted around that word for the past year, and now you can't stop saying it?" Her expression is smug as she looks up at me. I have no defense because it's entirely true.

"What can I say, you've broken me. I'm completely irreparable." I grab her wrist and drag her on top of me again. Like a starved man, I can't get my fill of feeling her naked body against mine. "And speaking of, who knew bastinado would be the catalyst to break the great Kara Caine?"

Kara's brows scrunch into a particularly adorable expression of confusion as she looks down at me. "What's *bastinado*?"

I smirk up at her. "Foot torture." If I'd had any idea that hitting her feet would get her to admit the ultimate surrender, I would have tried it a long time ago. I'm not a mastermind of sadism; I merely wanted to ensure that not a single part of her body escaped unscathed.

"What the fuck? Why is that a thing?"

"I thought you didn't kink shame?" And for the most part, she never has. Kara has always been very accepting of other people's kinks, even if they aren't to her personal tastes. I suppose all it takes is for someone to do something that you find abhorrent, and then the judgment comes out.

"I don't—but you would have to be insane to enjoy that," Kara answers, having the good manners to look slightly guilty.

"I believe I've found a new punishment for you," I threaten with a laugh.

"You're a fucking bastard." She attempts to shove my arm off her waist, but I dig my fingers tighter into her skin, holding her still against me. I won't let her get away from me—not now or ever again. "I wear heels twenty four-seven, you asshole."

Oh yes, that thought did cross my malevolent mind when I was hitting her soles with the belt. She'll likely be sore when she has to put on her heels to leave, the high arches chafing at her tender skin.

"Excellent idea," I announce. "We can combine bastinado *with* a high heels kink. Then you'll really think twice before touting your smart mouth and calling your master a fucking bastard." I see her grit her teeth and seethe at the word *master*, and her irritation brings infinite happiness to my cold, black heart.

"No bastinado," she orders, poking her index finger into my chest so hard that it almost hurts. "No *whatever the fuck* a high heels kink is. Hard limits." She's wearing her authoritative, *I'm Dr. Caine the stern librarian* expression, and it's positively precious that she thinks she has any say on the matter.

"As much as I appreciate your newfound ability to express your limitations," I inform her, plucking her errant finger from my chest and twisting it back until it's bent at an uncomfortable angle, "you don't get to have hard limits when it comes to punishments. You'll take what I give you because it's what you deserve." I'm being an arsehole, and I won't apologize for it. She knows what she signed up for—and it's her, on her fucking knees, willing to do as I command or suffer the goddamn consequences.

"And if I safeword?" she asks, her tone baiting as she arches her brow in challenge.

"Then I'll kiss your feet for having finally learned your lesson." I would be more proud of her using her safeword than I would be if she took the whole punishment without a word. But saying "Thornfield" won't get her completely out of trouble. "And then I'll beat your bloody arse instead."

"You're a cruel Dom," she says with a pout.

"But I'm *your* Dom, so you'll suffer me anyway." I chuck her under the chin. "Come love, it's time for me to take you home and fuck you properly in my bed."

Finn can find his own damn way home.

Chapter 37

KARA

I hurriedly sidestep a murky puddle as I cross the street, heading toward the warm haze of the candles flickering in the windows of my favorite cafe. Of course, it has to be pissing rain the first time I've managed to escape the manor in a week. Any desperate attempts to keep my heels from getting soaked were given up three streets ago, and my wet feet squish loudly in my shoes with each step. At least I had the good sense to wear a proper raincoat, even if my choice of footwear is characteristically insensible. Mrs. Hughes would have had a fit if she'd seen me go out in this state—and not only because Cade has forbidden me from leaving Ashford Manor at all.

Controlling bastard. You'd think I'd be used to his ridiculous demands after he kidnapped me and held me captive. Or the following twelve months that I stayed willingly. Shockingly, I still find myself seething anytime Cade oversteps the bounds of his sanity. Which is very, very often.

I make a run for the welcome warmth of Hallowed Grounds, casually pondering how long it will take for my babysitter to realize I've left. As usual, Declan has been tasked with keeping an eye on me in Cade's absence; the poor kid has the hardest job of them all. It's a wonder Cade leaves me behind at all given my less than commending track record of following orders.

There was something off about Cade this morning, a conflict in his eyes as he bent down and kissed me goodbye. His kiss was desperate, his arms gripping me tighter, as though I might disintegrate the second he let me go. When he pulled away, there was an indescribable darkness in his hazel eyes. If I had to name it, it looked like dread. I tried asking him about what kind of job he was working on, but he said he couldn't say. I asked him if it was dangerous and was met with a long pause of silence. It was obvious that he didn't feel inclined to tell me the truth, but he was hesitant to tell me a lie to soothe my fears.

I get the distinct feeling that Cade's recent, sudden excursions entail activities that I wouldn't approve of. The most obvious answer is that he's engaging in illegal shit even though he promised me he wouldn't. Since I'm currently breaking my promise to meet with someone he most definitely wouldn't approve of, I suppose we both have grievances to sort out with each other. Given what I know of my strict Dom, I can guarantee my disobedience will be paid in pain as soon as I return to the manor. But how will Cade atone for his sins?

The rich, intoxicating scent of coffee settles into my lungs the moment I open the door to the cafe. I shiver as warmth seeps into my chilled bones and start to unwrap my damp scarf and unbutton my coat. I screech with surprise as a pair of strong arms twist around my hips and lift me into the air. "Miss me, little sub?" a warm, familiar voice whispers in my ear.

"Greyson," I chide, trying and failing to sound stern as I swat his hands away. Because he's a prick, he doesn't let me go right away. "Greyson, get off. I'm soaked." I try squirming against him, embarrassed that we're starting to attract the curious attention of other people in the cafe.

"What do you say?" he asks, and I can hear the mischievous amusement in his tone. Petty bastard.

"*Please* let me go," I grind out with an eye roll. Why do all Doms have to be such power tripping assholes?

"Aww, no "master" this time? I'm hurt." He releases me with a laugh and has the chivalry to help me out of my dripping coat. Skilled hands sweep the scarf from around my neck, and he uses it to brush some of the rain from my drenched hair. "There," he says, stepping back to look at me with my wet coat and scarf hanging off his right arm. "Perfect, as usual."

I blush, fairly certain that he's complimenting me to make me uncomfortable rather than to actually be sweet. Though from the warm glint in his crystal blue eyes, I can't be sure. Greyson hangs my things on a coat rack beside a blazer that I recognize as his and leads me to the spot he's picked out.

It's a lounge with fluffy, earth colored pillows tucked away in one of the corners. There's a low table beside it decorated with a lit candle in an amber glass votive and a bunch of wildflowers in a small vase. The seclusion offers privacy along with a bit of romantic ambiance. Thank God we never slept together, or I would be a little suspicious of Greyson's intentions at the moment. I settle onto the far end of the lounge, trying to put a bit of space between us. As usual, Greyson ignores my personal boundaries.

"Since I can practically hear the insults you're mentally shouting at me," Greyson says as he nearly sits on top of me rather than taking the other end of the couch, "sorry for being a dick when you walked in." His tone doesn't sound the least bit apologetic, but I'll take what I can get.

"It's fine. I'm used to it at this point." And it's true. None of the men in my life have a scrap of manners between them. Except Declan, and he's bound to be corrupted by the rest of them at some point.

"Of course you are," he teases with a smile. "Speaking of dicks, how has Lord Twat been treating you? Was he very angry that you'd been fucking around with the peasants?"

"We didn't *fuck around*," I answer, shooting him a deadly glare.

"Semantics," Greyson says with a dismissive wave of his hand. "I'm sure it didn't make much difference to him. I could have been taking you to mass every Sunday, and the British prick would still want my guts on a silver platter."

I can't argue with that logic. I'm pretty sure Cade fantasizes about a mysterious accident relieving Greyson of his cock since he knows I'd never let him retaliate himself. Whenever I catch Cade with the ghost of a smile on his lips, I'm almost certain he's imagining torturing Greyson for his audacity to touch his things. "We should probably both be appreciative that you're still breathing," I respond in agreement.

"I assure you, no one is more appreciative of that fact than me." Greyson takes my hand and begins to trace a soothing pattern over my fingers. "Honestly though, how bad was it?"

I look up to see that his expression is entirely serious, a little furrow of concern between his brows. He actually cares, and the thought touches me more than I thought it would. "It was…bad," I answer truthfully, thinking back to the night Cade found me with Greyson at The Sanctuary. "Of course, he was livid that I'd been playing with you rather than walking away from the lifestyle he didn't want me in."

"You didn't do anything wrong, Kara." His hold on my hand turns from relaxing to firm as his features turn harsh. "He set you loose. You had every right to seek out comfort elsewhere." He looks down at me with something akin to vulnerability in his bright blue eyes. "I was honored to be your solace. And I will always be here if you need it again."

"Thank you," I answer, squeezing his hand back. "I don't regret anything. At the time, you were exactly what I needed. And I am very grateful for your friendship. I just wish the universe hadn't decided to fill my life with a bunch of damn Doms." I playfully knock my shoulder into his. "I swear, the stress of trying to meet the petty demands of all of you is taking years off my life."

Greyson laughs, the cheerful sound of it filling the air with warmth. "Oh shut up, you're such a greedy slut of a sub that you love all of our *petty demands*. Admit it." He pinches my thigh like an obnoxious older brother trying to rile up an annoying little sister.

"No comment," I deadpan. "And don't mark the merchandise." I brush his hand off my thigh. "I'll be in enough trouble as it is without Cade finding evidence of manhandling on his precious property."

"Did the little rebel break daddy's rules and sneak out of the house just for me? That's almost enough to warm my stone cold heart. What's he going to do when you get home? Put you over his knee and spank your naughty little ass?"

I cringe as I think of what punishment might be waiting for me when I get home. "I'm pretty sure I'd get off easy with a spanking. Cade tends to be *harsh* when he thinks I've broken rules that are in place for my safety." I don't think I'll be getting it easy this time.

"Sounds like a cunt. You should dump him."

"Grey!" I scold in surprise. "That's awful. And I can't."

"Why not? Did he fuck the next Ashford heir into you?"

"Jesus, *no*. No babies. Ever." I shiver in horror at the thought.

"Then why can't you dump his sorry British ass?"

"Because I love him." I let out a sigh of relief at the declaration. Greyson is the first person I've told. Well, other than Cade, of course.

Greyson looks down at me with pity in his eyes. "My condolences. I hear that illness is fatal."

I roll my eyes because he's the furthest thing from a romantic that I can think of. "It's actually amazing, and the sex is even better. You should try it."

"What, sex?" he asks with an expression of pure innocence. I arch a brow and glare at him. "Oh, the *other* thing. Yeah, no thanks. I'd rather chop off my own cock than fall in love."

"But that would be such a disservice to the women of the world," I answer with another eye roll. I'm only half joking. His metal studded cock *is* pretty. Maybe I should ask Cade if he has any interest in piercings.

"Wouldn't it, though?" His tone is pure arrogance. "So for the sake of pussies everywhere, I'll be keeping my black heart under wraps, thanks."

"Suit yourself," I reply with a little less bitchiness than I would like because a server comes over to the table with a tray of drinks and food. I wait for her to set everything on the table before flinging a look of irritation at Greyson. "You ordered for me?" He's done it before, but I thought it was purely part of the Dom/sub dynamic.

"Obviously," he replies as though there wasn't any other option while he picks up his cappuccino. "I'm not going to trust a novice with the menu."

"Hallowed Grounds is *my* favorite cafe. I'm the one who picked it. I know the menu from memory."

"Yes, which probably means that you order the same boring thing every single time." He levels a condemning scowl at me. He's exactly right, so I refuse to answer and try not to pout as I reach for the drink he ordered me, which smells undeniably delicious. "As I thought," he continues. "Now, be a good girl and drink what chef got you."

"Fine, but only because you have three Michelin stars. Any fewer and I would be deeply insulted that you didn't let me order."

"I'll have to be careful not to lose any then," he answers with a smirk.

"You can lose a Michelin star?"

"Of course. Otherwise people would rest on their laurels and stop innovating. I'm elevating the menus all the time. It helps keep me sharp. Now drink," he orders again with a nod toward my untouched drink.

"What is it?" I ask in suspicion as I raise the brown mug to my lips.

"Taste it, and you tell me."

Annoying bastard. I take a sip that's a little too hot, and it burns on the way down. I smack my lips in that pretentious way that wine connoisseurs do as I try to sort out the flavors. "Pumpkin spice latte?" I guess. "Am I that much of a basic white girl to you?"

"No," he answers slowly with a glare that suggests he'd still like the liberty to spank me every now and then. "And it's a chai latte, not a *psl*."

"It's good," I admit as I sip on the spiced drink and let the warmth banish the cold from my bones.

"Naturally," Greyson teases. "Be sure to eat too. You look half-starved."

"I always look half-starved. It's genetics. Trust me, Mrs. Hughes tries to fatten me up every chance she gets." Greyson gives me a quizzical look, and I realize he has no idea who she is. "Mrs. Hughes is Cade's cook and housekeeper, although that sounds a bit too pretentious. She's the matriarch of the manor really."

"Of course, the pampered prince can't even cook for himself," he scoffs.

"I'll admit, you have him beat there."

"I imagine I have him beat in a lot of areas."

"No need to pull out your cock. This isn't a dick measuring contest."

"I'd be more than happy to take that challenge," Greyson replies with a very suggestive smile before gesturing to the uneaten muffin in front of me.

"Don't sound so confident. You're about the same size, and the piercing doesn't count." I take a bite of muffin and moan as the delicious flavors of cinnamon, sugar, and butter melt in my mouth.

"Reminiscing about that pierced cock hitting the back of your throat, are you?"

That heavenly mouthful of muffin turns suffocating in my throat as I start choking in horror. "Christ, Greyson, you can't talk like that in public," I scold when I've finally stopped making a scene with my coughing fit. "Also, ick. I have no intention of letting—that—anywhere near my throat again."

"Shame. Guess I'll just have to ask your boyfriend then. Tell me, does the man you *love* still pass around your body like it's a party favor?" Greyson's tone has turned cold, and his words sting exactly like he wants.

"That's not fair," I answer in a low voice. "You don't get to judge him for doing the exact same things you do."

"Well, no one has entrusted me with their heart. If they did, I would be a little more careful with it."

Now it's my turn to scoff. "You're a sadist. If someone gave you their heart, you'd want to flay it apart piece by piece to see what makes it beat."

Greyson gives me a proud smile. "Looks like you really do know me, little sub."

I blush at the compliment as my praise kink kicks in at full force. "I'll admit, you have me down pretty well too." I wave the cinnamon streusel muffin in his face before taking another bite. "This is my favorite. Guess your attempt to prevent me from ordering the *same boring thing* was unsuccessful." I shoot him a self-satisfied smirk.

"I suppose I can't help it if you have good taste in everything but men," Greyson retorts with an equally smug smile before swooping down and stealing a bite of my muffin.

"Hey, get your own." I can't help but laugh at the sight of Greyson with streusel crumbs in his stubble. "Here, if you want some, at least eat it like a civilized human," I say, splitting the muffin in half and handing him a portion.

"If I was a gentleman, I'd decline. As it is," he takes the other half from my hand, "I never turn down good pastry."

We both eat in relaxed silence as I gather the bravery to say what I've come to say. "So, I probably won't be able to see you again. At least, not for a while. The only reason I was able to make it today was because Cade was unexpectedly called away."

"Yeah, I figured. His Lordship has you locked away in his castle doesn't he?"

"It's not like that. And trust me, I have something to compare it to."

"Oh yes, the good old "captive turned girlfriend" story is a classic," he retorts, his tone dripping with sarcasm.

"I'm aware that it's unorthodox—"

"It's fucking insane is what it is," he interrupts. His expression is a mixture of anger and frustration; I can't tell which is more dominant.

"I'm happy, Grey. I know it's hard for you to wrap your head around, but I am. Cade is everything I ever wanted, and everything I didn't know I needed. He knows me better than anyone, sometimes even better than I know myself. He understands how to damper my tendency toward self-destruction. He knows how to lead me when I'm too stubborn to ask for help or guidance. He knows how to force my weakness when my determination to appear strong is wearing me down. He knows how to break me and put me back together, so I don't have to blame myself for coming apart. He knows how to make me laugh when I need happiness and how to make me cry when I need release. He makes me feel more balanced than I've ever felt before. Also," a wicked smile pulls at the corners of my mouth as I look up at Greyson, "the sex is outrageously good."

"Damn, how is a man to compete with all of that," Greyson replies as he strokes his chin thoughtfully. "Guess I'm going to have to let you go, little sub. It was fun while it lasted."

"It was," I reply with a small hint of nostalgia. "You are, without a doubt, the best sadist I've ever known."

"High praise, I'm sure," Greyson answers with a laugh. "You're quite the little bundle of fun; I'll miss getting to torture you."

"I'm sure you have lots of subs lined up to fill my spot."

"Of course I do, but they won't be you." His eyes are warm pools of blue as he looks down at me, and I'm almost certain his compliment is genuine.

"I'll miss you." I allow a dramatic pause to let him worry I might have caught feelings for him. "Who else will make me a Michelin star grilled cheese in the middle of the night when I need it?" I finish with a giggle.

"For you, little sub, my kitchen is always open. The restaurant too; anytime you and your lover boy want a reservation, I'll have a table for you."

"I don't think you can promise that. GREY'S is practically booked through the next decade."

"Then I'll just have to throw someone out. I'd probably even enjoy it, so feel free to give me the excuse."

"Thank you. Truly. I don't think I would have survived last month without you." I try and fail to keep my eyes from misting over as I struggle to convey how much Greyson has meant to me, even though we won't be able to see each other much anymore. His kindness and particular brand of therapy is a debt I can never repay.

"Anytime. And if that British cunt ever hurts you in a way you don't like, tell me. I'll storm the castle as soon as you say the word."

"My own knight in shining armor," I swoon with a laugh even as emotion clogs my throat. "Don't you know I prefer the villain?"

"Don't they all," he quips with an eye roll. "Now, shouldn't the princess get back to the castle before the evil lord returns?"

"Probably." I heave a loud sigh at the thought of having to pay for the privilege of Greyson's company when I get home. I love Cade, but I wish he didn't have such a hard-on for rules.

"Wait here," Greyson commands before getting up and heading toward the counter. I guess he still needs to pay for our order.

I watch the flame of the candle flicker back and forth, contemplating how much of a shit storm I'll be walking into when I get home. When I catch sight of Greyson walking back, I realize he's carrying a large brown bag that's stuffed full. "What's all of that?" I ask, waving a finger at the bag in his hands.

"Cinnamon streusel muffins. I asked them to give me every one they had." He hands the bag to me. "It's an apology for whatever punishment you've earned for meeting with me."

I open the brown bag and count out seven of my favorite baked goods.

"That's incredibly sweet of you, but what am I going to do with *seven* muffins?" I can't help but laugh at the adorably over the top gesture. His love language is clearly food.

"Eat every last one. And that's an order. You're far too slim, and it hurts my little chef's heart."

"I'll do my best, but I guarantee it won't add any padding. I've tried for years, and I'm afraid I'm stuck this way."

Greyson gives me an apologetic smile. "You're beautiful, Kara. I didn't mean to imply that you weren't. I just grew up with a very different connotation of skinny. Most of the people in our burrow were thin by necessity rather than choice. It's been a hard concept to unlearn. That being said, I still expect you to eat every crumb."

"Yes, chef," I tease.

Begrudgingly, I decide it's time to leave and get up from the lounge with a sigh. Following my lead, Greyson walks us toward the coat rack at the front of the cafe. He helps me into my coat before reaching for his own. When I finish with the buttons, he takes my red scarf and wraps it delicately around my neck. Now, only the awkwardness of goodbye remains.

Before I have a moment to ponder the best approach to part ways, Greyson wraps me in his arms. I breathe in his familiar scent of spice and bergamot as he hugs me, knowing that this could be the last time I see him for ages. Who knows if Cade will ever let me out of his sight after this. And God knows he and Finn won't be very welcoming of him at Pandemonium right now, even if Greyson is a member of the demon club. And if I suggested going to GREY'S, Cade would probably shun the renowned restaurant as though they served smallpox with a side of poison.

If I'm being honest, this could be the last time I see Greyson, and it hurts my heart to lose him as a friend.

Greyson pulls away first, and I'm thankful that the hug was brief enough that I can hold off on being weepy until I'm in the privacy of my own car.

"Ladies first," he says as he opens the door and ushers me out. It's still raining like crazy. "Where did you park?"

"At the south side garage. You?"

"The other end," he answers with a slight grimace.

"Well, I guess this is it then. See you around, Grey." I wrap my arms around my chest to stave off the cold as my hair starts to soak through again. I make a run for the garage before I drown in the dreary Chicago downpour.

"Laters, little sub," I hear him shout back.

Chapter 38

KARA

There's a hesitant knock on the library door, and I know already that the time of my reckoning has come. I heard Cade get back around thirty minutes ago, and like an absolute coward, I hid in the library rather than going out to greet him. He's come for me sooner than expected.

"Come in," I call out, making no move to avoid the unavoidable.

Declan walks in with a very sheepish expression on his face as he avoids my gaze. "H-hi, Kara. Umm...Ashford would like to see you in his study. Now." He shifts uncomfortably as he waits for me to get up and obey my master's order.

Cade's study. I don't think anything good has ever come of being summoned to Cade's private office. It's where I'm always sent for scoldings when Cade doesn't have the time to deal with my misdemeanors right away, and it's my least favorite room in the manor. With a sigh of resignation, I get up from the couch and meet Declan by the door. He glances at me with an apology in his eyes, probably having guessed Cade's summons mean I'm in trouble.

"Don't look so worried," I chide, patronizingly patting him on the back as he escorts me to my doom. "I know I'm in for it. I broke his rules knowing there would be a price, and I'm okay with that. So stop looking like you're walking me to my death."

"I'm sorry—it's just that...never mind. I'm sorry." Declan glances away guiltily, like he's to blame for what's to come. He knows that Cade has unorthodox methods of keeping me in line. They all do. Cade is hardly discreet, probably because it adds another layer of humiliation to have the others know that he spanks and dominates me.

"Don't apologize, Declan. This one is on me. Let's just get it over with." We're nearly there, and I trudge on with determination. I've learned by now that I won't do myself any favors by delaying the inevitable. The doors to Cade's study are closed, so he's clearly still in the middle of working. Declan knocks twice before opening the doors at Cade's admittance.

Cade's expression is devoid of his usual fury when he looks at me for the first time since he kissed me goodbye early this morning. He's angry, that much is obvious from the icy glare he fixes on me, but there's no violence in his stance or fire in his eyes. Something about him feels off; I don't recognize this version of Cade. He's closed off rather than explosive, and I just wish he'd start shouting to put my mind at ease.

"You can go, Declan. Thank you for your assistance today. I'll be preoccupied the rest of the evening, so you can take an early night off, and I'll see you tomorrow."

Shit, I guess he's going to draw this out.

"Yes, sir," Declan responds with his usual formality. "Sorry, Kara," he whispers one more time before walking out and closing the doors.

"Come here, Kara," Cade orders, his voice stern but exhausted. If I didn't know any better, I'd say his heart isn't in punishing me tonight, but that would be as unfathomable as Stephen King developing an affinity for adverbs.

I follow his command without argument, going to the side of his desk and kneeling at his feet. He didn't ask for me to get into position, but I figure a little humility can't hurt me in this situation.

"Look at me."

I obey, lifting my eyes up to his. I'm startled to find that his expression is more sadness than anger, and guilt twists in my gut at having disappointed him with my disobedience today. His anger I can handle with ferocity, but this inexplicable devastation makes me want to grovel at his feet and beg his forgiveness. His hand reaches out to touch my cheek, but there's none of the threat I would have expected in the gesture. He runs his knuckles over my cheekbone, and I can't resist the urge to lean into his touch.

"Why did you disobey me, love?" Cade asks, continuing to caress my cheek. And in this moment, as he handles me with such tenderness, I wish with my whole heart that I could say I didn't.

"I wanted to see Greyson." My explanation sounds condemning to my own ears, and I hold my breath waiting for him to explode.

"I suppose I should be grateful that you grant me your honesty, if not your obedience. And why was seeing your ex-rebound-Dom worth breaking my rules?" Cade's voice is spiteful, and I can hear him silently contemplating whether I've told him the truth about the extent of my relationship with Greyson.

The subtle suggestion of Cade's mistrust is like the small nick of a dagger to my heart, and it stings. "Because I didn't want him to think that I used him," I answer in a low whisper, turning my eyes to the floor as I try not to betray my injured feelings.

"And why would you care what he thinks? He is nothing to you." Cade startles me by grabbing my hair and jerking my head back up. Rather than being frightened, I feel a jolt of relief at seeing the fierce version of Cade that I'm used to. "And he will never be anything more than nothing to you."

"I can't just shut off my feelings like you do, Cade."

"Oh, so you have feelings for him now?" His tone is sharp as shards of glass.

"He was there for me at a very low point in my life when no one else was." Cade has the decency to look a touch guilty at the insinuation. "And I'm grateful for that. I'm not going to dismiss Greyson just because you're possessive of my time. He's my friend."

"I am possessive of a good deal more than your time, Kara, and it would do you well to remember it." Cade's eyes start to heat as his hand on my hair goes from soft to punishing.

"It's not a competition, Cade. I belong to you; there will never be anyone else. But I'm allowed to have friends."

"Not those kinds of friends. I forbid you from seeing him again." The coldness of his tone offers not a sliver of room for argument.

I pause, biting my lip in indecision. Cade's never given me that kind of ultimatum before, at least, not since I've been free. I'm torn between wanting to submit to my Dom and wanting to fight for my freedom as I feel the walls of Cade's control closing in with suffocating force. Finally, I pull myself from his grasp. "You can't do that." My voice is firm as I plead with my eyes for him to see reason and stop being such a prick.

"I bloody well can do that. If you disagree, you can become very well-acquainted with the chains in the hideaway."

"You wouldn't." I try to ignore the tremble of panic in my bones as I realize he probably *would*.

"Fucking try me, Kara. I dare you."

Tears fill my eyes, but they have nothing to do with sadness. "You're not being fair."

"I never claimed to be fair." Cade sinks back into his chair, allowing some of the previous exhaustion to creep back into his face. He digs his fingers into his hair, looking so lost that I just want to climb into his lap and hold his head against my chest so he can hear how it beats only for him. Cade falters for the briefest of moments—a flicker of softness crossing his features—before he banishes any leniency with icy resolve. "But you did claim to be mine. Now prove it. Promise you won't see him again."

"I can't promise that unless you want me to break it," I whisper, barely able to draw breath as devastation wraps around my chest like a vice.

With a sudden strike of movement, Cade's fingers dig into my jaw with bruising strength as he lowers himself within a few inches of my face. "You will not. See. Him. Again."

"I can't agree to that." I can't explain the source of my sudden bravery, but it warms my blood like a mounting fire within my body. I tilt my chin up, leaning into Cade's harsh touch rather than pulling away from him. "Punish me if you must."

Cade looks startled for a moment before reconstructing his cold mask of dominance. "Oh don't worry, you'll be punished." Cade shoves me away and leans back in his chair. "Go to the hideaway and wait for me. I'll come down eventually. And when I do, you better be on your fucking knees and ready to beg for mercy."

"Yes, sir," I respond, my voice stiff and mechanical. I rise to my feet and walk with as much dignity as I can toward whatever hell awaits me below.

◆

I shiver against the cold as I continue to hold my position on my knees. According to Cade's protocol, I removed my clothes as soon as I entered the hideaway and placed them on the desk. The temperature down here can be freezing, especially in the winter months. When we use the room for play, Cade always adjusts the thermostat digitally and allows it to heat up beforehand; he likes me to be comfortable when he knows I'll be fully naked for several hours. When we use the hideaway for punishment, the temperature adjustment is more minimal. From the coolness of the air, I'm fairly certain Cade hasn't touched the thermostat today. It's about as damn cold as the archival room at the university.

It feels as though I've been waiting for ages. Another one of Cade's preferred methods of enhancing punishments—waiting in solitude. He knows the lack of productivity drives me mad as my mind goes over all of the things I could be doing while I sit uselessly on my knees. I already feel tortured, and he hasn't even begun. With morbid amusement, I ponder what form my punishment will take. A whipping? A caning? Since I outright disobeyed a direct order, it'll certainly be more than a spanking. I hope to God it's not the bastinado that he threatened to start implementing out of spite. Feet should be off limits—that's just common sense.

There's a raucous from above as the hidden door in the library opens. *Shit.* I hear the heavy thud of Cade's leather shoes on the steps as he makes his way down. If I had to guess from his gate alone, I'd say he is still moderately seething after our disagreement in his study. I try to compose my face to appear repentant—I'm not, but he doesn't need to know that. See, in spite of what Cade likes to tease, I *do* have a sense of self-preservation, thank you very much.

I feel him come up behind me, his body emanating a welcome warmth that I know doesn't show on his face at the moment. Like most times before I'm subjected to punishment, I have to resist my body's natural urge to seduce Cade in an attempt to save myself. As it is, I allow myself to lean back into the firmness of his muscular legs as he reaches down and brushes my hair to one side.

"Hold your hair." It's a command rather than the tender foreplay I've been enjoying the entirety of the week. I haven't been punished since the night Cade took me back, and I hadn't even disobeyed to earn the brutality that time. Considering my current sins, this will probably be far worse. I shudder at the thought as I take my hair in one hand and hold it up.

I feel something cold and heavy wrap around my neck and latch close with a sharp click. It's tight but familiar, and I'm desperate to reach up and see if it is what I think it is. I feel the pressure of it with every breath, and it's a nearly uncomfortable sensation.

"You may touch it." Cade's voice is reserved, and I can tell very little from it.

With a bit of hesitance, I raise trembling fingers to touch the object encircling my neck. I let out a soft sob when I realize what it is—my collar. I've felt so empty without it, so hollow since the moment Cade took it off of my neck. A single tear slides down my cheek as I reacquaint myself with the choker proclaiming Cade's ownership, running my fingers over the smooth facets of the rubies with reverence and gratitude. "T-thank you, sir," I manage to say when I've regained my voice.

"You are welcome. Maybe the constant weight of it can help remind you who you belong to when you decide to make reckless decisions that go against my explicit orders." His tone is stern, exacting, and it flays me.

"I'm sorry, sir," I answer with sorrow. Even if I don't regret my decision today, I fully regret having disappointed him and made him worry.

Cade walks around until he's standing in front of me, his expression contemplative. "Well, if you aren't now, you will be soon." It's like he can read the dissonance in my apology, and he doesn't approve. "There have been some modifications to the collar."

"Why?" I ask in surprise. The ruby choker was already custom made from antique jewels passed down through the Ashford family. What more could he have done to it?

"The necklace shattered." I shoot him an incredulous look. "I was… distraught after you were gone. I'm afraid the collar bore the brunt of my frustration at the time."

Oh, Cade. I forget that, even though he was the one who left, he still experienced the pain of the absence as much as I did. I want to take him into my arms and apologize that he had to deal with the heartbreak alone, but I'm not permitted to leave my knees. The distance between us at the moment stings like a fresh cut.

"I kept the broken pieces in my pocket," he continues. "Carried them everywhere I went. It made me feel close to you, even when I wasn't. After I found you again, I had the choker reconstructed with a few changes."

"It feels different," I comment, still running my fingers over the jewels. "It's—tighter. I can feel it when I breathe."

"Yes," Cade responds with a wicked smile. "I thought you could do with a shorter leash. Most of the rubies broke from their settings when they crashed into the wall. I didn't have them all re-added, so the length of the choker is shorter now. And the clasp in the back? It doesn't come undone. You'll be wearing it permanently. No more taking it off when you go to work or shower or sleep. You will see and feel that you're mine every second of every day." Cade looks down at me with victory shining in his hazel eyes.

"That feels excessive." The ruby choker suddenly seems even tighter, and I have to fight the tendrils of claustrophobia vying to root themselves in my mind.

"Love is an excessive emotion." It certainly doesn't sound like a compliment coming from his lips, but it's true all the same.

I close my eyes and let my body absorb the weight of the collar, allowing it to become part of me once more. When I open my eyes, I'm completely at ease for the first time in ages. Having Cade's collar around my neck was the final piece in banishing that heavy emptiness for good. I'm overwhelmed with gratitude, tears thickening in my throat. "T-thank you—for fixing it." I look up at him, my eyes full of relief. "I missed it."

Cade gives me a knowing smile. "I know you did, love." His fingers reach out and trace a line over my neck above the collar. "It killed me to take this off you. To see your neck bare and empty." His fingers wrap around my throat possessively as his eyes darken. "It will never be empty again. You'll always have a piece of me with you, to remind you that you're mine. Always."

"Thank you, sir." I'll always be his, and he'll always be mine. The knowledge that I belong to him clicks in my heart like a long lost piece of a puzzle finally sliding into place to make a complete picture. The perfect picture of happiness.

Cade gives me an appreciative nod before his features turn stern. "Get on the bed. Lie on your back."

Shit, I forgot this was meant to be a punishment. Cade came in with his collar, making me feel all weepy and sentimental, and I forgot I was supposed to be apprehensive of what comes next. Shuffling to obey, I get to my feet and walk to the bed, trying to settle in as comfortably as possible in the middle. I stretch out my legs, rest my hands at my sides, and wait.

I hear rummaging, which is never a good sign—the scrape of a drawer, the click of the cabinet door, the telltale sound of something being removed from the rack of hanging implements. I take bets with myself on what Cade will come back with. Whip? Flogger? Cane? Belt? Something I've never even been tortured with before? I feel the mattress dip and look over to see Cade mounting the bed with his hands full. He lays the items out and allows me to take stock.

Leather cuffs—standard and expected. A spreader bar—not wholly unusual when he has me on the bed. His favorite leather riding crop—not the worst thing he could have chosen. Two different vibrators and a dildo—decidedly *unexpected*. And a butt plug—that looks way, way too big to fit in my ass. I haven't even trained my ass in over a month. That huge thing will certainly rip me open. I look up at Cade with panic in my eyes.

"Hey, no one made you break my rules," Cade says without a touch of sympathy, his hands raised as though denying any guilt in the torture that is about to ensue. "My job is to make sure it doesn't happen again."

I sit in silence as he wraps the leather cuffs around my wrists and secures them to the bed posts. There is a bit of strain in my shoulders as my muscles try to accommodate the stretched position, but it's bearable. Next, he moves to my ankles and latches me to the spreader bar before tying down my legs to the bedposts as well. I hate feeling this exposed; there's something about not being able to do something as simple as close your legs that leaves an ache of helplessness in your chest.

"Like it?" Cade asks as he sits back and assesses his work with sadistic glee. And this is the happiest I've seen the British bastard all night. I shake my head. "Really?" he asks in feigned surprise. "But you look so pretty all trussed up and at my mercy. It's quite an improvement on the naughty girl running around town against her Dom's wishes." Cade's eyes glitter with devilish intent. "Maybe I should just keep you like this." He runs his fingers up the length of my legs that are spread wide. Even though his touch tickles, I don't have the option to squirm away from him. "That would keep my girl from getting into trouble, wouldn't it?"

Again, I shake my head, trying not to panic at the idea of this helplessness being made a standard part of our relationship.

"Well, it's a pity for you that you don't get to make the rules, isn't it?" Without warning, Cade thrusts one of his fingers into my wide open pussy. I flinch at the contact even as a part of me welcomes it. "Tsk, tsk, I thought you said you didn't like this, love?" Cade chides while his finger moves in and out of me. To my great mortification, I can feel my own arousal lubricating his intrusion. "You didn't lie to your master, did you? Because this cunt feels pretty bloody soaked."

I moan as Cade adds another finger, twisting and stroking them inside of me. "Well, Kara, do you *like* this?" he asks again. I grit my teeth, knowing that another lie would be useless.

"Yes," I admit, my tone begrudging and acerbic.

"Yes, you like what?" Suddenly there are three fingers thrusting inside of me, and I can barely breathe beneath the delicious intrusion.

"Yes, I like having your fingers in my pussy while I'm bound and helpless beneath you.

"Good girl," he says with a languid smile before removing his fingers and wiping the wetness across my bare thighs. I'm tempted to beg him to stuff them back inside of me, but since we're not in the hideaway for my pleasure, I don't think Cade will be very acquiescing.

"Now," he picks up the crop and taps the flat leather tip against his open palm, "how do you like this?"

I tense, waiting for my true punishment to begin. In general, the crop doesn't hurt too badly unless the shaft is used for the brunt of the blow; at that point, it's basically a cane and hurts like hell. Judging from Cade's anger in his office, I'm pretty sure he'll strive to make it hurt as much as possible.

The tip of the crop slaps against my breast; I flinch, even though the hit is so light that it's nearly playful. I look up at Cade in surprise, not the least bit placated to see a wide smirk of mischief on his face. Before I can contemplate whatever scheme has him smiling like a Cheshire Cat, the crop slaps out again and catches my other breast. To my great, unbearable humiliation, I moan at the stimulation, feeling my nipples grow stiff as though trying to make themselves better targets for Cade's assault.

"Does that feel good, love?" he purrs, and the sound of it shoots a bolt of desperate heat straight to my core.

"Yes." It's more a sob for release than an answer. Cade continues to tap the crop against my skin, always light enough to tease but never hard enough to hurt. The leather slaps over my breasts and down my stomach and hips, spreading warmth everywhere it touches. I whimper when the crop brushes against my thighs; I'm languishing with the need to feel its pleasant bite just a little bit higher. Cade slaps each of my thighs a handful of times, being very meticulous to avoid the needy spot between my legs. With my patience blown to bits, I start to tug against the restraints. I huff with frustration when I can't move an inch.

Cade laughs, the sound crueler than anything he's actually done to me. "What's wrong, Kara? Don't you like your beating?" He brings the crop against my thighs again, raining down a torrent of delicious little stinging kisses that never get any closer to where I need it. I'm wound so tightly I feel I could explode from the slightest pressure on my clit. "Or maybe," he trails the crop up to my pussy and slips the leather tip between my slick lips, "maybe I'm not hitting you where you need it."

I sigh breathlessly as Cade drags the crop up and down my slit. But it's too light. I need more. "Please," I plead in anguish. Even though I'm pinned down, I try to buck up my hips to get some friction from the crop.

"*Please*?" he scoffs. "This is a punishment, and my naughty girl is trying to make demands of her master?" Cade slips the crop from my pussy, and I whimper with the loss.

Of course, that's why he looks so smug. He's not going to give me pain as punishment for my disobedience. He's going to deny me pleasure until I'm a quivering, wet mess begging for anything to alleviate the ache between my thighs. That knowledge isn't enough to stop me from trying. "Please punish me, sir. Please spank my clit."

Cade's eyes ignite with twin flames of wickedness as he appears to consider my request. "You want me to hit you here?" he asks, tapping the crop over my mound far too lightly.

"Y-yes, please." My lips are trembling so much with starved arousal that I can barely form the words.

"You know I'm a weak man when you beg, love." Cade leans over me and uses his fingers to spread my pussy wide, leaving my glistening clit out in the open like the perfect target. Without hesitating, he slaps the crop against my sensitive flesh with a wet *smack*. The bite of the leather is blissful, sweet agony, and I can feel the fire in my blood mounting.

He hits me again right on the clit; I moan, half in pleasure and half in dread. I feel my orgasm building, and I know he'll torture me with denial rather than letting me come. Another slap brings tears of desperation to my eyes. My body rises as much as possible beneath the restraints to meet the next blow. When the crop lands against my clit again, sparks scatter across my nerves, the prelude to the explosion.

I know the next slap will send me over the edge. Cade knows my body well enough to realize it too. I brace from him to pull away, to torture me with the loss of an orgasm as his form of cruel and unusual punishment. I cry out in shock when he lashes out one more time, hitting my clit with more force than he's doled out the rest of the night. I detonate, shattering into pulsing fragments of pleasure and adrenaline as my vision darkens with an overload of sensation. Cade continues to lightly tap the crop against my pussy as I ride out my orgasm. Before I come down from the high, I feel another overwhelming stimulus against my sensitive core—a vibrator.

I writhe in pain as the full-powered vibrator forces more pleasure from my overused nerves than I want to give. Rather than being allowed to relax in the wake of my orgasm, my body is instantly being forced higher. I whimper as I crash toward the precipice of another orgasm, desperately waiting for Cade to pull me back from the edge. He doesn't. He continues his assault on my clit as I feel the unexpected penetration of a large dildo being shoved inside me. Against my will, I come again, screaming as he fucks me with the dildo and keeps the vibrating pressure on my clit.

I realize with absolute horror that I wholly misjudged Cade's method of punishment. He's not going to deny me; he's going to fucking kill me with orgasms.

"Isn't this fun, Kara?" Cade asks with venom in his voice, never stopping his assault.

Fuck, that's not even fair. He's turning my own body against me as he uses pleasure to bring agony. I shake my head violently, unable to believe that he would be this cruel. I would rather he beat me than manipulate my pussy to bring me overstimulated pain.

"No?" he questions with an arched brow. Without removing the pressure of the vibrator, Cade pulls out the dildo and waves the dripping silicon in front of my face. "Seems like you're enjoying it. Why don't you open that mouth and taste how much fun you're having."

Cade presses the dildo against my lips, and I turn my head away in disgust. "Open your fucking mouth, Kara." He grabs my jaw and digs his fingers into my cheeks, forcing me to open. Without a shred of gentleness, Cade shoves the dildo into my mouth, thrusting it deep until it reaches the back of my throat. I gag at the intrusion and the taste and the fucking humiliation of being fed the same toy that was just inside my pussy.

"Uh-uh, I've taught you better than that," he chides. "Relax your throat.

I want you to take it all the way down." Glaring daggers of hatred, I obey as much as I can, letting go of the tension in my body. "There you go," he praises as he starts to fuck my throat with the dildo. The room fills with the obscene sounds of me choking on a sex toy while the vibrator on my clit drags me unwillingly toward another release.

"Do you taste your cum, naughty girl?" he asks, adding another layer to the degradation. I give him a short nod. I can't escape the tangy, earthy taste of my own arousal in my mouth. It makes me want to vomit as much as the dildo triggering my gag reflex every few seconds. "Good. The next time you try to lie to me about being turned on, I'll just use your mouth to prove you wrong. Now, are you going to come again?" I nod pitifully as tears of frustration fill my eyes. How is coming again even possible? My body is already spent from the first two, but I can't deny the warmth that's building in my core once more.

"Give me another, Kara," Cade demands. Left with no other option, I shatter again as he muffles my screams with the dildo down my throat. My eyes roll into the back of my head, and when the spike of pleasure passes, all I want to do is sleep. A light slap on my cheek startles my eyes open once more. "Wake up. You're not nearly done yet."

He lets go of the dildo, but doesn't take it out yet. "Keep it in your mouth." Obediently, I wrap my teeth around the silicon, cringing at the amount of drool rolling down my chin and over my tits and throat. I avoid his gaze, feeling disgusting and repulsive. I hate for him to see me like this.

"Hey," he says, gently capturing my jaw and forcing me to meet his eyes. "You're gorgeous. The fucking prettiest little mess I ever saw." How did he even know I was feeling insecure? The man is a mind reader and almost always uses it to his own advantage.

I sigh in relief when he finally gives me a break from the onslaught of the vibrator. But I don't let myself get too comfortable as he stares down at me with cruel intent before turning to the pile of tools that he left on the bed. Cade chooses something and waves it in front of me with malicious satisfaction. Sure enough, he's moved on to worse forms of torture. He's holding the butt plug that's nearly the size of the damn dildo.

"Cade..." I whimper around the dildo in my mouth, pleading with my eyes for him to go easy on me. But I know he won't. He thinks I've earned this, and this is his sick idea of justice. I brace as I feel him slide the butt plug between my legs, coating it in my arousal. He hasn't brought any lube, so thank God I'm wet or this would really hurt.

He presses the plug into my entrance, and my pussy instinctively clamps down around it. He fucks me with it for a minute before pulling out and sliding the plug toward my puckered hole. There's the smallest bit of pressure, and I can already tell it's not going to fucking fit. I scream in panic against the dildo still stuffed in my mouth.

"Do you need to use your safeword?" Cade asks, his voice concerned. The plug is pulled away as he gives me a moment to consider my tolerance.

Is a butt plug really worth using my safeword? Sure, I'm panicked as hell, and I know it will hurt, but it's not enough to break me. At least, I don't *think* it will break me. I shake my head, not entirely sure I've made the right decision.

Cade drags the plug through my arousal one more time before sliding down to circle my asshole. He presses against me, and there's very little give. "Relax, Kara. You've done this before," he assures as he continues to press down, demanding entrance into my body. "Bear down."

Swallowing the thickness of humiliation, I do as he says and push down against the plug, allowing it to penetrate further. "Good job, love. Almost there," he praises. I squeak as I feel the plug slip all the way in. It's terribly uncomfortable, but it's manageable. I suppose I should be happy that he didn't decide to shove his dick in my asshole as punishment instead. Not yet, anyway.

After plugging my ass, Cade pulls the dildo from my mouth. I take a deep breath of relief to finally have my mouth free. My reprieve is short-lived as I feel Cade line the spit-covered dildo with my entrance. Before I can scream a word of protest, Cade sheathes the dildo inside of me. I cry out in agony. I'm too full; I'm going to burst at the seams. I'm overwhelmed and over-sensitized, and I can't seem to get enough air in my lungs as I start to hyperventilate.

"Shh, shh, shh, calm down," Cade orders in a low voice. I've closed my eyes in panic, but I feel his fingers in my hair, stroking and soothing. "I'm not going to move until you're ready. I've got you." He sounds so tender and composed that I forget this is meant to be a punishment and lean into his touch. When Cade feels me relax against him, he starts to move the dildo at a languid pace. Even though it's uncomfortable at first, my body starts to adjust. In less time than I would like to admit, I feel my body rise to welcome the thrusts of the dildo as it rubs against the plug in my ass, separated by only the thinnest layer of skin.

"That's it, love. Ride it." Cade's eyes burn with arousal as he watches me move my hips with the dildo as he fucks me with it. Unbelievably, I feel the stirrings of fire within my core once more. I've already come three times in a half hour. Surely there's a statute of limitations on such things? I hear a faint buzzing noise moments before Cade presses the vibrator to my clit, and I'm bursting into pleasure again as I come with a dildo in my pussy and a plug in my ass. There are tears on my cheeks when I come down from the high and mumble and plead for relief from the stimulation.

Cade's eyes turn dark and merciless as he feeds off my tears and anguish. This is my punishment, and he's determined to make me suffer. "Again," he demands, his voice black with brutality.

Chapter 39

KARA

Is it a problem if you keep track of the time of day by whether you're orgasming in bed or in another room of the house? It's an honest question. Morning is coming on Cade's face as he eats me for breakfast. Afternoon is coming on his fingers while we're both trying to get work done in the library or in his study. Evening is when I'm coming on his cock while he does delicious, kinky things to me in the hideaway. The days have all bled into one, long, continuous round of sex.

Thankfully, Cade has kept all of the orgasms to a reasonable limit since the day I snuck out to meet Greyson. After coming nine times on everything but his cock, I wasn't sure if I would ever recover. Cade was kind enough to grant me a day's reprieve before going back to wrecking my body with pleasure—the good kind.

And now, I'm fairly certain Cade thinks if he distracts me with his cock I won't go back to New York. But as persuasive as multi-orgasm days are, I'm too much of a professional to play hooky just to get banged.

"Cade," I half-moan, half-plead as he trails his warm mouth up and down my neck. We're in the library—so it must be the afternoon, although a slight rumble in my stomach tells me it's almost dinner time.

"Yes?" he answers with a smile against my skin before nibbling on my throat.

The sharpness of his teeth has me keening, and it's utterly devastating for my concentration. "As perfect as these last few days have been—" I gasp as he bites harder. "I will have to go back to New York—" I whimper when he runs his tongue along my collar bone, his stubble chaffing my over-sensitive skin, "once spring break is over."

"Never," he answers immediately, his grip on my hips growing tighter. "I won't allow it."

"Cade, I have to finish out the semester of research." I pull away, and he groans in discontent. "I signed a contract."

"Fuck the contract," he says angrily, pulling me back down beneath him. "I'll have you sign a new one that overrides any useless work agreement. Your place is here with me, and I refuse to let you leave again."

"This isn't negotiable." Ugh, he's so damned stubborn and far too heavy as he lies on top of me. "You agreed to this, remember?"

"I rescind my agreement," he retorts in a firm tone as he captures my wrists and pins them above my head. "Now, shut the fuck up before I take you down to the hideaway make good use of the cuffs on the bed."

"Caden Ashford, you do not get to kink your way out of this." I struggle against him, but it's useless. If he wants me trapped, there's no way I'm getting free. "We live in the real world where people are allowed to be separated from their partners for more than five minutes," I huff.

"If you think I am going to let you go back to that university without being marked as my goddamn property, you are out of your mind." He glares down at me.

"What the hell does that even mean? You want to mark me?" I roll my eyes. "If letting your inner sadist come out to play is what it takes to get permission to leave, then by all means, take me to the hideaway and do your worst."

Cade stills, his expression going dark and terrifying. "Would you like to consider that suggestion a little more seriously before I take you at your word and do something that can't be undone?"

"Do. Your. Worst," I spit back. Self-preservation? Yeah, she's a fickle bitch that comes and goes.

"I don't know if you can handle my worst, love." He grabs my hair and forces my head up. "But you'll fucking take it anyway."

◆

The temperature grows colder as we make our way down the steps to the hideaway. We're earlier than our usual playtime, so Cade hadn't adjusted the temperature yet. And given his current mood, I don't think he plans on making it any more comfortable for me down here.

"Strip," he commands, his voice rough.

I take off my clothes slowly, mourning each warm layer as they're stripped from my body and I'm left in naked shivers. I lay everything in a folded pile on the desk.

"Lie down."

"Aren't you going to tie me up or something?"

Cade growls in irritation. "If I wanted you to be tied up, you'd be tied up. Now get on the fucking bed."

"Yes, sir," I answer, hurrying to the bed.

Cade walks toward the wooden chest and comes back holding a long, narrow box.

"Your weapon of choice is rather small today," I tease.

"Do I need to gag you, or are you going to behave?" Cade snaps.

"I guess it depends on what's in the box," I answer with an arched brow.

He sighs and runs his fingers through his dark hair. "Christ, every minute with you is like a dance with mutual destruction." He steps closer, his eyes such a dark green that no fleck of gold remains. "You really should stop goading the monster before it decides it wants blood in return."

I giggle—I can't help it. "That's very Jekyll and Hyde of you, but I'm not scared."

"You should be." Cade opens the lid on the box, and inside is a smooth, ebony handle attached to a very sharp, steel blade.

"And what exactly do you plan on doing with that?" I ask, my voice trembling as every ounce of my previous bravery disappears.

"Maybe I'll shove the handle up your cunt and fuck you until you lack the mental capacity to question me," Cade retorts, his expression fierce. I can't tell if he's joking.

"*Is* that what you're going to do?" I'm not entirely sure of what I want his answer to be. Is the idea of taking a knife handle up my pussy terrifying? Yes. Is it better than any alternative involving the pointy end of the knife? Also yes. There are only bad options here, and I'm pissed at myself for taunting him so flippantly. I never expected him to bring out a goddamn knife.

"Not at the moment, no." His even tone gives very little indication of his intentions as he carefully takes out the knife and grips it just below the blade. I feel my pulse quicken as Cade captures my gaze, his hazel eyes molten with desire. Without a word, he brings the knife to my skin, the touch of the metal cold yet searing at the same time.

Keeping his eyes locked on mine, Cade takes the knife and drags the blade down my bare stomach. He doesn't press deep enough to cut, but there's a light sting left behind like a cat scratch. I can't help but squirm beneath his touch, my anxiety heightening as the knife travels lowers. "Don't move," he commands, his voice stern. "I don't want to cut you. Yet."

Did he just say cut me? *Fuck.*

I panic, trying to roll away from the sharp tip and end up nicking myself just like he warned. There's an instant burst of pain as I feel the reprimanding slap of his palm on my upper thigh.

"I told you not to move. Now look what you've done." I take my eyes from him to look down at my abdomen. There's a little trickle of blood right below my belly button. And a fucking Cade sized handprint on my thigh because he's an absolute dick.

"Why don't you let me slide a knife around your balls and see how well you sit still?" I bite back as I rub the stinginess from my thigh.

"That's not how this works though, is it Kara? Only one of us is the master, and it certainly isn't you." Cade's hand shoots to my neck, his fingers wrapping tightly around my throat. His other hand still holds the knife, and I'm not sure which is the greater threat at the moment.

I try to shove him off me, but my attempts are as useful as battering a stone wall with bare fists. Going for the element of surprise, I throw my right knee upward, trying to catch any of his vulnerable spots. He anticipates the move, all too easily knocking my leg to the side and straddling my hips to prevent any more struggling.

His hand tightens, continuing to choke me until dark spots dance in my vision and a lovely sort of weightlessness overcomes me. The fight leaves me as my body is starved of oxygen. I always have the option to tap out, but I don't. As far as kinks go, I love breath play; it's soothing to just let go and submit to the darkness. Right when I think Cade is going to make me pass out, his fingers around my throat loosen, allowing me hungry, desperate gulps of air as my organs try to regain their balance.

"Who do you belong to?" Cade asks, his tone vicious and carnal as he brings the knife up to my neck.

"You," I whisper, my voice hoarse.

"Louder." I feel the tip of the knife press in above my clavicle.

"I belong to you." My voice is clear and strong when I admit the one thing in life I know with absolute certainty.

"That's right. You're *mine*." The blade slides down from my neck until it hovers above the concave space between my hip bone and my pelvis. "And I'm going to mark what's mine." I flinch as I feel him lightly trace something into my skin. "And what do you think is a suitable mark for my property?"

"I-I don't know." *Nothing* seems like a reasonable answer, but he's never been a reasonable man.

"What do you usually write on your toys to keep other people from taking them?"

The blade is still moving softly over my skin, and the unnerving sensation is scattering my train of thought. "Your...your name?" Jesus, what the fuck was *that*? Stupid over-sensitized brain. I take it back. Please let me take it back.

"That's right," Cade answers, his dark voice equal parts smugness and sadism. "Wouldn't you look gorgeous with my name carved into your pretty skin?"

I shake my head violently, all ability to speak vanquished in horror of what he is suggesting. He wants to mark me with his name—to brand me like a slave. My head is reeling from the archaic, chauvinistic absurdity of his suggestion. My pussy—well, that traitor doesn't need to be addressed at the moment.

"Ah, you don't agree, love?" He laughs, and it's a dangerous, predatory sound. "Well, there's a word for that. So use it, or beg your master to mark you as his. Permanently."

Shit, I'm conflicted. Why the hell am I conflicted? This should be the easiest choice in the world. Use my safeword, or let a madman with a knife carve me up to feed some insatiable desire to own me. But something is stopping me from dismissing his suggestion with a logical, outright no. And in some small, dark corner of my mind, I'm battling a need that I didn't know existed until this exact moment. His mark would be a visible, tangible reminder that he will never let me go again. And the idea of him writing his name on my skin in blood? It does crazy, indescribable things to my pussy.

"Please," I whisper, half-trying to smother the words before they make their way out of my stupid mouth.

"You know me well enough to know that "please" won't save you." He digs the knife in a little bit deeper, and I feel my skin pleading to break beneath it.

The faintest smile tugs at my lips as my resolve strengthens, and it feels like victory. "Please, mark me."

At my request, Cade falters, jerking the knife away from me like he's afraid he'll cut me. I scoff; it's a little late for that. "What the fuck did you just say?" He's staring down at me in shock, and I don't know if I should find his blatant surprise insulting or not.

"Please mark me, sir."

Cade closes his eyes, his chest rising and falling deeply as he takes heavy breaths. When he opens his eyes, they're burning with demonic glee, molten amber snuffing out nearly any hint green in his irises. He bites his lip hard, looking as though he wants to devour me and he's just barely restraining himself.

"You can't help but feed the darkness, can you?" He says it lovingly, like he's finally accepted that there's no escaping the twisted tug of our bond. Now, all he has to do is make the bond permanent.

He brings the knife back to the spot by my pelvis and stabs the tip into the skin a few inches to the right of my pussy. "I'm going to cut you here. It will hurt. I don't want my mark fading, so I'll cut deep enough to scar. Are you okay with that?" I nod my head in agreement. "Verbal answers, Kara."

"Yes, sir." My voice is steady, and I know this is what I want.

"Fuck, you never cease to surprise me." Cade seems to forget the blade as he bends down to claim my mouth, his lips gentle and tender as his tongue licks and caresses almost reverently. "You're perfect." He whispers the words into my mouth as he continues to lap and suck and nip with his teeth. "My perfectly tailored ruin." He bites his way across my jaw and down my throat, stopping directly above the pulse I can feel throbbing to the point of nearly bursting through my skin. "Did heaven send you, or did hell?" His tone turns violent right before he sinks teeth into the flesh protecting my carotid artery. I whimper helplessly as he grinds his sharp teeth together, like he's actually trying to tear into me. He tugs hard before ripping himself off me. "It doesn't really matter, does it? Either way, you're mine to keep. My lovely little harbinger of chaos."

My pulse quickens as Cade takes the knife in a firm grasp and points it toward my bare, defenseless skin. Without any warning, the sharp tip of the blade pricks into the softness of my pelvis; time seems to pause for the smallest of moments before the cut starts to bleed. I'm so mesmerized by the tiny trail of red dripping down from the shallow wound that I forget to be scared of what comes next.

"There's no escape for you now, love. But then, you never really wanted your freedom, did you?" With that, Cade digs the blade in deep and rotates his wrist in a circular motion, stopping halfway around. The pain of the cut is searing, and I can't help but cry out in response. Cade holds the knife away from me, giving me a moment to breathe through the burn. I'm too anxious to look down and witness what I've allowed him to do to me, but I can see the tip of the knife is tinged with blood. My blood.

"Fuck, that's pretty," Cade says in awe, looking down at his handiwork. "Look at you, bleeding for your master like a good girl." My pussy was already wet at the twisted thought of letting him mark me, but his warm words of praise have me completely soaked. "That was the easy one. Are you ready for the next?"

That was the easy one? How much worse can it get? I suddenly remember Cade's exact intentions and realize the next will be three cuts rather than one. Shit.

"Do you need a minute?" Cade asks in concern after his first question goes unanswered.

"N-no. I'm okay. Just do it." Before I have enough time to come to my senses and run.

I close my eyes and brace for the worst as I feel Cade line the blade up an inch to the left of his first cut. This time, he cuts upward slowly, aiming for precision, and I feel tears gather in my eyes from the sting of it.

"Breathe, Kara," he orders in a firm voice. I hadn't even realized I was holding my breath. Following his instruction, I inhale deeply before exhaling a shaky huff of air. "Another," he commands. Again, I obey. "Two more, love." By the time I've worked my way through four deep breaths, I'm feeling calm and centered. "Ready?"

"Yes, sir." And I am.

The tip of the blade having never left my skin, Cade drags the knife downward, creating two sides of a triangle. I take a relaxing breath, knowing that the worst of it is over. Just one more. Without pausing, Cade completes the A with a short, deep slice through the middle before pulling away.

I wait a moment, then unclench my eyes and hazard a glance downward. It's a bloody mess, streaks of red dripping down from the two initials carved into my skin. I flinch as Cade rubs his thumb over the cuts to clear away some of the excess blood from his mark. C and A permanently etched into my body.

There's something so right in the twisted wrongness of bearing his ownership in blood. It makes me want to kiss him and fuck him and keep him forever. A little laugh bubbles out of me, for no other reason than I've likely gone a bit dizzy with love. My feelings of sheer ecstasy are shattered when I see Cade reach for the knife again. "W-what are you doing?" I ask, eying the weapon with trepidation.

"Exactly what I said I was going to do: writing my name into your skin. I'll put the D, E, and N here." He has the audacity to trace out three more letters beside the first two. "And then ASHFORD can go below."

He's lost his goddamn mind if he thinks *that's* going to happen. My penchant for insanity maxes out at two fucking scars. "I think we've had quite enough mutilation for one day, Caden Ashford. *Thornfield*. Now, get that fucking knife away from me before I decide to take it and use all eight inches of your beautiful cock as a canvas to write out my own name."

"There's my vicious girl," Cade says with adoration in his eyes as he throws the knife to the other side of the bed. "I just had to be sure."

"Be sure of what?"

"That you remembered to give me your weakness along with your strength." He slides down between my thighs, throwing both of my legs over his shoulders as his mouth hovers above my pussy and the fresh cuts beside it. "Because I love you for both."

My mind fractures in overwhelming lust as I watch Cade bend down and run his tongue over his marks, lapping at the blood until his lips are smeared with red. It stings, but it's an intoxicating sharpness of pain that sends my hips thrusting against his mouth, begging for more. He continues until the wounds have been licked clean and the red C and A stand out clear and stark against my pale skin.

"You surprised me, you know," he says as he lifts my hips until they hover off the bed.

"Why?" I ask, breathless and needy. "Because I didn't let you write out your whole name on my body like a piece of chattel?"

"No," he answers with a touch of amusement. "Because I expected you to scream *Thornfield* the moment I revealed the blade." Before I have a chance to be outraged, Cade slips his tongue between my folds and licks the length of me all the way up to my clit. I moan with abandon, any witty retorts completely evicted from my repertoire with one skillful lash of his tongue. He uses his thumbs to spread me wide open and thrusts his warm tongue into my entrance. I keen, shivering beneath the pleasure while he laps at my cunt like a man dying of thirst.

"I never dreamed I'd get to look at my initials branded into your skin as I fucked you. And that makes me so fucking hard," he whispers against my clit before sucking it against his teeth. I writhe in sweet agony, the pressure of his teeth somehow too much and just right at the same time. His stubbled jaw scrapes against my labia as he runs his tongue in a circular motion around my clit, dragging me toward release.

"Who owns this cunt?" he asks, and I'm thrown off balance when I feel his mouth move to the initials he carved into my pelvis.

I whimper at the loss of his tongue where I wanted it. Where I *needed* it. Cade runs his mouth over his marks, tracing them obsessively with his tongue. Before I can complain about the neglect of my pussy, he slips three fingers into my slick entrance, thrusting deep and hard. Moaning, I clench around him, grateful to be filled for the first time tonight. He finger fucks me without mercy, and when his thumb reaches up to stroke my clit, I see white behind my eyes. I shatter like glass, bursting into a thousand shards of pleasure, my mouth gaping with a silent scream. When my orgasm is finally spent, I'm gasping for breath.

"Who owns this cunt, love?" he asks again, his voice dark and desperate.

"You do," I reply without a second thought. As if there could be any other answer while my pussy is still clenching around his fingers.

He growls in approval, his lips vibrating against my skin. Without warning, his teeth tear into my skin, reopening the cuts. Rather than pulling away, I thrust my hips toward his mouth, begging him to take what he needs from me. My consciousness is floating somewhere just beyond my body, and everything is bright and blurred. I feel high, or rather, what I imagine being high feels like. It's tingly and weightless and warm.

In the distance, I feel a sudden emptiness as Cade removes his fingers. And then there's something cool being dragging between my folds. I open heavy eyes and glance down between my thighs. To my surprise, I see Cade gently running the knife along my slit. When I look up, his eyes are endless pits of darkness, raptorial and starving.

"Which end should I give you, love?" he questions, continuing to caress my cunt with the blade. "The sharp or the blunt?"

I shudder beneath him as my pussy clenches with need. He doesn't give me an option that doesn't involve having a weapon thrust inside me, and somehow, that floods my core with heat and sets my over-sensitized nerves aflame. I drag my teeth over my bottom lip as I look up at the man who owns every fragment of my soul. "You choose."

Cade's eyes turn a darker shade of black, his pupils expanding until only the thinnest sliver of his hazel irises remains. "*Christ*, you never cease to amaze me." He flips the knife in the air, catching the blade with a quick clench of his fist. "I'll take the edge for you love," he answers, squeezing his right hand tightly around the sharp side to shield me from any damage. "You bled for me, it's only fitting I do the same."

And he does. A thin trail of blood slips down his wrist and seeps into his white shirt. I'm transfixed as I watch the red blot spread over the material.

"Do you like that, Kara?" Cade says, his voice rough. "Do you like seeing me split open for you?" Cade uses his other hand to make quick work of his belt and pants, pulling them low on his hips and letting his cock spring out. His shaft is thick and pulsing, and the tip is swollen and nearly purple with the need for release.

I lick my lips. "Yes," I admit, my voice just as raw as his. He dips his left hand down to stroke himself, and I whimper with the need to feel him inside me. "Cade, please," I beg, tilting my hips up toward him.

"Does your needy cunt want to be filled, love?"

"Yes, please," I breathe, the words barely formed.

As promised, he thrusts the blunt end of the knife inside me while his hand keeps a strangling hold on his cock, pumping up and down. I wince, the sensation of being penetrated with the thick, slightly curved handle strange and unusual. It's not unpleasant, just different. Because I just orgasmed, I'm still tight, and I can feel the hard ridges of the handle as he slides it inside me.

"Are you okay?" he asks, driving the knife in slow but deep. I feel his knuckles brush against my entrance with every thrust, and I wish he'd stop teasing and give me more.

"Yes," I moan desperately, and he starts to pick up speed. "I-I like it."

He laughs sharply, his eyes focused on the knife disappearing inside my pussy. "Of course you do. You've never been able to avoid a little brush with danger." He slams the handle into me even harder, like he's punishing me for my lack of sense. Cade has a knack for making punishments feel like rewards sometimes.

A guttural shriek leaves my throat when the tip of the handle pierces my g-spot. Cade groans as my pussy clamps down, and he hits the same spot again. Over. And over. I bite down on my lip to keep from screaming—the sensation is growing too sharp too quick. I'm either going to come or pass out or do both at the same time. I feel a pressure in my bladder, like I need to relieve myself, and I fight the instinct to close my thighs and hold it in. Three more overwhelming, delicious stabs to my g-spot, and I can't hold back anymore. The floodgates open, and I'm coming again, drenching the knife, Cade's bloody hand, and the bed beneath us.

"That's it, love. Fucking soak my fingers like my good little slut," Cade gasps. I feel warm spurts of cum land on my thighs and belly as he finds his release alongside me.

Chapter 40

CADEN

We're both covered in blood and cum. Hers and mine intertwined as though they belong together. Which they do.

I look down at the cuts I carved into Kara's skin—cuts that will turn into scars—and I don't know how I got so goddamn lucky. This gorgeous, ferocious woman just had my knife inside her skin and her cunt. That confounding knowledge does inexplicable, feral things to every hormone, blood vessel, and atom in my body. I feel like a Neanderthal wanting to claim my woman in every goddamn way possible.

Which leaves me with the other small box I brought into this room. The one I'd planned on leading with before Kara decided to take my breath away and accept the mark of ownership I didn't even have the right to ask for.

This one, I assure you, is a little less drastic.

"So, I'm afraid this will feel a little anticlimactic," I announce, grabbing her by the hips and dragging her on top of me so that she's straddling my abdomen. "You know, after all the stabbing, blood play, and taking a sharp weapon up the cunt."

She giggles, still drunk off the adrenaline of orgasming and edge play. "Don't tell me you want me to slice you up with my initials too?"

I pull her down for a kiss, her mouth warm and laced with an addictive substance I just can't seem to get enough of. "Not at the moment." I kiss my way down her throat. "But I'd be more than up for it if you ever want to take a stab at it." She laughs again, and *God* I wish I could bottle the sound and listen to it over and over. "No, this is something for you. A present of sorts, though it comes with a rather heavy obligation if you choose to accept."

She sits up with a furrow of confusion between her brows, her thighs still wrapped around my hips. "A present?" she asks, latent excitement lingering in her tone. Of course, *those* are the only two words she hears.

"Check my pocket," I order, feeling the smallest tinge of nervousness as her hands immediately start palming at my thighs.

"Oh my God, are you already hard again?" she asks when her fingers land on the package I hadn't intended on her finding.

I roll my eyes. "You're straddling me naked, of course I'm bloody hard. I said check my damned pocket, not the state of my cock."

"Fine," she huffs, leaving my cock at attention while she digs her hands into my pockets. Her expression twists when she finds the small black box and pulls it out, staring at it dumbly.

"Open it," I command, anxious energy crackling beneath my skin.

The box opens with a loud *pop*, and Kara just gazes at it looking stunned.

"To be exact, your collar is short one ruby. I had my jeweler start working on it the day after you came back to me. That night at The Sanctuary was when I knew I wanted you to be my forever."

Kara blinks at me, but she says nothing. I take the box from her hand and pull out the engagement ring from the black, silk cushion. The oval ruby is huge. Emerson suggested I cut it down to be more proportionate with the size of Kara's hand, but I declined. I wanted it to be big enough that anyone who looks at her can see that she's taken from a kilometer away. Clusters of diamonds encircle the ruby in an Edwardian style, and there's an intricate gold band inlaid with diamonds. It's feminine and timeless, and it's perfect for her.

"I could get on my knees, but I figured that was more your area of expertise," I tease as I reach for her left hand. She pulls away, and my heart plummets in my chest.

"So you're…proposing?" she asks in a tone that could never be misconstrued as joyous. She sounds as though I've asked her to cut off her hand rather than give it to me in marriage. Actually, she sounds like she would prefer the mutilation option.

I balk at the blatant superfluity of her question. "That is the general idea when someone pulls out a ring and talks about forever, yes. Do I need to say the actual words?" I grab her wrists and throw her down on the bed, maneuvering so that I'm the one on top now. Technically, I'm on my knees, although I'm not sure it's much of a gesture when she's on her back below me. As romantic gestures go, my hard cock grinding against her bare pussy will have to do.

"Will you, Kara Caine, do me the very great honor of becoming Lady Ashford of Whitford Hall and Ashford Manor?" I ask dramatically, holding her left hand over my pulsing heart.

"No."

My thought processes malfunction for the briefest of moments before I realize I must have misheard her. "I'm sorry, no?"

"No," she answers in a sure tone devoid of any fragments of regret or sympathy. "Never. A thousand times no." I search her dark eyes and come to the startling conclusion that she's bloody serious.

I gape at her, completely thrown by her sudden rejection. "You took a *knife* to your skin without a word of protest—you'll wear my fucking *scars* for the rest of your life. But *marriage* is crossing a line?" I laugh, the sound of it bitter and tinged with anger. "Is a signature on a piece of paper a little too extreme a commitment for you, darling?"

"Goading me isn't going to change my mind, Caden. I said no."

"And may I ask why *not*?" I grit out, my devastation turning my mood instantly harsh. What is the point of any of this if she doesn't want to be mine permanently?

"Because marriage is a patriarchal construct established and perpetuated for the sake of sustaining male dominance and propagating a legitimate male line of succession," she retorts pretentiously, as though the reason for her rejection should be fucking obvious. Which it isn't because her *logic* is damned madness.

"Christ, I should have known I'd have your ridiculous ideologies to contend with," I snarl as I drag my fingers through my hair and try to decide what to do with her. I always have the cage…

"My ideologies are founded on facts and thousands of years of history," she snaps back, trying to squirm out from under me. I lock my knees tighter around her hips. She not going fucking anywhere until she's wearing my ring.

"This is the twenty-first century, darling." She squeals when I bend down and nip at her bottom lip. "If you actually got your head out of dusty books, you'd see your objections are antiquated by about a century." I run my tongue along the column of her neck. "I'm not offering to buy you from your family for a bloody cow."

"Same principles," Kara answers, her breathing growing a little unsteady. "You've just traded in livestock for diamonds."

I grab her jaw with one hand and dig my fingers into her skin. "Kara, the ring is a symbol of my love for you. It is not a bride price." I hold her gaze, not allowing her to look away.

"My answer stands," Kara responds, her voice faltering just a touch. A touch of indecision is all I need.

"Well I don't accept your answer," I declare without an ounce of mercy. I snatch up both of her wrists in one hand and force them above her head. With her arms trapped and my weight holding her down, she can't move.

"Jesus, Caden. You can't fucking Dom someone into marrying you!" she snaps in anger. She struggles against me even though she knows it's pointless. Fighting me will always be futile. She should save herself the trouble and give in now.

"I believe I can."

"That goes well beyond the bounds of my submission." She glares up at me, a sparkle of hatred in her eyes.

"You said you love me," I remind her, wrapping my hand around her throat.

"I do," she admits sullenly as though she's being forced to. "I just don't think I need to be a legally enslaved wife to prove it."

I groan as lust swirls in my mind and strokes at my cock. "Now you're just trying to turn me on," I accuse.

"Oh, so you find the idea of domestic oppression sexually stimulating?" She arches a brow, acting as though she's insulted me. Truly, she's just turning me on more.

"Absolutely." I buck my hips against her, letting her feel just how hard I am at the idea of her being my wife.

"You really are a sick bastard," she says with a shake of her head and a roll of her eyes.

"Never denied it," I agree, leaning down to force my tongue past her full lips. I thrust into her deeply, like I'm trying to fuck her mouth as I bite down on her tongue and steal the air from her lungs. She tries to fight me, but I feel the exact moment her body submits to me, and she melts beneath my touch. She's mine; every fucking cell in her body answers to me as though I'm her master.

When I finally pull away, she's gasping, her pupils are blown, and her cheeks are tinged with red. She looks positively high on lust. And highly susceptible to suggestion. I just need to push her over the edge.

"Want to know what life as Lady Ashford would look like?" I breathe against her ear.

She nods, her expression dazed.

I grab her by the thighs and push her legs up until her knees touch her chin. Then I push my cock into her, groaning as I feel her cunt clamp down on me for the first time tonight. "I would spend every minute of every day trying to make you the happiest woman in the world." I ram into her hard, sparing no patience for delicacy or sweetness.

"Really?" Kara sighs as she lets me wreck her, her eyes closing in rapture as I force my way further into her body.

"I would fuck you every day." *Thrust.*

"Yes," she moans.

"And every night." *Thrust.*

"Yes. God yes. I'm so close," she whimpers, her hips rising to meet me on every thrust.

"That's it, Lady Ashford. Ride your husband's cock," I command, lost to the illusion of Kara as my wife. As mine forever. And the fantasy is intoxicating. With one hand still strangling her wrists, I slide my other hand between her slick thighs and press against her clit.

"Fuck, I'm about to come," she nearly screams.

I keep my strokes steady on her clit while I angle my hips up and aim to penetrate her g-spot. Her guttural groan of pleasure is a sign that I've succeeded. I pin her down with my full weight and fuck her to the point of violence—to the point where she'll have cock shaped bruises in her womb when I'm finished.

"And then one day, when your body is so stuffed full with my cum that you can't take anymore, I'll fuck my baby into you."

"Shit—I'm coming," she cries, her cunt squeezing my cock so hard I come a few thrusts after. I pump into her until my seed is leaking out of her pussy and dripping down her thighs with her own arousal, leaving her sticky and used. With her hands still trapped, I grab the ring from the bed and force it on the fourth finger on her left hand.

Fucking mine.

"Cade—" she starts to protest, but I cut her off with a tight hold on her throat.

"Shut the fuck up, darling, and wear my goddamn ring."

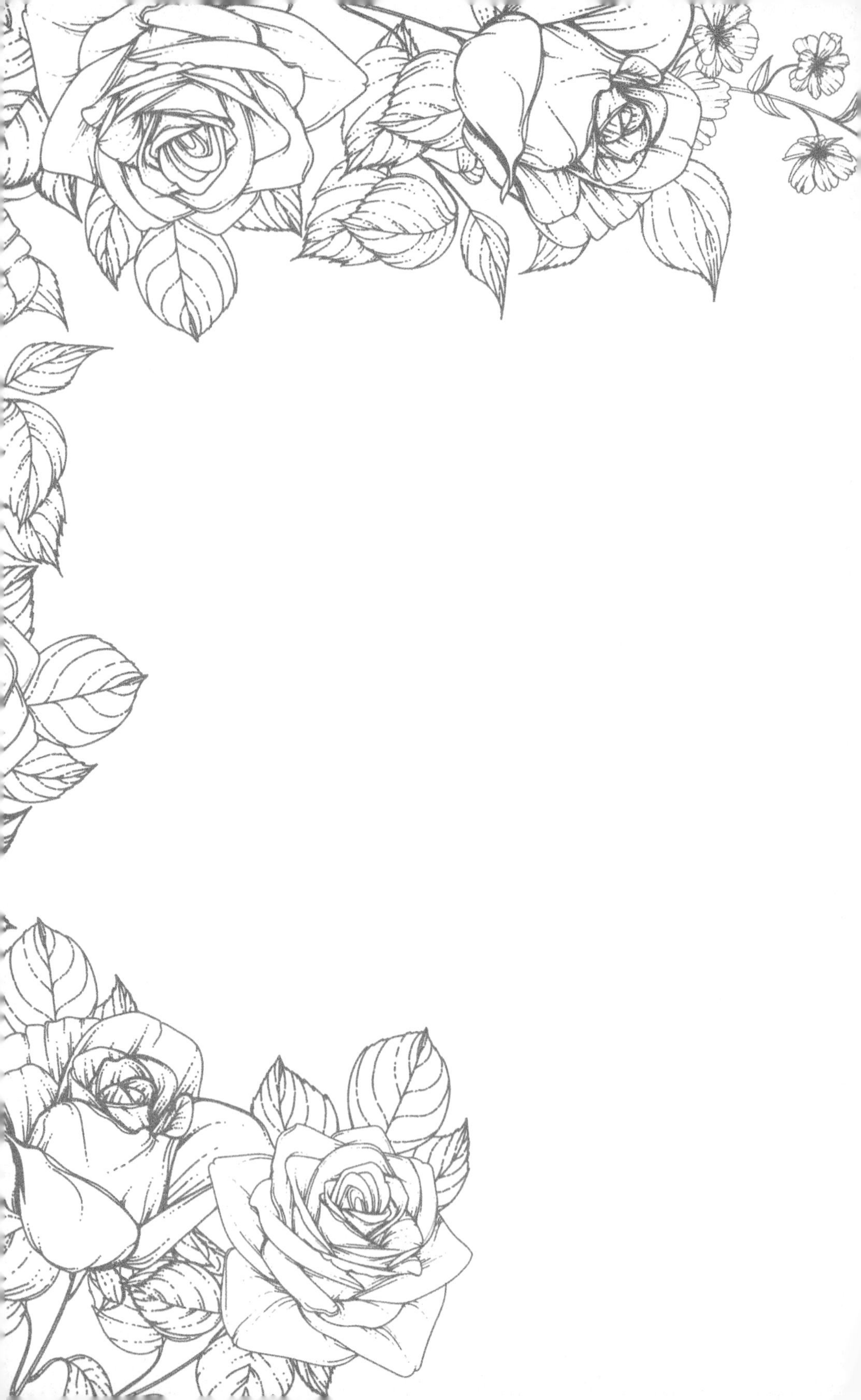

Chapter 41

KARA

And just like that, I'm Caden Ashford's captive once more. There's a goddamn ring on my finger that I didn't accept willingly. And I wear it *very* begrudgingly. At least it's pretty, and that is my one consolation as I go through my days with my hand weighed down by a five carat sign to anyone who looks at me that I've been *claimed*.

Not that I see anyone because I'm not allowed to leave the manor. Ever. It's as though nothing has changed from the day Cade walked down the steps of the library archives and stole me away from everything. At least now I can admit the bastard stole my damn heart too.

Cade won't let me go back to New York. I've begged and pleaded on my fucking knees, but nothing will move him. At this point, I feel like I've tried everything. As much as it pains me to say it, it might be time for me to admit defeat.

I open my laptop with the intention of offering my sincerest apologies to the head of the English department for my absence and regrets for not being able to finish my research on campus this term. With any luck, they'll let me continue my work remotely, and I should still have the academic journal and the course syllabus completed before the end of summer.

Given the state of my inbox, I probably should have checked my emails sooner. I skip past the most recent ones and scroll down to an email from the department head sent last week. It's unusual for Dr. Harding to be emailing me directly as I usually communicate with her assistant regarding any research updates. I told her assistant I've had the flu to make up for the two weeks of absence I had before spring break. The whole "my Dom is a control freak and won't let me leave the house" is a little bit harder to explain.

I open the email and skim before panic slips into my veins like ice water, and I have to start from the beginning to make sure I didn't misunderstand something.

Dear Dr. Caine,

Thank you for your email. Allow me to express my deepest regrets on behalf of the whole department regarding your decision to resign before completing your full term of research. Of course, you have my utmost respect for your decision to put your career on hold and focus on starting a family. I'm sure the decision must not have been an easy one.

I appreciate your recommendation of Dr. Westford to take over the literary research, and he has assured me he is more than willing to publish the journal and complete the course for the advanced level class. To our great delight, he has also agreed to teach the course for the fall and spring semesters.

I was surprised at your request for your work on this project to remain anonymous in favor of granting full accreditation to Dr. Westford, but I understand if this is the easiest way for you to break ties with your current academic obligations.

We wish you the best of luck in growing your family. Please feel free to reach out to me personally if you ever have an interest in pursuing an academic career again.

Warm regards,

Dr. Harding

What *the fuck* is this bullshit? I knew Cade was crazy, but *this*? Impersonating me and writing to my superior to sabotage my fucking career? To *grow my goddamn family*? This is the most traitorous betrayal I could ever imagine. Hell, it's *beyond* my imagination.

I'm going to kill him. I don't care if I love him. The British bastard is a dead man.

"Caden!" I shout as I tear my way through the manor like a lioness on a rampage. "Cade!" I scream again as I head toward his study, knowing he's probably holed up in there making more dastardly plots to keep me trapped within his grasp for all eternity. I throw open the doors of his study and am surprised to find his leather chair empty. "Caden!" I roar into the empty room purely because it makes me feel marginally better to express my anger in a tangible way.

I storm through the manor, continuing to shout his name as I barge into room after room only to find them empty. I check the library, the hideaway, the garage, the dining room. I'm about to put on my coat and brave the cold to search the stables when I hear a clatter from the kitchen. Even though that's the last place he would be, I push through the swinging door just to check.

And there he is—my beautiful betrayer. He's by the sink adding tap water to a cup that appears to be steaming. I'm perplexed enough by his current state that my fury is forgotten for the briefest of moments. And then the moment passes. "Caden Atticus Ashford, what the fuck have you done?" I thunder at him loud enough that he spills a bit of his drink in surprise.

Cade takes a tea towel from beside the sink and brushes the small spot of wetness from his pants. "This is one of the very rare moments in which I can honestly say I have no idea," Cade replies in a tone that seems sincere. He leans back against the counter and stares at me thoughtfully. "Enlighten me, and I will apologize profusely for whatever it is I've done to upset you this time."

"No apology will ever fix *this*, Caden," I bite out, walking across the kitchen and slamming my phone in his hand with the damning evidence up on the screen for him to see. Cade eyes flicker over the email as he reads the result of his damn handiwork.

"I'm confused," Cade says after a moment of studying Dr. Harding's reply. "You resigned?"

"No, I didn't *fucking resign*, you asshole! *You* did that for me. You couldn't bear to let me go back to New York, so you made sure I didn't have a job to go back to!"

"You're out of your bloody mind if you think I had anything to do with this," Cade scoffs as he pushes my phone back toward me.

"So you're denying it?" I ask with an arch of my eyebrow. As if anyone else would have suggested I was retiring from my work to "grow my family."

"Of course I'm denying it. Because I didn't fucking do it. I'm not that subtle, Kara. If I wanted to prevent you from going back, I wouldn't do it with an email. I'd just throw you in the cage I had custom made for you and lock the damn door."

"A cage?" Claustrophobic panic pulses through my chest, turning my heartbeat erratic. "Why the fuck do you have a cage?"

Cade smiles wickedly. "Technically speaking, I have two cages. You've seen the other. And a necessity for their use hasn't arisen yet. But I'm sure you'll present an opportunity one of these days."

I don't like the sadistic gleam in his eye, and I definitely don't like the possibility that he's stored a cage somewhere in the manor just in case I get a little too unruly for him to handle with his usual methods. "Can I just safeword on the damn cage now and save myself some trouble? Because there's no way in hell that's happening."

Cade considers for a moment. "Hmm, I think safewords should be more of an in the moment thing. Makes playing with you so much more fun, don't you think?"

"No, I fucking don't," I snap. "But back to the betrayal at hand. I'm going to need some rock solid proof that you didn't pull this shit." I wave my phone in the air. "Because the way I see it, you have means, opportunity, and definitely fucking motive."

"Where is this email that I've supposedly written?" Cade asks, happening upon the first hole in my theory. "You haven't shown me that."

"I can't find it anywhere," I admit sullenly. "It's like it doesn't exist."

"So you're hurling accusations based on what? *Nothing*?"

"Dr. Harding's reply is enough to know that there *was* an email saying that I'm not coming back—which is *your* ultimate prerogative. I apparently suggested that I wanted to grow my family—again, that's undeniably *your* intentions, even if they aren't mine. The disappearance of the original email is even more damning because *you* could have just had Braxton wipe it from my phone or whatever that tech shit is that he does. And *you* have access to all my devices. Hell, you probably even have all my passwords. From where I'm sitting, *you* are the only logical option."

"Looks like you have it all figured out, Detective Caine," Cade retorts. "The only problem is: I didn't do it. So your theories are about as substantial as that email that doesn't exist."

"Then who the fuck did?" I shout, frustration cutting my insides to ribbons.

Cade levels a stern look at me. "What about the fucking perverse professor who's apparently going to receive all the credit you earned? Did you ever even *consider* him before choosing to make me your villain?" Cade sighs. "I would rather crawl on my hands and knees through broken glass than bring any harm to you or your career."

Shit, the realization dawns on me the moment the words are out of Cade's mouth. Grant. *Fucking* Grant. He promised me ruin would come sooner than I thought. And somehow, he orchestrated this whole thing. To confirm my theory—or rather Cade's theory—I open my phone and search Grant's name in connection to any literary publications on kink in classics. And in an instant, I have all the proof I need.

"He stole it," I confirm with devastation.

"Who stole what?" Cade comes over to my side of the kitchen to look over my shoulder.

"Grant. He stole my research." I skim through the twenty page document for any hint that this isn't exactly what it seems—a petty piece of revenge by a scheming prick hell-bent on wrecking my life because I wouldn't let him touch my cunt. When I reach the bottom of the academic journal, I have my answer.

> *Thank you to Dr. Harding, Dr. Brown, my research assistant Kara Caine, and everyone else who helped make this study possible.*

He left off the title in front of my name. Grant of all people knows how hard I worked to become Dr. Caine, and he casually tossed in my name as though I was some undergrad student working to fetch him coffee for extra credit.

"He published it all under his name and gave me a small crumb of credit that feels more like an insult," I admit as anger curdles in my stomach.

"I'll kill him," Cade offers with the same casual ease of offering someone a pen or a piece of gum.

I groan. "Jesus, Cade. *Not* helping. You can't go around killing people." And he doesn't even know the worst of what Grant's done. If he knew what happened in my office a couple months ago, he actually *might* kill him.

"Why not?" Cade answers with a shrug. "He's near the top of my list anyway."

"You have a fucking hit list?"

"Of course," Cade says, wrapping his arms around me and hugging me close to his chest. Even though I can't logically explain it, the gesture somehow feels more tender as he speaks of being willing to kill for me. "Anyone who hurts you. Or touches you. Or looks at you in a way I disapprove of goes on it."

I roll my eyes as I nestle into his chest. "That's insane. You can't kill people for *looking* at me."

"Don't worry. I'm discreet."

I pull back just enough to look up at him. "I'm not worried about you getting caught, you British bastard. God knows you haven't been caught for any of your other crimes. I'm worried about your fucking black soul if you think it's such an easy thing to take a life."

"I don't think it's easy." His eyes go a little darker. "I think it's a goddamn travesty. But I'm honest enough to admit that some bloody twats deserve it anyway."

"Yeah, I can't argue with you there." If I toed the line of morality a little less carefully, I might even consider letting him do it. "So why on earth were you in the kitchen? I searched the whole house and this is the last place I expected you to be."

"Mrs. Hughes has a cold," he answers, as if that explains why I found him in the one room in the manor he never uses.

"Yes, I know Mrs. Hughes has a cold," I retort. That's why I ate toast for breakfast instead of scones. "That doesn't explain whatever that is." I wave my hand in the direction of the cup sitting forgotten on the edge of the counter.

He looks down at me with a mixture of frustration and embarrassment. "It's tea time." He nods toward the stove. "I got the damn kettle to boil, but the tea was too scorching to drink, so I added some cold water. And then it was all rather a mess."

"Oh my God," I respond with a giggle. "Lord Ashford really *doesn't* know how to make a cup of tea."

"But he *does* know how to spank your arse, so you better watch it," Cade snaps with a light swat on my ass.

"Come on, you helpless little rich boy," I tease, untangling myself from his arms and dragging him toward the stove to grab the kettle. "Let's make you a cuppa."

Chapter 42

CADEN

The passing street lights flicker over the large, diamond encircled ruby on Kara's left ring finger as I hold her hand captive against my thigh. Even though she's refused to give me her promise, I refused to let her leave the goddamn house without wearing my claim on her where everyone could see it. The initials carved into her skin are for me. The unavoidably large engagement ring on her hand is for everyone else.

To her, wearing my ring is an empty gesture meant to placate me. To me, it's a symbol of the future we will share together, even if she's too stubborn to admit it yet. And it's a symbol to every man and woman who sets their eyes on her to *back the fuck off*.

Kara Caine is mine—body, heart, and soul.

We're driving to Pandemonium tonight. I thought Kara could use a distraction after the shit she went through with that cunt, Dr. Westford—who I might still kill. It's our first time back at the club since I made the worst decision of my life. There's a symmetry in returning after I've made the best. Kara is mine, and she will be by my side until death do us part. And it's high time everyone at the club knew it. Think of it as an engagement party, but without the bride-to-be's consent.

Finn greets us at the doors, beaming with joy like a bloody mum when he sees the ring on Kara's hand.

"Congratulations, lovebirds," he says with a smug smile, as though he expected this outcome all along. I told him I was asking her to marry me; I don't think it ever occurred to him that she could say no.

"We're not engaged," Kara bites back as she glares at me and tries to cover her ring with her other hand.

I snatch her left hand and display it very prominently against my chest. "Come now, darling, no need to play coy," I chide. "Tell Satan 'thank you' for the well wishes on our betrothal." Kara's beautiful brown eyes are sharp like daggers glinting with the light of the fire surrounding us.

"Thank you, my lord, for the unwarranted congratulations on a very non-existent engagement and non-eventual nuptials." She rips her hand from my grasp and takes two steps back from both of us. "Also, thank you for upholding the asinine assumption that if a woman wears a piece of jewelry on a designated finger she's been claimed as another person's property. I've always been particularly fond of the antiquated exchange of goods for a lifetime of loyalty and servitude. Seeming like a fitting trade, don't you think?"

Finn's gaze flickers between Kara and me, a furrow of confusion between his brows. "Did she say *no*?" he asks, his eyes widened in surprise. Clearly, he's as shocked as I was.

"No," I answer at the same time Kara says, "yes."

Finn chortles, the cacophonous sound of glee grating on my nerves. "You just can't break this one, can you Ashford? She's fucking indestructible."

Kara smiles as though she's received a compliment of the highest order. Damned brat. I'm instantly overcome with a primal need to bring her back down to her knees where she belongs.

"Kara, darling?" I call, already knowing the term of endearment will drive her mad. I've used it ever since I put the ring on her finger, and she looks as though she wants to murder me every time she hears it. Of course, that means it's become my new favorite torment. I certainly can't be calling her Miss Caine when she's about to be Lady Ashford.

"Yes, *sir*?" she answers through gritted teeth.

I grasp her jaw and squeeze those clenched teeth until she winces. "Be a good girl and go get me a ball gag from my room," I command.

"Why?" she asks warily, her sudden trepidation overcoming her submission.

I glare down at her. "If you can't use your mouth to say pretty things, then I'll take it away and let you drool all over your lovely chin in silence."

Kara pouts, biting her lip as she tries to think of a way to get out of following my orders. She hates the gag, probably because mouthing off is one of her favorite pastimes. But tonight is meant to be a celebration, and she's taking all the bloody fun out of it.

"Go on," I order, swatting her arse in the direction of the stairs. With a sigh of resignation, she trudges toward my room. I watch her leave, admiring the view as she walks up the staircase and disappears out of sight.

"So what the hell happened?" Finn asks when Kara is out of earshot.

I slip my hands into the pockets of my trousers and lean against one of the gold columns depicting the battle of the angels in Heaven. "She was—less than thrilled at the idea of marriage," I answer with a shrug. "I'd go so far as to say she was offended by the idea of becoming my wife. Like it was some sort of attack on her fucking 'independence.' Bloody feminists."

Finn laughs. "Can you really be a feminist if you let a man collar you, own you, and treat you like a sex-slave?"

"Don't ask me *how* she does it, but she fucking does. The damned woman can be on her knees and still looking down on you from the moral high ground." Kara is somehow a brilliant submissive and also the least tractable woman I know. It's fucking ironic, and not the humorous kind. "I thought marriage and babies were the sort of bullshit every girl wanted." I rake my fingers through my hair. "I suppose my mistake was expecting Kara to be like every other girl."

"Well, she did decide to fuck and date her kidnapper, so she was bound to deviate from other norms too." Finn's expression turns contemplative. "Maybe she wanted a cage and not a ring?"

"I've got one on hand. It wouldn't hurt to try it," I agree darkly as I watch my submissive return with a ball gag as requested. She's lucky she's not getting the inflatable one. It's exceedingly unpleasant to socialize with a blown up cock shoved down your throat, or so I've been told.

"What are you two discussing so secretively?" Kara asks with a suspicious gleam in her eyes.

"Your possible sleeping arrangements if you don't start behaving," I snap back, holding out my hand for the gag. Reluctantly, Kara places the leather strap with the black silicon ball attachment in my palm. "Kneel."

Rolling her eyes, Kara gets down on her knees. She must assume that the gag is punishment enough that I'll let a little cheekiness slide. I won't, and I'll make sure she gets everything she deserves and more when I take her upstairs. For now, a little degradation will have to suffice.

"Open up," I command, tapping her closed mouth. Those perfect, red lips will be ruined before she leaves this room. Kara obeys, opening wide enough that her jaw grows taut. I slip the silicon ball behind her teeth and wrap the leather straps around her cheeks, pulling tight enough that the metal rings on either side dig into her skin before fastening the gag behind her head. She looks like a gorgeous mess already.

"What's your safety signal?" I ask, making sure she remembers how to tap out if she gets too uncomfortable or overwhelmed. She taps my thigh three times, our agreed non-verbal safeword. "Good girl," I praise with a soft pat on her head. I can see her eyes glaze with lust; as much as she hates to be used like this, she loves it too.

"Now, let's go share the good news." I help Kara to her feet, appreciating the absolute panic in her eyes. I lead her toward the bar and order two glasses of champagne, requesting that champagne be distributed throughout the club. Finn shakes his head with a small laugh, but he doesn't say a thing. As long as it's on my tab, he doesn't care what I do with his alcohol.

I hand one glass to Kara, well aware that she won't be able to drink it with a gag in her mouth. It's just for show anyway. She glares at me and accepts the champagne sullenly. I grab her left hand and use her new ring to tap against the glass and draw the attention of the crowded room. Nearly everyone has a glass of champagne in their hands now. The blood drains from Kara's face the second she realizes what I'm about to do.

Her hand taps against my thigh once. I still, looking down at her and waiting for the other two taps. If she gives the signal, I'll stop. I study her face, waiting until I see resignation overtake the dread in her dark eyes. And with her begrudging permission, I trudge her toward her own personal hell. "Attention everyone," I call out with a raised voice, wrapping my arm around Kara and drawing her close to me. "Kara and I have an announcement we'd like to make." She goes stiff as a marble statue in my arms.

"Kara has done me the very great honor of agreeing to be mine *officially*." The room erupts into a roaring applause, and I feel the sharp heel of Kara's stiletto dig into my foot. The smile never leaves my face as I bend down to whisper in her ear, "you'll get a spanking for that later, darling." She whimpers at the warning and has the good sense to remove her damned foot from mine.

"We wanted all of you to be the first to know. Of course, Kara wishes she could tell you how happy she is, but her mouth is a little full at the moment." I laugh, and the room joins me. "So, cheers to my lovely sub making me the happiest Dom in the world." We all raise our glasses and drink to my and Kara's happy future while she's probably planning ways to make herself a widow as soon as possible.

Finn comes over and clinks his glass against mine. "Cheers, mate." He clinks his glass against the superfluous one in Kara's right hand. I still hold her left one in mine so that everyone can see the ring she somewhat willingly accepted even if she hasn't quite agreed to the rest of it. Yet. "You know she'll probably try to kill you in your sleep tonight, right?" he comments in a stage whisper.

"Oh, I'd expect nothing less of my vicious girl," I reply, kissing Kara's leather adorned cheek. She's begun to drool down her neck. She mumbles something against the gag that bears a vague resemblance to *fuck you*. "I love you, too, darling," I respond, tapping the center of the silicone ball currently stuffing her stretched open mouth smeared with spit and lipstick. God, she's bloody gorgeous when she's messy. I need to take her upstairs and do filthy things to her this goddamn minute.

"Now, if you'll excuse me, I need to go fuck the future Lady Ashford." I pull Kara toward the stairs, her feet dragging the whole way there as the champagne in her glass spills on her dress. She'll soon be wearing nothing but her collar and her matching engagement ring anyway.

I throw open the door to my private suit and toss Kara inside. Announcing our engagement has set the blood pounding in my veins, and it's all heading in one direction. Desperate to get her naked, I grab the bodice of Kara's black dress in both hands and tear it down the middle. She grunts in protest when I turn the damn thing to a pile of threads on the floor. She's always bemoaned my ravaging of her clothes during sex—but she knows I can just buy her a new one. Or twenty.

I reach to remove the gag next, but I pause with my hands on the leather as I remember the tongue lashing I'm likely to receive for being somewhat misleading regarding the truth of our engagement. Or lack thereof. Well, I suppose she can take a lashing in return.

"I'm going to take this off," I tell her with my hand gripping her jaw. "But I will cane you for each filthy curse word that leaves your lovely mouth. Do you understand?"

She doesn't nod her head or grunt in response. She merely glowers at me with an unspoken challenge in her dark eyes. I've warned her. What she does afterward is up to her. Bidding farewell to the last seconds of blissful silence, I unbuckle the gag and pull the ball from her mouth. She stretches her jaw and rubs at the sore muscles for a moment before launching her attack.

"What the *fuck* was that, Caden Ashford?" she screams in outrage. To be honest, the outrage is fair, but I've never claimed to be a just man.

"That's one. And what was what, darling?" I ask, feigning innocence. I like to think it sounds believable, but from the murderous look on her face, it probably doesn't.

"You *know* what. That fucking farce of an engagement announcement when you know full well I have no intention of marrying you—ever."

"That's two. And I have every intention of changing your mind, so my announcement today was merely preemptive."

"Get this through your thick skull, you damned British bastard. I *will not* marry you. No matter how many times you ask in however many ways, I will not sign my name on a piece of paper that says I belong to you until I die. Marriage isn't romantic. It's fucking slavery."

"That's five. And I was under the impression that you enjoyed a bit of slavery. In fact, I'm fairly certain it gets your cunt wet. Shall we test my theory?"

She remains silent, glaring up at me through her dark lashes.

"Brilliant," I say, assuming she's accepted my challenge if she has no plans to deny my accusation. "Come here."

Kara clenches her fists at her sides and starts to walk toward me.

"Uh, uh, uh," I tsk, pointing to the dark, marble floor. "Crawl to me. On your knees." I arch a brow, daring her to challenge me.

After a small internal struggle, she obeys, getting down on her hands and knees and crawling toward me. She stops in front of my leather shoes and slips into a kneeling position at my feet. Whether she admits it or not, she finds great peace in kneeling beneath me. I stroke her hair, and she instantly leans into my touch like a loving pet. I let my hand trail down to her choker and slip my index finger beneath it, pulling her closer to me. It's a tight fit, and I know her breath will be restricted slightly.

"What's this around your neck, love?" I ask pointedly.

"My collar, sir," she chokes out with the air that I allow her to breathe.

"Mhmm," I agree, tugging on the ruby necklace a bit more. "And what is the significance of you wearing my collar?"

"It means—" She coughs against the strain on her throat. "It means you o-own me."

"Correct," I reply, granting her a little more oxygen. "I own you. Like a slave, isn't that right?" I use my hold on her bejeweled collar to drag her backwards toward the bed. I stop when her back hits the bedpost. "Isn't that right, Kara?" I reiterate.

"Yes, sir," she answers, her voice small.

"Say the words, Kara. I want to hear you say it." I lift her up by her collar and throw her on the bed, rolling her over onto her stomach.

"You own me like a slave," she answers, her tone full of humiliation and something much more searing. She's horny as hell.

I leave her on her stomach and go to fetch a thin, whippy cane with a curved handle from one of the racks. I promised her five. And she's going to get every single one. Without warning, I flick the cane against her arse, the thin rattan flying through the air with very little force. She shrieks when it unexpectedly slices against her skin, leaving a stripe of red.

"Count them out, Kara," I demand in a stern tone. "You earned every one."

"One," she says in a near whisper.

Swish. "Louder, Kara."

"Two," she calls out in a firmer voice.

The next two come down hard against the middle of her thighs.

"Three," she chokes out. "Four."

Just to be a bastard, I give her the final one in the delicate crease just below her arse.

She cries out and has to take a steadying breath before counting out her last. "Five."

I drop the cane to the ground and rub my hands over the gorgeous marks left behind on Kara's skin. She flinches at the contact, but lets me continue to caress her without protest. She always looks so damn pretty after a caning, and I love the heat that lingers on her skin as the blood rises to the surface. I let my hand slip between the cleft of her arse cheeks and dip down to her hot cunt. As expected, she's as slick as a rose in a rainstorm.

"What did I tell you?" I ask, thrusting my middle finger inside her and stroking at her wet inner walls. "Does acting like my perfect little slave get you wet?" She struggles beneath me, trying to lift her hips off the bed to get me to finger her deeper. I push her back down and continue my pace—nice and slow. "I asked you a question, Kara."

"Yes, sir," she answers, sounding like she had to cough up broken glass along with the words.

I lay my body on top of her, using my full weight to crush her into the mattress. "You're already mine until you die, darling," I growl against her ear. "Does writing it down on a piece of paper really make it so much worse?"

Kara stays silent, breathing heavily beneath me as I continue to thrust my finger into her at a languid pace. I'm not sure if her lack of response is because she's considering changing her mind about the proposal, or because she knows she doesn't have a solid argument for refusing me.

Well, if she can't meet me halfway, then I don't feel the need to do half the work either. I slip my hand from her cunt, and she moans from the loss. I turn her onto her back and am met with the full force of Kara Caine's scowling displeasure.

"None of that," I chide, slapping her lightly on the cheek. "If you won't submit to being my wife, you can get your own self off."

Kara glares at me, her lovely brown eyes glimmering with thoughts of torture and revenge. Her viciousness is as precious as a kitten with its claws out.

"That wasn't a bloody suggestion, Kara. Touch your clit. Now." She is going to get an orgasm, but I'm going make her work for it.

With a groan of annoyance, Kara obeys, lazily running her fingers over her clit. I give her pussy a quick slap. "If you don't touch yourself properly, I will edge you all goddamn night and not let you come at all," I warn.

She flinches. In an effort to escape her least favorite punishment, she renews her efforts with her pussy, this time stroking the bundle of nerves the way she likes it. She moans in pleasure as her fingers trace soft circles over her clit. But pleasure isn't all she's going to get.

"Slide your middle finger inside your cunt. I want to hear how fucking wet you are," I command. She obeys, sliding her left hand up between her thighs and slipping a finger inside. Her ring looks damn pretty glittering against her glistening cunt. I have a sudden, insatiable need to see the ruby and diamonds disappear inside of her. "Good girl. Now add another."

She thrusts two fingers into her pussy, arching her hips to penetrate deeper. Her cheeks are flushed with arousal, and she keens with the pleasure of being filled while she strums at her clit.

"Does that feel good, darling?" She nods. "Add one more, I think you can take three inside that needy pussy." She does as I ask, and I feel my cock get hard as a goddamn rock at the sight of her engagement ring sliding inside her and getting sticky with her cum. "Are you full, love?" I ask, barely able to concentrate as I watch her fingers thrust in and out. It's fucking hypnotic.

"Uh-huh," she whimpers.

"Can you feel your tight cunt clamping down on your hand?"

"Yes," she moans, her fingers working faster.

"Another," I demand.

She stills in shock. "I-I can't."

"Yes, you can."

"It's too tight."

"You can stretch. Slip your little finger inside. Look at your greedy hole gaping for more, desperate to be filled." A deep, strangled sound between a moan and a whimper erupts from her chest as she stuffs a fourth finger inside her cunt. "Fuck yourself with them, love. I want to see you thrust into that soaking wet pussy. Do you hear the slickness of your cum sliding against your fingers? It's like a fucking symphony." Kara cries out when she begins to move her fingers in and out of her pussy. "Keep touching that fucking clit," I remind her. I want to see her come undone while riding her own hand.

I crawl onto the bed and lay down beside her, taking a moment to enjoy the sight of my beautiful girl stuffing herself to the brim on my command. Well, almost.

"Make it five," I demand, my voice raw with the need to be inside her. But not yet. First, I want to see her get herself off.

"W-what?" she asks, startled by my request. Both of her hands still as she looks up at me with terror in her eyes.

"I want to see you shove your whole hand inside your cunt."

"That's not even possible!" she says in frustration, removing all of her fingers from between her legs and trying to sit up. Not the best decision on her part, since she'll have to fit them all back in again.

"Believe me, it *is*. Now lay the fuck back down." Shooting me a murderous glare, she lays back with a pout on her adorable face. "Five fingers. Now, Kara." With a huff of exasperation, she hesitantly starts filling herself again. She pauses when she gets to four, clearly not sure if adding another is feasible.

"Take a deep breath, love," I coax, brushing my knuckles against the soft skin of her cheek. She complies, taking oxygen into her lungs and holding it in until I fear she might burst. Finally, she exhales with a gasp, taking multiple heaving breaths to steady herself. Her eyes are wide and her pupils are dilated when she stares up at me, waiting for my next command. "Pull your knees up and spread your legs as wide as they will go."

Again, she obeys, spreading herself as she continues to hold my gaze, her eyes shining with the warmth of unadulterated submission.

"Now, squeeze your fingers together tightly and slip your thumb inside."

She groans in what sounds like a mixture of discomfort and something indescribable as she manages to fit her whole fist inside her cunt. And fuck, if it isn't the most beautiful fucking sight I've ever seen. My cock quivers with need as I stare down at her pussy swallowing her entire hand.

"Push them in further, love. Like you're trying to punch through." Cautiously, she follows my instructions, moving her hand in and out at a slow pace. "Don't forget to rub your clit."

While she's busy with her cunt, I bend down and take one of her pretty pink nipples into my mouth, swirling my tongue around the hard bud and teasing it with my teeth. Kara squeals with the overload of sensation, her hands stilling as she writhes beneath me.

"Don't stop. I want you to come on your hand." She resumes her attention to her pussy while I continue my assault with my mouth, sucking hard on her nipple as I pinch and twist at the other one with my fingers. It doesn't take long before I feel Kara stiffen beneath me, her hips rising off the bed as she tries to meet her orgasm.

"Are you going to come, darling?" I ask, barely keeping myself from coming as I rub my cock against the side of her arse.

"Yes, sir," she answers with a gasp, her hand pounding into her pussy hard and fast.

"Then come, love. Fuck that pretty cunt with your fist." I know she's coming when a guttural scream fills the air, her arousal soaking the sheets beneath us while she continues to ride her hand and drain every last ounce of pleasure from her swollen clit.

Jesus fucking Christ.

I don't think I've ever been harder in my whole bloody life. My cock is so fucking swollen it might actually explode if I don't bury myself in her dripping cunt this instant. "Pull your hand out, darling. I need to fuck you." I make quick work of my belt and drag my trousers and pants down my hips.

Kara does as I ask, flinching slightly when she retracts all of her fingers. Her cunt gapes at the sudden emptiness, just begging for my cock to stuff her full again. Not wasting any time, I grab her hips—my fingers brutally digging into the soft skin—and twist her onto her stomach. Wrapping my hands around her narrow waist, I pull her up so she's on all fours in front of me. The keen little cockslut arches her back and pushes her arse against me, silently begging me to fill her. So, like a gentleman, I give her what she fucking needs.

Digging one hand into her hair and the other into her hip, I pull her against me, impaling her with one, sharp thrust into her slick opening. She cries out, and the sound merely feeds the lust burning in my blood. I pound into her in a frenzy, desperate to reach the deepest parts of her body and tear pleasure from her very soul. Knowing my sweet little whore likes to have all her holes filled, I spit on her arse and watch it trickle down between her cheeks. I feel her stiffen when I use my fingers to smear the wetness over her back hole. Continuing to thrust into her, I slip my middle finger down to the knuckle inside her arse and fuck both holes at once.

Kara's moans turn deep and low as I use her body like I own it. Because I fucking do. "You like that, dirty girl? You like having me in your cunt and arse, stuffing you full?" I ask, my voice rough and raw from lust at the unholy sight of her.

"Yes, sir," she answers, the words barely formed through her moans of pleasure.

"Bet you want me to fill you up with my cum, too. Do you want to feel my cum dripping out of your sweet little cunt?" I drive into her deep, loving the way she trembles around me. She's so fucking close.

"Y-yes, please. Please give it to me. Stuff me full, sir," Kara begs. My eyes roll into the back of my skull at the sound of those filthy pleas on her lips.

"Take it, darling," I command her, pulling my fingers from her arse and reaching between her legs to rub her clit. Almost instantly, I feel her spasm beneath me, her breaths rapid and desperate. Racing to join her, I pound into her at a crazed pace, the room filling with the sound of my balls slapping against her arse. I tense as I shoot my cum deep inside her, thrusting a couple times before pulling out and wanking my cock over her arse and lower back, painting her in my cum. The sight of her drenched in my seed is a fucking masterpiece.

After wiping myself on the sheets, I walk over to the bathroom and bring back a warm washcloth for Kara. Gently, I brush the cloth over her skin, wiping away the traces of me left behind. She doesn't ever stir or shift as I wash her, her breathing deep and even. A quick glance at her face tells me what I already guessed: my little demon-angel fell asleep. Her expression is always so soft when she slumbers, and it immediately stirs an overwhelming barrage of tenderness.

I allow myself a moment to feel the full, intoxicating, utterly destructive depth of my emotions for the gorgeous girl lying peacefully in my bed. I run my fingers down her spine, loving her little subconscious moan at the sensation. I trace my thumb over her barely parted lips, shoving down the desire to stick my cock in her mouth while she sleeps. I brush my knuckles over the small silver scars along her hairline, a beautiful symbol of her strength and survival. Because my brave girl can survive anything life throws at her. Even me.

In every aspect of her life, Kara fights and conquers with no hint of surrender, like a dauntless Amazonian warrior in a constant battle. So when I get her in the bedroom, I like to strip away that determination and stubbornness and damned belligerence and see what lies beneath. Because my little warrior without her armor is the most beautiful goddamn thing I've ever seen.

When I finish tending, I stand back to appreciate the sight of Kara sleeping and clean in my bed. I frown as I find a small reason for discontent.

She looked better filthy and covered in me.

Chapter 43

KARA

If bruises and bite marks are the signs of a good time, then our reunion at Pandemonium was an absolute rave.

I glance down at the ring Cade insists I wear in spite of refusing his proposal. I'm half-expecting to wake up one morning tied to the bed in a white wedding dress with my forged signature on a marriage license. I wouldn't put it past the bastard.

The house is quiet. Cade left before dawn, kissing me when I was half asleep and mumbling something about an unexpected work emergency. I'm not an idiot—I know he's not conducting legitimate business deals in the middle of the night. I suppose it might have been unfair of me to expect Cade to change his interests and his income stream in an instant, but it's been over a year. He's had more than enough time to cut ties with his illegal contacts for good. Then again, I don't see Caden Ashford as the type to sit at home and bask in his wealth. He needs the thrill of something dangerous.

If he's been finding that danger by continuing to steal from innocent people, I'll give him hell when he gets home. And he can pay me back in orgasms after.

When I finally crawl out of bed to go foraging for breakfast, there's a large black box waiting for me on the kitchen island. It reminds me of the little presents Cade would sneak into my office in New York during the times we were separated, although this one is much bigger.

I cut open the tape, the suspense putting me in a bit of a rush. Cade's other four gifts were jewelry, so I have no idea what could fit in a box of this size. It's not like he could give me anything bigger or more extravagant than the collar around my neck and the ring on my finger. And what's the occasion? An apology for leaving me on my own again? A thank you for putting up with that fake engagement hell he put me through last night?

To my surprise, inside the packaging is two dozen white roses in a simple black vase. I don't think Cade has ever given me anything white. In fact, I'm not sure he even owns anything white. He's always favored luxurious colors over somber elegance.

And then I realize with horror one very well-known association with white roses—weddings.

Bloody freaking hell, if that damned man has gotten it into his head that he *can* dominate me into marrying him, he's got another thing coming. I thought our night at Pandemonium was a bit of play-acting, letting him pretend like I was the future Lady Ashford for a night and act out his marriage kink. A fake engagement party for our non-eventual nuptials. If he thought that it was real…

I notice a piece of paper tucked in between the roses. Balancing the vase on my hip, I pluck out the note, hoping it isn't more spoutings of matrimony. I'm already wearing his damned ring on my damned finger. That's the best the British bastard is going to get.

My brow furrows when I notice the paper that the message has been written on. There are words printed on the front and back. Not just any words, it's an excerpt from the Reeve's Tale from The Canterbury Tales. And it hasn't been printed out on a page; it's been torn from a physical book. I gasp in horror. Certainly Cade knows not to slaughter books and use them as stationary? The gesture doesn't feel thoughtful. In all honesty, it feels like an assault.

Plagued by an indescribable sense of unease, I flip open the folded page and read the poem that has been scribbled over Chaucer's brilliant words.

Roses are red
Like veins that have bled
You'll look so pretty when you're dead

My hands tremble, the vase slipping from my fingers and falling to the marble floor. The black glass shatters with a loud *crash* as roses and shards scatter over the floor. And red. There is red everywhere. Spread over the floor, streaking down the walls, painting the white roses in splatters of bright color. It looks like—my eyes drop down to the paper still clutched in my hand—blood.

The black vase was filled with blood.

I cover my mouth with my hand, stifling a scream as horror fills my belly with gnawing dread. Quickly, I read the next lines.

Your sister will lead
And how she will plead
Before I make her body bleed

This time, I do try to scream, but no sound leaves my mouth. Why would anyone threaten my sister? How would anyone even know about Harper?

Terror claws at every cell in my body, like necrosis spreading through my limbs and leaving them dead and useless. I can't move. I'm paralyzed with terror.

Tick Tock
I'm coming

I can't breathe.

Tick Tock
Start running

I can't breathe.

Tick Tock
Time's almost up

I distantly acknowledge that my vision is spotting. I watch as the world turns sideways without any power to stop it. And then it's dark.

When my eyes open again, I'm on the floor. There's a vague recognition that I've fallen on glass, and there's blood on my hands. I can't tell if it's mine or someone else's.

I turn my hands palms up, frowning when I see shards of black glass embedded in the skin. The blood gathering in the creases of my palms is mine. Looking down, I see that the red bleeding into the skirt of my lavender dress isn't. There's so much red.

Should I be relieved that I'm not sitting in a pool of my own blood? Or is it worse that it is someone else's? I can't be sure at the moment.

My fingers are shaking so badly that it takes me a minute to pull my phone from my pocket. I don't know what's happening, but I know I need Cade. I need to hear the steady control of his voice before I give in to panic again.

"Hello?" comes the deep timbre of Cade's voice, soothing my anxiety with a single pair of syllables.

"Cade," I almost cry in relief.

"Kara, what is it? What's wrong?" His voice is tinged with panic. It sounds strange on him.

"I d-don't know," I stutter through sobs.

"Damnit, Kara, are you safe? *Get Declan on the phone, now!*" I hear him shout to someone in the room with him. Probably Ortega.

"Kara! Fucking answer me, goddamnit," Cade yells through the phone. The sharp sound of it makes my ears ring.

"I'm here," I mumble back. "I—fell." I'm not really sure how to explain the rest of it.

"Kara, focus," Cade snaps. "How did you fall? *Why isn't Declan there, yet?*" Cade yells at the other person on his end again.

"There's blood. So much blood…" I pull my legs up to my chest, my bare feet scraping across broken glass. In my state of shock, I can't feel it, but I can hear as the shards scratch across my skin. I wrap my arms around my knees, squeezing tightly. In this moment, all I want to be is small and safe.

I flinch when I feel a hand on my shoulder. When I peek up, I'm staring into Declan's dark eyes full of horror and something else. Something that tells me he might know more than I do.

Gently, Declan takes the phone from my bleeding hand. I can still hear Cade shouting over the speaker, but it's muffled when Declan puts the phone to his ear. I lean my head back against the kitchen island and close my eyes, letting the boys handle things. Right now, I want to sleep and let the horror in front of me fade away.

"Kara?" Declan asks.

"Hmm?" I force open my heavy lids to see Declan bending down in front of me. I'm glad he's wearing shoes so he doesn't get cut when he moves toward me.

"Are you hurt, Kara?" he inquires calmly. His voice sounds older than usual. More serious. I'm afraid he's grown up while I've been away in New York.

"Not really," I answer, shaking my head. "My hands…" I offer him my injured hands. He touches them lightly, being careful not to disturb the glass or the cuts.

"Anywhere else?" His tone is clinical, like he's not the least bit concerned by all the blood on the floor. *The blood that isn't mine.*

I slide my legs out toward him, wordlessly pointing to my bloody, bare feet. He frowns down at me, surveying the damage with the same detached analysis he did my hands.

"Superficial injuries on her hands and feet from the glass," Declan informs Cade on the phone. "I don't see anything too serious. There's blood all over the kitchen—it looks like a massacre, but none of it is from her."

Cade responds with something loud and angry.

"It's him," Declan replies. "Yes, I'm sure. He left a fucking note."

I startle, looking down at my hands and finding them empty. I didn't even notice him take it. He must have slipped it from my fingers when he examined my hands. I let my consciousness drift as Declan goes over the details of the note. I don't think I can bear to witness the vile threats again.

"You've got to tell her, sir. You can't wait any longer. Things are getting dangerous. She has a right to know."

There's another angry blast from the phone as Cade tears into Declan.

I'm mildly aware that they're arguing about me. After a brief and heated discussion, Declan bends down beside me and offers me my phone back.

"Kara?" Cade calls, his voice distorted with emotions I've never heard from him before. Without cause, I feel my skin prickle with fear. "Kara, I need to tell you something. And I need you to stay calm. Can you do that for me, love?" The warmth in his last question is forced, like throwing a blanket over an iceberg to disguise the chill.

"Y-yes," I answer, my teeth chattering. I'm not entirely sure I can keep my promise even as I speak it.

"It's Jace."

My heart stops functioning for one beat. Two. "What?" I ask finally. Even though his answer makes logical sense, it's not computing in my head.

"I let you think I was hunting him for the first edition. And for what he did to you. But the truth is, Jace is hunting *you*. He has been for a long time. But I'm not going to let anything happen to you. Do you hear me? That sick bastard isn't going to touch you again."

The shock of Cade's words sinks beneath my skin and burrows like shards of ice. This whole time, I've been stalked like prey, and I didn't even realize. A terrible realization dawns on me as I stare at the black box lying inconspicuously on the counter. "Cade," I swallow hard against the lump in my throat, "did you send me presents while I was in New York? Little black boxes left on top of the desk in my office or tucked into the drawers?"

"No—" There's a charged pause, and my heart squeezes with panic knowing I already have my answer of *who* left those boxes.

"*Christ*, I thought we had cameras on her office," Cade calls to someone else. "Get fucking Braxton in here. If he missed something, I'm going to *fucking* flay him."

Oh my God. Feeling sick, I look down at the small bracelet on my wrist tucked beneath the one with a heart charm from Cade. "Get it off. Get it *off!*" I shriek in panic as I try to claw the plain gold chain off me with glass still stuck in my hands. Finally, the thin metal tears, and I rip the bracelet off and throw it across the room. It hits the wall and lands in a splotch of blood marring the marble floor.

I've been wearing something *he* touched for months. He was in *my office*. Fuck, he could have been in my apartment—watching, waiting.

"Oh my God, Harper," I gasp when I remember I'm not the only one who was threatened. I've put my own sister in danger.

"I know, love. We'll get her."

"But what if we don't get there in time?"

"We will, Kara. I promise."

"But how can you be sure?"

Cade sighs heavily. "Because we're already in California."

I pause, picking at the glass in my left hand. Cade's ring sits heavy and unfamiliar on my fourth finger. "Why are you in California, Cade?" I ask, already knowing I won't like the answer.

I can hear Cade deciding whether to tell me a pretty lie or the truth for once. He curses before deciding on the more painful of the two options. "Because they found a dead girl drained of blood and an eighteenth century edition of The Canterbury Tales with a page missing in her hands."

Epilogue

JACE

Her pale blonde hair blows in the wind, whipping across her cheeks before she brushes it back behind her ear. The color is a perfect match for *hers*, but longer. How I imagine she must have worn it before she turned cold and hard.

Her cheeks are pink, like she gets too much sun for her fair skin, but she doesn't really care. She's warm, vibrant, the opposite of the frigid bitch. She laughs at her friend's joke as they walk along the beach—not too loud, just the right amount to sound amused but not annoying like most of the kids her age.

She's so young, so innocent. A little thing of seventeen without a care in the world. Well, her parents are dead. And she will be soon too, but little blondie doesn't know that. Not yet.

Something stirs below my waist as I watch her flick her tongue over the green ice cream dripping down the side of her cone. She twists her wrist, licking at every side while the hot sun melts her treat faster than she can eat it.

Does she know what she's doing? Is she a fucking tease like *her*? Taunting me with something she never plans on dishing out? Or is she still too naive to know the effect she has on other people's cocks? I adjust my pants, thinking about how I can teach her exactly what she does to me. With any luck, I can be her first. And her last.

I wasn't attached to any of the others. They were worms—lowly bait used to draw out my true prey. And though hunting them was fun, they were minor entertainment—the opening acts. This girl—this perfect, sweet thing—is the main attraction.

Maybe I'll play with her first. I think I've more than earned the right to enjoy myself. I didn't touch the others. I was tempted, of course, but it's not smart to mix your fluids with the bodies. You can't be too careful. I don't want them to find me. Not yet.

Her creamy thighs peek out of her short, white skirt, thick and tempting. My mouth waters for just a taste. Or maybe more. Will she taste like *her*?

She looks so soft, so delicate, so breakable. I want to rip her apart bit by bit and lay out all the pieces like the prettiest little present. My perfect surprise for *her*.

She's my true masterpiece. But it's not time. Not yet.

Tick tock, sweetheart. I'm coming for you next.

Note from the Author

Thank you so much for reading! This book has my whole heart, and I truly hope you fell in love with these characters as much as I did while writing them. If you enjoyed it, please consider taking a bit of time to write a review. Nothing makes my day like getting to see what readers think of my dark and cozy little world.

I apologize for leaving you with a bit of a cliffhanger. I didn't *want* to do it, but some things are worth waiting for, I promise! You'll definitely be seeing more from Kara Caine and Caden Ashford. And if our favorite kinky chef Gavin Greyson wormed his way into your dark hearts, don't worry—his story is just getting started.

If you haven't read Hideaway yet (I really hope you did, otherwise this story would be confusing as hell), you can find it on amazon or read for free Kindle Unlimited.

Acknowledgements

A huge thank you to my absolutely amazing beta readers, Lindsey and Lauren. You guys made sure I dotted every I, crossed every T, and put the cocks where they needed to be. Your feedback and support has meant the world to me, and I could not have written this book without you. Thank you for helping make this story and these characters be the best version of themselves…even if it meant convincing me to delete five of Kara's orgasms.

So much thanks to Mary, Val, and Julie at Books and Moods for this stunning cover and formatting. You guys always do an incredible job of bringing all of my dreams to life, and your designs are to die for. Thank you for creating covers that I can't wait to get on my bookshelf.

Thank you to my sister for being the first one to believe I could actually do this thing. There is no way I could have made it this far without you cheering from the sidelines every step of the way. Thank you for always being my number one fan even if you will never read any of my books and the word *cock* gives you the ick.

A very heart-felt thank you to the rest of my family for being shockingly supportive when I came out as a kinky romance author. I have never been so proud (or horrified) that some of you actually managed to suffer through reading it. I love you all, and I am sorry for any unintentional scarring.

And lastly, an extra special thank you for every single reader who took the time to venture into this twisted universe of mine. I know TBR lists are endless, and we'll never have enough hours in the day to read all the books we want, so I am incredibly honored that you devoted some of those hours to Kara and Caden. You all are the stars that fill my world with light!

About the Author

Willow has a degree in English lit that she takes great delight in using to twist together smut and the classics in deliciously perverse ways that would make the professors of her former Christian university cry blasphemy.

She lives in Amsterdam with her husband and small coven of mini monsters. She spends her nights in a caffeine haze dreaming up kinky sexcapades and morally grey bastards who make you get on your knees and beg for more.

Willow loves to connect with her readers! If you want to keep up with the latest news on upcoming books and projects, follow Willow here:

- @willowprescottbooks
- @willowprescottbooks
- Willow Prescott
- http://Willowprescott.com
- willowprescottbooks@gmail.com

Printed in Great Britain
by Amazon